THE
COMPLETE
PARATIME

Ace Science Fiction Books by H. Beam Piper

THE COMPLETE FUZZY
THE COMPLETE PARATIME

THE
COMPLETE
PARATIME

H. Beam Piper

ACE BOOKS, NEW YORK

This is a work of fiction. Names, characters, places, and incidents either are the product of the author's imagination or are used fictitiously, and any resemblance to actual persons, living or dead, business establishments, events, or locales is entirely coincidental.

THE COMPLETE PARATIME

PRINTING HISTORY
Ace trade paperback edition / March 2001

All rights reserved.
Paratime copyright © 1981 by Charter Communications, Inc.
Introduction to *Paratime* copyright © 1981 by John F. Last
Lord Kalvan of Otherwhen copyright © 1965 by Ace Books, Inc.
Cover art by Dave Dorman

This book, or parts thereof, may not be reproduced
in any form without permission.
For information address: The Berkley Publishing Group,
a division of Penguin Putnam Inc.,
375 Hudson Street, New York, New York 10014.

The Penguin Putnam Inc. World Wide Web site address is
http://www.penguinputnam.com

Check out the ACE Science Fiction & Fantasy newsletter
and much more on the Internet at Club PPI!

ISBN: 0-441-00801-1

ACE®
Ace Books are published by The Berkley Publishing Group,
a division of Penguin Putnam Inc., 375 Hudson Street,
New York, New York 10014.
ACE and the "A" design are trademarks
belonging to Penguin Putnam Inc.

Printed in the United States of America

10 9 8 7 6 5 4 3 2 1

THE
COMPLETE
PARATIME

PARATIME

—

Contents

INTRODUCTION

John F. Carr

HERE, at long last, are the Paratime tales (with the exception of the Lord Kalvan stories*) by H. Beam Piper together in one volume. These stories, first published in *Astounding Science Fiction* during the late forties and early fifties, are the foundation of Piper's reputation as one of the great sf adventure writers. Together they display Piper's lifelong interest in history, reincarnation and alternate worlds, and the time theories of J. W. Dunne.

Interestingly enough, H. Beam Piper's first published story, "Time and Time Again," was a time travel piece: It begins with a soldier in a World War III battlefield who is at the point of death when he is projected back into his childhood persona. The rest of the story deals with his attempts to influence the "future" of his childhood, and later of mankind. The story has an autobiographical feel and Piper does a good job of evoking rural Pennsylvania, where he himself was raised.

Until the late fifties, most of H. Beam Piper's fiction was concerned with time travel and alternate worlds, stories such as "He Walked Around the Horses," "Genesis," "Police Operation," "Flight from Tomorrow," and others. Other science-fiction writers, Philip K. Dick, Robert Silverberg, Keith Laumer,

*The first two Lord Kalvan novelettes, "Gunpowder God" and "Down Styphon," were published in *Analog* in the sixties. In 1965 they were collected, together with a third novelette, and published as *Lord Kalvan of Otherwhen* by Ace Books. [Ed. note: *Lord Kalvan of Otherwhen* is reprinted in this volume, beginning on page 247.]

Poul Anderson, etc., have dealt with time travel and paradox, but none—with the possible exception of Richard Meredith—have been so obsessed with it.

There may be an explanation: At a science fiction convention in Seattle in the early sixties, Jerry Pournelle asked Piper whether he believed in reincarnation or not. Beam's answer was yes, and he added that the story "He Walked Around the Horses" was one that had occurred in a past life. Well aware of Piper's wry sense of humor, Jerry questioned him further, but could elicit no more information. Jerry left convinced that Piper was serious.

A little over five years ago, I rode an RTD bus into Los Angeles and sat next to a bearded man in his late twenties. It was a long ride and after a while we fell into conversation; the talk turned to reincarnation. This man, a former Vietnam soldier, claimed that he was the reincarnation of a World War II lieutenant who had died somewhere in Normandy. All his life he had been fascinated by war toys and games of war, and had sometimes dreamed of battles and long marches. No one, including himself, had thought his interests unusual as they were quite common among his peers. It wasn't until he joined the Marines that he began to have actual flashbacks of World War II battlefields and firefights.

They continued, predominately in dreams, throughout his tour of 'Nam. He had thought they would stop when he returned to the United States, but they didn't. They intensified.

When I talked with him, he was working in a carwash, living at home with his parents, and saving every cent he could toward a pilgrimage to Normandy. His free time was spent in the library researching World War II and trying to identify that young lieutenant. He was certain that once he found the young officer's name he would be able to lay his ghost to rest, or possibly find his real identity. He wasn't sure. He admitted that with every passing year his own life grew more faint and the young lieutenant's grew stronger. He was even beginning to relive his youth in the Midwest. I left the bus convinced that he believed every word of what he'd told me, and certain that I wouldn't want to be in his place.

DAVID Chamberlain, a San Diego psychologist who completed a study on birth memories under hypnosis, claims that people can remember their own births in great detail. A large number of his subjects, during hypnotic age regression, remembered their painful birth experiences, complaining bitterly about harsh treatment by their doctors and separation from their mothers.

Some of these memories had led to lifelong traumas: psychological maladaption brought on by chance remarks, headaches resulting from rough handling with forceps, digestive problems caused by the mother's refusal to breastfeed, and asthma provoked by the panic of delivery. In nine out of ten cases, Dr. Chamberlain found that these memories were corroborated by the mothers during independent questioning.

In an interview in the *Los Angeles Times,* Dr. Chamberlain said: "The fact that a child's mind is actually working at birth upsets a lot of theories . . . obviously, we're not dealing with the brain at all . . . I don't think that birth memory has anything whatever to do with the brain. What we're dealing with is mind. It's a non-physical aspect of every person. And mind has an all-or-nothing quality. It doesn't develop cell by cell over the years so that it's competent to do something at six years that it can't do at two. It's just not that way." Reincarnation is one possible explanation for the retention of birth memories.

I think H. Beam Piper would have been very interested in Dr. Chamberlain's work. In "Last Enemy" Hadron Dalla is doing research on reincarnation, although she is attempting to communicate with the recently dead rather than the newly born.

On the Akor-Neb time-line where Dalla is doing her research, we have a culture where reincarnation is an accepted scientific truth, while death is considered no more than a somewhat disruptive event—more an inconvenience than anything else. When Dalla establishes communication with a recently dead who has not yet picked a new incarnation, she starts a political crisis between the Volitionalists (the party that believes you return in the body of your choice) and the Statisticalists (who believe that one is reincarnated in the first available human host). Not only does she undermine the belief in statistical reincarnation but she opens up a literal Pandora's box over inheritance laws and guilt over crimes in past lives.

If H. Beam Piper did believe in volitional reincarnation, it goes a long way to explain his own suicide. While an inconvenience, death does clean the slate of debts and financial obligations, and Piper at the time of his death felt weighed down by both. I hope for his sake he was right.

*   *   *

THE idea of parallel worlds is an old one in human mythology and folk tales, with roots in mythical fairylands and astral planes. Edgar Rice Burroughs, A. Merritt, and Henry Kuttner were some of the first writers to use this theme in science fiction. A major treatment of the parallel worlds theme has been to create a series of alternate worlds as part of a continuum of increasing social and historical variation from a template world—usually a present or future version of our own civilization. These variations are based on alternate historical branchings at some time in the past; for example, Carthage winning the Punic Wars with Rome or Germany defeating the Allies in World War II. The farther in the past these historical branchings take place, the more bizarre the alternate world appears to the travelers from the template world.

Piper's template world, the Home Time-Line, is an advanced civilization based on Martian colonization of the earth some seventy-five to one hundred thousand years in the past. The Home Time-Line paratimers use the Ghaldron-Hesthor Transposition Field to travel between the ten-to-the-hundred-thousandth time-lines. Piper created the Paratime Police primarily to guard the secret of the transpositional field and to enforce the laws of the Paratime Commission and Home Time-Line society. As for the Home Time-Line and what it uses the transposition travel for: "For over twelve millennia, the people of her race . . . had been existing as parasites on all the innumerable other worlds of alternate probability on the lateral dimension of time. Smart parasites never injure their hosts, and try never to reveal their existence."

Like with many writers, Piper freely used autobiographical incidents in his work. In *Murder in the Gunroom,* a mystery novel, Piper gives us a clue as to the basis for his Ghaldron-Hesthor Transposition Field, when he has one of the characters—a pulp science-fiction writer—give the following answer as to what he is writing:

"Science fiction. I do a lot of stories for the pulps . . . *Space Trails,* and *Other Worlds,* and *Wonder Stories;* mags like that. Most of it's standardized formula-stuff; what's known in the trade as space-operas. My best stuff goes to *Astonishing.* Parenthetically, you mustn't judge any of these magazines by their names. It seems to be a convention to use hyperbolic names for science-fiction magazines; a heritage from what might be called an earlier and ruder day. What I do for *Astonishing* is really hard work, and I enjoy it. I'm working now on one of them, based on J. W. Dunne's time theories . . ."

After noticing a strange mixture of past and future events in his dreams, J. W. Dunne began to systematically study his dreams and noted that there was a fifty-fifty split in them between the future and the past. This precognitive element of dreams led him to speculate that there must exist a second-level "supertime" which measures the rate at which time passes. This of course implies the existence of other supertimes, which lead him to the idea of serial time, an infinite series of different "times." Dunne went on to create the supermind to explain how we could survive in an infinite number of "times."

Piper took Dunne's supermind and called it the extraphysical ego component. The Ghaldron-Hesthor Transposition Field was a collaboration between Ghaldron (who was working to develop a spacewarp drive) and Hesthor (who was working on the possibility of linear time travel, that is to get back to the past) and Rhogom (who was studying precognition). Rhogom's Doctrine—which is based directly on J. W. Dunne's time theories—states: "We exist perpetually at all moments within our life-span; our extraphysical ego component passes from the ego existing at one moment to the ego existing at the next. During unconsciousness, the EPC (extraphysical ego component) is 'time-free'; it may detach, and connect at some other moment, with the ego existing at that time-point. That's how we precog. We take an autohypno and recover memories brought back from the future moment and buried in the subconscious mind."

In "Police Operation," the first Paratime story, Piper postulates a near infinity of First Level Time-Lines with a Verkan Vall varient in each one. This and the extraphysical ego component are glossed over in later stories, probably because of the paradox that if there is more than one Home Time-Line there is no transpositional time secret. It is doubtful—there is no existing evidence either way—that Piper ever realized that first story would ever become the basis of a popular series, and, as Asimov did with his Foundation series, he found himself with some elements he had to either modify or ignore.

Using Dunne's time-theories, Piper explains the concept of time-lines in this manner: "*All* time-lines are totally present, in perpetual co-existence. The theory is that the EPC (extraphysical ego component) passes from one moment, on one time-line, to the next moment on the next time-line, so that the true passage of the EPC from moment to moment is a two-dimensional diagonal. . . . Now, what we do, in paratime transposition, is to build up a hypertemporal field to include the time-line we want to reach, and then shift over to it. Some point in the plenum; same point in primary time—plus primary time elapsed during mechanical and electronic lag in the relays—but a different line of secondary time."

He explains the operation of the Ghaldron-Hesthor field-generator thus: "The Ghaldron-Hesthor field-generator is like every other mechanism; it can operate only in the area of primary time in which it exists. It can transpose to any other time-line, and carry with it anything inside its field, but it can't go outside its own temporal area of existence, any more than a bullet from that rifle can hit the target a week before it's fired. . . . Anything inside the field is supposed to be unaffected by anything outside. *Supposed to be* is the way to put it; it doesn't always work. Once in a while, something pretty nasty gets picked up in transit."

The transpositional field is impenetrable except when two paratime conveyors, going in opposite "directions," interpenetrate. When this occurs, far more often than the Paratime Police like because of the volume of conveyors traveling between time-lines, the field weakens and material objects and life forms can enter the field. *Lord Kalvan of Otherwhen* is about what happens to a police officer from our own time-line who gets picked up by a paratemporal field and dropped off on a primitive time-line.

Travel between time-lines is measured in parayears, which consist of ten thousand time-lines. The transposition from one line to another takes half an hour, which is the time required to build up and collapse the transpositional field. It is impossible therefore to make transtemporal jumps of less than ten parayears, or a hundred thousand time-lines. This creates some real difficulties in "Time Crime," where the Paratime cops have to chase down a large band of First Level time slavers who have bases on several levels and sectors.

PIPER divided the Paratime alternate worlds into levels, sectors, and belts. There are five primary levels all based on the different outcomes of the Martians' attempt to colonize Terra over seventy-five to a hundred thousand years ago. Areas on different time levels that show common cultural origins and characteristics are called sectors. Sectors are then somewhat arbitrarily divided into sub-sectors, which are further broken into belts—areas within sub-sectors that share common conditions resulting from recent probabilities.

After having depleted their own planet of resources, the Martians attempted to colonize Terra. The five primary levels are indicative of the success or failure of that colonization. On the First Level the colony was a complete success, and begins to repeat the mistakes that devastated the planet Mars. Verkan Vall, special assistant to the Chief of the Paratime Police, gives this overview of First Level history in "Police Operation": "We've been paratiming for the past ten thousand years. When the Ghaldron-Hesthor transtemporal field was discovered, our ancestors had pretty well exhausted the resources of this planet [Terra]. We had a world population of half a billion, and it was all they could do to keep alive. After we began paratime transportation, our population climbed to ten billion, and there it stayed for the last eight thousand years. . . . We've tapped the resources of those other worlds on other time-lines, a little here, a little there, and not enough to really hurt anybody. We've left our mark in a few places—the Dakota Badlands, and the Gobi, on the Fourth Level, for instance . . ."

The First Level civilization is the ultimate parasite culture, drawing secretly on the resources and populations of other time-lines. No wonder the Paratime Secret is so well guarded by the Paratime Police, who have only one inflexible law regarding outtime ventures: "The secret of paratime transposition must be kept inviolate, and any activity tending to endanger it is prohibited."

First Level society is a rational one, based on the fundamental laws and rules of science. They have, in Piper's words, "forgotten all the taboos and terminologies of naturalistic religion and sex inhibition." The government appears to be loosely patterned on the British parliamentary system, without the monarchy. They have an Executive Council which passes laws and is powerful enough to censure the Paratime Police. There is also a hereditary nobility which commands some respect, although Piper never makes it clear whether or not they have any governing function.

We find that perfect memories are common among the First Level Population and Piper often alludes to their superiority over the other outtime peoples. There is also a high degree of social and mental stability due to the efforts of the Bureau of Psychological Hygiene. Piper uses this advanced civilization in the early stories to satirize some of our own political and social conventions. For a man who believed that *Homo sapiens* was more or less ungovernable, Piper's First Level civilization comes as close to a utopia as any science-fiction society he ever created.

However, by the mid-fifties when he wrote "Time Crime," First Level civilization was beginning to show some warts. Utopias are inherently dull—if the human condition is perfected, there's not much for conflict—and don't make for good stories. And Piper was first and foremost a good storyteller. Furthermore, Piper—as reflected in his letters and fiction—was growing increasingly cynical about the nature of the human beast and the future of democratic institutions.

In "Time Crime" we learn about the steel fist behind the velvet glove of psycho-rehabilitation, which is described as "a year of unremitting agony, physical and mental, worse than a Khiftan torture rack," leaving the victim a new personality. Yet despite the Bureau of Psychological Hygiene's testing and hypno-conditioning, it has been infiltrated and compromised by a criminal conspiracy. We also learn that there is a large subject population of indentured servants, who appear little more than slaves. "As far as that goes, what's the difference between that [what the slave dealers are doing] and the way we drag those Fourth Level Primitive Sector-Complex people off to Fifth Level Service Sector to work for us?" The First Level rationale is: "We need a certain amount of human labor, for tasks requiring original thought and decision that are beyond the ability of robots, and most of it is work our Citizens simply wouldn't perform."

There's a good deal of prejudice against these Fourth Level servants and it takes many generations before they can earn First Level citizenship. The Proles have their own subculture and live in ghettos. Guard units are needed to prevent Prole insurrections. By the end of "Time Crime," First Level society, far from being a utopia, looks like a funhouse mirror image of our own society.

Second Level civilization is almost as well established as First Level, although there have been several dark-age interludes. As on the First Level, there is contact on most sectors with Venus and Mars. On some of the sectors, with the exception of paratime transposition, technology is advanced over that of the First Level—on a few time-lines they are working on a space drive.

The Third Level probability is the result of an abortive attempt to colonize Terra by a few survivors. The colonists lose all traces of Martian civilization and culture, even the memory of their mother world, while on Mars, civilization falls apart and withers away. Civilization here is more recent, and has taken some different directions, than on the first two levels.

On the Fourth Level we find our own time-line: the Europo-American Sector. Here some disaster occurred to the original colonists and all civilization and technology were lost. Most Fourth Level time-lines believe they are an indigenous race with a long history of savagery. Fourth Level is the big one; the maximum probability. On most of the sectors civilization began in the valleys of the Nile and Tigris-Euphrates, or on the Indus and Yangtze. Civilization on the Fourth Level ranges from pikes and matchlocks to thermonuclear weapons.

Some of the sectors that Piper mentions are: the Alexandrian-Roman Sector, the Alexandrian-Punic Sector, the Sino-Hindic Sector, the Indo-Turanian Sector, and the Aryan sectors—Aryan-Oriental, Proto-Aryan, and Aryan-

Transpacific. Piper mentions enough exotic combinations of cultures to tantalize any history buff and keep him anxious for more stories. With ten to the hundred thousandth possible time-lines, Piper could justify about any historical possibility imaginable, as in the Aryan-Transpacific Sector where he turned the Aryan migrations around, provided the Aryans with ships, and sent them to the coast of North America where they slaughtered the American Indians and began a civilization that was not to change for thousands of years. Considering the breadth of Piper's Terro-Human Future History and his interest in history, it's surprising he didn't write more stories on Fourth Level sectors.

*   *   *

LIKE many other writers of the late forties and early fifties, including Leigh Brackett and Ray Bradbury, Piper seemed fascinated by the red world and its Lost Civilizations. Besides the Paratime stories, there are mentions of the Old Martians in several of his Terro-Human Future History yarns, including "Omnilingual," where an archaeological expedition to Mars attempts to decipher some ancient Martian writing. Some Piper researchers, such as John F. Costello in his "H. Beam Piper: An Infinity of Worlds," have used the Martians to link the Paratime series to Piper's Terro-Human Future History. As further proof, they mention that both series share certain advanced technologies—contragravity and collapsium.

It is my opinion that both series are separate. If Piper had meant to bridge the two series, he would have done so in a more obvious manner—mentioning their common origin or having the paratimers appear in his future history. While Piper does mention a time-line where they are working on a spacewarp, this is a Second Level world rather than a Fourth Level Europo-American time-line—as is Piper's Terro-Human Future History world, since it clearly doesn't begin to differ from our own time-line until the seventies. This of course is more a problem of time catching up to the series rather than Piper trying to create an "alternate" time-line. Furthermore, when "When in the Course . . ." (a Terro-Human Future History story reprinted in *Federation* by H. Beam Piper, Ace Books) was expanded and modified into *Lord Kalvan of Otherwhen,* all references to the Federation and Piper's Terro-Human Future History were dropped, and its background became pure Paratime.

Nor does the argument that Piper's use of common concepts in both series proves they are linked stand up when one scrutinizes Piper's entire body of work. A number of early stories, such as "Genesis," "Flight from Tomorrow," "Mercenary," "Hunter Patrol," and "Day of the Moron," clearly do not belong to either series, yet they too share common concepts and themes.

But what did H. Beam Piper have to say on the subject? In a letter dated June 14, 1964, to Charlie and Marcia Brown, Piper states: "Paratime stories to date:

'Police Operation'

'Last Enemy'

'Temple Trouble'

'Time Crime'

Campbell has just bought another Paratime story, 'Gunpowder God,' and since then I have finished another which is still unreported ('Down Styphon'), and am working on a third at present." (These are the three stories that make up the novel *Lord Kalvan of Otherwhen*.) It is apparent from this letter that Piper saw the Paratime stories as distinct from those of his Terro-Human Future History. Unless some new evidence is uncovered, I suspect this should end the unnatural mating of these two series.

Introduction to
"He Walked Around the Horses"

"He Walked Around the Horses" is an alternate-worlds story based on a true incident—the disappearance of Benjamin Bathurst outside an inn in Prussia. He was never seen again. Piper offers a most interesting explanation—one he claimed was autobiographical in a talk with Jerry Pournelle!

While this is not a Paratime story—there is no mention of the Paratime Police—it is based on the same idea and was published just a month before the first Paratime story in Astounding.

HE WALKED AROUND
THE HORSES

*In November 1809, an Englishman named Benjamin Bathurst van-
ished, inexplicably and utterly.*

*He was en route to Hamburg from Vienna, where he had been serv-
ing as his government's envoy to the court of what Napoleon had left
of the Austrian Empire. At an inn in Perleburg, in Prussia, while examining a change of horses for his coach, he casually stepped out of
sight of his secretary and his valet. He was not seen to leave the inn
yard. He was not seen again, ever.*

At least, not in this continuum . . .

(FROM Baron Eugen von Krutz, Minister of Police, to His Excellency the
Count von Berchtenwald, Chancellor to His Majesty Friedrich Wilhelm III of
Prussia.)

25 November, 1809

Your Excellency:

A circumstance has come to the notice of this Ministry, the significance of
which I am at a loss to define, but, since it appears to involve matters of State,
both here and abroad, I am convinced that it is of sufficient importance to be
brought to your personal attention. Frankly, I am unwilling to take any further
action in the matter without your advice.

Briefly, the situation is this: We are holding, here at the Ministry of Police, a person giving his name as Benjamin Bathurst, who claims to be a British diplomat. This person was taken into custody by the police at Perleburg yesterday, as a result of a disturbance at an inn there; he is being detained on technical charges of causing disorder in a public place, and of being a suspicious person. When arrested, he had in his possession a dispatch case, containing a number of papers; these are of such an extraordinary nature that the local authorities declined to assume any responsibility beyond having the man sent here to Berlin.

After interviewing this person and examining his papers, I am, I must confess, in much the same position. This is not, I am convinced, any ordinary police matter; there is something very strange and disturbing here. The man's statements, taken alone, are so incredible as to justify the assumption that he is mad. I cannot, however, adopt this theory, in view of his demeanor, which is that of a man of perfect rationality, and because of the existence of these papers. The whole thing is mad; incomprehensible!

The papers in question accompany, along with copies of the various statements taken at Perleburg, a personal letter to me from my nephew, Lieutenant Rudolf von Tarlburg. This last is deserving of your particular attention; Lieutenant von Tarlburg is a very level-headed young officer, not at all inclined to be fanciful or imaginative. It would take a good deal to affect him as he describes.

The man calling himself Benjamin Bathurst is now lodged in an apartment here at the Ministry; he is being treated with every consideration, and, except for freedom of movement, accorded every privilege.

I am, most anxiously awaiting your advice, et cetera, et cetera,

Krutz

(Report of Traugott Zeller, *Oberwachtmeister, Staatspolizei,* made at Perleburg, 25 November, 1809.)

At about ten minutes past two of the afternoon of Saturday, 25 November, while I was at the police station, there entered a man known to me as Franz Bauer, an inn servant employed by Christian Hauck, at the sign of the Sword & Scepter, here in Perleburg. This man Franz Bauer made complaint to *Staatspolizeikapitan* Ernst Hartenstein, saying that there was a madman making trouble at the inn where he, Franz Bauer, worked. I was, therefore, directed, by *Staatspolizeikapitan* Hartenstein, to go to the Sword & Scepter Inn, there to act at my discretion to maintain the peace.

Arriving at the inn in company with the said Franz Bauer, I found a considerable crowd of people in the common room, and, in the midst of them, the innkeeper, Christian Hauck, in altercation with a stranger. This stranger was a gentlemanly-appearing person, dressed in traveling clothes, who had under his arm a small leather dispatch case. As I entered, I could hear him, speaking in German with a strong English accent, abusing the innkeeper, the said Christian Hauck, and accusing him of having drugged his, the stranger's, wine, and of having stolen his, the stranger's, coach-and-four, and of having abducted his, the stranger's, secretary and servants. This the said Christian Hauck was loudly denying, and the other people in the inn were taking the innkeeper's part, and mocking the stranger for a madman.

On entering, I commanded everyone to be silent, in the king's name, and then, as he appeared to be the complaining party of the dispute, I required the foreign gentleman to state to me what was the trouble. He then repeated his accusations against the innkeeper, Hauck, saying that Hauck, or, rather, another man who resembled Hauck and who had claimed to be the innkeeper, had drugged his wine and stolen his coach and made off with his secretary and his servants. At this point, the innkeeper and the bystanders all began shouting denials and contradictions, so that I had to pound on a table with my truncheon to command silence.

I then required the innkeeper, Christian Hauck, to answer the charges which the stranger had made; this he did with a complete denial of all of them, saying that the stranger had had no wine in his inn, and that he had not been inside the inn until a few minutes before, when he had burst in shouting accusations, and that there had been no secretary, and no valet, and no coachman, and no coach-and-four, at the inn, and that the gentleman was raving mad. To all this, he called the people who were in the common room to witness.

I then required the stranger to account for himself. He said that his name was Benjamin Bathurst, and that he was a British diplomat, returning to England from Vienna. To prove this, he produced from his dispatch case sundry papers. One of these was a letter of safe-conduct, issued by the Prussian Chancellery, in which he was named and described as Benjamin Bathurst. The other papers were English, all bearing seals and appearing to be official documents.

Accordingly, I requested him to accompany me to the police station, and also the innkeeper, and three men whom the innkeeper wanted to bring as witnesses.

Traugott Zeller
Oberwachtmeister

Report approved,

Ernst Hartenstein
Staatspolizeikapitan

(Statement of the self-so-called Benjamin Bathurst, taken at the police station at Perleburg, 25 November, 1809.)

My name is Benjamin Bathurst, and I am Envoy Extraordinary and Minister Plenipotentiary of the government of his Britannic Majesty to the court of His Majesty Franz I, Emperor of Austria, or, at least, I was until the events following the Austrian surrender made necessary my return to London. I left Vienna on the morning of Monday, the 20th, to go to Hamburg to take ship home; I was traveling in my own coach-and-four, with my secretary, Mr. Bertram Jardine, and my valet, William Small, both British subjects, and a coachman, Josef Bidek, an Austrian subject, whom I had hired for the trip. Because of the presence of French troops, whom I was anxious to avoid, I was forced to make a detour west as far as Salzburg before turning north toward Magdeburg, where I crossed the Elbe. I was unable to get a change of horses for my coach after leaving Gera, until I reached Perleburg, where I stopped at the Sword & Scepter Inn.

Arriving there, I left my coach in the inn yard, and I and my secretary, Mr. Jardine, went into the inn. A man, not this fellow here, but another rogue, with more beard and less paunch, and more shabbily dressed, but as like him as though he were his brother, represented himself as the innkeeper, and I dealt with him for a change of horses, and ordered a bottle of wine for myself and my secretary, and also a pot of beer apiece for my valet and the coachman, to be taken outside to them. Then Jardine and I sat down to our wine, at a table in the common room, until the man who claimed to be the innkeeper came back and told us that the fresh horses were harnessed to the coach and ready to go. Then we went outside again.

I looked at the two horses on the off side, and then walked around in front of the team to look at the two nigh-side horses, and as I did, I felt giddy, as though I were about to fall, and everything went black before my eyes. I thought I was having a fainting spell, something I am not at all subject to, and I put out my hand to grasp the hitching bar, but could not find it. I am sure, now, that I was unconscious for some time, because when my head cleared, the coach and horses were gone, and in their place was a big farm wagon, jacked up in front, with the right front wheel off, and two peasants were greasing the detached wheel.

I looked at them for a moment, unable to credit my eyes, and then I spoke to them in German, saying, "Where the devil's my coach-and-four?"

They both straightened, startled; the one who was holding the wheel almost dropped it.

"Pardon, excellency," he said, "there's been no coach-and-four here, all the time we've been here."

"Yes," said his mate, "and we've been here since just after noon."

I did not attempt to argue with them. It occurred to me—and it is still my opinion—that I was the victim of some plot; that my wine had been drugged, that I had been unconscious for some time, during which my coach had been removed and this wagon substituted for it, and that these peasants had been put to work on it and instructed what to say if questioned. If my arrival at the inn had been anticipated, and everything put in readiness, the whole business would not have taken ten minutes.

I therefore entered the inn, determined to have it out with this rascally innkeeper, but when I returned to the common room, he was nowhere to be seen, and this other fellow, who has given his name as Christian Hauck, claimed to be the innkeeper and denied knowledge of any of the things I have just stated. Furthermore, there were four cavalrymen, Uhlans, drinking beer and playing cards at the table where Jardine and I had had our wine, and they claimed to have been there for several hours.

I have no idea why such an elaborate prank, involving the participation of many people, should be played on me, except at the instigation of the French. In that case, I cannot understand why Prussian soldiers should lend themselves to it.

Benjamin Bathurst

(Statement of Christian Hauck, innkeeper, taken at the police station at Perleburg, 25 November, 1809.)

May it please your honor, my name is Christian Hauck, and I keep an inn at the sign of the Sword & Scepter, and have these past fifteen years, and my father, and his father, before me, for the past fifty years, and never has there been a complaint like this against my inn. Your honor, it is a hard thing for a man who keeps a decent house, and pays his taxes, and obeys the laws, to be accused of crimes of this sort.

I know nothing of this gentleman, nor of his coach, nor his secretary, nor his servants; I never set eyes on him before he came bursting into the inn from the yard, shouting and raving like a madman, and crying out, "Where the devil's that rogue of an innkeeper?"

I said to him, "I am the innkeeper; what cause have you to call me a rogue, sir?"

The stranger replied:

"You're not the innkeeper I did business with a few minutes ago, and he's the rascal I want to see. I want to know what the devil's been done with my coach, and what's happened to my secretary and my servants."

I tried to tell him that I knew nothing of what he was talking about, but he would not listen, and gave me the lie, saying that he had been drugged and robbed, and his people kidnaped. He even had the impudence to claim that he and his secretary had been sitting at a table in that room, drinking wine, not fifteen minutes before, when there had been four noncommissioned officers of the Third Uhlans at that table since noon. Everybody in the room spoke up for me, but he would not listen, and was shouting that we were all robbers, and kidnapers, and French spies, and I don't know what all, when the police came.

Your honor, the man is mad. What I have told you about this is the truth, and all that I know about this business, so help me God.

Christian Hauck

(Statement of Franz Bauer, inn servant, taken at the police station at Perleburg, 25 November, 1809.)

May it please your honor, my name is Franz Bauer, and I am a servant at the Sword & Scepter Inn, kept by Christian Hauck.

This afternoon, when I went into the inn yard to empty a bucket of slops on the dung heap by the stables, I heard voices and turned around, to see this gentleman speaking to Wilhelm Beick and Fritz Herzer, who were greasing their wagon in the yard. He had not been in the yard when I had turned away to empty the bucket, and I thought that he must have come in from the street. This gentleman was asking Beick and Herzer where was his coach, and when they told him they didn't know, he turned and ran into the inn.

Of my own knowledge, the man had not been inside the inn before then, nor had there been any coach, or any of the people he spoke of, at the inn, and none of the things he spoke of happened there, for otherwise I would know, since I was at the inn all day.

When I went back inside, I found him in the common room, shouting at my master, and claiming that he had been drugged and robbed. I saw that he was mad, and was afraid that he would do some mischief, so I went for the police.

Franz Bauer
his (x) mark

(Statements of Wilhelm Beick and Fritz Herzer, peasants, taken at the police station at Perleburg, 25 November, 1809.)

May it please your honor, my name is Wilhelm Beick, and I am a tenant on the estate of the Baron von Hentig. On this day, I and Fritz Herzer were sent into Perleburg with a load of potatoes and cabbages which the innkeeper at the Sword & Scepter had bought from the estate superintendent. After we had unloaded them, we decided to grease our wagon, which was very dry, before going back, so we unhitched and began working on it. We took about two hours, starting just after we had eaten lunch, and in all that time, there was no coach-and-four in the inn yard. We were just finishing when this gentleman spoke to us, demanding to know where his coach was. We told him that there had been no coach in the yard all the time we had been there, so he turned around and ran into the inn. At the time, I thought that he had come out of the inn before speaking to us, for I know that he could not have come in from the street. Now I do not know where he came from, but I know that I never saw him before that moment.

Wilhelm Beick
his (x) mark

I have heard the above testimony, and it is true to my own knowledge, and I have nothing to add to it.

Fritz Herzer
his (x) mark

(From *Staatspolizeikapitan* Ernst Hartenstein, to His Excellency, the Baron von Krutz, Minister of Police.)

25 November, 1809

Your Excellency:

The accompanying copies of statements taken this day will explain how the prisoner, the self-so-called Benjamin Bathurst, came into my custody. I have charged him with causing disorder and being a suspicious person, to hold him until more can be learned about him. However, as he represents himself to be a British diplomat, I am unwilling to assume any further responsibility, and am having him sent to your excellency, in Berlin.

In the first place, your excellency, I have the strongest doubts of the man's story. The statement which he made before me, and signed, is bad enough, with a coach-and-four turning into a farm wagon, like Cinderella's coach into a pumpkin, and three people vanishing as though swallowed by the earth. But all this is perfectly reasonable and credible, beside the things he said to me of which no record was made.

Your excellency will have noticed, in his statement, certain allusions to the Austrian surrender, and to French troops in Austria. After his statement had been taken down, I noticed these allusions, and I inquired, what surrender, and what were French troops doing in Austria. The man looked at me in a pitying manner, and said:

"News seems to travel slowly, hereabouts; peace was concluded in Vienna on the 14th of last month. And as for what French troops are doing in Austria, they're doing the same things Bonaparte's brigands are doing everywhere in Europe."

"And who is Bonaparte?" I asked.

He stared at me as though I had asked him, "Who is the Lord Jehovah?" Then, after a moment, a look of comprehension came into his face.

"So, you Prussians concede him the title of Emperor, and refer to him as Napoleon," he said. "Well, I can assure you that His Britannic Majesty's government haven't done so, and never will; not so long as one Englishman has a finger left to pull a trigger. General Bonaparte is a usurper; His Britannic Majesty's government do not recognize any sovereignty in France except the House of Bourbon." This he said very sternly, as though rebuking me.

It took me a moment or so to digest that, and to appreciate all its implications. Why, this fellow evidently believed, as a matter of fact, that the French Monarchy had been overthrown by some military adventurer named Bonaparte, who was calling himself the Emperor Napoleon, and who had made war on Austria and forced a surrender. I made no attempt to argue with him— one wastes time arguing with madmen—but if this man could believe that, the transformation of a coach-and-four into a cabbage wagon was a small matter indeed. So, to humor him, I asked him if he thought General Bonaparte's agents were responsible for his trouble at the inn.

"Certainly," he replied. "The chances are they didn't know me to see me, and took Jardine for the minister, and me for the secretary, so they made off with poor Jardine. I wonder, though, that they left me my dispatch case. And that reminds me; I'll want that back. Diplomatic papers, you know."

I told him, very seriously, that we would have to check his credentials. I promised him I would make every effort to locate his secretary and his servants and his coach, took a complete description of all of them, and persuaded him to go into an upstairs room, where I kept him under guard. I did start inquiries, calling in all my informers and spies, but, as I expected, I could learn nothing. I could not find anybody, even, who had seen him anywhere in Perleburg before he appeared at the Sword & Scepter, and that rather surprised me, as somebody should have seen him enter the town, or walk along the street.

In this connection, let me remind your excellency of the discrepancy in the statements of the servant, Franz Bauer, and of the two peasants. The former is certain the man entered the inn yard from the street; the latter are just as positive that he did not. Your excellency, I do not like such puzzles, for I am sure that all three were telling the truth to the best of their knowledge. They are ignorant common folk, I admit, but they should know what they did or did not see.

After I got the prisoner into safekeeping, I fell to examining his papers, and I can assure your excellency that they gave me a shock. I had paid little heed to his ravings about the King of France being dethroned, or about this General Bonaparte, who called himself the Emperor Napoleon, but I found all these things mentioned in his papers and dispatches, which had every appearance of being official documents. There was repeated mention of the taking, by the French, of Vienna, last May, and of the capitulation of the Austrian Emperor to this General Bonaparte, and of battles being fought all over Europe, and I don't know what other fantastic things. Your excellency, I have heard of all sorts of madmen—one believing himself to be the Archangel Gabriel, or Mohammed, or a werewolf, and another convinced that his bones are made of glass, or that he is pursued and tormented by devils—but, so help me God, this is the first time I have heard of a madman who had documentary proof for his delusions! Does your excellency wonder, then, that I want no part of this business?

But the matter of his credentials was even worse. He had papers, sealed with the seal of the British Foreign Office, and to every appearance genuine—but they were signed, as Foreign Minister, by one George Canning, and all the world knows that Lord Castlereagh has been Foreign Minister these last five years. And to cap it all, he had a safe-conduct, sealed with the seal of the Prussian Chancellery—the very seal, for I compared it, under a strong magnifying glass, with one that I knew to be genuine, and they were identical!—and yet, this letter was signed, as Chancellor, not by Count von Berchtenwald, but by Baron Stein, the Minister of Agriculture, and the signature, as far as I could see, appeared to be genuine! This is too much for me, your excellency; I must ask to be excused from dealing with this matter, before I become as mad as my prisoner!

I made arrangements, accordingly, with Colonel Keitel, of the Third Uhlans, to furnish an officer to escort this man into Berlin. The coach in which they come belongs to this police station, and the driver is one of my men. He should be furnished expense money to get back to Perleburg. The guard is a corporal of Uhlans, the orderly of the officer. He will stay with the *Herr Oberleutnant,* and both of them will return here at their own convenience and expense.

I have the honor, your excellency, to be, et cetera, et cetera.

Ernst Hartenstein
Staatspolizeikapitan

(From *Oberleutnant* Rudolf von Tarlburg, to Baron Eugen von Krutz.)

26 November, 1809

Dear Uncle Eugen:

This is in no sense a formal report; I made that at the Ministry, when I turned the Englishman and his papers over to one of your officers—a fellow with red hair and a face like a bulldog. But there are a few things which you should be told, which wouldn't look well in an official report, to let you know just what sort of a rare fish has got into your net.

I had just come in from drilling my platoon, yesterday, when Colonel Keitel's orderly told me that the colonel wanted to see me in his quarters. I found the old fellow in undress in his sitting room, smoking his big pipe.

"Come in, lieutenant; come in and sit down, my boy!" he greeted me, in that bluff, hearty manner which he always adopts with his junior officers when he has some particularly nasty job to be done. "How would you like to take a little trip in to Berlin? I have an errand, which won't take half an hour, and you can stay as long as you like, just so you're back by Thursday, when your turn comes up for road patrol."

Well, I thought, this is the bait. I waited to see what the hook would look like, saying that it was entirely agreeable with me, and asking what his errand was.

"Well, it isn't for myself, Tarlburg," he said. "It's for this fellow Hartenstein, the *Staatspolizeikapitan* here. He has something he wants done at the Ministry of Police, and I thought of you because I've heard you're related to the Baron von Krutz. You are, aren't you?" he asked, just as though he didn't know all about who all his officers are related to.

"That's right, colonel; the baron is my uncle," I said. "What does Hartenstein want done?"

"Why, he has a prisoner whom he wants taken to Berlin and turned over at the Ministry. All you have to do is to take him in, in a coach, and see he doesn't escape on the way, and get a receipt for him, and for some papers. This is a very important prisoner; I don't think Hartenstein has anybody he can trust to handle him. The prisoner claims to be some sort of British diplomat, and for all Hartenstein knows, maybe he is. Also, he is a madman."

"A madman?" I echoed.

"Yes, just so. At least, that's what Hartenstein told me. I wanted to know what sort of a madman—there are various kinds of madmen, all of whom must be handled differently—but all Hartenstein would tell me was that he had unrealistic beliefs about the state of affairs in Europe."

"Ha! What diplomat hasn't?" I asked.

Old Keitel gave a laugh, somewhere between the bark of a dog and the croaking of a raven.

"Yes, exactly! The unrealistic beliefs of diplomats are what soldiers die of," he said. "I said as much to Hartenstein, but he wouldn't tell me anything more. He seemed to regret having said even that much. He looked like a man who's seen a particularly terrifying ghost." The old man puffed hard at his famous pipe for a while, blowing smoke through his mustache. "Rudi, Hartenstein has pulled a hot potato out of the ashes, this time, and he wants to toss it to your uncle, before he burns his fingers. I think that's one reason why he got me to furnish an escort for his Englishman. How, look; you must take this unrealistic diplomat, or this undiplomatic madman, or whatever in blazes he is, to Berlin. And understand this." He pointed his pipe at me as though it were a pistol. "Your orders are to take him there and turn him over at the Ministry of Police. Nothing has been said about whether you turn him over alive, or dead, or half one and half the other. I know nothing about this business, and want to know nothing; if Hartenstein wants us to play gaol warders for him, then he must be satisfied with our way of doing it!"

Well, to cut short the story, I looked at the coach Hartenstein had placed at my disposal, and I decided to chain the left door shut on the outside, so that it couldn't be opened from within. Then, I would put my prisoner on my left, so that the only way out would be past me. I decided not to carry any weapons which he might be able to snatch from me, so I took off my saber and locked it in the seat box, along with the dispatch case containing the Englishman's papers. It was cold enough to wear a greatcoat in comfort, so I wore mine, and in the right side pocket, where my prisoner couldn't reach, I put a little leaded bludgeon, and also a brace of pocket pistols. Hartenstein was going to furnish me a guard as well as a driver, but I said that I would take a servant, who could act as guard. The servant, of course, was my orderly, old Johann; I gave him my double hunting gun to carry, with a big charge of boar shot in one barrel and an ounce ball in the other.

In addition, I armed myself with a big bottle of cognac. I thought that if I could shoot my prisoner often enough with that, he would give me no trouble.

As it happened, he didn't, and none of my precautions—except the cognac—were needed. The man didn't look like a lunatic to me. He was a rather stout gentleman, of past middle age, with a ruddy complexion and an intelligent face. The only unusual thing about him was his hat, which was a peculiar contraption, looking like a pot. I put him in the carriage, and then offered him a drink out of my bottle, taking one about half as big myself. He smacked his lips over it and said, "Well, that's real brandy; whatever we think of their detestable politics, we can't criticize the French for their liquor." Then, he said, "I'm glad they're sending me in the custody of a military gentleman, instead of a confounded gendarme. Tell me the truth, lieutenant; am I under arrest for anything?"

"Why," I said, "Captain Hartenstein should have told you about that. All I know is that I have orders to take you to the Ministry of Police, in Berlin, and not to let you escape on the way. These orders I will carry out; I hope you don't hold that against me."

He assured me that he did not, and we had another drink on it—I made sure, again, that he got twice as much as I did—and then the coachman cracked his whip and we were off for Berlin.

Now, I thought, I am going to see just what sort of a madman this is, and why Hartenstein is making a State affair out of a squabble at an inn. So I decided to explore his unrealistic beliefs about the state of affairs in Europe.

After guiding the conversation to where I wanted it, I asked him:

"What, *Herr* Bathurst, in your belief, is the real, underlying cause of the present tragic situation in Europe?"

That, I thought, was safe enough. Name me one year, since the days of Julius Caesar, when the situation in Europe hasn't been tragic! And it worked, to perfection.

"In my belief," says this Englishman, "the whole mess is the result of the victory of the rebellious colonists in North America, and their blasted republic."

Well, you can imagine, that gave me a start. All the world knows that the American Patriots lost their war for independence from England; that their army was shattered, that their leaders were either killed or driven into exile. How many times, when I was a little boy, did I not sit up long past my bedtime, when old Baron von Steuben was a guest at Tarlburg-Schloss, listening open-mouthed and wide-eyed to his stories of that gallant lost struggle! How I used to shiver at his tales of the terrible winter camp, or thrill at the battles, or weep as he told how he held the dying Washington in his arms, and listened to his noble last words, at the Battle of Doylestown! And here, this man was telling me that the Patriots had really won, and set up the republic for which they had fought! I had been prepared for some of what Hartenstein had called unrealistic beliefs, but nothing as fantastic as this.

"I can cut it even finer than that," Bathurst continued. "It was the defeat of Burgoyne at Saratoga. We made a good bargain when we got Benedict Arnold to turn his coat, but we didn't do it soon enough. If he hadn't been on the field that day, Burgoyne would have gone through Gates' army like a hot knife through butter."

But Arnold hadn't been at Saratoga. I know; I have read much of the American War. Arnold was shot dead on New Year's Day of 1776, during the storming of Quebec. And Burgoyne had done just as Bathurst had said; he had gone through Gates like a knife, and down the Hudson to join Howe.

"But, *Herr* Bathurst," I asked, "how could that affect the situation in Europe? America is thousands of miles away, across the ocean."

"Ideas can cross oceans quicker than armies. When Louis XVI decided to come to the aid of the Americans, he doomed himself and his regime. A successful resistance to royal authority in America was all the French Republicans needed to inspire them. Of course, we have Louis's own weakness to blame, too. If he'd given those rascals a whiff of grapeshot, when the mob tried to storm Versailles in 1790, there'd have been no French Revolution."

But he had. When Louis XVI ordered the howitzers turned on the mob at Versailles, and then sent the dragoons to ride down the survivors, the Republican movement had been broken. That had been when Cardinal Talleyrand, who was then merely Bishop of Autun, had come to the fore and become the power that he is today in France; the greatest King's Minister since Richelieu.

"And, after that, Louis's death followed as surely as night after day," Bathurst was saying. "And because the French had no experience in self-government, their republic was foredoomed. If Bonaparte hadn't seized power, somebody else would have; when the French murdered their king, they delivered themselves to dictatorship. And a dictator, unsupported by the prestige of royalty, has no choice but to lead his people into foreign war, to keep them from turning upon him."

It was like that all the way to Berlin. All these things seem foolish, by daylight, but as I sat in the darkness of that swaying coach, I was almost convinced of the reality of what he told me. I tell you, Uncle Eugen, it was frightening, as though he were giving me a view of Hell. *Gott im Himmel,* the things that man talked of! Armies swarming over Europe; sack and massacre, and cities burning; blockades, and starvation; kings deposed, and thrones tumbling like tenpins; battles in which the soldiers of every nation fought, and in which tens of thousands were mowed down like ripe grain; and, over all, the Satanic figure of a little man in a gray coat, who dictated peace to the Austrian Emperor in Schoenbrunn, and carried the Pope away a prisoner to Savona.

Madman, eh? Unrealistic beliefs, says Hartenstein? Well, give me madmen who drool spittle, and foam at the mouth, and shriek obscene blasphemies. But not this pleasant-seeming gentleman who sat beside me and talked of horrors in a quiet, cultured voice, while he drank my cognac.

But not all my cognac! If your man at the Ministry—the one with red hair and the bulldog face—tells you that I was drunk when I brought in that Englishman, you had better believe him!

Rudi.

(From Count von Berchtenwald, to the British Minister.)

28 November, 1809

Honored Sir:

The accompanying dossier will acquaint you with the problem confronting this Chancellery, without needless repetition on my part. Please to understand that it is not, and never was, any part of the intentions of the government of His Majesty Friedrich Wilhelm III to offer any injury or indignity to the government of His Britannic Majesty George III. We would never contemplate holding in arrest the person, or tampering with the papers, of an accredited envoy of your government. However, we have the gravest doubt, to make a considerable understatement, that this person who calls himself Benjamin Bathurst is any such envoy, and we do not think that it would be any service to the government of His Britannic Majesty to allow an impostor to travel about Europe in the guise of a British diplomatic representative. We certainly should not thank the government of His Britannic Majesty for failing to take steps to deal with some person who, in England, might falsely represent himself to be a Prussian diplomat.

This affair touches us as closely as it does your own government; this man had in his possession a letter of safe-conduct, which you will find in the accompanying dispatch case. It is of the regular form, as issued by this Chancellery, and is sealed with the Chancellery seal, or with a very exact counterfeit of it. However, it has been signed, as Chancellor of Prussia, with a signature indistinguishable from that of the Baron Stein, who is the present Prussian Minister of Agriculture. Baron Stein was shown the signature, with the rest of the letter covered, and without hesitation acknowledged it for his own writing. However, when the letter was uncovered and shown to him, his surprise and horror were such as would require the pen of a Goethe or a Schiller to describe, and he denied categorically ever having seen the document before.

I have no choice but to believe him. It is impossible to think that a man of Baron Stein's honorable and serious character would be party to the fabrication of a paper of this sort. Even aside from this, I am in the thing as deeply as he; if it is signed with his signature, it is also sealed with my seal, which has not been out of my personal keeping in the ten years that I have been Chancellor here. In fact, the word "impossible" can be used to describe the entire business. It was impossible for the man Benjamin Bathurst to have entered the inn yard—yet he did. It was impossible that he should carry papers of the sort found in his dispatch case, or that such papers should exist—yet I am sending them to you with this letter. It is impossible that Baron von Stein should sign a paper of the sort he did, or that it should be sealed by the Chancellery—yet it bears both Stein's signature and my seal.

You will also find in the dispatch case other credentials, ostensibly originating with the British Foreign Office, of the same character, being signed by persons having no connection with the Foreign Office, or even with the government, but being sealed with apparently authentic seals. If you send these papers to London, I fancy you will find that they will there create the same situation as that caused here by this letter of safe-conduct.

I am also sending you a charcoal sketch of the person who calls himself Benjamin Bathurst. This portrait was taken without its subject's knowledge. Baron von Krutz's nephew, Lieutenant von Tarlburg, who is the son of our mutual friend Count von Tarlburg, has a little friend, a very clever young lady who is, as you will see, an expert at this sort of work; she was introduced into a room at the Ministry of Police and placed behind a screen, where she could sketch our prisoner's face. If you should send this picture to London, I think that there is a good chance that it might be recognized. I can vouch that it is an excellent likeness.

To tell the truth, we are at our wits' end about this affair. I cannot understand how such excellent imitations of these various seals could be made, and the signature of the Baron von Stein is the most expert forgery that I have ever seen, in thirty years' experience as a statesman. This would indicate careful and painstaking work on the part of somebody; how, then, do we reconcile this with such clumsy mistakes, recognizable as such by any schoolboy, as signing the name of Baron Stein as Prussian Chancellor, or Mr. George Canning, who is a member of the opposition party and not connected with your government, as British Foreign secretary.

These are mistakes which only a madman would make. There are those who think our prisoner is mad, because of his apparent delusions about the great conqueror, General Bonaparte, alias the Emperor Napoleon. Madmen have been known to fabricate evidence to support their delusions, it is true, but I shudder to think of a madman having at his disposal the resources to manufacture the papers you will find in this dispatch case. Moreover, some of our foremost medical men, who have specialized in the disorders of the mind, have interviewed this man Bathurst and say that, save for his fixed belief in a nonexistent situation, he is perfectly sane.

Personally, I believe that the whole thing is a gigantic hoax, perpetrated for some hidden and sinister purpose, possibly to create confusion, and to undermine the confidence existing between your government and mine, and to set against one another various persons connected with both governments, or else as a mask for some other conspiratorial activity. Only a few months ago, you will recall, there was a Jacobin plot unmasked at Kölin.

But, whatever this business may portend, I do not like it. I want to get to the bottom of it as soon as possible, and I will thank you, my dear sir, and your government, for any assistance you may find possible.

I have the honor, sir, to be, et cetera, et cetera, et cetera,

Berchtenwald

FROM BARON VON KRUTZ, TO THE COUNT VON BERCHTENWALD. MOST URGENT; MOST IMPORTANT.

TO BE DELIVERED IMMEDIATELY AND IN PERSON, REGARDLESS OF CIRCUMSTANCES.

28 November, 1809

Count von Berchtenwald:

Within the past half hour, that is, at about eleven o'clock tonight, the man calling himself Benjamin Bathurst was shot and killed by a sentry at the Ministry of Police, while attempting to escape from custody.

A sentry on duty in the rear courtyard of the Ministry observed a man attempting to leave the building in a suspicious and furtive manner. This sentry, who was under the strictest orders to allow no one to enter or leave without written authorization, challenged him; when he attempted to run, the sentry fired his musket at him, bringing him down. At the shot, the Sergeant of the Guard rushed into the courtyard with his detail, and the man whom the sentry had shot was found to be the Englishman, Benjamin Bathurst. He had been hit in the chest with an ounce ball, and died before the doctor could arrive, and without recovering consciousness.

An investigation revealed that the prisoner, who was confined on the third floor of the building, had fashioned a rope from his bedding, his bed cord, and the leather strap of his bell pull. This rope was only long enough to reach to the window of the office on the second floor, directly below, but he managed to enter this by kicking the glass out of the window. I am trying to find out how he could do this without being heard. I can assure you that somebody is going to smart for this night's work. As for the sentry, he acted within his orders; I have commended him for doing his duty, and for good shooting, and I assume full responsibility for the death of the prisoner at his hands.

I have no idea why the self-so-called Benjamin Bathurst, who, until now, was well-behaved and seemed to take his confinement philosophically, should suddenly make this rash and fatal attempt, unless it was because of those infernal dunderheads of madhouse doctors who have been bothering him. Only this afternoon they deliberately handed him a bundle of newspapers—Prussian, Austrian, French, and English—all dated within the last month. They wanted, they said, to see how he would react. Well, God pardon them, they've found out!

What do you think should be done about giving the body burial?

Krutz

(From the British Minister, to the Count von Berchtenwald.)

December 20th, 1809

My dear Count von Berchtenwald:

Reply from London to my letter of the 28th, which accompanied the dispatch case and other papers, has finally come to hand. The papers which you wanted returned—the copies of the statements taken at Perleburg, the letter to the Baron von Krutz from the police captain, Hartenstein, and the personal letter of Krutz's nephew, Lieutenant von Tarlburg, and the letter of safe-conduct found in the dispatch case—accompany herewith. I don't know what the people at Whitehall did with the other papers; tossed them into the nearest fire, for my guess. Were I in your place, that's where the papers I am returning would go.

I have heard nothing, yet, from my dispatch of the 29th concerning the death of the man who called himself Benjamin Bathurst, but I doubt very much if any official notice will ever be taken of it. Your government had a perfect right to detain the fellow, and, that being the case, he attempted to escape at his own risk. After all, sentries are not required to carry loaded muskets in order to discourage them from putting their hands in their pockets.

To hazard a purely unofficial opinion, I should not imagine that London is very much dissatisfied with this denouement. His Majesty's government are a hard-headed and matter-of-fact set of gentry who do not relish mysteries, least of all mysteries whose solution may be more disturbing than the original problem.

This is entirely confidential, but those papers which were in that dispatch case kicked up the devil's own row in London, with half the government bigwigs protesting their innocence to high Heaven, and the rest accusing one another of complicity in the hoax. If that was somebody's intention, it was literally a howling success. For a while, it was even feared that there would be questions in Parliament, but eventually, the whose vexatious business was hushed.

You may tell Count Tarlburg's son that his little friend is a most talented young lady; her sketch was highly commended by no less an authority than Sir Thomas Lawrence, and here comes the most bedeviling part of a thoroughly bedeviled business. The picture was instantly recognized. It is a very fair likeness of Benjamin Bathurst, or, I should say, Sir Benjamin Bathurst, who is King's lieutenant governor for the Crown Colony of Georgia. As Sir Thomas Lawrence did his portrait a few years back, he is in an excellent position to criticize the work of Lieutenant von Tarlburg's young lady. However, Sir Benjamin Bathurst was known to have been in Savannah, attending to the duties of his office, and in the public eye, all the while that his double was in Prussia. Sir Benjamin does not have a twin brother. It has been suggested that this fellow might be a half-brother, but, as far as I know, there is no justification for this theory.

The General Bonaparte, alias the Emperor Napoleon, who is given so much mention in the dispatches, seems also to have a counterpart in actual life; there is, in the French army, a Colonel of Artillery by that name, a Corsican who Gallicized his original name of Napolione Buonaparte. He is a most brilliant military theoretician; I am sure some of your own officers, like General Scharnhorst, could tell you about him. His loyalty to the French monarchy has never been questioned.

This same correspondence to fact seems to crop up everywhere in that amazing collection of pseudo-dispatches and pseudo-State papers. The United States of America, you will recall, was the style by which the rebellious colonies referred to themselves, in the Declaration of Philadelphia. The James Madison who is mentioned as the current President of the United States is now living, in exile, in Switzerland. His alleged predecessor in office, Thomas Jefferson, was the author of the rebel Declaration; after the defeat of the rebels, he escaped to Havana, and died, several years ago, in the Principality of Lichtenstein.

I was quite amused to find our old friend Cardinal Talleyrand—without the ecclesiastical title—cast in the role of chief adviser to the usurper, Bonaparte. His Eminence, I have always thought, is the sort of fellow who would land on his feet on top of any heap, and who would as little scruple to be Prime Minister to His Satanic Majesty as to His Most Christian Majesty.

I was baffled, however, by one name, frequently mentioned in those fantastic papers. This was the English general, Wellington. I haven't the least idea who this person might be.

I have the honor, your excellency, et cetera, et cetera, et cetera.

Sir Arthur Wellesley

Introduction to
"Police Operation"

"Police Operation" is the first Paratime Police story and the only story that gives a detailed explanation of lateral time travel. In this story we are introduced to the Chief of Paratime Police, Tortha Karf, and his special assistant, Verkan Vall, whose career is almost brought to an untimely end before it really begins.

POLICE OPERATION

". . . there may be something in the nature of an occult police force, which operates to divert human suspicions, and to supply explanations that are good enough for whatever, somewhat in the nature of minds, human beings have—or that, if there be occult mischief makers and occult ravagers, they may be of a world also of other beings that are acting to check them, and to explain them, not benevolently, but to divert suspicion from themselves, because they, too, may be exploiting life upon this earth, but in ways more subtle, and in orderly, or organized, fashion."

Charles Fort: "LO!"

JOHN Strawmyer stood, an irate figure in faded overalls and sweat-whitened black shirt, apart from the others, his back to the weathered farm-buildings and the line of yellowing woods and the cirrus-streaked blue October sky. He thrust out a work-gnarled hand accusingly.

"That there heifer was worth two hund'rd, two hund'rd an' fifty dollars!" he clamored. "An' that there dog was just like one uh the fam'ly; an' now look at'm! I don't like t' use profane language, but you'ns gotta *do* some'n about this!"

Steve Parker, the district game protector, aimed his Leica at the carcass of the dog and snapped the shutter. "We're doing something about it," he said shortly. Then he stepped ten feet to the left and edged around the mangled heifer, choosing an angle for his camera shot.

The two men in the gray whipcords of the state police, seeing that Parker was through with the dog, moved in and squatted to examine it. The one with the triple chevrons on his sleeves took it by both forefeet and flipped it over on its back. It had been a big brute, of nondescript breed, with a rough black-and-brown coat. Something had clawed it deeply about the head, its throat was slashed transversely several times, and it had been disemboweled by a single slash that had opened its belly from breastbone to tail. They looked at it carefully, and then went to stand beside Parker while he photographed the dead heifer. Like the dog, it had been talon-raked on either side of the head, and its throat had been slashed deeply several times. In addition, flesh had been torn from one flank in great strips.

"I can't kill a bear outa season, no!" Strawmyer continued his plaint. "But a bear comes an' kills my stock an' my dog; that there's all right! That's the kinda deal a farmer always gits, in this state! I don't like t' use profane language—"

"Then don't!" Parker barked at him, impatiently. "Don't use any kind of language. Just put in your claim and shut up!" He turned to the men in whipcords and gray Stetsons. "You boys seen everything?" he asked. "Then let's go."

THEY walked briskly back to the barnyard, Strawmyer following them, still vociferating about the wrongs of the farmer at the hands of a cynical and corrupt State government. They climbed into the state police car, the sergeant and the private in front and Parker into the rear, laying his camera on the seat beside a Winchester carbine.

"Weren't you pretty short with that fellow back there, Steve?" the sergeant asked as the private started the car.

"Not too short. 'I don't like t' use profane language,'" Parker mimicked the bereaved heifer owner, and then he went on to specify: "I'm morally certain that he's shot at least four illegal deer in the last year. When and if I ever get anything on him, he's going to be sorrier for himself than he is now."

"They're the characters that always beef their heads off," the sergeant agreed. "You think that whatever did this was the same as the others?"

"Yes. The dog must have jumped it while it was eating at the heifer. Same superficial scratches about the head, and deep cuts on the throat or belly. The bigger the animal, the farther front the big slashes occur. Evidently something grabs them by the head with front claws, and slashes with hind claws; that's why I think it's a bobcat."

"You know," the private said, "I saw a lot of wounds like that during the war. My outfit landed on Mindanao, where the guerrillas had been active. And this looks like bolo-work to me."

"The surplus-stores are full of machetes and jungle knives," the sergeant considered. "I think I'll call up Doc Winters, at the County Hospital, and see if all his squirrel-fodder is present and accounted for."

"But most of the livestock was eaten at, like the heifer," Parker objected.

"By definition, nuts have abnormal tastes," the sergeant replied. "Or the eating might have been done later, by foxes."

"I hope so; that'd let me out," Parker said.

"Ha, listen to the man!" the private howled, stopping the car at the end of the lane. "He thinks a nut with a machete and a Tarzan complex is just good clean fun. Which way, now?"

"Well, let's see." The sergeant had unfolded a quadrangle sheet; the game protector leaned forward to look at it over his shoulder. The sergeant ran a finger from one to another of a series of variously colored crosses that had been marked on the map.

"Monday night, over here on Copperhead Mountain, that cow was killed," he said. "The next night, about ten o'clock, that sheep-flock was hit, on this side of Copperhead, right about here. Early Wednesday night, that mule got slashed up in the woods back of the Weston farm. It was only slightly injured; must have kicked the whatzit and got away, but the whatzit wasn't too badly hurt, because a few hours later, it hit that turkey-flock on the Rhymer farm. And last night, it did that." He jerked a thumb over his shoulder at the Strawmyer farm. "See, following the ridges, working toward the southeast, avoiding open ground, killing only at night. Could be a bobcat, at that."

"Or Jink's maniac with the machete," Parker agreed. "Let's go up by Hindman's Gap and see if we can see anything."

THEY turned, after a while, into a rutted dirt road, which deteriorated steadily into a grass-grown track through the woods. Finally, they stopped, and the private backed off the road. The three men got out; Parker with his Winchester, the sergeant checking the drum of a Thompson, and the private pumping a buckshot shell into the chamber of a riot gun. For half an hour, they followed the brush-grown trail beside the little stream; once, they passed a dark gray commercial-model jeep, backed to one side. Then they came to the head of the gap.

A man, wearing a tweed coat, tan field boots, and khaki breeches, was sitting on a log, smoking a pipe; he had a bolt-action rifle across his knees, and a pair of binoculars hung from his neck. He seemed about thirty years old, and any bobby-soxer's idol of the screen would have envied him the handsome regularity of his strangely immobile features. As Parker and the two State policemen approached, he rose, slinging his rifle, and greeted them.

"Sergeant Haines, isn't it?" he asked pleasantly. "Are you gentlemen out hunting the critter, too?"

"Good afternoon, Mr. Lee. I thought that was your jeep I saw, down the road a little." The sergeant turned to the others. "Mr. Richard Lee; staying at the old Kinchwalter place, the other side of Rutter's Fort. This is Mr. Parker, the district game protector. And Private Zinkowski." He glanced at the rifle. "Are you out hunting for it, too?"

"Yes. I thought I might find something up here. What do you think it is?"

"I don't know," the sergeant admitted. "It could be a bobcat. Canada lynx. Jink, here, has a theory that it's some escapee from the paper-doll factory, with a machete. Me, I hope not; but I'm not ignoring the possibility."

The man with the matinee-idol's face nodded. "It could be a lynx. I understand they're not unknown, in this section."

"We paid bounties on two in this county, in the last year," Parker said. "Odd rifle you have, there; mind if I look at it?"

"Not at all." The man who had been introduced as Richard Lee unslung and handed it over. "The chamber's loaded," he cautioned.

"I never saw one like this," Parker said. "Foreign?"

"I think so. I don't know anything about it; it belongs to a friend of mine, who loaned it to me. I think the action's German, or Czech; the rest of it's a custom job, by some West Coast gunmaker. It's chambered for some ultra-velocity wildcat load."

The rifle passed from hand to hand; the three men examined it in turn, commenting admiringly.

"You find anything, Mr. Lee?" the sergeant asked, handing it back.

"Not a trace." The man called Lee slung the rifle and began to dump the ashes from his pipe. "I was along the top of this ridge for about a mile on either side of the gap, and down the other side as far as Hindman's Run; I didn't find any tracks, or any indication of where it had made a kill."

The game protector nodded, turning to Sergeant Haines.

"There's no use us going any farther," he said. "Ten to one, it followed that line of woods back of Strawmyer's, and crossed over to the other ridge. I think our best bet would be the hollow at the head of Lowrie's Run. What do you think?"

The sergeant agreed. The man called Richard Lee began to refill his pipe methodically.

"I think I shall stay here for a while, but I believe you're right. Lowrie's Run, or across Lowrie's Gap into Coon Valley," he said.

AFTER Parker and the state policemen had gone, the man whom they had addressed as Richard Lee returned to his log and sat smoking, his rifle across his knees. From time to time, he glanced at his wristwatch and raised his head to listen. At length, faint in the distance, he heard the sound of a motor starting.

Instantly, he was on his feet. From the end of the hollow log on which he had been sitting, he produced a canvas musette-bag. Walking briskly to a patch of damp ground beside the little stream, he leaned the rifle against a tree and opened the bag. First, he took out a pair of gloves of some greenish, rubberlike substance and put them on, drawing the long gauntlets up over his coat sleeves. Then he produced a bottle and unscrewed the cap. Being careful to avoid splashing his clothes, he went about, pouring a clear liquid upon the ground in several places. Where he poured, white vapors rose, and twigs and grass grumbled into brownish dust. After he had replaced the cap and returned the bottle to the bag, he waited for a few minutes, then took a spatula from the musette and dug where he had poured the fluid, prying loose four black, irregular-shaped lumps of matter, which he carried to the running water and washed carefully, before wrapping them and putting them in the bag, along with the gloves. Then he slung bag and rifle and started down the trail to where he had parked the jeep.

Half an hour later, after driving through the little farming village of Rutter's Fort, he pulled into the barnyard of a rundown farm and backed through the open doors of the barn. He closed the double doors behind him, and barred them from within. Then he went to the rear wall of the barn, which was much closer to the front than the outside dimensions of the barn would have indicated.

He took from his pocket a black object like an automatic pencil. Hunting over the rough plank wall, he found a small hole and inserted the pointed end of the pseudo-pencil, pressing on the other end. For an instant, nothing happened. Then a ten-foot-square section of the wall receded two feet and slid noiselessly to one side. The section which had slid inward had been built of three-inch steel, masked by a thin covering of boards; the wall around it was two-foot concrete, similarly camouflaged. He stepped quickly inside.

Fumbling at the right side of the opening, he found a switch and flicked it. Instantly, the massive steel plate slid back into place with a soft, oily click. As it did, lights came on within the hidden room, disclosing a great semiglobe of some fine metallic mesh, thirty feet in diameter and fifteen in height. There was a sliding door at one side of this; the man called Richard Lee opened and entered through it, closing it behind him. Then he turned to the center of the hollow dome, where an armchair was placed in front of a small desk below a large instrument panel. The gauges and dials on the panel, and the levers and switches and buttons on the desk control board, were all lettered and numbered with characters not of the Roman alphabet or the Arabic notation, and, within instant reach of the occupant of the chair, a pistol-like weapon lay on the desk. It had a conventional index-finger trigger and a hand-fit grip, but instead of a tubular barrel, two slender parallel metal rods extended about four inches forward of the receiver, joined together at what would correspond to the muzzle by a streamlined knob of some light blue ceramic or plastic substance.

THE man with the handsome immobile face deposited his rifle and musette on the floor beside the chair and sat down. First, he picked up the pistol-like weapon and checked it, and then he examined the many instruments on the panel in front of him. Finally, he flicked a switch on the control board.

At once, a small humming began, from some point overhead. It wavered and shrilled and mounted in intensity, and then fell to a steady monotone. The dome about him flickered with a queer, cold iridescence and slowly vanished. The hidden room vanished, and he was looking into the shadowy interior of a deserted barn. The barn vanished; blue sky appeared above, streaked with wisps of high cirrus cloud. The autumn landscape flickered unreally. Buildings appeared and vanished, and other buildings came and went in a twinkling. All around him, half-seen shapes moved briefly and disappeared.

Once, the figure of a man appeared, inside the circle of the dome. He had an angry, brutal face, and he wore a black tunic piped with silver, and black breeches, and polished black boots, and there was an insignia, composed of a cross and thunderbolt, on his cap. He held an automatic pistol in his hand.

Instantly, the man at the desk snatched up his own weapon and thumbed off the safety, but before he could lift and aim it, the intruder stumbled and passed outside the force-field which surrounded the chair and instruments.

For a while, there were fires raging outside, and for a while, the man at the desk was surrounded by a great hall, with a high, vaulted ceiling, through which figures flitted and vanished. For a while, there were vistas of deep forests, always set in the same background of mountains and always under the same blue cirrus-laced sky. There was an interval of flickering blue-white light, of unbearable intensity. Then the man at the desk was surrounded by the interior of vast industrial works. The moving figures around him slowed and became more distinct. For an instant, the man in the chair grinned as he found himself looking into a big washroom, where a tall blond girl was taking a shower bath, and a pert little redhead was vigorously drying herself with a towel. The dome grew visible, coruscating with many-colored lights, and then the humming died and the dome became a cold and inert mesh of fine white metal. A green light above flashed on and off slowly.

He stabbed a button and flipped a switch, then got to his feet, picking up his rifle and musette and fumbling under his shirt for a small mesh bag, from which he took an inch-wide disk of blue plastic. Unlocking a container on the instrument panel, he removed a small roll of solidograph-film, which he stowed in his bag. Then he slid open the door and emerged into his own dimension of space-time.

Outside was a wide hallway, with a pale green floor, paler green walls, and a ceiling of greenish off-white. A big hole had been cut to accommodate the dome, and across the hallway a desk had been set up, and at it sat a clerk in a pale blue tunic, who was just taking the audio-plugs of a music-box out of his ears. A couple of policemen in green uniforms, with ultrasonic paralyzers dangling by thongs from their left wrists and holstered sigma-ray needlers like the one on the desk inside the dome, were kidding with some girls in vivid orange and scarlet and green smocks. One of these, in bright green, was a duplicate of the one he had seen rubbing herself down with a towel.

"Here comes your boss-man," one of the girls told the cops, as he approached. They both turned and saluted casually. The man who had lately been using the name of Richard Lee responded to their greeting and went to the desk. The policemen grasped their paralyzers, drew their needlers, and hurried into the dome.

Taking the disk of blue plastic from his packet, he handed it to the clerk at the desk, who dropped it into a slot in the voder in front of him. Instantly, a mechanical voice responded:

"Verkan Vall, blue-seal noble, hereditary Mavrad of Nerros. Special Chief's Assistant, Paratime Police, special assignment. Subject to no orders below those of Tortha Karf, Chief of Paratime Police. To be given all courtesies and co-operation within the Paratime Transposition Code and the Police Powers Code. Further particulars?"

The clerk pressed the "no" button. The blue sigil fell out of the release-slot and was handed back to its bearer, who was drawing up his left sleeve.

"You'll want to be sure I'm *your* Verkan Vall, I suppose?" he said, extending his arm.

"Yes, quite, sir."

The clerk touched his arm with a small instrument which swabbed it with antiseptic, drew a minute blood-sample, and medicated the needle prick, all in one almost painless operation. He put the blood-drop on a slide and inserted it at one side of a comparison microscope, nodding. It showed the same distinctive permanent colloid pattern as the sample he had ready for comparison; the colloid pattern given in infancy by injection to the man in front of him, to set him apart from all the myriad other Verkan Valls on every other probability-line of paratime.

"Right, sir," the clerk nodded.

The two policemen came out of the dome, their needlers holstered and their vigilance relaxed. They were lighting cigarettes as they emerged.

"It's all right, sir," one of them said. "You didn't bring anything in with you, this trip."

The other cop chuckled. "Remember that Fifth Level wild-man who came in on the freight conveyor at Jandar last month?" he asked.

If he was hoping that some of the girls would want to know, what wild-man, it was a vain hope. With a blue-seal Mavrad around, what chance did a couple of ordinary coppers have? The girls were already converging on Verkan Vall.

"When are you going to get that monstrosity out of our restroom," the little redhead in green coveralls was demanding. "If it wasn't for that thing, I'd be taking a shower right now."

"You were just finishing one, about fifty paraseconds off, when I came through," Verkan Vall told her.

The girl looked at him in obvious feigned indignation.

"Why, you—You *parapeeper!*"

Verkan Vall chuckled and turned to the clerk. "I want a strato-rocket and pilot for Dhergabar, right away. Call Dhergabar Paratime Police Field and give them my ETA; have an air-taxi meet me, and have the chief notified that I'm coming in. Extraordinary report. Keep a guard over the conveyor; I think I'm going to need it again, soon." He turned to the little redhead. "Want to show me the way out of here, to the rocket field?" he asked.

OUTSIDE, on the open landing field, Verkan Vall glanced up at the sky, then looked at his watch. It had been twenty minutes since he had backed the jeep into the barn, on that distant other time-line; the same delicate lines of white cirrus were etched across the blue above. The constancy of the weather, even across two hundred thousand parayears of perpendicular time, never failed to impress him. The long curve of the mountains was the same, and they were mottled with the same autumn colors, but where the little village of Rutter's Fort stood on that other line of probability, the white towers of an apartment-city rose—the living quarters of the plant personnel.

The rocket that was to take him to headquarters was being hoisted with a crane and lowered into the firing-stand, and he walked briskly toward it, his rifle and musette slung. A boyish-looking pilot was on the platform, opening the door of the rocket; he stood aside for Verkan Vall to enter, then followed and closed it, dogging it shut while his passenger stowed his bag and rifle and strapped himself into a seat.

"Dhergabar Commercial Terminal, sir?" the pilot asked, taking the adjoining seat at the controls.

"Paratime Police Field, back of the Paratime Administration Building."

"Right, sir. Twenty seconds to blast, when you're ready."

"Ready now." Verkan Vall relaxed, counting seconds subconsciously.

The rocket trembled, and Verkan Vall felt himself being pushed gently back against the upholstery. The seats, and the pilot's instrument panel in front of them, swung on gimbals, and the finger of the indicator swept slowly over a ninety-degree arc as the rocket rose and leveled. By then, the high cirrus clouds Verkan Vall had watched from the field were far below; they were well into the stratosphere.

There would be nothing to do, now, for the three hours in which the rocket sped northward across the pole and southward to Dhergabar; the navigation was entirely in the electronic hands of the robot controls. Verkan Vall got out his pipe and lit it; the pilot lit a cigarette.

"That's an odd pipe, sir," the pilot said. "Outtime item?"

"Yes, Fourth Probability Level; typical of the whole paratime belt I was working in." Verkan Vall handed it over for inspection. "The bowl's natural brier-root; the stem's a sort of plastic made from the sap of certain tropical trees. The little white dot is the maker's trademark; it's made of elephant tusk."

"Sounds pretty crude to me, sir." The pilot handed it back. "Nice workmanship, though. Looks like good machine production."

"Yes. The sector I was on is really quite advanced, for an electro-chemical civilization. That weapon I brought back with me—that solid-missile projector—is typical of most Fourth Level culture. Moving parts machined to the closest tolerances, and interchangeable with similar parts of all similar weapons. The missile is a small bolt of cupro-alloy coated lead, propelled by expanding gases from the ignition of some nitro-cellulose compound. Most of their scientific advance occurred within the past century, and most of that in the past forty years. Of course, the life-expectancy on that level is only about seventy years."

"Humph! I'm seventy-eight, last birthday," the boyish-looking pilot snorted. "Their medical science must be mostly witchcraft!"

"Until quite recently, it was," Verkan Vall agreed. "Same story there as in everything else—rapid advancement in the past few decades, after thousands of years of cultural inertia."

"You know, sir, I don't really understand this paratime stuff," the pilot confessed. "I know that all time is totally present, and that every moment has its own past-future line of event-sequence, and that all events in space-time occur according to maximum probability, but I just don't get this alternate probability stuff at all. If something exists, it's because it's the maximum-probability effect of prior causes; why does anything else exist on any other time-line?"

Verkan Vall blew smoke at the air-renovator. A lecture on paratime theory would nicely fill in the three-hour interval until the landing at Dhergabar. At least this kid was asking intelligent questions.

"Well, you know the principal of time-passage, I suppose?" he began.

"Yes, of course: Rhogom's Doctrine. The basis of most of our psychical science. We exist perpetually at all moments within our life-span; our extraphysical ego component passes from the ego existing at one moment to the ego existing at the next. During unconsciousness, the EPC is 'time-free'; it may detach, and connect at some other moment, with the ego existing at that time-point. That's how we precog. We take an autohypno and recover memories brought back from the future moment and buried in the subconscious mind."

"That's right," Verkan Vall told him. "And even without the autohypno, a lot of precognitive matter leaks out of the subconscious and into the conscious mind, usually in distorted forms, or else inspires 'instinctive' acts, the motivation for which is not brought to the level of consciousness. For instance, suppose you're walking along North promenade, in Dhergabar, and you come to the Martian Palace Café, and you go in for a drink and meet some girl and strike up an acquaintance with her. This chance acquaintance develops into a love affair, and a year later, out of jealousy, she rays you half a dozen times with a needler."

"Just about that happened to a friend of mine, not long ago," the pilot said. "Go on, sir."

"Well, in the microsecond or so before you die—or afterward, for that matter, because we know that the extraphysical component survives physical destruction—your EPC slips back a couple of years, and re-connects at some point pastward of your first meeting with this girl, and carries with it memories of everything up to the moment of detachment, all of which are indelibly recorded in your subconscious mind. So, when you re-experience the event of standing outside the Martian palace with a thirst, you go on to the Starway, or Nhergal's, or some other bar. In both cases, on both time-lines, you follow the line of maximum probability; in the second case, your subconscious future memories are an added causal factor."

"And when I back-slip, after I've been needled, I generate a new time-line? Is that it?"

Verkan Vall made a small sound of impatience. "No such thing!" he exclaimed. "It's semantically inadmissible to talk about the total presence of time with one breath and about generating new time-lines with the next. *All* time-lines are totally present, in perpetual co-existence. The theory is that the EPC passes from one moment on one time-line to the next moment on the next line, so that the true passage of the EPC from moment to moment is a two-dimensional diagonal. So, in the case we're using, the event of your going into the Martian Palace exists on one time-line, and the event of your passing along to the Starway exists on another, but both are events in real existence.

"Now, what we do in paratime transposition is to build up a hyper-temporal field to include the time-line we want to reach, and then shift over to it. Same point in the plenum; same point in primary time—plus primary time elapsed during mechanical and electronic lag in the relays—but a different line of secondary time."

"Then why don't we have past-future time travel on our own time-line?" the pilot wanted to know.

THAT was a question every paratimer has to answer, every time he talks paratime to the laity. Verkan Vall had been expecting it; he answered patiently.

"The Ghaldron-Hesthor field-generator is like every other mechanism; it can operate only in the area of primary time in which it exists. It can transpose to any other time-line, and carry with it anything inside its field, but it can't go outside its own temporal area of existence, any more than a bullet from that rifle can hit the target a week before it's fired," Verkan Vall pointed out. "Anything inside the field is supposed to be unaffected by anything outside. *Supposed to be* is the way to put it; it doesn't always work. Once in a while, something pretty nasty gets picked up in transit." He thought, briefly, of the man in the black tunic. "That's why we have armed guards at terminals."

"Suppose you pick up a blast from a nucleonic bomb," the pilot asked, "or something red-hot, or radioactive?"

"We have a monument, at Paratime Police Headquarters, in Dhergabar, bearing the names of our own personnel who didn't make it back. It's a large monument; over the past ten thousand years, it's been inscribed with quite a few names."

"You can have it: I'll stick to rockets!" the pilot replied. "Tell me another thing, though: What's all this about levels, and sectors, and belts? What's the difference?"

"Purely arbitrary terms. There are five main probability levels, derived from the five possible outcomes of the attempt to colonize this planet seventy-five thousand years ago. We're on the First Level—complete success, and colony fully established. The Fifth Level is the probability of complete failure—no human population established on this planet, and indigenous quasi-human life evolved indigenously. On the Fourth Level, the colonists evidently met with some disaster and lost all memory of their extraterrestrial origin, as well as all extraterrestrial culture. As far as they know, they are an indigenous race; they have a long prehistory of Stone-Age savagery.

"Sectors are areas of paratime on any level in which the prevalent culture has a common origin and common characteristics. They are divided more or less arbitrarily into sub-sectors. Belts are areas within sub-sectors where conditions are the result of recent alternate probabilities. For instance, I've just come from the Europo-American Sector of the Fourth Level, an area of about ten thousand parayears in depth, in which the dominant civilization developed on the North-West Continent of the Major Land Mass, and spread from there to the Minor Land Mass. The line on which I was operating is also part of a sub-sector of about three thousand parayears' depth, and a belt developing from one of several probable outcomes of a war concluded about three elapsed years ago. On that time-line, the field at the Hagraban Synthetics Works, where we took off, is part of an abandoned farm; on the site of Hagraban City is a little farming village. Those things are there, right now, both in primary time and in the plenum. They are about two hundred and fifty thousand parayears perpendicular to each other, and each is of the same general order of reality."

The red light overhead flashed on. The pilot looked into his visor and put his hands to the manual controls, in case of failure of the robot controls. The rocket landed smoothly, however; there was a slight jar as it was grappled by the crane and hoisted upright, the seats turning in their gimbals. Pilot and passenger unstrapped themselves and hurried through the refrigerated outlet and away from the glowing-hot rocket.

AN air-taxi, emblazoned with the device of the Paratime Police, was waiting. Verkan Vall said good-by to the rocket-pilot and took his seat beside the pilot of the aircab; the latter lifted his vehicle above the building level and then set it down on the landing-stage of the Paratime Police Building in a long, side-swooping glide. An express elevator took Verkan Vall down to one of the middle stages, where he showed his sigil to the guard outside the door of Tortha Karf's office and was admitted at once.

The Paratime Police chief rose from behind his semicircular desk, with its array of keyboards and viewing-screens and communicators. He was a big man, well past his two hundredth year; his hair was iron-gray and thinning in front, he had begun to grow thick at the waist, and his calm features bore the lines of middle age. He wore the dark-green uniform of the Paratime Police.

"Well, Vall," he greeted. "Everything secure?"

"Not exactly, sir." Verkan Vall came around the desk, deposited his rifle and bag on the floor, and sat down in one of the spare chairs. "I'll have to go back again."

"So?" His chief lit a cigarette and waited.

"I traced Gavran Sarn." Verkan Vall got out his pipe and began to fill it. "But that's only the beginning. I have to trace something else. Gavran Sarn exceeded his Paratime permit, and took one of his pets along. A Venusian nighthound."

Tortha Karf's expression did not alter; it merely grew more intense. He

used one of the short, semantically ugly terms which serve, in place of pro-
fanity, as the emotional release of a race that has forgotten all the taboos and
terminologies of supernaturalistic religion and sex-inhibition.

"You're sure of this, of course." It was less a question than a statement.

Verkan Vall bent and took cloth-wrapped objects from his bag, unwrap-
ping them and laying them on the desk. They were casts, in hard black plastic, of the footprints of some large three-toed animal.

"What do these look like, sir?" he asked.

Tortha Karf fingered them and nodded. Then he became as visibly angry
as a man of his civilization and culture-level ever permitted himself.

"What does that fool think we have a Paratime Code for?" he demanded.
"It's entirely illegal to transpose any extraterrestrial animal or object to any
time-line on which space-travel is unknown. I don't care if he is a green-seal
Thavrad; he'll face charges, when he gets back, for this!"

"He *was* a green-seal Thavrad," Verkan Vall corrected. "And he won't be
coming back."

"I hope you didn't have to deal summarily with him," Tortha Karf said.
"With his title, and social position, and his family's political importance, that
might make difficulties. Not that it wouldn't be all right with me, of course,
but we never seem to be able to make either the Management or the public realize the extremities to which we are forced, at times." He sighed. "We probably never shall."

Verkan Vall smiled faintly. "Oh, no, sir; nothing like that. He was dead before I transposed to that time-line. He was killed when he wrecked a self-
propelled vehicle he was using. One of those Fourth Level automobiles. I
posed as a relative and tried to claim his body for the burial-ceremony observed on that cultural level, but was told that it had been completely destroyed by fire when the fuel tank of this automobile burned. I was given
certain of his effects which had passed through the fire; I found his sigil concealed inside what appeared to be a cigarette case." He took a green disk from
the bag and laid it on the desk. "There's no question; Gavran Sarn died in the
wreck of that automobile."

"And the nighthound?"

"It was in the car with him, but it escaped. You know how fast those things
are. I found that track"—he indicated one of the black casts—"in some dried
mud near the scene of the wreck. As you see, the cast is slightly defective.
The others were fresh this morning, when I made them."

"And what have you done so far?"

"I rented an old farm near the scene of the wreck, and installed my field-generator there. It runs through to the Hagraban Synthetics Works, about a hundred miles east of Thalna-Jarvizar. I have my this-line terminal in the girls' rest room at the durable plastics factory; handled that on a local police-power writ. Since then, I've been hunting for the nighthound. I think I can find it, but I'll need some special equipment, and a hypno-mech indoctrination. That's why I came back."

HAS it been attracting any attention?" Tortha Karf asked anxiously.

"Killing cattle in the locality; causing considerable excitement. Fortunately, it's a locality of forested mountains and valley farms, rather than a built-up industrial district. Local police and wild-game protection officers are concerned; all the farmers excited, and going armed. The theory is that it's either a wildcat of some sort, or a maniac armed with a cutlass. Either theory would conform, more or less, to the nature of its depredations. Nobody has actually seen it."

"That's good!" Tortha Karf was relieved. "Well, you'll have to go and bring it out, or kill it and obliterate the body."

Verkan knew why, as well as his superior did. In a primitive culture, such an incursion would be assigned supernatural explanations, and embedded in the locally accepted religion. But this culture, while nominally religious, was highly rationalistic in practice. Typical lag-effect, characteristic of all expanding cultures. A hundred and fifty years ago, the inhabitants of this Europo-American Sector didn't even know how to apply steam power.

"Did you know," Vall asked, "that now it has begun to release nuclear energy in a few crude forms?"

Tortha Karf whistled, softly. "That's quite a jump. There's a sector that'll be in for trouble in the next few centuries."

"That is realized locally, sir." Verkan Vall concentrated on relighting his pipe for a moment, then continued: "I would predict space-travel on that sector within the next half century. Maybe the next quarter century, at least to the Moon. And the art of taxidermy is very highly developed. Now, suppose some farmer shoots that thing; what would he do with it, sir?"

Tortha Karf grunted. "Nice logic, Vall. On a most uncomfortable possibility. He'd have it mounted, and it'd be put in a museum, somewhere. And as soon as the first starship reaches Venus, and they find those things in a wild state, they'll have the mounted specimen identified."

"Exactly. And then, instead of beating their brains about *where* their specimen came from, they'll begin asking *when* it came from. They're quite capable of such reasoning, even now."

"A hundred years isn't a particularly long time," Tortha Karf considered. "I'll be retired then, but you'll have my job, and it'll be your headache. You'd better get this cleaned up now, while it can be handled. What are you going to do?"

"I'm not sure, now, sir. I want a hypno-mech indoctrination, first." Verkan Vall gestured toward the communicator on the desk. "May I?" he asked.

"Certainly." Tortha Karf slid the instrument across the desk. "Anything you want."

"Thank you, sir." Verkan Vall snapped on the code-index, found the symbol he wanted, and then punched it on the keyboard. "Special Chief's Assistant Verkan Vall," he identified himself. "Speaking from office of Tortha Karf, Chief of Paratime Police. I want a complete hypno-mech on Venusian nighthounds, emphasis on wild state, special emphasis domesticated nighthounds reverted to wild state in terrestrial surroundings, extra-special emphasis hunting techniques applicable to same. The word 'nighthound' will do for trigger-symbol." He turned to Tortha Karf. "Can I take it here?"

Tortha Karf nodded, pointing to a row of booths along the far wall of the office.

"Make set-up for wired transmission; I'll take it here."

"Very well, sir; in fifteen minutes," a voice replied out of the communicator.

Verkan Vall slid the communicator back. "By the way, sir, I had a hitch-hiker on the way back. Carried him about a hundred or so parayears; picked him up about three hundred parayears after leaving my other-line terminal. Nasty-looking fellow, in a black uniform; looked like one of these private-army storm troopers you find all through that sector. Armed, and hostile. I thought I'd have to ray him, but he blundered outside the field almost at once. I have a record, if you'd care to see it."

"Yes, put it on." Tortha Karf gestured toward the solidograph-projector. "It's set for miniature reproduction here on the desk; that be all right?"

VERKAN Vall nodded, getting out the film and loading it into the projector. When he pressed a button, a dome of radiance appeared on the desk top, two feet in width and a foot in height. In the middle of this appeared a small soli-dograph image of the interior of the conveyor, showing the desk, and the control board, and the figure of Verkan Vall seated at it. The little figure of the storm trooper appeared, pistol in hand. The little Verkan Vall snatched up his tiny needler; the storm trooper moved into one side of the dome and vanished.

Verkan Vall flipped a switch and cut out the image.

"Yes. I don't know what causes that, but it happens, now and then," Tortha Karf said. "Usually at the beginning of a transposition. I remember, when I was just a kid, about a hundred and fifty years ago—a hundred and thirty-nine, to be exact—I picked up a fellow on the Fourth Level, just about where you're operating, and dragged him a couple of hundred parayears. I went back to find him and return him to his own time-line, but before I could locate him, he'd been arrested by the local authorities as a suspicious character, and got himself shot trying to escape. I felt badly about that, but—" Tortha Karf shrugged. "Anything else happen on the trip?"

"I ran through a belt of intermittent nucleonic bombing on the Second Level." Verkan Vall mentioned an approximate paratime location.

"Aaagh! That Khiftan civilization—by courtesy so called!" Tortha Karf pulled a wry face. "I suppose the intra-family enmities of the Hvadka Dynasty have reached critical mass again. They'll fool around till they blast themselves back to the Stone Age."

"Intellectually, they're about there now. I had to operate in that sector once—Oh, yes, another thing, sir. This rifle." Verkan Vall picked it up, emptied the magazine and handed it to his superior. "The supplies office slipped up on this; it's not appropriate to my line of operation. It's a lovely rifle, but it's about two hundred percent in advance of existing arms design on my line. It excited the curiosity of a couple of police officers and a game-protector, who should be familiar with the weapons of their own time-line. I evaded by disclaiming ownership or intimate knowledge, and they seemed satisfied, but it worried me."

"Yes. That was made in our duplicating shops, here in Dhergabar." Tortha Karf carried it to a photographic bench behind his desk. "I'll have it checked while you're taking your hypno-mech. Want to exchange it for something authentic?"

"Why, no, sir. It's been identified to me, and I'd excite less suspicion with it than I would if I abandoned it and mysteriously acquired another rifle. I just wanted a check, and Supplies warned to be more careful in the future."

Tortha Karf nodded approvingly. The young Mavrad of Nerros Verkan Vall was thinking as a paratimer should.

"What's the designation of your line again?"

Verkan Vall told him. It was a short numerical term of six places, but it expressed a number of the order of ten to the fortieth power, exact to the last digit. Tortha Karf repeated it into his stenomemograph, with explanatory comment.

"There seems to be quite a few things going wrong in that area," he said. "Let's see, now."

HE punched the designation on a keyboard; instantly, it appeared on a translucent screen in front of him. He punched another combination and, at the top of the screen, under the number, there appeared:

EVENTS, PAST ELAPSED FIVE YEARS.

He punched again; below this line appeared the sub-heading:

EVENTS INVOLVING PARATIME TRANSPOSITION.

Another code-combination added a third line:

(ATTRACTING PUBLIC NOTICE AMONG INHABITANTS.)

He pressed the "start" button; the headings vanished, to be replaced by page after page of print, succeeding one another on the screen as the two men read. They told strange and apparently disconnected stories—of unexplained fires and explosions; of people vanishing without trace; of unaccountable disasters to aircraft. There were many stories of an epidemic of mysterious disk-shaped objects seen in the sky, singly or in numbers. To each account was appended one or more reference-numbers. Sometimes Tortha Karf or Verkan Vall would punch one of these and read, on an adjoining screen, the explanatory matter referred to.

Finally Tortha Karf leaned back and lit a fresh cigarette.

"Yes, indeed, Vall; very definitely we will have to take action in the matter of the runaway nighthound of the late Gavran Sarn," he said. "I'd forgotten that that was the time-line onto which the *Ardrath* expedition launched those antigrav disks. If this extraterrestrial monstrosity turns up on the heels of that 'flying saucer' business, everybody above the order of intelligence of a cretin will suspect some connection."

"What really happened in the *Ardrath* matter?" Verkan Vall inquired. "I was on the Third Level, on that Luvarian Empire operation, at the time."

"That's right; you missed that. Well, it was one of these joint-operation things. The Paratime Commission and the Space Patrol were experimenting with a new technique for throwing a spaceship into paratime. They used the cruiser *Ardrath,* Kalzarn Jann commanding. Went into space about halfway to the Moon and took up orbit, keeping on the sunlit side of the planet to avoid being observed. That was all right. But then Captain Kalzarn ordered away a flight of antigrav disks, fully manned, to take pictures, and finally authorized a landing in the western mountain range, Northern Continent, Minor Land Mass. That's when the trouble started."

He flipped the run-back switch, till he had recovered the page he wanted. Verkan Vall read of a Fourth Level aviator, in his little airscrew-drive craft, sighting nine high-flying saucerlike objects.

"That was how it began," Tortha Karf told him. "Before long, as other incidents of the same sort occurred, our people on that line began sending back to know what was going on. Naturally, from the different descriptions of these 'saucers,' they recognized the objects as antigrav landing-disks from a spaceship. So I went to the Commission and raised atomic blazes about it, and the *Ardrath* was ordered to confine operations to the lower areas of the Fifth Level. Then our people on that time-line went to work with corrective action. Here."

He wiped the screen and then began punching combinations. Page after page appeared, bearing accounts of people who had claimed to have seen the mysterious disks, and each report was more fantastic than the last.

THE standard smother-out technique," Verkan Vall grinned. "I only heard a little talk about the 'flying saucers,' and all of that was in joke. In that order of culture, you can always discredit one true story by setting up ten others, palpably false, parallel to it. Wasn't that the time-line the Tharmax Trading Corporation almost lost their paratime license on?"

"That's right; it was! They bought up all the cigarettes and caused a conspicuous shortage, after Fourth Level cigarettes had been introduced on this line and had become popular. They should have spread their purchases over a number of lines, and kept them within the local supply-demand frame. And they also got into trouble with the local government for selling unrationed petrol. We had to send in a special-operations group, and they came closer to having to engage in out-time local politics than I care to think of." Tortha Karf quoted a line from a currently popular song about the sorrows of a policeman's life. "We're jugglers, Vall; trying to keep our traders and sociological observers and tourists and plain idiots like the late Gavran Sarn out of trouble; trying to prevent panics and disturbances and dislocations of local economy as a result of our operations; trying to keep out of out-time politics—and, at all times, at all costs and hazards, by all means, guarding the secret of paratime transposition. Sometimes I wish Ghaldron Karf and Hesthor Ghrom had strangled in their cradles!"

Verkan Vall shook his head. "No, chief," he said. "You don't mean that; not really," he said. "We've been paratiming for the past ten thousand years. When the Ghaldron-Hesthor transtemporal field was discovered, our ancestors had pretty well exhausted the resources of this planet. We had a world population of half a billion, and it was all they could do to keep alive. After we began paratime transposition, our population climbed to ten billion, and there it stayed for the last eight thousand years. Just enough of us to enjoy our planet and the other planets of the system to the fullest; enough of everything for everybody that nobody need fight anybody for anything. We've tapped the resources of those other worlds on other time-lines, a little here, a little there, and not enough to really hurt anybody. We've left our mark in a few places— the Dakota Badlands, and the Gobi, on the Fourth Level, for instance—but we've done no great damage to any of them."

"Except the time they blew up half the Southern Island Continent, over about five hundred parayears on the Third Level," Tortha Karf mentioned.

"Regrettable accident, to be sure," Verkan Vall conceded. "And look how much we've learned from the experiences of those other time-lines. During the Crisis, after the Fourth Interplanetary War, we might have adopted Palnar Sarn's 'Dictatorship of the Chosen' scheme, if we hadn't seen what an exactly similar scheme had done to the Jak Hakka Civilization, on the Second Level. When Palnar Sarn was told about that, he went into paratime to see for himself, and when he returned, he renounced his proposal in horror."

Tortha Karf nodded. He wouldn't be making any mistake in turning his post over to the Mavrad of Nerros on his retirement.

"Yes, Vall; I know," he said. "But when you've been at this desk as long as I have, you'll have a sour moment or two, now and then, too."

A blue light flashed over one of the booths across the room. Verkan Vall got to his feet, removing his coat and hanging it on the back of his chair, and crossed the room, rolling up his left shirt sleeve. There was a relaxer-chair in the booth, with a blue plastic helmet above it. He glanced at the indicator-screen to make sure he was getting the indoctrination he called for, and then sat down in the chair and lowered the helmet over his head, inserting the ear plugs and fastening the chin strap. Then he touched his left arm with an injector which was lying on the arm of the chair, and at the same time flipped the starter switch.

Soft, slow music began to chant out of the earphones. The insidious fingers of the drug blocked off his senses, one by one. The music diminished, and the words of the hypnotic formula lulled him to sleep.

He woke, hearing the lively strains of dance music. For a while, he lay relaxed. Then he snapped off the switch, took out the ear plugs, removed the helmet and rose to his feet. Deep in his subconscious mind was the entire body of knowledge about the Venusian nighthound. He mentally pronounced the word, and at once it began flooding into his conscious mind. He knew the animal's evolutionary history, its anatomy, it characteristics, it dietary and reproductive habits, how it hunted, how it fought its enemies, how it eluded pursuit, and how best it could be tracked down and killed. He nodded. Already, a plan for dealing with Gavran Sarn's renegade pet was taking shape in his mind.

He picked a plastic cup from the dispenser, filled it from a cooler-tap with amber-colored spiced wine, and drank, tossing the cup into the disposal-bin. He placed a fresh injector on the arm of the chair, ready for the next user of the booth. Then he emerged, glancing at his Fourth Level wristwatch and mentally translating to the First Level time-scale. Three hours had passed; there had been more to learn about his quarry than he had expected.

Tortha Karf was sitting behind his desk, smoking a cigarette. It seemed as though he had not moved since Verkan Vall had left him, though the special agent knew that he had dined, attended several conferences, and done many other things.

"I checked up on your hitchhiker, Vall," the chief said. "We won't bother about him. He's a member of something called the Christian Avengers—one of those typical Europo-American race-and-religious hate groups. He belongs in a belt that is the outcome of the Hitler victory of 1940, whatever that was. Something unpleasant, I daresay. We don't owe him anything; people of that sort should be stepped on, like cockroaches. And he won't make any more trouble on the line where you dropped him than they have there already. It's in a belt of complete social and political anarchy; somebody probably shot him as soon as he emerged because he wasn't wearing the right sort of uniform. Nineteen-forty what, by the way?"

"Elapsed years since the birth of some religious leader," Verkan Vall explained. "And did you find out about my rifle?"

"Oh, yes. It's a reproduction of something that's called a Sharp's Model '37,235 Ultraspeed-Express. Made on an adjoining paratime belt by a company that went out of business sixty-seven years ago, elapsed time, on your line of operation. What made the difference was the Second War between the States. I don't know what that was, either—I'm not too well up on Fourth Level history—but whatever, your line of operation didn't have it. Probably just as well for them, though they very likely had something else, as bad or worse. I put in a complaint to Supplies about it, and got you some more ammunition and reloading tools. Now, tell me what you're going to do about this nighthound business."

TORTHA Karf was silent for a while, after Verkan Vall had finished.

"You're taking some awful chances, Vall," he said at length. "The way you plan doing it, the advantages will all be with the nighthound. Those things can see as well at night as you can in daylight. I suppose you know that, though; you're the nighthound specialist, now."

"Yes. But they're accustomed to hotland marshes; it's been dry weather for the last two weeks all over the northeastern section of the Northern Continent. I'll be able to hear it long before it gets close to me. And I'll be wearing an electric headlamp. When I snap that on, it'll be dazzled for a moment."

"Well, as I said, you're the nighthound specialist. There's the communicator; order anything you need." He lit a fresh cigarette from the end of the old one before crushing it out. "But be careful, Vall. It took me close to forty years to make a paratimer out of you; I don't want to have to repeat the process with somebody else before I can retire."

THE grass was wet as Verkan Vall—who reminded himself that here he was called Richard Lee—crossed the yard from the farmhouse to the ramshackle barn in the early autumn darkness. It had been raining that morning when the strato-rocket from Dhergabar had landed him at the Hagraban Synthetics Works, on the First Level; unaffected by the probabilities of human history, the same rain had been coming down on the old Kinchwalter farm, near Rutter's Fort, on the Fourth Level. And it had persisted all day, in a slow, deliberate drizzle.

He didn't like that. The woods would be wet, muffling his quarry's footsteps, and canceling his only advantage over the night-prowler he hunted. He had no idea, however, of postponing the hunt. If anything, the rain had made it all the more imperative that the nighthound be killed at once. At this season, a falling temperature would speedily follow. The nighthound, a creature of the hot Venus marshes, would suffer from the cold, and, taught by years of domestication to find warmth among human habitations, it would invade some isolated farmhouse or, worse, one of the little valley villages. If it were not killed tonight, the incident he had come to prevent would certainly occur.

Going to the barn, he spread on old horse blanket on the seat of the jeep, laid his rifle on it, and then backed the jeep outside. Then he took off his coat, removing his pipe and tobacco from the pockets, and spread it on the wet grass. He unwrapped a package and took out a small plastic spray-gun he had brought with him from the First Level, aiming it at the coat and pressing the trigger until it blew itself empty. A sickening, rancid fetor tainted the air—the scent of the giant poison-roach of Venus, the one creature for which the nighthound bore an inborn, implacable hatred. It was because of this compulsive urge to attack and kill the deadly poison-roach that the first human settler of Venus, long millennia ago, had domesticated the ugly and savage nighthound. He remembered that the Gavran family derived their title from their vast hotlands estates; that Gavran Sarn, the man who had brought this thing to the Fourth Level, had been born on that planet. When Verkan Vall donned that coat, he would become his own living bait for the murderous fury of the creature he sought. At the moment, mastering his queasiness and putting on the coat, he objected less to that danger than to the hideous stench of the scent, to obtain which a valuable specimen had been sacrificed at the Dhergabar Museum of Extraterrestrial Zoology the evening before.

Carrying the wrapper and the spray-gun to an outside fireplace, he snapped his lighter to them and tossed them in. They were highly inflammable, blazing up and vanishing in a moment. He tested the electric headlamp on the front of his cap; checked his rifle; drew the heavy revolver, an authentic product of his line of operation, and flipped the cylinder out and in again. Then he got into the jeep and drove away.

For half an hour, he drove quickly along the valley roads. Now and then he passed farmhouses, and dogs, puzzled and angered by the alien scent his coat bore, barked furiously. At length, he turned into a back road, and from this to the barely discernible trace of an old log road. The rain had stopped, and in order to be ready to fire in any direction at any time, he had removed the top of the jeep. Now he had to crouch below the windshield to avoid over-hanging branches. Once three deer—a buck and two does—stopped in front of him and stared for a moment, then bounded away with a flutter of white tails.

He was driving slowly, now; laying behind him a reeking trail of scent. There had been another stock-killing the night before, while he had been on the First Level. The locality of this latest depredation had confirmed his esti-mate of the beast's probable movements, and indicated where it might be prowling tonight. He was certain that it was somewhere near; sooner or later, it would pick up the scent.

Finally, he stopped, snapping out his lights. He had chosen this spot care-fully while studying the Geological Survey map that afternoon; he was on the grade of an old railroad line, now abandoned and its track long removed, which had served the logging operations of fifty years ago. On one side, the mountain slanted sharply upward; on the other, it fell away sharply. If the nighthound were below him, it would have to climb that forty-five degree slope, and could not avoid dislodging loose stones or otherwise making a noise. He would get out on that side; if the nighthound were above him, the jeep would protect him when it charged. He got to the ground, thumbing off the safety of his rifle, and an instant later he knew that he had made a mistake that might easily cost him his life; a mistake from which neither his comprehensive logic nor his hypnot-ically acquired knowledge of the beast's habits had saved him.

As he stepped to the ground, facing toward the front of the jeep, he heard a low, whining cry behind him, and a rush of padded feet. He whirled, snap-ping on the headlamp with his left hand and thrusting out his rifle pistol-wise in his right. For a split second, he saw the charging animal, its long, lizardlike head split in a toothy grin, it talon-tipped forepaws extended.

He fired, and the bullet went wild. The next instant, the rifle was knocked from his hand. Instinctively, he flung up his left arm to shield his eyes. Claws raked his left arm and shoulder, something struck him heavily along the left side, and his cap-light went out as he dropped and rolled under the jeep, drawing in his legs and fumbling under his coat for the revolver.

In that instant, he knew what had gone wrong. His plan had been entirely too much of a success. The nighthound had winded him as he had driven up the old railroad grade, and had followed. Its best running speed had been just good enough to keep it a hundred or so feet behind the jeep, and the motor-noise had covered the padding of its feet. In the few moments between stopping the little car and getting out, the nighthound had been able to close the distance and spring upon him.

IT was characteristic of First-Level mentality that Verkan Vall wasted no moments on self-reproach or panic. While he was still rolling under his jeep, his mind had been busy with plans to retrieve the situation. Something touched the heel of one boot, and he froze his leg into immobility, at the same time trying to get the big Smith & Wesson free. The shoulder holster, he found, was badly torn, though made of the heaviest skirting leather, and the spring which retained the weapon in place had been wrenched and bent until he needed both hands to draw. The eight-inch slashing-claw of the nighthound's right intermediary limb had raked him; only the instinctive motion of throwing up his arm, and the fact that he wore the revolver in a shoulder holster, had saved his life.

The nighthound was prowling around the jeep, whining frantically. It was badly confused. It could see quite well, even in the close darkness of the starless night; its eyes were of a nature capable of perceiving infrared radiations as light. There were plenty of these; the jeep's engine, lately running on four-wheel drive, was quite hot. Had he been standing alone, especially on this raw, chilly night, Verkan Vall's own body-heat would have lighted him up like a jack-o'-lantern. Now, however, the hot engine above him masked his own radiations. Moreover, the poison-roach scent on his coat was coming up through the floor board and mingling with the scent on the seat, yet the nighthound couldn't find the two-and-a-half foot insectlike thing that should have been producing it. Verkan Vall lay motionless, wondering how long the next move would be in coming. Then he heard a thud above him, followed by a furious tearing as the nighthound ripped the blanket and began rending at the seat cushion.

"Hope it gets a paw-full of seat-springs," Verkan Vall commented mentally. He had already found a stone about the size of his two fists, and another slightly smaller, and had put one in each of the side pockets of the coat. Now he slipped his revolver into his waist-belt and writhed out of the coat, shedding the ruined shoulder holster at the same time. Wriggling on the flat of his back, he squirmed between the rear wheels, until he was able to sit up, behind the jeep. Then, swinging the weighted coat, he flung it forward, over the nighthound and the jeep itself, at the same time drawing his revolver.

Immediately the nighthound, lured by the sudden movement of the principal source of the scent, jumped out of the jeep and bounded after the coat, and there was considerable noise in the brush on the lower side of the railroad grade. At once, Verkan Vall swarmed into the jeep and snapped on the lights.

His stratagem had succeeded beautifully. The stinking coat had landed on the top of a small bush, about ten feet in front of the jeep and ten feet from the ground. The nighthound, erect on its haunches, was reaching out with its front paws to drag it down, and slashing angrily at it with its single-clawed intermediary limbs. Its back was to Verkan Vall.

His sights clearly defined by the lights in front of him, the paratimer centered them on the base of the creature's spine, just above its secondary shoulders, and carefully squeezed the trigger. The big .357 Magnum bucked in his hand and belched flame and sound—if only these Fourth Level weapons weren't so confoundedly boisterous!—and the nighthound screamed and fell. Recocking the revolver, Verkan Vall waited for an instant, then nodded in satisfaction. The beast's spine had been smashed, and its hind quarters, and even its intermediary fighting limbs, had been paralyzed. He aimed carefully for a second shot and fired into the base of the thing's skull. It quivered and died.

GETTING a flashlight, he found his rifle, sticking muzzle-down in the mud a little behind and to the right of the jeep, and swore briefly in the local Fourth Level idiom, for Verkan Vall was a man who loved good weapons, be they sigma-ray needlers, neutron-disruption blasters, or the solid-missile projectors of the lower levels. By this time, he was feeling considerable pain from the claw-wounds he had received. He peeled off his shirt and tossed it over the hood of the jeep.

Tortha Karf had advised him to carry a needler, or a blaster, or a neurostat-gun, but Verkan Vall had been unwilling to take such arms onto the Fourth Level. In event of mishap to himself, it would be all to easy for such a weapon to fall into the hands of someone able to deduce from it scientific principles too far in advance of the general Fourth Level culture. But there had been one First Level item which he had permitted himself, mainly because, suitably packaged, it was not readily identifiable as such. Digging a respectable Fourth-Level leatherette case from under the seat, he opened it and took out a pint bottle with a red poison-label, and a towel. Saturating the towel with the contents of the bottle, he rubbed every inch of his torso with it, so as not to miss even the smallest break made in his skin by the septic claws of the nighthound. Whenever the lotion-soaked towel touched raw skin, a pain like the burn of a hot iron shot through him; before he was through, he was in agony. Satisfied that he had disinfected every wound, he dropped the towel and clung weakly to the side of the jeep. He grunted out a string of English oaths, and capped them with an obscene Spanish blasphemy he had picked up among the Fourth Level inhabitants of his island home of Nerros, to the south, and a thundering curse in the name of Mogga, Fire God of Dool, in a Third-Level tongue. He mentioned Fasif, Great God of Khift, in a manner which would have gotten him an acid-bath if the Khiftan priests had heard him. He alluded to the baroque amatory practices of the Third-Level Illyalla people, and soothed himself, in the classical Dar-Halma tongue, with one of those rambling genealogical insults favored in the Indo-Turanian Sector of the Fourth Level.

By this time, the pain had subsided to an over-all smarting itch. He'd have to bear with that until his work was finished and he could enjoy a hot bath. He got another bottle out of the first-aid kit—a flat pint, labeled "Old Oberholt," containing a locally manufactured specific for inward and subjective wounds—and medicated himself copiously from it, corking it and slipping it into his hip pocket against future need. He gathered up the ruined shoulder holster and threw it under the back seat. He put on his shirt. Then he went and dragged the dead nighthound onto the grade by its stumpy tail.

It was an ugly thing, weighing close to two hundred pounds, with powerfully muscled hind legs, which furnished the bulk of its motive-power, and sturdy three-clawed front legs. Its secondary limbs, about a third of the way back from its front shoulders, were long and slender; normally, they were carried folded closely against the body, and each was armed with a single curving claw. The revolver-bullet had gone in at the base of the skull and emerged under the jaw; the head was relatively undamaged. Verkan Vall was glad of that; he wanted that head for the trophy-room of his home on Nerros. Grunting and straining, he got the thing into the back of the jeep, and flung his almost shredded tweed coat over it.

A last look around assured him that he had left nothing unaccountable or suspicious. The brush was broken where the nighthound had been tearing at the coat; a bear might have done that. There were splashes of the viscid stuff the thing had used for blood, but they wouldn't be there long. Terrestrial rodents liked nighthound blood, and the woods were full of mice. He climbed in under the wheel, backed, turned, and drove away.

INSIDE the paratime-transposition dome, Verkan Vall turned from the body of the nighthound, which he had just dragged in, and considered the inert form of another animal—a stump-tailed, tuft-eared, tawny Canada lynx. That particular animal had already made two paratime transpositions; captured in the vast wilderness of Fifth-Level North America, it had been taken to the First Level and placed in the Dhergabar Zoological Gardens, and then, requisitioned on the authority of Tortha Karf, it had been brought to the Fourth Level by Verkan Vall. It was almost at the end of all its travels.

Verkan Vall prodded the supine animal with the toe of his boot; it twitched slightly. Its feet were cross-bound with straps, but when he saw that the narcotic was wearing off, Verkan Vall snatched a syringe, parted the fur at the base of its neck, and gave it an injection. After a moment, he picked it up in his arms and carried it out to the jeep.

"All right, pussy cat," he said, placing it under the rear seat, "this is the one-way ride. The way you're doped up, it won't hurt a bit."

He went back and rummaged in the debris of the long-deserted barn. He picked up a hoe, and discarded it as too light. An old plowshare was too unhandy. He considered a gratebar from a heating furnace, and then he found the poleax, lying among a pile of worm-eaten boards. Its handle had been shortened, at some time, to about twelve inches, converting it into a heavy hatchet. He weighed it, and tried it on a block of wood, and then, making sure that the secret door was closed, he went out again and drove off.

An hour later, he returned. Opening the secret door, he carried the ruined shoulder holster, and the straps that had bound the bobcat's feet, and the ax, now splotched with blood and tawny cat-hairs, into the dome. Then he closed the secret room, and took a long drink from the bottle on his hip.

The job was done. He would take a hot bath, and sleep in the farmhouse till noon, and then he would return to the First Level. Maybe Tortha Karf would want him to come back here for a while. The situation on this time-line was far from satisfactory, even if the crisis threatened by Gavran Sarn's renegade pet had been averted. The presence of a chief's assistant might be desirable.

At least, he had a right to expect a short vacation. He thought of the little redhead at the Hagraban Synthetics Works. What was her name? Something Kara—Morvan Kara; that was it. She'd be coming off shift about the time he'd make First Level tomorrow afternoon.

The claw-wounds were still smarting vexatiously. A hot bath, and a night's sleep—he took another drink, lit his pipe, picked up his rifle and started across the yard to the house.

PRIVATE Zinkowski cradled the telephone and got up from the desk, stretching. He left the orderly-room and walked across the hall to the recreation room, where the rest of the boys were loafing. Sergeant Haines, in a languid gin-rummy game with Corporal Conner, a sheriff's deputy, and a mechanic from the service station down the road, looked up.

"Well, Sarge, I think we can write off those stock-killings," the private said.

"Yeah?" The sergeant's interest quickened.

"Yeah. I think the whatzit's had it. I just got a buzz from the railroad cops at Logansport. It seems a track-walker found a dead bobcat on the Logan River branch, about a mile or so below MMY signal tower. Looks like it tangled with that night freight upriver, and came off second best. It was near chopped to hamburger."

"MMY signal tower; that's right below Yoder's Crossing," the sergeant considered. "The Strawmyer farm night-before-last, the Amrine farm last night—yeah, that would be about right."

"That'll suit Steve Parker; bobcats aren't protected, so it's not his trouble. And they're not a violation of state law, so it's none of our worry," Conner said. "Your deal, isn't it, Sarge?"

"Yeah. Wait a minute." The sergeant got to his feet. "I promised Sam Kane, the AP man at Logansport, that I'd let him in on anything new." He got up and started for the phone. "Phantom Killer!" He blew an impolite noise.

"Well, it was a lot of excitement while it lasted," the deputy sheriff said. "Just like that flying saucer thing."

Introduction to
"Last Enemy"

In "Last Enemy," the only Paratime story set on the Second Level, Piper introduces us to the fascinating Akor-Neb civilization and the Society of Assassins. While reincarnation is an accepted scientific fact on this time-line, no one is prepared for the consequences of communication with the unreincarnated dead—reverberations of which reach even to the First Level and threaten the Paratime Secret.

"Last Enemy" has my own personal nomination as the best Paratime story in this volume.

LAST ENEMY

ALONG the U-shaped table, the subdued clatter of dinnerware and the buzz of conversation was dying out; the soft music that drifted down from the overhead sound outlets seemed louder as the competing noises diminished. The feast was drawing to a close, and Dallona of Hadron fidgeted nervously with the stem of her wineglass as last-moment doubts assailed her.

The old man at whose right she sat noticed, and reached out to lay his hand on hers.

"My dear, you're worried," he said softly. "You, of all people, shouldn't be, you know."

"The theory isn't complete," she replied. "And I could wish for more positive verification. I'd hate to think I'd gotten you into this—"

Garnon of Roxor laughed. "No, no!" he assured her. "I'd decided upon this long before you announced the results of your experiments. Ask Girzon; he'll bear me out."

"That's true," the young man who sat at Garnon's left said, leaning forward. "Father has meant to take this step for a long time. He was waiting until after the election, and then he decided to do it now, to give you an opportunity to make experimental use of it."

The man on Dallona's right added his voice. Like the others at the table, he was of medium stature, brown-skinned and dark-eyed, with a wide mouth, prominent cheekbones and a short, square jaw. Unlike the others, he was armed, with a knife and pistol on his belt, and on the breast of his black tunic he wore a scarlet oval patch on which a pair of black wings, with a tapering silver object between them, had been superimposed.

"Yes, Lady Dallona; the Lord Garnon and I discussed this, oh, two years ago at the least. Really, I'm surprised that you seem to shrink from it now. Of course, you're Venus-born, and customs there may be different, but with your scientific knowledge—"

"That may be the trouble, Dirzed," Dallona told him. "A scientist gets in the way of doubting, and one doubts one's own theories most of all."

"That's the scientific attitude, I'm told," Dirzed replied, smiling. "But somehow, I cannot think of you as a scientist." His eyes traveled over her in a way that would have made most women, scientists or otherwise, blush. It gave Dallona of Hadron a feeling of pleasure. Men often looked at her that way, especially here at Darsh. Novelty had something to do with it—her skin was considerably lighter than usual, and there was a pleasing oddness about the structure of her face. Her alleged Venusian origin was probably accepted as the explanation of that, as of so many other things.

As she was about to reply, a man in dark gray, one of the upper-servants who were accepted as social equals by the Akor-Neb nobles, approached the table. He nodded respectfully to Garnon of Roxor.

"I hate to seem to hurry things, sir, but the boy's ready. He's in a trance-state now," he reported, pointing to the pair of visiplates at the end of the room.

Both of the ten-foot-square plates were activated. One was a solid luminous white; on the other was the image of a boy of twelve or fourteen, seated at a big writing machine. Even allowing for the fact that the boy was in a hypnotic trance, there was an expression of idiocy on his loose-lipped, slack-jawed face, a pervading dullness.

"One of our best sensitives," a man with a beard, several places down the table on Dallona's right, said. "You remember him, Dallona; he produced that communication from the discarnate Assassin, Sirzim. Normally, he's a low-grade imbecile, but in trance-state he's wonderful. And there can be no argument that the communications he produces originate in his own mind; he doesn't have mind enough, of his own, to operate that machine."

Garnon of Roxor rose to his feet, the others rising with him. He unfastened a jewel from the front of his tunic and handed it to Dallona.

"Here, my dear Lady Dallona; I want you to have this," he said. "It's been in the family of Roxor for six generations, but I know that you will appreciate and cherish it." He twisted a heavy ring from his left hand and gave it to his son. He unstrapped his wristwatch and passed it across the table to the gray-clad upper-servant. He gave a pocket case, containing writing tools, slide rule and magnifier, to the bearded man on the other side of Dallona. "Something you can use, Dr. Harnosh," he said. Then he took a belt, with a knife and holstered pistol, from a servant who had brought it to him, and gave it to the man with the red badge. "And something for you, Dirzed. The pistol's by Farnor of Yand, and the knife was forged and tempered on Luna."

The man with the winged-bullet badge took the weapons, exclaiming in appreciation. Then he removed his own belt and buckled on the gift.

"The pistol's fully loaded," Garnon told him.

Dirzed drew it and checked—a man of his craft took no statement about weapons without verification—then slipped it back into the holster.

"Shall I use it?" he asked.

"By all means; I'd had that in mind when I selected it for you."

Another man, to the left of Girzon, received a cigarette case and lighter. He and Garnon hooked fingers and clapped shoulders.

"Our views haven't been the same, Garnon," he said, "but I've always valued your friendship. I'm sorry you're doing this now; I believe you'll be disappointed."

Garnon chuckled. "Would you care to make a small wager on that, Nirzav?" he asked. "You know what I'm putting up. If I'm proven right, will you accept the Volitionalist theory as verified?"

Nirzav chewed his mustache for a moment. "Yes, Garnon, I will." He pointed toward the blankly white screen. "If we get anything conclusive on that, I'll have no other choice."

"All right, friends," Garnon said to those around him. "Will you walk with me to the end of the room?"

Servants removed a section from the table in front of him, to allow him and a few others to pass through; the rest of the guests remained standing at the table, facing toward the inside of the room. Garnon's son, Girzon, and the gray-mustached Nirzav of Shonna walked on his left; Dallona of Hadron and Dr. Harnosh of Hosh on his right. The gray-clad upper-servant, and two or three ladies, and a nobleman with a small chin-beard, and several others, joined them; of those who had sat close to Garnon, only the man in the black tunic with the scarlet badge hung back. He stood still, by the break in the table, watching Garnon of Roxor walk away from him. Then Dirzed the Assassin drew the pistol he had lately received as a gift, hefted it in his hand, thumbed off the safety, and aimed at the back of Garnon's head.

They had nearly reached the end of the room when the pistol cracked. Dallona of Hadron started, almost as though the bullet had crashed into her own body, then caught herself and kept on walking. She closed her eyes and laid a hand on Dr. Harnosh's arm for guidance, concentrating her mind upon a single question. The others went on as though Garnon of Roxor were still walking among them.

"Look!" Harnosh of Hosh cried, pointing to the image in the visiplate ahead. "He's under control!"

They all stopped short, and Dirzed, holstering his pistol, hurried forward to join them. Behind, a couple of servants had approached with a stretcher and were gathering up the crumpled figure that had, a moment ago, been Garnon.

A change had come over the boy at the writing machine. His eyes were still glazed with the stupor of the hypnotic trance, but the slack jaw had stiffened, and the loose mouth was compressed in a purposeful line. As they watched, his hands went out to the keyboard in front of him and began to move over it, and as they did, letters appeared on the white screen on the left.

Garnon of Roxor, discarnate, communicating, they read. The machine stopped for a moment, then began again. *To Dallona of Hadron: The question you asked, after I discarnated, was: What was the last book I read, before the feast? While waiting for my valet to prepare my bath, I read the first ten verses of the fourth canto of "Splendor of Space," by Larnov of Horka, in my bedroom. When the bath was ready, I marked the page with a strip of message tape, containing a message from the bailiff of my estate on the Shevva River, concerning a breakdown at the power plant, and laid the book on the ivory-inlaid table beside the big red chair.*

Harnosh of Hosh looked at Dallona inquiringly; she nodded.

"I rejected the question I had in my mind, and substituted that one, after the shot," she said.

He turned quickly to the upper-servant. "Check on that right away, Kirzon," he directed.

As the upper-servant hurried out, the writing machine started again.

And to my son, Girzon: I will not use your son, Garnon, as a reincarnation-vehicle; I will remain discarnate until he is grown and has a son of his own; if he has no male child, I will reincarnate in the first available male child of the family of Roxor, or of some family allied to us by marriage. In any case, I will communicate before reincarnating.

To Nirzav of Shonna: Ten days ago, when I dined at your home, I took a small knife and cut three notches, two close together and one a little apart from the others, on the underside of the table. As I remember, I sat two places down on the left. If you find them, you will know that I have won that wager that I spoke of a few minutes ago.

"I'll have my butler check on that right away," Nirzav said. His eyes were wide with amazement, and he had begun to sweat; a man does not casually watch the beliefs of a lifetime invalidated in a few moments.

To Dirzed the Assassin: the machine continued. *You have served me faithfully, in the last ten years, never more so than with the last shot you fired in my service. After you fired, the thought was in your mind that you would like to take service with the Lady Dallona of Hadron, whom you believe will need the protection of a member of the Society of Assassins. I advise you to do so, and I advise her to accept your offer. Her work, since she has come to Darsh, has not made her popular in some quarters. No doubt Nirzav of Shonna can bear me out on that.*

"I won't betray things told me in confidence, or said at the Councils of the Statisticalists, but he's right," Nirzav said. "You need a good Assassin, and there are few better than Dirzed."

I see that this sensitive is growing weary, the letters on the screen spelled out. *His body is not strong enough for prolonged communication. I bid you all farewell, for the time; I will communicate again. Good evening, my friends, and I thank you for your presence at the feast.*

The boy, on the other screen, slumped back in his chair, his face relaxing into its customary expression of vacancy.

"Will you accept my offer of service, Lady Dallona?" Dirzed asked. "It's as Garnon said; you've made enemies."

Dallona smiled at him. "I've not been too deep in my work to know that. I'm glad to accept your offer, Dirzed."

NIRZAV of Shonna had already turned away from the group and was hurrying from the room to call his home for confirmation on the notches made on the underside of his dining table. As he went out the door, he almost collided with the upper-servant, who was rushing in with a book in his hand.

"Here it is," the latter exclaimed, holding up the book. "Larnov's 'Splendor of Space,' just where he said it would be. I had a couple of servants with me as witnesses; I can call them in now, if you wish." He handed the book to

Harnosh of Hosh. "See, a strip of message tape in it, at the tenth verse of the fourth canto."

Nirzav of Shonna re-entered the room; he was chewing his mustache and muttering to himself. As he rejoined the group in front of the now dark visi-plates, he raised his voice, addressing them all generally.

"My butler found the notches, just as the communication described," he said. "This settles it! Garnon, if you're where you can hear me, you've won. I can't believe in the Statisticalist doctrines after this, or in the political program based upon them. I'll announce my change of attitude at the next meeting of the Executive Council, and resign my seat. I was elected by Statisticalist votes, and I cannot hold office as a Volitionalist."

"You'll need a couple of Assassins, too," the nobleman with the chin-beard told him. "Your former colleagues and fellow-party-members are regrettably given to the forcible discarnation of those who differ with them."

"I've never employed personal Assassins before," Nirzav replied, "but I think you're right. As soon as I get home, I'll call Assassins' Hall and make the necessary arrangements."

"Better do it now," Girzon of Roxor told him, lowering his voice. "There are over a hundred guests here, and I can't vouch for all of them. The Statisticalists would be sure to have a spy planted among them. My father was one of their most dangerous opponents when he was on the Council; they've always been afraid he'd come out of retirement and stand for re-election. They'd want to make sure he was really discarnate. And if that's the case, you can be sure your change of attitude is known to old Mirzark of Bashad by this time. He won't dare allow you to make a public renunciation of Statisticalism." He turned to the other nobleman. "Prince Jirzyn, why don't you call the Volitionalist headquarters and have a couple of our Assassins sent here to escort Lord Nirzav home?"

"I'll do that immediately," Jirzyn of Starpha said. "It's as Lord Girzon says; we can be pretty sure there was a spy among the guests, and now that you've come over to our way of thinking, we're responsible for your safety."

He left the room to make the necessary visiphone call. Dallona, accompanied by Dirzed, returned to her place at the table, where she was joined by Harnosh of Hosh and some of the others.

"There's no question about the results," Harnosh was exulting. "I'll grant that the boy might have picked up some of that stuff telepathically from the carnate minds present here; even from the mind of Garnon, before he was discarnated. But he could not have picked up enough data, in that way, to make a connected and coherent communication. It takes a sensitive with a powerful mind of his own to practice telesthesia, and that boy's almost an idiot." He turned to Dallona. "You asked a question, mentally, after Garnon was discarnate, and got an answer that could have been contained only in Garnon's mind. I think it's conclusive proof that the discarnate Garnon was fully conscious and communicating."

"Dirzed also asked a question, mentally, after the discarnation, and got an answer. Dr. Harnosh, we can state positively that the surviving individuality is fully conscious in the discarnate state, is telepathically sensitive, and is capable of telepathic communication with other minds," Dallona agreed. "And in view of our earlier work with memory-recalls, we're justified in stating positively that the individual is capable of exercising choice in reincarnation vehicles."

"My father had been considering voluntary discarnation for a long time," Girzon of Roxor said. "Ever since the discarnation of my mother. He deferred that step because he was unwilling to deprive the Volitionalist Party of his support. Now it would seem that he has done more to combat Statisticalism by discarnating than he ever did in his carnate existence."

"I don't know, Girzon," Jirzyn of Starpha said, as he joined the group. "The Statisticalists will denounce the whole thing as a prearranged fraud. And if they can discarnate the Lady Dallona before she can record her testimony under truth hypnosis or on a lie detector, we're no better off than we were before. Dirzed, you have a great responsibility in guarding the Lady Dallona; some extraordinary security precautions will be needed."

IN his office, in the First Level city of Dhergabar, Tortha Karf, Chief of Paratime Police, leaned forward in his chair to hold his lighter for his special assistant, Verkan Vall, then lit his own cigarette. He was a man of middle age—his three hundredth birthday was only a decade or so off—and he had begun to acquire a double chin and a bulge at his waistline. His hair, once black, had turned a uniform iron-gray and was beginning to thin in front.

"What do you know about the Second Level Akor-Neb Sector, Vall?" he inquired. "Ever work in that paratime-area?"

Verkan Vall's handsome features became even more immobile than usual as he mentally pronounced the verbal trigger symbols which should bring hypnotically acquired knowledge into his conscious mind. Then he shook his head.

"Must be a singularly well-behaved sector, sir," he said. "Or else we've been lucky so far. I never was on an Akor-Neb operation; don't even have a hypno-mech for that sector. All I know is from general reading.

"Like all the Second Level, its time-lines descend from the probability of one or more shiploads of colonists having come to Terra from Mars about seventy-five to a hundred thousand years ago, and then having been cut off from the home planet and forced to develop a civilization of their own here. The Akor-Neb civilization is of a fairly high culture-order, even for Second Level. An atomic-power, interplanetary culture; gravity-counteraction, direct conversion of nuclear energy to electrical power, that sort of thing. We buy fine synthetic plastics and fabrics from them." He fingered the material of his smartly cut green police uniform. "I think this cloth is Akor-Neb. We sell a lot of Venusian *zerfa*-leaf; they smoke it, straight and mixed with tobacco. They have a single System-wide government, a single race, and a universal language. They're a dark-brown race, which evolved in its present form about fifty thousand years ago; the present civilization is about ten thousand years old, developed out of the wreckage of several earlier civilizations which decayed or fell through wars, exhaustion of resources, et cetera. They have legends, maybe historical records, of their extraterrestrial origin."

Tortha Karf nodded. "Pretty good, for consciously acquired knowledge," he commented. "Well, our luck's run out on that sector; we have troubles there now. I want you to go iron them out. I know you've been going pretty hard, lately—that nighthound business, on the Fourth Level Europo-American Sector, wasn't any picnic. But the fact is that a lot of my ordinary and deputy assistants have a little too much regard for the alleged sanctity of human life, and this is something that may need some pretty drastic action."

"Some of our people getting out of line?" Verkan Vall asked.

"Well, the data isn't too complete, but one of our people has run into trouble on that sector, and needs rescuing—a psychic-science researcher, a young lady named Hadron Dalla. I believe you know her, don't you?" Tortha Karf asked innocently.

"Slightly," Verkan Vall deadpanned. "I enjoyed a brief but rather hectic companionate-marriage with her, about twenty years ago. What sort of a jam's little Dalla got herself into now?"

"Well, frankly, we don't know. I hope she's still alive, but I'm not unduly optimistic. It seems that about a year ago, Dr. Hadron transposed to the Second Level to study alleged proof of reincarnation, which the Akor-Neb people were reported to possess. She went to Gindrabar, on Venus, and transposed to the Second Paratime Level, to a station maintained by Outtime Import & Export Trading Corporation—a *zerfa* plantation just east of the High Ridge country. There she assumed an identity as the daughter of a planter, and took the name of Dallona of Hadron. Parenthetically, all Akor-Neb family names are prepositional; family names were originally place names. I believe that ancient Akor-Neb marital relations were too complicated to permit exact establishment of paternity. And all Akor-Neb men's personal names have -*irz*- or -*arn*- inserted in the middle, and women's names end in -*itra*- or -*ona*. You could call yourself Virzal of Verkan, for instance.

"Anyhow, she made the Second Level Venus-Terra trip on a regular passenger liner, and landed at the Akor-Neb city of Ghamma, on the upper Nile. There she established contact with the Outtime Trading Corporation representative, Zortan Brend, locally known as Brarnend of Zorda. He couldn't call himself Brarnend of Zortan—in the Akor-Neb language, *zortan* is a particularly nasty dirty-word. Hadron Dalla spent a few weeks at his residence, briefing herself on local conditions. Then she went to the capital city, Darsh, in eastern Europe, and enrolled as a student at something called the Independent Institute for Reincarnation Research, having secured a letter of introduction to its director, a Dr. Harnosh of Hosh.

"Almost at once, she began sending in reports to her home organization, the Rhogom Memorial Foundation of Psychic Science, here at Dhergabar, through Zortan Brend. The people there were wildly enthusiastic. I don't have more than the average intelligent—I hope—layman's knowledge of psychics, but Dr. Volzar Darv, the director of Rhogom Foundation, tells me that even in the present incomplete form, her reports have opened whole new horizons in the science. It seems that these Akor-Neb people have actually demonstrated, as a scientific fact, that the human individuality reincarnates after physical death—that your personality, and mine, have existed, as such, for ages, and will exist for ages to come. More, they have means of recovering, from almost anybody, memories of past reincarnations.

"Well, after about a month, the people at this Reincarnation Institute realized that this Dallona of Hadron wasn't any ordinary student. She probably had trouble keeping down to the local level of psychic knowledge. So, as soon as she'd learned their techniques, she was allowed to undertake experimental work of her own. I imagine she let herself out on that; as soon as she'd mastered the standard Akor-Neb methods of recovering memories of past reincarnations, she began refining and developing them more than the local yokels had been able to do in the past thousand years. I can't tell you just what she did, because I don't know the subject, but she must have lit things up properly. She got quite a lot of local publicity; not only scientific journals, but general newscasts.

"Then, four days ago, she disappeared, and her disappearance seems to have been coincident with an unsuccessful attempt on her life. We don't know as much about this as we should; all we have is Zortan Brend's account.

"It seems that on the evening of her disappearance, she had been attending the voluntary discarnation feast—suicide party—of a prominent nobleman named Garnon of Roxor. Evidently when the Akor-Neb people get tired of their current reincarnation they invite in their friends, throw a big party, and then do themselves in in an atmosphere of general conviviality. Frequently they take poison or inhale lethal gas; this fellow had his personal trigger man shoot him through the head. Dalla was one of the guests of honor, along with this Harnosh of Hosh. They'd made rather elaborate preparations, and after the shooting they got a detailed and apparently authentic spirit-communication from the late Garnon. The voluntary discarnation was just a routine social event, it seems, but the communication caused quite an uproar, and rated top place on the System-wide newscasts, and started a storm of controversy.

"After the shooting and the communication, Dalla took the officiating gun artist, one Dirzed, into her own service. This Dirzed was spoken of as a generally respected member of something called the Society of Assassins, and that'll give you an idea of what things are like on that sector, and why I don't want to send anybody who might develop trigger-finger cramp at the wrong moment. She and Dirzed left the home of the gentleman who had just had himself discarnated, presumably for Dalla's apartment, about a hundred miles away. That's the last that's been heard of either of them.

"This attempt on Dalla's life occurred while the premortem revels were still going on. She lived in a six-room apartment, with three servants, on one of the upper floors of a three-thousand-foot tower—Akor-Neb cities are built vertically, with considerable interval between units—and while she was at this feast, a package was delivered at the apartment, ostensibly from the Reincarnation Institute and made up to look as though it contained record tapes. One of the servants accepted it from a service employee of the apartments. The next morning, a little before noon, Dr. Harnosh of Hosh called her on the visiphone and got no answer; he then called the apartment manager, who entered the apartment. He found all three of the servants dead, from a lethal-gas bomb which had exploded when one of them had opened this package. However, Hadron Dalla had never returned to the apartment the night before."

VERKAN Vall was sitting motionless, his face expressionless as he ran Tortha Karf's narrative through the intricate semantic and psychological processes of the First Level mentality. The fact that Hadron Dalla had been a former wife of his had been relegated to one corner of his consciousness and contained there; it was not a fact that would, at the moment, contribute to the problem or to his treatment of it.

"The package was delivered while she was at this suicide party," he considered. "It must, therefore, have been sent by somebody who either did not know she would be out of the apartment, or who did not expect it to function until after her return. On the other hand, if her disappearance was due to hostile action, it was the work of somebody who knew she was at the feast and did not want her to reach her apartment again. This would seem to exclude the sender of the package bomb."

Tortha Karf nodded. He had reached that conclusion himself.

"Thus," Verkan Vall continued, "if her disappearance was the work of an enemy, she must have two enemies, each working in ignorance of the other's plans."

"What do you think she did to provoke such enmity?"

"Well, of course, it just might be that Dalla's normally complicated love-life had gotten a little more complicated than usual and short-circuited on her," Verkan Vall said, out of the fullness of personal knowledge, "but I doubt that, at the moment. I would think that this affair has political implications."

"So?" Tortha Karf had not thought of politics as an explanation. He waited for Verkan Vall to elaborate.

"Don't you see, chief?" the special assistant asked. "We find a belief in reincarnation on many time-lines, as a religious doctrine, but these people accept it as a scientific fact. Such acceptance would carry much more conviction; it would influence a people's entire thinking. We see it reflected in their disregard for death—suicide as a social function, this Society of Assassins, and the like. It would naturally color their political thinking, because politics is nothing but common action to secure more favorable living conditions, and to these people, the term 'living conditions' includes not only the present life, but also an indefinite number of future lives as well. I find this title, 'Independent' Institute, suggestive. Independent of what? Possibly of partisan affiliation."

"But wouldn't these people be grateful to her for her new discoveries, which would enable them to plan their future reincarnations more intelligently?" Tortha Karf asked.

"Oh, chief!" Verkan Vall reproached. "You know better than that! How many times have our people gotten in trouble on other time-lines because they divulged some useful scientific fact that conflicted with the locally revered nonsense? You show me ten men who cherish some religious doctrine or political ideology, and I'll show you nine men whose minds are utterly impervious to any factual evidence which contradicts their beliefs, and who regard the producer of such evidence as a criminal who ought to be suppressed. For instance, on the Fourth Level Europo-American Sector, where I was just working, there is a political sect, the Communists, who, in the territory under their control, forbid the teaching of certain well-established facts of genetics and heredity, because those facts do not fit the world-picture demanded by their political doctrines. And on the same sector, a religious sect recently tried, in some sections successfully, to outlaw the teaching of evolution by natural selection."

Tortha Karf nodded. "I remember some stories my grandfather told me about his narrow escapes from an organization called the Holy Inquisition, when he was a paratime trader on the Fourth Level, about four hundred years ago. I believe that thing's still operating, on the Europo-American Sector, under the name of NKVD. So you think Dalla may have proven something that conflicted with local reincarnation theories, and somebody who had a vested interest in maintaining those theories is trying to stop her?"

"You spoke of a controversy over the communication alleged to have originated with this voluntarily discarnated nobleman. That would suggest a difference of opinion on the manner of nature of reincarnation or the discarnate state. This difference may mark the dividing line between the different political parties. Now, to get to this Darsh place, do I have to go to Venus, as Dalla did?"

"No. The Outtime Trading Corporation has transposition facilities at Ravvanan, on the Nile, which is spatially coexistent with the city of Ghamma on the Akor-Neb Sector, where Zortan Brend is. You transpose through there, and Zortan Brend will furnish you transportation to Darsh. It'll take you about two days here, getting your hypno-mech indoctrinations and having your skin pigmented and your hair turned black. I'll notify Zortan Brend at once that you're coming through. Is there anything special you'll want?"

"Why, I'll want an abstract of the reports Dalla sent back to Rhogom Foundation. It's likely that there is some clue among them as to whom her discoveries may have antagonized. I'm going to be a Venusian *zerfa*-planter, a friend of her father's; I'll want full hypno-mech indoctrination to enable me to play that part. And I'll want to familiarize myself with Akor-Neb weapons and combat techniques. I think that will be all, chief."

THE last of the tall city-units of Ghamma were sliding out of sight as the ship passed over them—shaftlike buildings that rose two or three thousand feet above the ground in clumps of three or four or six, one at each corner of the landing stages set in series between them. Each of these units stood in the middle of a wooded park some five miles from its nearest neighbor, and the land between was the uniform golden-brown of ripening grain, crisscrossed with the threads of irrigation canals and dotted here and there with studdy farm-village buildings and tall, stacklike granaries. There were a few other ships in the air at the fifty-thousand-foot level, and below, swarms of small air-boats darted back and forth on different levels, depending upon speed and direction. Far ahead, to the northeast, was the shimmer of the Red Sea and the hazy bulk of Asia Minor beyond.

Verkan Vall—the Lord Virzal of Verkan, temporarily—stood at the glass front of the observation deck, looking down. He was a different Verkan Vall from the man who had talked with Tortha Karf in the latter's office, two days before. The First Level cosmeticists had worked miracles upon him with their art. His skin was a soft chocolate-brown, now; his hair was jet-black, and so were his eyes. And in his subconscious mind, instantly available to consciousness, was a vast body of knowledge about conditions on the Akor-Neb Sector, as well as a complete command of the local language, all hypnotically acquired.

He knew that he was looking down upon one of the minor provincial cities of a very respectably advanced civilization. A civilization which built its cities vertically, since it had learned to counteract gravitation. A civilization which still depended upon natural cereals for food, but one which had learned to make the most efficient use of its soil. The network of dams and irrigation canals which he saw was as good as anything on his own paratime level. The wide dispersal of buildings, he knew, was a heritage of a series of disastrous atomic wars of several thousand years before; the Akor-Neb people had come to love the wide inter-vistas of open country and forest, and had continued to scatter their buildings, even after the necessity had passed. But the slim, towering buildings could only have been reared by a people who had banished nationalism and, with it, the threat of total war. He contrasted them with the ground-hugging dome cities of the Khiftan civilization, only a few thousand parayears distant.

Three men came out of the lounge behind him and joined him. One was, like himself, a disguised paratimer from the First Level—the Outtime Import & Export man, Zortan Brend, here known as Brarnend of Zorda. The other two were Akor-Neb people, and both wore the black tunics and the winged-bullet badges of the Society of Assassins. Unlike Verkan Vall and Zortan Brend, who wore shoulder holsters under their short tunics, the Assassins openly displayed pistols and knives on their belts.

"We heard that you were coming two days ago, Lord Virzal," Zortan Brend said. "We delayed the take-off of this ship, so that you could travel to Darsh as inconspicuously as possible. I also booked a suite for you at the Solar Hotel, at Darsh. And these are your Assassins—Olirzon and Marnik."

Verkan Vall hooked fingers and clapped shoulders with them.

"Virzal of Verkan," he identified himself. "I am satisfied to entrust myself to you."

"We'll do our best for you, Lord Virzal," the older of the pair, Olirzon, said. He hesitated for a moment, then continued: "Understand, Lord Virzal, I only ask for information useful in serving and protecting you. But is this of the Lady Dallona a political matter?"

"Not from our side," Verkan Vall told him. "The Lady Dallona is a scientist, entirely nonpolitical. The Honorable Brarnend is a businessman; he doesn't meddle with politics as long as the politicians leave him alone. And I'm a planter on Venus; I have enough troubles, with the natives, and the weather, and blue-rot in the *zerfa* plants, and poison roaches, and javelin bugs, without getting into politics. But psychic science is inextricably mixed with politics, and the Lady Dallona's work had evidently tended to discredit the theory of Statistical Reincarnation."

"Do you often make understatements like that, Lord Virzal?" Olirzon grinned. "In the last six months, she's knocked Statistical Reincarnation to splinters."

"Well, I'm not a psychic scientist, and as I said, I don't know much about Terran politics," Verkan Vall replied. "I know that the Statisticalists favor complete socialization and political control of the whole economy, because they want everybody to have the same opportunities in every reincarnation. And the Volitionalists believe that everybody reincarnates as he pleases, and so they favor continuance of the present system of private ownership of wealth and private profit under a system of free competition. And that's about all I do know. Naturally, as a landowner and the holder of a title of nobility, I'm a Volitionalist in politics, but the socialization issue isn't important on

Venus. There is still too much unseated land there, and too many personal opportunities, to make socialism attractive to anybody."

"Well, that's about it," Zortan Brend told him. "I'm not enough of a psychicist to know what the Lady Dallona's been doing, but she's knocked the theoretical basis from under Statistical Reincarnation, and that's the basis, in turn, of Statistical Socialism. I think we'll find that the Statisticalist Party is responsible for whatever happened to her."

Marnik, the younger of the two Assassins, hesitated for a moment, then addressed Verkan Vall:

"Lord Virzal, I know none of the personalities involved in this matter, and I speak without wishing to give offense, but is it not possible that the Lady Dallona and the Assassin Dirzed may have gone somewhere together voluntarily? I have met Dirzed, and he has many qualities which women find attractive, and he is by no means indifferent to the opposite sex. You understand, Lord Virzal—"

"I understand all too perfectly, Marnik," Verkan Vall replied, out of the fullness of experience. "The Lady Dallona has had affairs with a number of men, myself among them. But under the circumstances, I find that explanation unthinkable."

Marnik looked at him in open skepticism. Evidently, in his book, where an attractive man and a beautiful woman were concerned, that explanation was never unthinkable.

"The Lady Dallona is a scientist," Verkan Vall elaborated. "She is not above diverting herself with love affairs, but that's all they are—a not too important form of diversion. And, if you recall, she had just participated in a most significant experiment; you can be sure that she had other things on her mind at the time than pleasure jaunts with good-looking Assassins."

THE ship was passing around the Caucasus Mountains, with the Caspian Sea in sight ahead, when several of the crew appeared on the observation deck and began preparing the shielding to protect the deck from gunfire. Zortan Brend inquired of the petty officer in charge of the work as to the necessity.

"We've been getting reports of trouble at Darsh, sir," the man said. "Newscast bulletins every couple of minutes; rioting in different parts of the city. Started yesterday afternoon, when a couple of Statisticalist members of the Executive Council resigned and went over to the Volitionalists. Lord

Nirzav of Shonna, the only nobleman of any importance in the Statisticalist Party, was one of them; he was shot immediately afterward, while leaving the Council Chambers, along with a couple of Assassins who were with him. Some people in an airboat sprayed them with a machine rifle as they came out onto the landing stage."

The two Assassins exclaimed in horrified anger over this.

"That wasn't the work of members of the Society of Assassins!" Olirzon declared. "Even after he'd resigned, the Lord Nirzav was still immune till he left the Government Building. There's too blasted much illegal assassination going on!"

"What happened next?" Verkan Vall wanted to know.

"About what you'd expect, sir. The Volitionalists weren't going to take that quietly. In the past eighteen hours, four prominent Statisticalists were forcibly discarnated, and there was even a fight in Mirzark of Bashad's house, when Volitionalist Assassins broke in; three of them and four of Mirzark's Assassins were discarnated."

"You know, something is going to have to be done about that, too," Olirzon said to Marnik. "It's getting to a point where these political faction fights are being carried on entirely between members of the Society. In Ghamma alone last year, thirty or forty of our members were discarnated that way."

"Plug in a newscast visiplate, Karnil," Zortan Brend told the petty officer. "Let's see what's going on in Darsh now."

In Darsh, it seemed, an uneasy peace was being established. Verkan Vall watched heavily armed airboats and light combat ships patrolling among the high towers of the city. He saw a couple of minor riots being broken up by the blue-uniformed Constabulary, with considerable shooting and a ruthless disregard for who might get shot. It wasn't exactly the sort of policing that would have been tolerated in the First Level Civil Order Section, but it seemed to suit Akor-Neb conditions. And he listened to a series of angry recriminations and contradictory statements by different politicians, all of whom blamed the disorders on their opponents. The Volitionalists spoke of the Statisticalists as "insane criminals" and "underminers of social stability," and the Statisticalists called the Volitionalists "reactionary criminals" and "enemies of social progress." Politicians, he had observed, differed little in their vocabularies from one time-line to another.

This kept up all the while the ship was passing over the Caspian Sea; as they were turning up the Volga valley, one of the ship's officers came down from the control deck above.

"We're coming into Darsh now," he said, and as Verkan Vall turned from the visiplate to the forward windows, he could see the white and pastel-tinted towers of the city rising above the hardwood forests that covered the whole Volga basin on this sector. "Your luggage has been put into the airboat, Lord Virzal and Honorable Assassins, and it's ready for launching whenever you are." The officer glanced at his watch. "We dock at Commercial Center in twenty minutes; we'll be passing the Solar Hotel in ten."

They all rose, and Verkan Vall hooked fingers and clapped shoulders with Zortan Brend.

"Good luck, Lord Virzal," the latter said. "I hope you find the Lady Dallona safe and carnate. If you need help, I'll be at Mercantile House for the next day or so; if you get back to Ghamma before I do, you know who to ask for there."

A number of Assassins loitered in the hallways and offices of the Independent Institute of Reincarnation Research when Verkan Vall, accompanied by Marnik, called there that afternoon. Some of them carried submachine-guns or sleep-gas projectors, and they were stopping people and questioning them. Marnik needed only to give them a quick gesture and the words, "Assassins' Truce," and he and his client were allowed to pass. They entered a lifter tube and floated up to the office of Dr. Harnosh of Hosh, with whom Verkan Vall had made an appointment.

"I'm sorry, Lord Virzal," the director of the Institute told him, "but I have no idea what has befallen the Lady Dallona, or even if she is still carnate. I am quite worried; I admired her extremely, both as an individual and as a scientist. I do hope she hasn't been discarnated; that would be a serious blow to science. It is fortunate that she accomplished as much as she did, while she was with us."

"You think she is no longer carnate, then?"

"I'm afraid so. The political effects of her discoveries—" Harnosh of Hosh shrugged sadly. "She was devoted, to a rare degree, to her work. I am sure that nothing but her discarnation could have taken her away from us at this time, with so many important experiments still uncompleted."

Marnik nodded to Verkan Vall, as much as to say: "You were right."

"Well, I intend acting upon the assumption that she is still carnate and in need of help, until I am positive to the contrary," Verkan Vall said. "And in the latter case, I intend finding out who discarnated her, and send him to apologize for it in person. People don't forcibly discarnate my friends with impunity."

"Sound attitude," Dr. Harnosh commented. "There's certainly no positive evidence that she isn't still carnate. I'll gladly give you all the assistance I can, if you'll only tell me what you want."

"Well, in the first place," Verkan Vall began, "just what sort of work was she doing?" He already knew the answer to that, from the reports she had sent back to the First Level, but he wanted to hear Dr. Harnosh's version. "And what, exactly, are the political effects you mentioned? Understand, Dr. Harnosh, I am really quite ignorant of any scientific subject unrelated to *zerfa* culture, and equally so of Terran politics. Politics on Venus is mainly a question of who gets how much graft out of what."

Dr. Harnosh smiled; evidently he had heard about Venusian politics. "Ah, yes, of course. But you are familiar with the main differences between Statistical and Volitional reincarnation theories?"

"In a general way. The Volitionalists hold that the discarnate individuality is fully conscious, and is capable of something analogous to sense-perception, and is also capable of exercising choice in the matter of reincarnation vehicles, and can reincarnate or remain in the discarnate state as it chooses. They also believe that discarnate individualities can communicate with one another, and with at least some carnate individualities, by telepathy," he said. "The Statisticalists deny all this; their opinion is that the discarnate individuality is in a more or less somnambulistic state, that it is drawn by a process akin to tropism to the nearest available reincarnation vehicle, and that it must reincarnate in and only in that vehicle. They are labeled Statisticalists because they believe that the process of reincarnation is purely at random, or governed by unknown and uncontrollable causes, and is unpredictable except as to aggregates."

"That's a fairly good generalized summary," Dr. Harnosh of Hosh grudged, unwilling to give a mere layman too much credit. He dipped a spoon into a tobacco humidor, dusted the tobacco lightly with dried *zerfa,* and rammed it into his pipe. "You must understand that our modern Statisticalists are the intellectual heirs of those ancient materialistic thinkers who denied the possibility of any discarnate existence, or of any extraphysical mind, or even of extrasensory perception. Since all these things have been demonstrated to be facts, the materialistic dogma has been broadened to include them, but always strictly within the frame of materialism.

"We have proven, for instance, that the human individuality can exist in a discarnate state, and that it reincarnates into the body of an infant, shortly after birth. But the Statisticalists cannot accept the idea of discarnate consciousness, since they conceive of consciousness purely as a function of the physical brain. So they postulate an unconscious discarnate personality or, as you put it, one in a somnambulistic state. They have to concede memory to this discarnate personality, since it was by recovery of memories of previous reincarnations that discarnate existence and reincarnation were proven to be facts. So they picture the discarnate individuality as a material object, or physical event, of negligible but actual mass, in which an indefinite number of memories can be stored as electrical charges. And they picture it as being drawn irresistibly to the body of the nearest non-incarnated infant. Curiously enough, the reincarnation vehicle chosen is almost always of the same sex as the vehicle of the previous reincarnation, the exceptions being cases of persons who had a previous history of psychological sex-inversion."

Dr. Harnosh remembered the unlighted pipe in his hand, thrust it into his mouth, and lit it. For a moment, he sat with it jutting out of his black beard, until it was drawing to his satisfaction. "This belief in immediate reincarnation leads the Statisticalists, when they fight duels or perform voluntary discarnation, to do so in the neighborhood of maternity hospitals," he added. "I know, personally, of one reincarnation memory-recall, in which the subject, a Statisticalist, voluntarily discarnated by lethal-gas inhaler in a private room at one of our local maternity hospitals, and reincarnated twenty years later in the city of Jeddul, three thousand miles away." The square black beard jiggled as the scientist laughed.

"Now, as to the political implications of these contradictory theories: Since the Statisticalists believe that they will reincarnate entirely at random, their aim is to create an utterly classless social and economic order, in which, theoretically, each individuality will reincarnate into a condition of equality with everybody else. Their political program, therefore, is one of complete socialization of all means of production and distribution, abolition of hereditary titles and inherited wealth—eventually, all private wealth—and total government control of all economic, social and cultural activities. Of course," Dr. Harnosh apologized, "politics isn't my subject; I wouldn't presume to judge how that would function in practice."

"I would," Verkan Vall said shortly, thinking of all the different time-lines on which he had seen systems like that in operation. "You wouldn't like it, doctor. And the Volitionalists?"

"Well, since they believe that they are able to choose the circumstances of their next reincarnations for themselves, they are the party of the *status quo*.

Naturally, almost all the nobles, almost all the wealthy trading and manufac- turing families, and almost all professional people are Volitionalists; most of the workers and peasants are Statisticalists. Or, at least, they were, for the most part, before we began announcing the results of the Lady Dallona's ex- perimental work."

"Ah; now we come to it," Verkan Vall said, as the story clarified.

"Yes. In somewhat oversimplified form, the situation is rather like this," Dr. Harnosh of Hosh said. "The Lady Dallona introduced a number of re- finements and some outright innovations into our technique of recovering memories of past reincarnations. Previously, it was necessary to keep the sub- ject in a hypnotic trance, during which he or she would narrate what was re- membered of past reincarnations, and this would be recorded. On emerging from the trance, the subject would remember nothing; the tape-recording would be all that would be left. But the Lady Dallona devised a technique by which these memories would remain in what might be called the fore part of the subject's subconscious mind, so that they could be brought to the level of consciousness at will. More, she was able to recover memories of past dis- carnate existences, something we had never been able to do heretofore." Dr. Harnosh shook his head. "And to think, when I first met her, I thought that she was just another sensation-seeking young lady of wealth, and was almost about to refuse her enrollment!"

He wasn't the only one whom little Dalla had surprised, Verkan Vall thought. At least he had been pleasantly surprised.

"You see, this entirely disproves the Statistical Theory of Reincarnation. For example, we got a fine set of memory-recalls from one subject, for four previous reincarnations and four intercarnations. In the first of these, the sub- ject had been a peasant on the estate of a wealthy noble. Unlike most of his fellows, who reincarnated into other peasant families almost immediately af- ter discarnation, this man waited for fifty years in the discarnate state for an opportunity to reincarnate as the son of an over-servant. In his next reincar- nation, he was the son of a technician, and received a technical education; he became a physics researcher. For his next reincarnation, he chose the son of a nobleman by a concubine as his vehicle; in his present reincarnation, he is a member of a wealthy manufacturing family, and married into a family of the nobility. In five reincarnations, he has climbed from the lowest to the next-to- highest rung of the social ladder. Few individuals of the class from whence he began this ascent possess so much persistence or determination. Then, of course, there was the case of Lord Garnon of Roxor."

He went on to describe the last experiment in which Hadron Dalla had participated.

"Well, that all sounds pretty conclusive," Verkan Vall commented. "I take it the leaders of the Volitionalist Party here are pleased with the result of the Lady Dallona's work?"

"Pleased? My dear Lord Virzal, they're fairly bursting with glee over it!" Harnosh of Hosh declared. "As I pointed out, the Statisticalist program of socialization is based entirely on the proposition that no one can choose the circumstances of his next reincarnation, and that's been demonstrated to be utter nonsense. Until the Lady Dallona's discoveries were announced, they were the dominant party, controlling a majority of the seats in Parliament and on the Executive Council. Only the Constitution kept them from enacting their entire socialization program long ago, and they were about to legislate constitutional changes which would remove that barrier. They had expected to be able to do so after the forthcoming general elections. But now, social inequality has become desirable; it gives people something to look forward to in the next reincarnation. Instead of wanting to abolish wealth and privilege and nobility, the proletariat want to reincarnate into them." Harnosh of Hosh laughed happily. "So you can see how furious the Statisticalist Party organization is!"

"There's a catch to this, somewhere," Marnik the Assassin, speaking for the first time, declared. "They can't all reincarnate as princes, there aren't enough vacancies to go 'round. And no noble is going to reincarnate as a tractor driver to make room for a tractor driver who wants to reincarnate as a noble."

"That's correct," Dr. Harnosh replied. "There is a catch to it; a catch most people would never admit, even to themselves. Very few individuals possess the willpower, the intelligence or the capacity for mental effort displayed by the subject of the case I just quoted. The average man's interests are almost entirely on the physical side; he actually finds mental effort painful, and makes as little of it as possible. And that is the only sort of effort a discarnate individuality can exert. So, unable to endure the fifty or so years needed to make a really good reincarnation, he reincarnates in a year or so, out of pure boredom, into the first vehicle he can find, usually one nobody else wants." Dr. Harnosh dug out the heel of his pipe and blew through the stem. "But nobody will admit his own mental inferiority, even to himself. Now every machine operator and field hand on the planet thinks he can reincarnate as a prince or a millionaire. Politics isn't my subject, but I'm willing to bet that since Statistical Reincarnation is an exploded psychic theory, Statisticalist Socialism has been caught in the blast area and destroyed along with it."

OLIRZON was in the drawing room of the hotel suite when they returned, sitting on the middle of his spinal column in a reclining chair, smoking a pipe, dressing the edge of his knife with a pocket-hone, and gazing lecherously at a young woman in the visiplate. She was an extremely well-designed young woman, in a rather fragmentary costume, and she was heaving her bosom at the invisible audience in anger, sorrow, scorn, entreaty, and numerous other emotions.

". . . this revolting crime," she was declaiming, in a husky contralto, as Verkan Vall and Marnik entered, "foul even for the criminal beasts who conceived and perpetrated it!" She pointed an accusing finger. "This murder of the beautiful Lady Dallona of Hadron!"

Verkan Vall stopped short, considering the possibility of something having been discovered lately of which he was ignorant. Olirzon must have guessed his thought; he grinned reassuringly.

"Think nothing of it, Lord Virzal," he said, waving his knife at the visiplate. "Just political propaganda; strictly for the sparrows. Nice propagandist, though."

"And now," the woman with the magnificent natural resources lowered her voice reverently, "we bring you the last image of the Lady Dallona, and of Dirzed, her faithful Assassin, taken just before they vanished, never to be seen again."

The plate darkened, and there were strains of slow, dirgelike music; then it lighted again, presenting a view of a broad hallway, thronged with men and women in bright vari-colored costumes. In the foreground, wearing a tight skirt of deep blue and a short red jacket, was Hadron Dalla, just as she had looked in the solidographs taken in Dhergabar after her alteration by the First Level cosmeticians to conform to the appearance of the Malayoid Akor-Neb people. She was holding the arm of a man who wore the black tunic and red badge of an Assassin, a handsome specimen of the Akor-Neb race. Trust little Dalla for that, Verkan Vall thought. The figures were moving with exaggerated slowness, as though a very fleeting picture were being stretched out as far as possible. Having already memorized his former wife's changed appearance, Verkan Vall concentrated on the man beside her until the picture faded.

"All right, Olirzon; what did you get?" he asked.

"Well, first of all, at Assassins' Hall," Olirzon said, rolling up his left sleeve, holding his bare forearm to the light, and shaving a few fine hairs from it to test the edge of his knife. "Of course, they never tell one Assassin anything about the client of another Assassin; that's standard practice. But I was in the Lodge Secretary's office, where nobody but Assassins are ever admitted. They have a big panel in there, with the names of all the Lodge members on it in light-letters; that's standard in all Lodges. If an Assassin is unattached and free to accept a client, his name's in white light. If he has a client, the light's changed to blue, and the name of the client goes up under his. If his whereabouts are unknown, the light's changed to amber. If he is discarnated, his name's removed entirely, unless the circumstances of his discarnation are such as to constitute an injury to the Society. In that case, the name's in red light until he's been properly avenged, or, as we say, till his blood's been mopped up. Well, the name of Dirzed is up in blue light, with the name of Dallona of Hadron under it. I found out that the light had been amber for two days after the disappearance, and then had been changed back to blue. Get it, Lord Virzal?"

Verkan Vall nodded. "I think so. I'd been considering that as a possibility from the first. Then what?"

"Then I was about and around for a couple of hours, buying drinks for people—unattached Assassins, Constabulary detectives, political workers, newscast people. You owe me fifteen System Monetary Units for that, Lord Virzal. What I got, when it's all sorted out—I taped it in detail, as soon as I got back—reduces to this: The Volitionalists are moving mountains to find out who was the spy at Garnon of Roxor's discarnation feast, but are doing nothing but nothing at all to find the Lady Dallona or Dirzed. The Statisticalists are making all sorts of secret efforts to find out what happened to her. The Constabulary blame the Statistos for the package bomb; they're interested in that because of the discarnation of the three servants by an illegal weapon of indiscriminate effect. They claim that the disappearance of Dirzed and the Lady Dallona was a publicity hoax. The Volitionalists are preparing a line of publicity to deny this."

Verkan Vall nodded. "That ties in with what you learned at Assassins' Hall," he said. "They're hiding out somewhere. Is there any chance of reaching Dirzed through the Society of Assassins?"

Olirzon shook his head. "If you're right—and that's the way it looks to me, too—he's probably just called in and notified the Society that he's still carnate and so is the Lady Dallona, and called off any search the Society might be making for him."

"And I've got to find the Lady Dallona as soon as I can. Well, if I can't reach her, maybe I can get her to send word to me," Verkan Vall said. "That's going to take some doing, too."

"What did you find out, Lord Virzal?" Olirzon asked. He had a piece of soft leather, now, and was polishing his blade lovingly.

"The Reincarnation Research people don't know anything," Verkan Vall replied. "Dr. Harnosh of Hosh thinks she's discarnate. I did find out that the experimental work she's done, so far, has absolutely disproved the theory of Statistical Reincarnation. The Volitionalists' theory is solidly established."

"Yes, what do you think, Olirzon?" Marnik added. "They have a case on record of a man who worked up from field hand to millionaire in five reincarnations. Deliberately, that is." He went on to repeat what Harnosh of Hosh had said; he must have possessed an almost eidetic memory, for he gave the bearded psychicist's words verbatim, and threw in the gestures and voice-inflections.

Olirzon grinned. "You know, there's a chance for the easy-money boys," he considered. " 'You, too, can Reincarnate as a millionaire! Let Dr. Nirzutz of Futzbutz Help You! Only 49.98 System Monetary Units for the Secret, Infallible, Autosuggestive Formula.' And would it sell!" He put away the hone and the bit of leather and slipped his knife back into its sheath. "If I weren't a respectable Assassin, I'd give it a try, myself."

Verkan Vall looked at his watch. "We'd better get something to eat," he said. "We'll go down to the main dining room; the Martian Room, I think they call it. I've got to think of some way to let the Lady Dallona know I'm looking for her."

THE Martian Room, fifteen stories down, was a big place, occupying almost half of the floor space of one corner tower. It had been fitted to resemble one of the ruined buildings of the ancient and vanished race of Mars who were the ancestors of Terran humanity. One whole side of the room was a gigantic cine-solidograph screen, on which the gullied desolation of a Martian landscape was projected; in the course of about two hours, the scene changed from sunrise through daylight and night to sunrise again.

It was high noon when they entered and found a table; by the time they had finished their dinner, the night was ending and the first glow of dawn was tinting the distant hills. They sat for a while, watching the light grow stronger, then got up and left the table.

There were five men at a table near them; they had come in before the stars had grown dim, and the waiters were just bringing their first dishes. Two were Assassins, and the other three were of a breed Verkan Vall had learned to recognize on any time-line—the arrogant, cocksure, ambitious, leftist politician, who knows what is best for everybody better than anybody else does, and who is convinced that he is inescapably right and that whoever differs with him is not only an ignoramus but a venal scoundrel as well. One was a beefy man in a gold-laced cream-colored dress tunic; he had thick lips and a too-ready laugh. Another was a rather monkish-looking young man who spoke earnestly and rolled his eyes upward, as though at some celestial vision. The third had the faint powdering of gray in his black hair, which was, among the Akor-Neb people, almost the only indication of advanced age.

"Of course it is; the whole thing is a fraud," the monkish young man was saying angrily. "But we can't prove it."

"Oh, Sirzob, here, can prove anything, if you give him time," the beefy one laughed. "The trouble is, there isn't too much time. We know that that communication was a fake, prearranged by the Volitionalists, with Dr. Harnosh and this Dallona of Hadron as their tools. They fed the whole thing to that idiot boy hypnotically, in advance, and then, on a signal, he began typing out this spurious communication. And then, of course, Dallona and this Assassin of hers ran off somewhere together, so that we'd be blamed with discarnating or abducting them, and so that they wouldn't be made to testify about the communication on a lie detector."

A sudden happy smile touched Verkan Vall's eyes. He caught each of his Assassins by an arm.

"Marnik, cover my back," he ordered. "Olirzon, cover everybody at the table. Come on!"

Then he stepped forward, halting between the chairs of the young man and the man with the gray hair and facing the beefy man in the light tunic.

"You!" he barked. "I mean **YOU.**"

The beefy man stopped laughing and stared at him; then sprang to his feet. His hand, streaking toward his left armpit, stopped and dropped to his side as Olirzon aimed a pistol at him. The others sat motionless.

"You," Verkan Vall continued, "are a complete, deliberate, malicious, and unmitigated liar. The Lady Dallona of Hadron is a scientist of integrity, incapable of falsifying her experimental work. What's more, her father is one of my best friends; in his name, and in hers, I demand a full retraction of the slanderous statements you have just made."

"Do you know who I am?" the beefy one shouted.

"I know *what* you are," Verkan Vall shouted back. Like most ancient languages, the Akor-Neb speech included an elaborate, delicately shaded, and utterly vile vocabulary of abuse; Verkan Vall culled from it judiciously and at length. "And if I don't make myself understood verbally, we'll go down to the object level," he added, snatching a bowl of soup from in front of the monkish-looking young man and throwing it across the table.

The soup was a dark brown, almost black. It contained bits of meat, and mushrooms, and slices of hard-boiled egg, and yellow Martian rock lichen. It produced, on the light tunic, a most spectacular effect.

For a moment, Verkan Vall was afraid the fellow would have an apoplectic stroke, or an epileptic fit. Mastering himself, however, he bowed jerkily.

"Marnark of Bashad," he identified himself. "When and where can my friends consult yours?"

"Lord Virzal of Verkan," the paratimer bowed back. "Your friends can negotiate with mine here and now. I am represented by these Gentlemen-Assassins."

"I won't submit my friends to the indignity of negotiating with them," Marnark retorted. "I insist that you be represented by persons of your own quality and mine."

"Oh, you do?" Olirzon broke in. "Well, is your objection personal to me, or to Assassins as a class? In the first case, I'll remember to make a private project of you, as soon as I'm through with my present employment; if it's the latter, I'll report your attitude to the Society. I'll see what Klarnood, our President-General, thinks of your views."

A crowd had begun to accumulate around the table. Some of them were persons in evening dress, some were Assassins on the hotel payroll, and some were unattached Assassins.

"Well, you won't have far to look for him," one of the latter said, pushing through the crowd to the table.

He was a man of middle age, inclined to stoutness; he made Verkan Vall think of a chocolate figure of Tortha Karf. The red badge on his breast was surrounded with gold lace, and instead of black wings and a silver bullet, it bore silver wings and a golden dagger. He bowed contemptuously at Marnark of Bashad.

"Klarnood, President-General of the Society of Assassins," he announced. "Marnark of Bashad, did I hear you say that you considered members of the Society as unworthy to negotiate an affair of honor with your friends, on behalf of this nobleman who has been courteous enough to accept your challenge?" he demanded.

Marnark of Bashad's arrogance suffered considerable evaporation-loss. His tone became almost servile.

"Not at all, Honorable Assassin-President," he protested. "But as I was going to ask these gentlemen to represent me, I thought it would be more fitting for the other gentleman to be represented by personal friends, also. In that way—"

"Sorry, Marnark," the gray-haired man at the table said. "I can't second you; I have a quarrel with the Lord Virzal, too." He rose and bowed. "Sirzob of Abo. Inasmuch as the Honorable Marnark is a guest at my table, an affront to him is an affront to me. In my quality as his host, I must demand satisfaction from you, Lord Virzal."

"Why, gladly, Honorable Sirzob," Verkan Vall replied. This was getting better and better every moment. "Of course, your friend, the Honorable Marnark, enjoys priority of challenge; I'll take care of you as soon as I have, shall we say, satisfied him."

The earnest and rather consecrated-looking young man rose also, bowing to Verkan Vall.

"Yirzol of Narva. I, too, have a quarrel with you, Lord Virzal; I cannot submit to the indignity of having my food snatched from in front of me, as you just did. I also demand satisfaction."

"And quite rightly, Honorable Yirzol," Verkan Vall approved. "It looks like such good soup, too," he sorrowed, inspecting the front of Marnark's tunic. "My seconds will negotiate with yours immediately; your satisfaction, of course, must come after that of Honorable Sirzob."

"If I may intrude," Klarnood put in smoothly, "may I suggest that as the Lord Virzal is represented by his Assassins, yours can represent all three of you at the same time. I will gladly offer my own good offices as impartial supervisor."

Verkan Vall turned and bowed as to royalty. "An honor, Assassin-President; I am sure no one could act in that capacity more satisfactorily."

"Well, when would it be most convenient to arrange the details?" Klarnood inquired. "I am completely at your disposal, gentlemen."

"Why, here and now, while we're all together," Verkan Vall replied.

"I object to that!" Marnark of Bashad vociferated. "We can't make arrangements here; why, all these hotel people, from the manager down, are nothing but tipsters for the newscast services!"

"Well, what's wrong with that?" Verkan Vall demanded. "You knew that when you slandered the Lady Dallona in their hearing."

"The Lord Virzal of Verkan is correct," Klarnood ruled. "And the offenses for which you have challenged him were also committed in public. By all means, let's discuss the arrangements now." He turned to Verkan Vall. "As the challenged party, you have the choice of weapons; your opponents, then, have the right to name the conditions under which they are to be used."

Marnark of Bashad raised another outcry over that. The assault upon him by the Lord Virzal of Verkan was deliberately provocative, and therefore tantamount to a challenge; he, himself, had the right to name the weapons. Klarnood upheld him.

"Do the other gentlemen make the same claim?" Verkan Vall wanted to know.

"If they do, I won't allow it," Klarnood replied. "You deliberately provoked Honorable Marnark, but the offenses of provoking him at Honorable Sirzob's table, and of throwing Honorable Yirzol's soup at him, were not given with intent to provoke. These gentlemen have a right to challenge, but not to consider themselves provoked."

"Well, I choose knives, then," Marnark hastened to say.

Verkan Vall smiled thinly. He had learned knife-play among the greatest masters of that art in all paratime, the Third Level Khanga pirates of the Caribbean Islands.

"And we fight barefoot, stripped to the waist, and without any parrying weapon in the left hand," Verkan Vall stipulated.

The beefy Marnark fairly licked his chops in anticipation. He outweighed Verkan Vall by forty pounds; he saw an easy victory ahead. Verkan Vall's own confidence increased at these signs of his opponent's assurance.

"And as for Honorable Sirzob and Honorable Yirzol, I choose pistols," he added.

Sirzob and Yirzol held a hasty whispered conference.

"Speaking both for Honorable Yirzol and for myself," Sirzob announced, "we stipulate that the distance shall be twenty meters, that the pistols shall be fully loaded, and that fire shall be at will after the command."

"Twenty rounds, fire at will, at twenty meters!" Olirzon hooted. "You must think our principal's as bad a shot as you are!"

The four Assassins stepped aside and held a long discussion about something, with considerable argument and gesticulation. Klarnood, observing Verkan Vall's impatience, leaned close to him and whispered:

"This is highly irregular; we must pretend ignorance and be patient. They're laying bets on the outcome. You must do your best, Lord Virzal; you don't want your supporters to lose money."

He said it quite seriously, as though the outcome were otherwise a matter of indifference to Verkan Vall.

Marnark wanted to discuss time and place, and proposed that all three duels be fought at dawn, on the fourth landing stage of Darsh Central Hospital; that was closest to the maternity wards, and statistics showed that most births occurred just before that hour.

"Certainly not," Verkan Vall vetoed. "We'll fight here and now; I don't propose going a couple of hundred miles to meet you at any such unholy hour. We'll fight in the nearest hallway that provides twenty meters' shooting distance."

Marnark, Sirzob and Yirzol all clamored in protest. Verkan Vall shouted them down, drawing on his hypnotically acquired knowledge of Akor-Neb dueling customs. "The code explicitly states that satisfaction shall be rendered as promptly as possible, and I insist on a literal interpretation. I'm not going to inconvenience myself and Assassin-President Klarnood and these four Gentlemen-Assassins just to humor Statisticalist superstitions."

The manager of the hotel, drawn to the Martian Room by the uproar, offered a hallway connecting the kitchens with the refrigerator rooms; it was fifty meters long by five in width, was well-lighted and soundproof, and had a bay in which the seconds and others could stand during the firing.

They repaired thither in a body, Klarnood gathering up several hotel servants on the way through the kitchen. Verkan Vall stripped to the waist, pulled off his ankle boots, and examined Olirzon's knife. Its tapering eight-inch blade was double-edged at the point, and its handle was covered with black velvet to afford a good grip, and wound with gold wire. He nodded approvingly, gripped it with his index finger crooked around the cross-guard, and advanced to meet Marnark of Bashad.

As he had expected, the burly politician was depending upon his greater brawn to overpower his antagonist. He advanced with a sidling, spread-legged gait, his knife hand against his right hip and his left hand extended in front. Verkan Vall nodded with pleased satisfaction; a wrist-grabber. Then he blinked. Why, the fellow was actually holding his knife reversed, his little finger to the guard and his thumb on the pommel!

Verkan Vall went briskly to meet him, made a feint at his knife hand with his own left, and then side-stepped quickly to the right. As Marnark's left hand grabbed at his right wrist, his left hand brushed against it and closed into a fist, with Marnark's left thumb inside of it. He gave a quick downward twist with his wrist, pulling Marnark off balance.

Caught by surprise, Marnark stumbled, his knife flailing wildly away from Verkan Vall. As he stumbled forward, Verkan Vall pivoted on his left heel and drove the point of his knife into the back of Marnark's neck, twisting it as he jerked it free. At the same time, he released Marnark's thumb. The politician continued his stumble and fell forward on his face, blood spurting from his neck. He gave a twitch or so, and was still.

Verkan Vall stooped and wiped the knife on the dead man's clothes—another Khanga pirate gesture—and then returned it to Olirzon.

"Nice weapon, Olirzon," he said. "It fit my hand as though I'd been born holding it."

"You used it as though you had, Lord Virzal," the Assassin replied. "Only eight seconds from the time you closed with him."

THE function of the hotel servants whom Klarnood had gathered up now became apparent; they advanced, took the body of Marnark by the heels, and dragged it out of the way. The others watched this removal with mixed emotions. The two remaining principals were impassive and frozen-faced. Their two Assassins, who had probably bet heavily on Marnark, were chagrined. And Klarnood was looking at Verkan Vall with a considerable accretion of respect. Verkan Vall pulled on his boots and resumed his clothing.

There followed some argument about the pistols; it was finally decided that each combatant should use his own shoulder-holster weapon. All three were nearly enough alike—small weapons, rather heavier than they looked, firing a tiny ten-grain bullet at ten thousand foot-seconds. On impact, such a bullet would almost disintegrate; a man hit anywhere in the body with one would be killed instantly, his nervous system paralyzed and his heart stopped by internal pressure. Each of the pistols carried twenty rounds in the magazine.

Verkan Vall and Sirzob of Abo took their places, their pistols lowered at their sides, facing each other across a measured twenty meters.

"Are you ready, gentlemen?" Klarnood asked. "You will not raise your pistols until the command to fire; you may fire at will after it. Ready. *Fire!*"

Both pistols swung up to level. Verkan Vall found Sirzob's head in his sights and squeezed; the pistol kicked back in his hand, and he saw a lance of blue flame jump from the muzzle of Sirzob's. Both weapons barked together, and with the double report came the whip-cracking sound of Sirzob's bullet passing Verkan Vall's head. Then Sirzob's face altered its appearance unpleasantly, and he pitched forward. Verkan Vall thumbed on his safety and stood motionless, while the servants advanced, took Sirzob's body by the heels, and dragged it over beside Marnark's.

"All right; Honorable Yirzol, you're next," Verkan Vall called out.

"The Lord Virzal has fired one shot," one of the opposing seconds objected, "and Honorable Yirzol has a full magazine. The Lord Virzal should put in another magazine."

"I grant him the advantage; let's get on with it," Verkan Vall said.

Yirzol of Narva advanced to the firing point. He was not afraid of death—none of the Akor-Neb people were; their language contained no word to express the concept of total and final extinction—and discarnation by gunshot was almost entirely painless. But he was beginning to suspect that he had made a fool of himself by getting into this affair, he had work in his present reincarnation which he wanted to finish, and his political party would suffer loss, both of his services and of prestige.

"Are you ready, gentlemen?" Klarnood intoned ritualistically. "You will not raise your pistols until the command to fire; you may fire at will after it. Ready, *Fire!*"

Verkan Vall shot Yirzol of Narva through the head before the latter had his pistol half raised. Yirzol fell forward on the splash of blood Sirzob had made, and the servants came forward and dragged his body over with the others. It reminded Verkan Vall of some sort of industrial assembly-line operation. He replaced the two expended rounds in his magazine with fresh ones and slid the pistol back into its holster. The two Assassins whose principals had been so expeditiously massacred were beginning to count up their losses and pay off the winners.

Klarnood, the President-General of the Society of Assassins, came over, hooking fingers and clapping shoulders with Verkan Vall.

"Lord Virzal, I've seen quite a few duels, but nothing quite like that," he said. "You should have been an Assassin!"

That was a considerable compliment. Verkan Vall thanked him modestly.

"I'd like to talk to you privately," the Assassin-President continued. "I think it'll be worth your while if we have a few words together."

Verkan Vall nodded. "My suite is on the fifteenth floor above; will that be all right?" He waited until the losers had finished settling their bets, then motioned to his own pair of Assassins.

As they emerged into the Martian Room again, the manager was waiting; he looked as though he were about to demand that Verkan Vall vacate his suite. However, when he saw the arm of the President-General of the Society of Assassins draped amicably over his guest's shoulder, he came forward bowing and smiling.

"Larnorm, I want you to put five of your best Assassins to guarding the approaches to the Lord Virzal's suite," Klarnood told him. "I'll send five more from Assassins' Hall to replace them at their ordinary duties. And I'll hold you responsible with your carnate existence for the Lord Virzal's safety in this hotel. Understand?"

"Oh, yes, Honorable Assassin-President; you may trust me. The Lord Virzal will be perfectly safe."

In Verkan Vall's suite, above, Klarnood sat down and got out his pipe, filling it with tobacco lightly mixed with *zerfa*. To his surprise, he saw his host light a plain tobacco cigarette.

"Don't you use *zerfa?*" he asked.

"Very little," Verkan Vall replied. "I grow it. If you'd see the bums who hang around our drying sheds on Venus, cadging rejected leaves and smoking themselves into a stupor, you'd be frugal in using it, too."

Klarnood nodded. "You know, most men would want a pipe of fifty percent, or a straight *zerfa* cigarette, after what you've been through," he said.

"I'd need something like that to deaden my conscience, if I had one to deaden," Verkan Vall said. "As it is, I feel like a murderer of babes. That overgrown fool, Marnark, handled his knife like a cow-butcher. The young fellow couldn't handle a pistol at all. I suppose the old fellow, Sirzob, was a fair shot, but dropping him wasn't any great feat of arms, either."

Klarnood looked at him curiously for a moment. "You know," he said at length, "I believe you actually mean that. Well, until he met you, Marnark of Bashad was rated as the best knife-fighter in Darsh. Sirzob had ten dueling victories to his credit, and young Yirzol four." He puffed slowly on his pipe. "I like you, Lord Virzal; a great Assassin was lost when you decided to reincarnate as a Venusian landowner. I'd hate to see you discarnated without proper warning. I take it you're ignorant of the intricacies of Terran politics?"

"To a large extent, yes."

"Well, do you know who those three men were?" When Verkan Vall shook his head, Klarnood continued: "Marnark was the son and right-hand associate of old Mirzark of Bashad, the Statisticalist Party leader. Sirzob of Abo was their propaganda director. And Yirzol of Narva was their leading socio-economic theorist, and their candidate for Executive Chairman. In six minutes, with one knife thrust and two shots, you did the Statisticalist Party an injury second only to that done them by the young lady in whose name you were fighting. In two weeks, there will be a planet-wide general election. As it stands, the Statisticalists have a majority of the seats in Parliament and on the Executive Council. As a result of your work and the Lady Dallona's, they'll lose that majority, and more, when the votes are tallied."

"Is that another reason why you like me?" Verkan Vall asked.

"Unofficially, yes. As President-General of the Society of Assassins, I must be nonpolitical. The Society is rigidly so; if we let ourselves become involved, as an organization, in politics, we could control the System Government inside of five years, and we'd be wiped out of existence in fifty years by the very forces we sought to control," Klarnood said. "But personally, I would like to see the Statisticalist Party destroyed. If they succeed in their program of socialization, the Society would be finished. A socialist state is, in its final development, an absolute, total, state; no total state can tolerate extra-legal and para-governmental organizations. So we have adopted the policy of giving a little inconspicuous aid, here and there, to people who are dangerous to the Statisticalists. The Lady Dallona of Hadron, and Dr. Harnosh of Hosh, are such persons. You appear to be another. That's why I ordered that fellow, Larnorm, to make sure you were safe in his hotel."

"Where is the Lady Dallona?" Verkan Vall asked. "From your use of the present tense, I assume you believe her to be still carnate."

Klarnood looked at Verkan Vall keenly. "That's a pretty blunt question, Lord Virzal," he said. "I wish I knew a little more about you. When you and your Assassins started inquiring about the Lady Dallona, I tried to check up on you. I found out that you had come to Darsh from Ghamma on a ship of the family of Zorda, accompanied by Brarnend of Zorda himself. And that's all I could find out. You claim to be a Venusian planter, and you might be. Any Terran who can handle weapons as you can would have come to my notice long ago. But you have no more ascertainable history than if you'd stepped out of another dimension."

That was getting uncomfortably close to the truth. In fact, it *was* the truth. Verkan Vall laughed.

"Well, confidentially," he said, "I'm from the Arcturus System. I followed the Lady Dallona here from our home planet, and when I have rescued her from among you Solarians, I shall, according to our customs, receive her hand in marriage. As she is the daughter of the Emperor of Arcturus, that'll be quite a good thing for me."

Klarnood chuckled. "You know, you'd only have to tell me that about three or four times and I'd start believing it," he said. "And Dr. Harnosh of Hosh would believe it the first time; he's been talking to himself ever since the Lady Dallona started her experimental work here. Lord Virzal, I'm going to take a chance on you. The Lady Dallona is still carnate, or was four days ago, and the same for Dirzed. They both went into hiding after the discarnation feast of Garnon of Roxor, to escape the enmity of the Statisticalists. Two days after they disappeared, Dirzed called Assassins' Hall and reported this, but told us nothing more. I suppose, in about three or four days, I could re-establish contact with him. We want the public to think that the Statisticalists made away with the Lady Dallona, at least until the election's over."

Verkan Vall nodded. "I was pretty sure that was the situation," he said. "It may be that they will get in touch with me; if they don't, I'll need your help in reaching them."

"Why do you think the Lady Dallona will try to reach you?"

"She needs all the help she can get. She knows she can get plenty from me. Why do you think I interrupted my search for her, and risked my carnate existence, to fight those people over a matter of verbalisms and political propaganda?" Verkan Vall went to the newscast visiplate and snapped it on. "We'll see if I'm getting results yet."

The plate lighted, and a handsome young man in a gold-laced green suit was speaking out of it:

". . . where he is heavily guarded by Assassins. However, in an exclusive interview with representatives of this service, the Assassin Hirzif, one of the two who seconded the men the Lord Virzal fought, said that in his opinion all of the three were so outclassed as to have had no chance whatever, and that he had already refused an offer of ten thousand System Monetary Units to discarnate the Lord Virzal for the Statisticalist Party. 'When I want to discarnate,' Hirzif the Assassin said, 'I'll invite in my friends and do it properly; until I do, I wouldn't go up against the Lord Virzal of Verkan for ten million S.M.U.' "

Verkan Vall snapped off the visiplate. "See what I mean?" he asked. "I fought those politicians just for the advertising. If Dallona and Dirzed are anywhere near a visiplate, they'll know how to reach me."

"Hirzif shouldn't have talked about refusing that retainer," Klarnood frowned. "That isn't good Assassin ethics. Why, yes, Lord Virzal; that was cleverly planned. It ought to get results. But I wish you'd get the Lady Dallona out of Darsh, and preferably off Terra, as soon as you can. We've benefited by this, so far, but I shouldn't like to see things go much further. A real civil war could develop out of this situation, and I don't want that. Call on me for help; I'll give you a code word to use at Assassins' Hall."

A real civil war was developing even as Klarnood spoke; by mid-morning of the next day, the fighting that had been partially suppressed by the Constabulary had broken out anew. The Assassins employed by the Solar Hotel—heavily re-enforced during the night—had fought a pitched battle with Statisticalist partisans on the landing-stage above Verkan Vall's suite, and now several Constabulary airboats were patrolling around the building. The rule on Constabulary interference seemed to be that while individuals had an unquestionable right to shoot out their differences among themselves, any fighting likely to endanger nonparticipants was taboo.

Just how successful in enforcing this rule the Constabulary were was open to some doubt. Ever since arising, Verkan Vall had heard the crash of small arms and the hammering of automatic weapons in other parts of the towering city-unit. There hadn't been a civil war on the Akor-Neb Sector for over five centuries, he knew, but then Hadron Dalla, Doctor of Psychic Science and intertemporal trouble-carrier extraordinary, had only been on this sector for a little under a year. If anything, he was surprised that the explosion had taken so long to occur.

One of the servants furnished to him by the hotel management approached him in the drawing room, holding a four-inch-square wafer of white plastic.

"Lord Virzal, there is a masked Assassin in the hallway who brought this under Assassins' Truce," he said.

Verkan Vall took the wafer and pared off three of the four edges, which showed black where they had been fused. Unfolding it, he found, as he had expected, that the pyrographed message within was in the alphabet and language of the First Paratime Level:

Vall, darling:

Am I glad you got here; this time I really *am* in the middle, but good! The Assassin, Dirzed, who brings this, is in my service. You can trust him implicitly; he's about the only person in Darsh you can trust. He'll bring you to where I am.

Dalla

P.S. I hope you're not still angry about that musician. I told you, at the time, that he was just helping me with an experiment in telepathy.

D.

Verkan Vall grinned at the postscript. That had been twenty years ago, when he'd been eighty and she'd been seventy. He supposed she'd expect him to take up his old relationship with her again. It probably wouldn't last any longer than it had the other time; he recalled a Fourth Level proverb about the leopard and his spots. It certainly wouldn't be boring, though.

"Tell the Assassin to come in," he directed. Then he tossed the message down on a table. Outside of himself, nobody in Darsh could read it but the woman who had sent it; if, as he thought highly probable, the Statisticalists had spies among the hotel staff, it might serve to reduce some cryptanalyst to gibbering insanity.

THE assassin entered, drawing off a cowl-like mask. He was the man whose arm Dalla had been holding in the visiplate picture; Verkan Vall even recognized the extremely ornate pistol and knife on his belt.

"Dirzed the Assassin," he named himself. "If you wish, we can visiphone Assassins' Hall for verification of my identity."

"Lord Virzal of Verkan. And my Assassins, Marnik and Olirzon." They all hooked fingers and clapped shoulders with the newcomer. "That won't be needed," Verkan Vall told Dirzed. "I know you from seeing you with the Lady Dallona, on the visiplate; you're 'Dirzed, her faithful Assassin.'"

Dirzed's face, normally the color of a good walnut gunstock, turned almost black. He used shockingly bad language.

"And that's why I have to wear this abomination," he finished, displaying the mask. "The Lady Dallona and I can't show our faces anywhere; if we did, every Statisticalist and his six-year-old brat would know us, and we'd be fighting off an army of them in five minutes."

"Where's the Lady Dallona, now?"

"In hiding, Lord Virzal, at a private dwelling dome in the forest; she's most anxious to see you. I'm to take you to her, and I would strongly advise that you bring your Assassins along. There are other people at this dome, and they are not personally loyal to the Lady Dallona. I've no reason to suspect them of secret enmity, but their friendship is based entirely on political expediency."

"And political expediency is subject to change without notice," Verkan Vall finished for him. "Have you an airboat?"

"On the landing stage below. Shall we go now, Lord Virzal?"

"Yes." Verkan Vall made a two-handed gesture to his Assassins, as though gripping a submachine-gun; they nodded, went into another room, and returned carrying light automatic weapons in their hands and pouches of spare drums slung over their shoulders. "And may I suggest, Dirzed, that one of my Assassins drives the airboat? I want you on the back seat with me, to explain the situation as we go."

Dirzed's teeth flashed white against his brown skin as he gave Verkan Vall a quick smile.

"By all means, Lord Virzal; I would much rather be distrusted than to find that my client's friends were not discreet."

There were a couple of hotel Assassins guarding Dirzed's airboat on the landing stage. Marnik climbed in under the controls, with Olirzon beside him; Verkan Vall and Dirzed entered the rear seat. Dirzed gave Marnik the co-ordinate reference for their destination.

"Now, what sort of a place is this, where we're going?" Verkan Vall asked. "And who's there whom we may or may not trust?"

"Well, it's a dome house belonging to the family of Starpha; they own a five-mile radius around it, oak and beech forest and underbrush, stocked with deer and boar. A hunting lodge. Prince Jirzyn of Starpha, Lord Girzon of Roxor, and a few other top-level Volitionalists know that the Lady Dallona's hiding there. They're keeping her out of sight till after the election, for propaganda purposes. We've been hiding there since immediately after the discarnation feast of the Lord Garnon of Roxor."

"What happened after the feast?" Verkan Vall wanted to know.

"Well, you know how the Lady Dallona and Dr. Harnosh of Hosh had this telepathic-sensitive there, in a trance and drugged with a *zerfa*-derivative alkaloid the Lady Dallona had developed. I was Lord Garnon's Assassin; I discarnated him, myself. Why, I hadn't even put my pistol away before he was in control of this sensitive, in a room five stories above the banquet hall; he began communicating at once. We had visiplates to show us what was going on."

"Right away, Nirzav of Shonna, one of the Statisticalist leaders who was a personal friend of Lord Garnon's in spite of his politics, renounced Statisticalism and went over to the Volitionalists, on the strength of this communication. Prince Jirzyn and Lord Girzon, the new family-head of Roxor, decided that there would be trouble in the next few days, so they advised the Lady Dallona to come to this hunting lodge for safety. She and I came here in her airboat, directly from the feast. A good thing we did, too; if we'd gone to her apartment, we'd have walked in before that lethal gas had time to clear.

"There are four Assassins of the family of Starpha, and six menservants, and an upper-servant named Tarnod, the gamekeeper. The Starpha Assassins and I have been keeping the rest under observation. I left one of the Starpha Assassins guarding the Lady Dallona when I came for you, under brotherly oath to protect her in my name till I returned."

The airboat was skimming rapidly above the treetops, toward the northern part of the city.

"What's known about that package bomb?" Verkan Vall asked. "Who sent it?"

Dirzed shrugged. "The Statisticalists, of course. The wrapper was stolen from the Reincarnation Research Institute; so was the case. The Constabulary are working on it." Dirzed shrugged again.

The dome, about a hundred and fifty feet in width and some fifty in height, stood among the trees ahead. It was almost invisible from any distance; the concrete dome was of mottled green and gray concrete, trees grew so close as to brush it with their branches, and the little pavilion on the flattened top was roofed with translucent green plastic. As the airboat came in, a couple of men in Assassins' garb emerged from the pavilion to meet them.

"Marnik, stay at the controls," Verkan Vall directed. "I'll send Olirzon up for you if I want you. If there's any trouble, take off for Assassins' Hall and give the code word, then come back with twice as many men as you think you'll need."

Dirzed raised his eyebrows over this. "I hadn't known the Assassin-President had given you a code word, Lord Virzal," he commented. "That doesn't happen very often."

"The Assassin-President has honored me with his friendship," Verkan Vall replied noncommittally, as he, Dirzed and Olirzon climbed out of the airboat. Marnik was holding it an unobtrusive inch or so above the flat top of the dome, away from the edge of the pavilion roof.

THE two Assassins greeted him, and a man in upper-servants' garb and wearing a hunting knife and a long hunting pistol approached.

"Lord Virzal of Verkan? Welcome to Starpha Dome. The Lady Dallona awaits you below."

Verkan Vall had never been in an Akor-Neb dwelling dome, but a description of such structures had been included in his hypno-mech indoctrination. Originally, they had been the standard structure for all purposes; about two thousand elapsed years ago, when nationalism had still existed on the Akor-Neb Sector, the cities had been almost entirely under ground, as protection from air attack. Even now, the design had been retained by those who wished to live apart from the towering city units, to preserve the natural appearance of the landscape. The Starpha hunting lodge was typical of such domes. Under it was a circular well, eighty feet in depth and fifty in width, with a fountain and a shallow circular pool at the bottom. The storerooms, kitchens and servants' quarters were at the top, the living quarters at the bottom, in segments of a wide circle around the well, back of balconies.

"Tarnod, the gamekeeper," Dirzed performed the introductions. "And Erarno and Kirzol, Assassins."

Verkan Vall hooked fingers and clapped shoulders with them. Tarnod accompanied them to the lifter tubes—two percent positive gravitation for descent and two percent negative for ascent—and they all floated down the former, like air-filled balloons, to the bottom level.

"The Lady Dallona is in the gun room," Tarnod informed Verkan Vall, making as though to guide him.

"Thanks, Tarnod; we know the way," Dirzed told him shortly, turning his back on the upper-servant and walking toward a closed door on the other side of the fountain. Verkan Vall and Olirzon followed; for a moment, Tarnod stood looking after them, then he followed the other two Assassins into the ascent tube.

"I don't relish that fellow," Dirzed explained. "The family of Starpha used him for work they couldn't hire an Assassin to do at any price. I've been here often, when I was with the Lord Garnon; I've always thought he had some-thing on Prince Jirzyn."

He knocked sharply on the closed door with the butt of his pistol. In a moment, it slid open, and a young Assassin with a narrow mustache and a tuft of chin beard looked out.

"Ah, Dirzed." He stepped outside. "The Lady Dallona is within; I return her to your care."

Verkan Vall entered, followed by Dirzed and Olirzon. The big room was fitted with reclining chairs and couches and low tables; its walls were hung with the heads of deer and boar and wolves, and with racks holding rifles and hunting pistols and fowling pieces. It was filled with the soft glow of indirect cold light. At the far side of the room, a young woman was seated at a desk, speaking softly into a sound transcriber. As they entered, she snapped it off and rose.

Hadron Dalla wore the same costume Verkan Vall had seen on the visiplate; he recognized her instantly. It took her a second or two to perceive Verkan Vall under the brown skin and black hair of the Lord Virzal of Verkan. Then her face lighted with a happy smile.

"Why, Va-a-a-ll!" she whooped, running across the room and tossing herself into his not particularly reluctant arms. After all, it had been twenty years—"I didn't know you at first!"

"You mean, in these clothes?" he asked, seeing that she had forgotten, for the moment, the presence of the two Assassins. She had even called him by his First Level name, but that was unimportant—the Akor-Neb affectionate diminutive was formed by omitting the -irz- or -arn-. "Well, they're not exactly what I generally wear on the plantation." He kissed her again, then turned to his companions. "Your pardon, Gentlemen-Assassins; it's been something over a year since we've seen each other."

Olirzon was smiling at the affectionate reunion; Dirzed wore a look of amused resignation, as though he might have expected something like this to happen. Verkan Vall and Dalla sat down on a couch near the desk.

"That was really sweet of you, Vall, fighting those men for talking about me," she began. "You took an awful chance, though. But if you hadn't, I'd never have known you were in Darsh—Oh, oh! That was why you did it, wasn't it?"

"Well, I had to do something. Everybody either didn't know or wasn't saying where you were. I assumed, from the circumstances, that you were hiding somewhere. Tell me, Dalla; do you really have scientific proof of reincarnation? I mean, as an established fact?"

"Oh, yes; these people on this sector have had that for over ten centuries. They have hypnotic techniques for getting back into a part of the subconscious mind that we've never been able to reach. And after I found out how they did it, I was able to adapt some of our hypno-epistemological techniques to it, and—"

"All right; that's what I wanted to know," he cut her off. "We're getting out of here, right away."

"But where?"

"Ghamma, in an airboat I have outside, and then back to the First Level. Unless there's a paratime-transposition conveyor somewhere nearer."

"But why, Vall? I'm not ready to go back; I have a lot of work to do here, yet. They're getting ready to set up a series of control-experiments at the Institute, and then, I'm in the middle of an experiment, a two-hundred-subject memory-recall experiment. See, I distributed two hundred sets of equipment for my new technique—injection-ampoules of this *zerfa*-derivative drug, and sound records of the hypnotic suggestion formula, which can be played on an ordinary reproducer. It's just a crude variant of our hypno-mech process, except that instead of implanting information in the subconscious mind, to be brought at will to the level of consciousness, it works the other way, and draws into conscious knowledge information already in the subconscious mind. The way these people have always done it has been to put the subject in a hypnotic trance and then record verbal statements made in the trance state; when the subject comes out of the trance, the record is all there is, because the memories of past reincarnations have never been in the conscious mind. But with my process, the subject can consciously remember everything about his last reincarnation, and as many reincarnations before that as he wishes to. I haven't heard from any of the people who received these auto-recall kits, and I really must—"

"Dalla, I don't want to have to pull Paratime Police authority on you, but so help me, if you don't come back voluntarily with me, I will. Security of the secret of paratime transposition."

"Oh, my eye!" Dalla exclaimed. "Don't give me that, Vall!"

"Look, Dalla. Suppose you get discarnated here," Verkan Vall said. "You say reincarnation is a scientific fact. Well, you'd reincarnate on this sector, and then you'd take a memory-recall, under hypnosis. And when you did, the paratime secret wouldn't be a secret any more."

"Oh!" Dalla's hand went to her mouth in consternation. Like every paratimer, she was conditioned to shrink with all her being from the mere thought of revealing to any out-time dweller the secret ability of her race to pass to other time-lines, or even the existence of alternate lines of probability. "And if I took one of the old-fashioned trance-recalls, I'd blat out everything; I wouldn't be able to keep a thing back. And I even know the principles of transposition!" She looked at him, aghast.

"When I get back, I'm going to put a recommendation through department channels that this whole sector be declared out of bounds for all paratime-transposition, until you people at Rhogom Foundation work out the problem of discarnate return to the First Level," he told her. "Now, have you any notes or anything you want to take back with you?"

She rose. "Yes; just what's on the desk. Find me something to put the tape spools and notebooks in, while I'm getting them in order."

He secured a large game bag from under a rack of fowling pieces, and held it while she sorted the material rapidly, stuffing spools of record tape and notebooks into it. They had barely begun when the door slid open and Olirzon, who had gone outside, sprang into the room, his pistol drawn, swearing vilely.

"They've double-crossed us!" he cried. "The servants of Starpha have turned on us." He holstered his pistol and snatched up his submachine-gun, taking cover behind the edge of the door and letting go with a burst in the direction of the lifter tubes. "Got that one!" he grunted.

"What happened, Olirzon?" Verkan Vall asked, dropping the game bag on the table and hurrying across the room.

"I went up to see how Marnik was making out. As I came out of the lifter tube, one of the obscenities took a shot at me with a hunting pistol. He missed me; I didn't miss him. Then a couple more of them were coming up, with fowling pieces; I shot one of them before they could fire, and jumped into the descent tube and came down heels over ears. I don't know what's happened to Marnik." He fired another burst, and swore. "Missed him!"

"Assassins' Truce! Assassins' Truce!" a voice howled out of the descent tube. "Hold your fire, we want to parley."

"Who is it?" Dirzed shouted, over Olirzon's shoulder. "You, Sarnax? Come on out; we won't shoot."

The young Assassin with the mustache and chin beard emerged from the descent tube, his weapons sheathed and his clasped hands extended in front of him in a peculiarly ecclesiastical-looking manner. Dirzed and Olirzon stepped out of the gun room, followed by Verkan Vall and Hadron Dalla. Olirzon had left his submachine-gun behind. They met the other Assassin by the rim of the fountain pool.

"Lady Dallona of Hadron," the Starpha Assassin began. "I and my colleagues, in the employ of the family of Starpha, have received orders from our clients to withdraw our protection from you, and to discarnate you, and all with you who undertake to protect or support you." That much sounded like a recitation of some established formula; then his voice became more conversational. "I and my colleagues, Erarno and Kirzol and Harnif, offer our apologies for the barbarity of the servants of the family of Starpha, in attacking without declaration of cessation of friendship. Was anybody hurt or discarnated?"

"None of us," Olirzon said. "How about Marnik?"

"He was warned before hostilities were begun against him," Sarnax replied. "We will allow five minutes until—"

Olirzon, who had been looking up the well, suddenly sprang at Dalla, knocking her flat, and at the same time jerking out his pistol. Before he could raise it, a shot banged from above and he fell on his face. Dirzed, Verkan Vall, and Sarnax all drew their pistols, but whoever had fired the shot had vanished. There was an outburst of shouting above.

"Get to cover," Sarnax told the others. "We'll let you know when we're ready to attack; we'll have to deal with whoever fired that shot first." He looked at the dead body on the floor, exclaimed angrily, and hurried to the ascent tube, springing upward.

Verkan Vall replaced the small pistol in his shoulder holster and took Olirzon's belt, with his knife and heavier pistol.

"Well, there you see," Dirzed said, as they went back to the gun room. "So much for political expediency."

"I think I understand why your picture and the Lady Dallona's were exhibited so widely," Verkan Vall said. "Now anybody would recognize your bodies, and blame the Statisticalists for discarnating you."

"That thought had occurred to me, Lord Virzal," Dirzed said. "I suppose our bodies will be atrociously but not unidentifiably mutilated, to further enrage the public," he added placidly. "If I get out of this carnate, I'm going to pay somebody off for it."

After a few minutes, there was more shouting of: "Assassins' Truce!" from the descent tube. The two Assassins, Erarno and Kirzol, emerged, dragging the gamekeeper, Tarnod, between them. The upper-servant's face was bloody, and his jaw seemed to be broken. Sarnax followed, carrying a long hunting pistol in his hand.

"Here he is!" he announced. "He fired during Assassins' Truce; he's subject to Assassins' Justice!"

He nodded to the others. They threw the gamekeeper forward on the floor, and Sarnax shot him through the head, then tossed the pistol down beside him. "Any more of these people who violate the decencies will be treated similarly," he promised.

"Thank you, Sarnax," Dirzed spoke up. "But we lost an Assassin; discarnating this lackey won't equalize that. We think you should retire one of your number."

"That at least, Dirzed; wait a moment."

The three Assassins conferred at some length. Then Sarnax hooked fingers and clapped shoulders with his companions.

"See you in the next reincarnation, brothers," he told them, walking toward the gun-room door, where Verkan Vall, Dalla and Dirzed stood. "I'm joining you people. You had two Assassins when the parley began, you'll have two when the shooting starts."

Verkan Vall looked at Dirzed in some surprise. Hadron Dalla's Assassin nodded.

"He's entitled to do that, Lord Virzal; the Assassins' Code provides for such changes of allegiance."

"Welcome, Sarnax," Verkan Vall said, hooking fingers with him. "I hope we'll all be together when this is over."

"We will be," Sarnax assured him cheerfully. "Discarnate. We won't get out of this in the body, Lord Virzal."

A submachine-gun hammered from above, the bullets lashing the fountain pool; the water actually steamed, so great was their velocity.

"All right!" a voice called down. "Assassins' Truce is over!"

Another burst of automatic fire smashed out the lights at the bottom of the ascent tube. Dirzed and Dalla struggled across the room, pushing a heavy steel cabinet between them; Verkan Vall, who was holding Olirzon's submachine-gun, moved aside to allow them to drop it on edge in the open doorway, then wedged the door half-shut against it. Sarnax came over, bringing rifles, hunting pistols, and ammunition.

"What's the situation up there?" Verkan Vall asked him. "What force have they, and why did they turn against us?"

"Lord Virzal!" Dirzed objected, scandalized. "You have no right to ask Sarnax to betray confidences!"

Sarnax spat against the door. "In the face of Jirzyn of Starpha!" he said.

"And in the face of his *zortan* mother, and of his father, whoever he was! Dirzed, do not talk foolishly; one does not speak of betraying betrayers." He turned to Verkan Vall. "They have three menservants of the family of Starpha; your Assassin, Olirzon, discarnated the other three. There is one of Prince Jirzyn's poor relations, named Girzad. There are three other men, Volitionalist precinct workers, who came with Girzad, and four Assassins, the three who were here, and one who came with Girzad. Eleven, against the three of us."

"The four of us, Sarnax," Dalla corrected. She had buckled on a hunting pistol, and had a light deer rifle under her arm.

Something moved at the bottom of the descent tube. Verkan Vall gave it a short burst, though it was probably only a dummy, dropped to draw fire.

"The four of us, Lady Dallona," Sarnax agreed. "As to your other Assassin, the one who stayed in the airboat, I don't know how he fared. You see, about twenty minutes ago, this Girzad arrived in an airboat, with an Assassin and these three Volitionalist workers. Erarno and I were at the top of the dome when he came in. He told us that he had orders from Prince Jirzyn to discarnate the Lady Dallona and Dirzed at once. Tarnod, the gamekeeper"—Sarnax spat ceremoniously against the door again—"told him you were here, and that Marnik was one of your men. He was going to shoot Marnik at once, but Erarno and I and his Assassin stopped him. We warned Marnik about the change in the situation, according to the code, expecting Marnik to go down here and join you. Instead, he lifted the airboat, zoomed over Girzad's boat, and let go a rocket blast, setting Girzad's boat on fire. Well, that was a hostile act, so we all fired after him. We must have hit something, because the boat went down, trailing smoke, about ten miles away. Girzad got another airboat out of the hangar and he and his Assassin started after your man. About that time, your Assassin, Olirzon—happy reincarnation to him—came up, and the Starpha servants fired at him, and he fired back and discarnated two of them, and then jumped down the descent tube. One of the servants jumped after him; I found his body at the bottom when I came down to warn you formally. You know what happened after that."

"But why did Prince Jirzyn order our discarnation?" Dalla wanted to know. "Was it to blame the Statisticalists with it?"

Sarnax, about to answer, broke off suddenly and began firing at the opening of the ascent tube with a hunting pistol.

"I got him," he said, in a pleased tone. "That was Erarno; he was always playing tricks with the tubes, climbing down against negative gravity and up against positive gravity. His body will float up to the top—why, Lady Dallona, that was only part of it. You didn't hear about the big scandal, on the newscast, then?"

"We didn't have it on. What scandal?"

Sarnax laughed. "Oh, the very father and family-head of all scandals! You ought to know about it because you started it; that's why Prince Jirzyn wants you out of the body—you devised a process by which people could give themselves memory-recalls of previous reincarnations, didn't you? And distributed apparatus to do it with? And gave one set to young Tarnov, the son of Lord Tirzov of Fastor?"

Dalla nodded. Sarnax continued:

"Well, last evening, Tarnov of Fastor used his recall outfit, and what do you think? It seems that thirty years ago, in his last reincarnation, he was Jirzid of Starpha, Jirzyn's older brother. Jirzid was betrothed to the Lady Annitra of Zabna. Well, his younger brother was carrying on a clandestine affair with the Lady Annitra, and he also wanted the title of Prince and family-head of Starpha. So he bribed this fellow Tarnod, whom I had the pleasure of discarnating, and who was an under-servant here at the hunting lodge. Between them, they shot Jirzid during a boar hunt. An accident, of course. So Jirzyn married the Lady Annitra, and when old Prince Jarnid, his father, discarnated a year later, he succeeded to the title. And immediately, Tarnod was made head gamekeeper here."

"What did I tell you, Lord Virzal? I knew that son of a *zortan* had something on Jirzyn of Starpha!" Dirzed exclaimed. "A nice family, this of Starpha!"

"Well, that's not the end of it," Sarnax continued. "This morning, Tarnov of Fastor, late Jirzid of Starpha, went before the High Court of Estates and entered suit to change his name to Jirzid of Starpha and laid claim to the title of Starpha family-head. The case has just been entered, so there's been no hearing, but there's the blazes of an argument among all the nobles about it—some are claiming that the individuality doesn't change from one reincarnation to the next, and others claiming that property and titles should pass along the line of physical descent, no matter what individuality has reincarnated into what body. They're the ones who want the Lady Dallona discarnated and her discoveries suppressed. And there's talk about revising the entire system of estate-ownership and estate-inheritance. Oh, it's an utter obscenity of a business!"

"This," Verkan Vall told Dalla, "is something we will not emphasize when we get home." That was as close as he dared come to it, but she caught his meaning. The working of major changes in outtime social structures was not viewed with approval by the Paratime Commission on the First Level. "*If* we get home," he added. Then an idea occurred to him.

"Dirzed, Sarnax; this place must have been used by the leaders of the Volitionalists for top-level conferences. Is there a secret passage anywhere?"

Sarnax shook his head. "Not from here. There is one, on the floor above, but they control it. And even if there were one down here, they would be guarding the outlet."

"That's what I was counting on. I'd hoped to simulate an escape that way, and then make a rush up the regular tubes." Verkan Vall shrugged. "I suppose Marnik's our only chance. I hope he got away safely."

"He was going for help? I was surprised that an Assassin would desert his client; I should have thought of that," Sarnax said. "Well, even if he got down carnate, and if Girzad didn't catch him, he'd still be afoot ten miles from the nearest city unit. That gives us a little chance—about one in a thousand."

"Is there any way they can get at us, except by those tubes?" Dalla asked.

"They could cut a hole in the floor, or burn one through," Sarnax replied. "They have plenty of thermite. They could detonate a charge of explosives over our heads, or clear out of the dome and drop one down the well. They could use lethal gas or radiodust, but their Assassins wouldn't permit such illegal methods. Or they could shoot sleep-gas down at us, and then come down and cut our throats at their leisure."

"We'll have to get out of this room, then," Verkan Vall decided. "They know we've barricaded ourselves in here; this is where they'll attack. So we'll patrol the perimeter of the well; we'll be out of danger from above if we keep close to the wall. And we'll inspect all the rooms on this floor for evidence of cutting through from above."

Sarnax nodded. "That's sense, Lord Virzal. How about the lifter tubes?"

"We'll have to barricade them. Sarnax, you and Dirzed know the layout of this place better than the Lady Dallona or I; suppose you two check the rooms, while we cover the tubes and the well," Verkan Vall directed. "Come on, now."

THEY pushed the door wide-open and went out past the cabinet. Hugging the wall, they began a slow circuit of the well, Verkan Vall in the lead with the submachine-gun, then Sarnax and Dirzed, the former with a heavy boar-rifle and the latter with a hunting pistol in each hand, and Hadron Dalla brought up the rear with her rifle. It was she who noticed a movement along the rim of the balcony above and snapped a shot at it; there was a crash above, and a shower of glass and plastic and metal fragments rattled on the pavement of the court. Somebody had been trying to lower a scanner or a visiplate-pickup, or something of the sort; the exact nature of the instrument was not evident from the wreckage Dalla's bullet had made of it.

The rooms Dirzed and Sarnax entered were all quiet; nobody seemed to be attempting to cut through the ceiling, fifteen feet above. They dragged furniture from a couple of rooms, blocking the openings of the lifter tubes, and continued around the well until they had reached the gun room again.

Dirzed suggested that they move some of the weapons and ammunition stored there to Prince Jirzyn's private apartment, halfway around to the lifter tubes, so that another place of refuge would be stocked with munitions in event of their being driven from the gun room.

Leaving him on guard outside, Verkan Vall, Dalla and Sarnax entered the gun room and began gathering weapons and boxes of ammunition. Dalla finished packing her game bag with the recorded data and notes of her experiments. Verkan Vall selected four more of the heavy hunting pistols, more accurate than his shoulder-holster weapon or the dead Olirzon's belt arm, and capable of either full- or semi-automatic fire. Sarnax chose a couple more boar-rifles. Dalla slung her bag of recorded notes, and another bag of ammunition, and secured another deer rifle. They carried this accumulation of munitions to the private apartment of Prince Jirzyn, dumping everything in the middle of the drawing room, except the bag of notes, from which Dalla refused to separate herself.

"Maybe we'd better put some stuff over in one of the rooms on the other side of the well," Dirzed suggested. "They haven't really begun to come after us; when they do, we'll probably be attacked from two or three directions at once."

They returned to the gun room, casting anxious glances at the edge of the balcony above and at the barricade they had erected across the openings to the lifter tubes. Verkan Vall was not satisfied with this last; it looked to him as though they had provided a breastwork for somebody to fire on them from, more than anything else.

He was about to step around the cabinet which partially blocked the gun-room door when he glanced up, and saw a six-foot circle on the ceiling turning slowly brown. There was a smell of scorched plastic. He grabbed Sarnax by the arm and pointed.

"Thermite," the Assassin whispered. "The ceiling's got six inches of spaceship-insulation between it and the floor above; it'll take them a few minutes to burn through it." He stooped and pushed on the barricade, shoving it into the room. "Keep back; they'll probably drop a grenade or so through, first, before they jump down. If we're quick, we can get a couple of them."

Dirzed and Sarnax crouched, one at either side of the door, with weapons ready. Verkan Vall and Dalla had been ordered, rather peremptorily, to stay behind them; in a place of danger, an Assassin was obliged to shield his client. Verkan Vall, unable to see what was going on inside the room, kept his eyes and his gun muzzle on the barricade across the openings to the lifter tubes, the erection of which he was now regretting as a major tactical error.

Inside the gun room, there was a sudden crash, as the circle of thermite burned through and a section of ceiling dropped out and hit the floor. Instantly, Dirzed flung himself back against Verkan Vall, and there was a tremendous explosion inside, followed by another and another. A second or so passed, then Dirzed, leaping around the corner of the door, began firing rapidly into the room. From the other side of the door, Sarnax began blazing away with his rifle. Verkan Vall kept his position, covering the lifter tubes.

Suddenly, from behind the barricade, a blue-white gun flash leaped into being, and a pistol banged. He sprayed the opening between a couch and a section of bookcase from whence it had come, releasing his trigger as the gun rose with the recoil, squeezing and releasing and squeezing again. Then he jumped to his feet.

"Come on, the other place; hurry!" he ordered.

Sarnax swore in exasperation. "Help me with her, Dirzed!" he implored.

Verkan Vall turned his head, to see the two Assassins drag Dalla to her feet and hustle her away from the gun room; she was quite senseless, and they had to drag her between them. Verkan Vall gave a quick glance into the gun room; two of the Starpha servants and a man in rather flashy civil dress were lying on the floor where they had been shot as they had jumped down from above. He saw a movement at the edge of the irregular, smoking, hole in the ceiling, and gave it a short burst, then fired another at the exit from the descent tube. Then he took to his heels and followed the Assassins and Hadron Dalla into Prince Jirzyn's apartment.

As he ran through the open door, the Assassins were letting Dalla down into a chair; they instantly threw themselves into the work of barricading the doorway so as to provide cover and at the same time allow them to fire out into the central well.

For an instant, as he bent over her, he thought Dalla had been killed, an assumption justified by his knowledge of the deadliness of Akor-Neb bullets. Then he saw her eyelids flicker. A moment later, he had the explanation of her escape. The bullet had hit the game bag at her side; it was full of spools of metal tape, in metal cases, and notes in written form, pyrographed upon sheets of plastic ring-fastened into metal binders. Because of their extreme velocity, Akor-Neb bullets were sure killers when they struck animal tissue, but for the same reason, they had very poor penetration on hard objects. The alloy-steel tape, and the steel spools and spool cases, and the notebook binders had been enough to shatter the little bullet into tiny splinters of magnesium-nickel alloy, and the stout leather back of the game bag had stopped all of these. But the impact, even distributed as it had been through the contents of the bag, had been enough to knock the girl unconscious.

He found a bottle of some sort of brandy and a glass on a serving table nearby and poured her a drink, holding it to her lips. She spluttered over the first mouthful, then took the glass from him and sipped the rest.

"What happened?" she asked. "I thought those bullets were sure death."

"Your notes. The bullet hit the bag. Are you all right now?"

She finished the brandy, "I think so." She put a hand into the game bag and brought out a snarled and tangled mess of steel tape. "Oh, *blast!* That stuff was important; all the records on the preliminary auto-recall experiments." She shrugged. "Well, it wouldn't have been worth much more if I'd stopped that bullet myself." She slipped the strap over her shoulder and started to rise.

As she did, a bedlam of firing broke out, both from the two Assassins at the door and from outside. They both hit the floor and crawled out of line of the partly open door; Verkan Vall recovered his submachine-gun, which he had set down beside Dalla's chair. Sarnax was firing with his rifle at some target in the direction of the lifter tubes; Dirzed lay slumped over the barricade, and one glance at his crumpled figure was enough to tell Verkan Vall that he was dead.

"You fill magazines for us," he told Dalla, then crawled to Dirzed's place at the door. "What happened, Sarnax?"

"They shoved over the barricade at the lifter tubes and came out into the well. I got a couple, they got Dirzed, and now they're holed up in rooms all around the circle. They—Aah!" He fired three shots, quickly, around the edge of the door. "That stopped that." The Assassin crouched to insert a fresh magazine into his rifle.

Verkan Vall risked one eye around the corner of the doorway, and as he did, there was a red flash and a dull roar, unlike the blue flashes and sharp cracking reports of the pistols and rifles, from the doorway of the gun room. He wondered, for a split second, if it might be one of the fowling pieces he had seen there, and then something whizzed past his head and exploded with a soft *plop* behind him. Turning, he saw a pool of gray vapor beginning to spread in the middle of the room. Dalla must have got a breath of it, for she was slumped over the chair from which she had just risen.

Dropping the submachine-gun and gulping a lungful of fresh air from outside, Verkan Vall rushed to her, caught her by the heels, and dragged her into Prince Jirzyn's bedroom, beyond. Leaving her in the middle of the floor, he took another deep breath and returned to the drawing room, where Sarnax was already overcome by the sleep-gas.

He saw the serving table from which he had gotten the brandy, and dragged it over to the bedroom door, overturning it and laying it across the doorway, its legs in the air. Like most Akor-Neb serving tables, it had a gravity-counteraction unit under it; he set this for double minus gravitation and snapped it on. As it was now above the inverted table, the table did not rise, but a tendril of sleep-gas, curling toward it, bent upward and drifted away from the doorway. Satisfied that he had made a temporary barrier against the sleep-gas, Verkan Vall secured Dalla's hunting pistol and spare magazines and lay down at the bedroom door.

For some time, there was silence outside. Then the besiegers evidently decided that the sleep-gas attack had been a success. An Assassin, wearing a gas mask and carrying a submachine-gun, appeared in the doorway, and behind him came a tall man in a tan tunic, similarly masked. They stepped into the room and looked around.

Knowing that he would be shooting over a two hundred percent negative gravitation-field, Verkan Vall aimed for the Assassin's belt-buckle and squeezed. The bullet caught him in the throat. Evidently the bullet had not only been lifted in the negative gravitation, but lifted point-first and deflected upward. He held his front sight just above the other man's knee, and hit him in the chest.

As he fired, he saw a wisp of gas come sliding around the edge of the inverted table. There was silence outside, and for an instant, he was tempted to abandon his post and go to the bathroom, back of the bedroom, for wet towels to improvise a mask. Then, when he tried to crawl backward, he could not. There was an impression of distant shouting which turned to a roaring sound in his head. He tried to lift his pistol, but it slipped from his fingers.

WHEN consciousness returned, he was lying on his back, and something cold and rubbery was pressing into his face. He raised his arms to fight off whatever it was, and opened his eyes, to find that he was staring directly at the red oval and winged bullet of the Society of Assassins. A hand caught his wrist as he reached for the small pistol under his arm. The pressure on his face eased.

"It's all right, Lord Virzal," a voice came to him. "Assassins' Truce!"

He nodded stupidly and repeated the words. "Assassins' Truce; I won't shoot. What happened?"

Then he sat up and looked around. Prince Jirzyn's bed-chamber was full of Assassins. Dalla, recovering from her touch of sleep-gas, was sitting groggily in a chair, while five or six of them fussed around her, getting in each others' way, handing her drinks, chaffing her wrists, holding damp cloths on her brow. That was standard procedure, when any group of males thought Dalla needed any help. Another Assassin, beside the bed, was putting away an oxygen-mask outfit, and the Assassin who had prevented Verkan Vall from drawing his pistol was his own follower, Marnik. And Klarnood, the Assassin-President, was sitting on the foot of the bed, smoking one of Prince Jirzyn's monogrammed and crested cigarettes, critically.

Verkan Vall looked at Marnik, and then at Klarnood, and back to Marnik.

"You got through," he said. "Good work, Marnik; I thought they'd downed you."

"They did; I had to crash-land in the woods. I went about a mile on foot, and then I found a man and woman and two children, hiding in one of these little log rain shelters. They had an airboat, a good one. It seemed that rioting had broken out in the city unit where they lived, and they'd taken to the woods till things quieted down again. I offered them Assassins' protection if they'd take me to Assassins' Hall, and they did."

"By luck, I was in when Marnik arrived," Klarnood took over. "We brought three boatloads of men, and came here at once. Just as we got here, two boatloads of Starpha dependents arrived; they tried to give us an argument, and we discarnated the lot of them. Then we came down here, crying 'Assassins' Truce.' One of the Starpha Assassins, Kirzol, was still carnate; he told us what had been going on." The President-General's face became grim. "You know, I take a rather poor view of Prince Jirzyn's procedure in this matter, not to mention that of his underlings. I'll have to speak to him about this. Now, how about you and the Lady Dallona? What do you intend doing?"

"We're getting out of here," Verkan Vall said. "I'd like air transport and protection as far as Ghamma, to the establishment of the family of Zorda. Brarnend of Zorda has a private space yacht; he'll get us to Venus."

Klarnood gave a sigh of obvious relief. "I'll have you and the Lady Dallona airborne and off for Ghamma as soon as you wish," he promised. "I will, frankly, be delighted to see the last of both of you. The Lady Dallona has started a fire here at Darsh that won't burn out in a half-century, and who knows what it may consume." He was interrupted by a heaving shock that made the underground dome dwelling shake like a light airboat in turbulence. Even eighty feet under the ground, they could hear a continued crashing roar. It was an appreciable interval before the sound and the shock ceased.

For an instant, there was silence and then an excited bedlam of shouting broke from the Assassins in the room. Klarnood's face was frozen in horror.

"That was a fission bomb!" he exclaimed. "The first one that has been exploded on this planet in hostility in a thousand years!" He turned to Verkan Vall. "If you feel well enough to walk, Lord Virzal, come with us. I must see what's happened."

They hurried from the room and went streaming up the ascent tube to the top of the dome. About forty miles away, to the south, Verkan Vall saw the sinister thing that he had seen on so many other time-lines, in so many other paratime sectors—a great pillar of varicolored fire-shot smoke, rising to a mushroom head fifty thousand feet above.

"Well, that's it," Klarnood said sadly. "That is civil war."

"May I make a suggestion, Assassin-President?" Verkan Vall asked. "I understand that Assassins' Truce is binding even upon non-Assassins; is that correct?"

"Well, not exactly; it's generally kept by such non-Assassins as want to remain in their present reincarnations, though."

"That's what I mean. Well, suppose you declare a general, planet-wide Assassins' Truce in this political war, and make the leaders of both parties responsible for keeping it. Publish lists of the top two or three thousand Statisticalists and Volitionalists, starting with Mirzark of Bashad and Prince Jirzyn of Starpha, and inform them that they will be assassinated, in order, if the fighting doesn't cease."

"Well!" A smile grew on Klarnood's face. "Lord Virzal, my thanks; a good suggestion. I'll try it. And furthermore, I'll withdraw all Assassin protection permanently from anybody involved in political activity, and forbid any Assassin to accept any retainer connected with political factionalism. It's about time our members stopped discarnating each other in these political squabbles." He pointed to the three airboats drawn up on the top of the dome; speedy black craft, bearing the red oval and winged bullet. "Take your choice, Lord Virzal. I'll lend you a couple of my men, and you'll be in Ghamma in three hours." He hooked fingers and clapped shoulders with Verkan Vall, and bent over Dalla's hand. "I still like you, Lord Virzal, and I have seldom met a more charming lady than you, Lady Dallona. But I sincerely hope I never see either of you again."

THE ship for Dhergabar was driving north and west; at seventy thousand feet, it was still daylight, but the world below was wrapping itself in darkness. In the big visiscreens, which served in lieu of the windows which could never have withstood the pressure and friction heat of the ship's speed, the sun was sliding out of sight over the horizon to port. Verkan Vall and Dalla sat together, watching the blazing western sky—the sky of their own First Level time-line.

"I blame myself terribly, Vall," Dalla was saying. "And I didn't mean any of them the least harm. All I was interested in was learning the facts. I know, that sounds like, 'I didn't know it was loaded,' but—"

"It sounds to me like those Fourth Level Europo-American Sector physicists who are giving themselves guilt-complexes because they designed an atomic bomb," Verkan Vall replied. "All you were interested in was learning the facts. Well, as a scientist, that's all you're supposed to be interested in. You don't have to worry about any social or political implications. People have to learn to live with newly discovered facts; if they don't, they die of them."

"But, Vall; that sounds dreadfully irresponsible—"

"Does it? You're worrying about the results of your reincarnation memory-recall discoveries, the shootings and riotings and the bombing we saw." He touched the pommel of Olirzon's knife, which he still wore. "You're no more guilty of that than the man who forged this blade is guilty of the death of Marnark of Bashad; if he'd never lived, I'd have killed Marnark with some other knife somebody else made. And what's more, you can't know the results of your discoveries. All you can see is a thin film of events on the surface of an immediate situation, so you can't say whether the long-term results will be beneficial or calamitous.

"Take this Fourth Level Europo-American atomic bomb, for example. I choose that because we both know that sector, but I could think of a hundred other examples in other paratime areas. Those people, because of deforestation, bad agricultural methods and general mismanagement, are eroding away their arable soil at an alarming rate. At the same time, they are breeding like rabbits. In other words, each successive generation has less and less food to divide among more and more people, and for inherited traditional and superstitious reasons, they refuse to adopt any rational program of birth-control and population-limitation.

"But, fortunately, they now have the atomic bomb, and they are developing radioactive poisons, weapons of mass-effect. And their racial, nationalistic and ideological conflicts are rapidly reaching the explosion point. A series of all-out atomic wars is just what that sector needs, to bring their population down to their world's carrying capacity; in a century or so, the inventors of the atomic bomb will be hailed as the saviors of their species."

"But how about my work on the Akor-Neb Sector?" Dalla asked. "It seems that my memory-recall technique is more explosive than any fission bomb. I've laid the train for a century-long reign of anarchy!"

"I doubt that; I think Klarnood will take hold, now that he has committed himself to it. You know, in spite of his sanguinary profession, he's the nearest thing to a real man of goodwill I've found on that sector. And here's something else you haven't considered. Our own First Level life expectancy is from four to five hundred years. That's the main reason why we've accomplished as much as we have. We have, individually, time to accomplish things. On the Akor-Neb Sector, a scientist or artist or scholar or statesman will grow senile and die before he's as old as either of us. But now, a young student of twenty or so can take one of your auto-recall treatments and immediately have available all the knowledge and experience gained in four or five previous lives. He can start where he left off in his last reincarnation. In other words, you've made those people time-binders, individually as well as racially. Isn't that worth the temporary discarnation of a lot of ward-heelers and plug-uglies, or even a few decent types like Dirzed and Olirzon? If it isn't, I don't know what scales of values you're using."

"Vall!" Dalla's eyes glowed with enthusiasm. "I never thought of that! And you said, 'temporary discarnation.' That's just what it is. Dirzed and Olirzon and the others aren't dead; they're just waiting, discarnate, between physical lives. You know, in the sacred writings of one of the Fourth Level peoples it is stated: 'Death is the last enemy.' By proving that death is just a cyclic condition of continued individual existence, these people have conquered their last enemy."

"Last enemy but one," Verkan Vall corrected. "They still have one enemy to go, an enemy within themselves. Call it semantic confusion, or illogic, or incomprehension, or just plain stupidity. Like Klarnood, stymied by verbal objections to something labeled 'political intervention.' He'd never have consented to use the power of his Society if he hadn't been shocked out of his inhibitions by that nuclear bomb. Or the Statisticalists, trying to create a classless order of society through a political program which would only result in universal servitude to an omnipotent government. Or the Volitionalist nobles, trying to preserve their hereditary feudal privileges, and now they can't even agree on a definition of the term 'hereditary.' Might they not recover all the silly prejudices of their past lives, along with the knowledge and wisdom?"

"But . . . I thought you said—" Dalla was puzzled, a little hurt.

Verkan Vall's arm squeezed around her waist, and he laughed comfortingly.

"You see? Any sort of result is possible, good or bad. So don't blame yourself in advance for something you can't possibly estimate." An idea occurred to him, and he straightened in the seat. "Tell you what; if you people at Rhogom Foundation get the problem of discarnate paratime transposition licked by then, let's you and I go back to the Akor-Neb Sector in about a hundred years and see what sort of a mess those people have made of things."

"A hundred years; that would be Year Twenty-Two of the next millennium. It's a date, Vall; we'll do it."

They bent to light their cigarettes together at his lighter. When they raised their heads again and got the flame glare out of their eyes, the sky was purple-black, dusted with stars, and dead ahead, spilling up over the horizon, was a golden glow—the lights of Dhergabar and home.

Introduction to
"Time Crime"

*"Time Crime" was Piper's longest Paratime story until the Lord Kalvan series of a decade later. In this short novel we find the Paratime Police at their best. Of all the Paratime stories, "Time Crime" comes closest to being a police procedural, possibly because of the two mysteries Piper had written several years earlier (*Murder in the Gun-Room *and its sequel).*

"Time Crime" gives us the most complete picture of First Level civilization of all the Paratime stories; here we learn that there are serpents even in the garden of a scientific society.

TIME CRIME

I

KIRO Soran, the guard captain, stood in the shadow of the veranda roof, his white cloak thrown back to display the scarlet lining. He rubbed his palm reflectively on the checkered butt of his revolver and watched the four men at the table.

"And ten tens are a hundred," one of the clerks in blue jackets said, adding another stack to the pile of gold coins.

"Nineteen hundreds," one of the pair in dirty striped robes agreed, taking a stone from the box in front of him and throwing it away. Only one stone remained. "One more hundred to pay."

One of the blue-jacketed plantation clerks made a tally mark; his companion counted out coins, ten and ten and ten.

Dosu Golan, the plantation manager, tapped impatiently on his polished boot leg with a thin riding whip.

"I don't like this," he said, in another and entirely different language. "I know, chattel slavery's an established custom on this sector, and we have to conform to local usages, but it sickens me to have to haggle with these swine over the price of human beings. On the Zarkantha Sector, we used nothing but free wage-labor."

"Migratory workers," the guard captain said. "Humanitarian considerations aside, I can think of a lot better ways of meeting the labor problem on a fruit plantation than by buying slaves you need for three months a year and have to feed and quarter and clothe and doctor the whole twelve."

"Twenty hundreds of *obus*," the clerk who had been counting the money said. "That is the payment, is it not, Coru-hin-Irigod?"

"That is the payment," the slave dealer replied.

The clerk swept up the remaining coins, and his companion took them over and put them in an iron-bound chest, snapping the padlock. The two guards who had been loitering at one side slung their rifles and picked up the chest, carrying it into the plantation house. The slave dealer and his companion arose, putting their money into a leather bag; Coru-hin-Irigod turned and bowed to the two men in white cloaks.

"The slaves are yours, noble lords," he said.

Across the plantation yard, six more men in striped robes, with carbines slung across their backs, approached; with them came another man in a hooded white cloak, and two guards in blue jackets and red caps, with bayoneted rifles. The man in white and his armed attendants came toward the house; the six Calera slavers continued across the yard to where their horses were picketed.

"If I do not offend the noble lords, then," Coru-hin-Irigod said, "I beg their sufferance to depart. I and my men have far to ride if we would reach Careba by nightfall. The Lord; the Great Lord, the Lord God Safar watch between us until we meet again."

Urado Alatana, the labor foreman, came up onto the porch as the two slavers went down.

"Have a good look at them, Radd?" the guard captain asked.

"You think I'm crazy enough to let those bandits out of here with two thousand *obus*—forty thousand Paratemporal Exchange Units—of the Company's money without knowing what we're getting?" the other parried. "They're all right—nice, clean, healthy-looking lot. I did everything but take them apart and inspect the pieces while they were being unshackled at the stockade. I'd like to know where this Coru-hin-Whatshisname got them, though. They're not local stuff. Lot darker, and they're jabbering among themselves in some lingo I never heard before. A few are wearing some rags of clothing, and they have odd-looking sandals. I noticed that most of them showed marks of recent whipping. That may mean they're troublesome, or it may just mean that these Caleras are a lot of sadistic brutes."

"Poor devils!" The man called Dosu Golan was evidently hoping that he'd never catch himself talking about fellow humans like that. The guard captain turned to him.

"Coming to have a look at them, Doth?" he asked.

"You go, Kirv; I'll see them later."

"Still not able to look the Company's property in the face?" the captain asked gently. "You'll not get used to it any sooner than now."

"I suppose you're right." For a moment Dosu Golan watched Coru-hin-Irigod and his followers canter out of the yard and break into a gallop on the road beyond. Then he tucked his whip under his arm. "All right, then. Let's go see them."

THE labor foreman went into the house; the manager and the guard captain went down the steps and set out across the yard. A big slat-sided wagon, drawn by four horses, driven by an old slave in a blue smock and a thing like a sunbonnet, rumbled past, loaded with newlypicked oranges. Blue woodsmoke was beginning to rise from the stoves at the open kitchen and a couple of slaves were noisily chopping wood. Then they came to the stockade of close-set pointed poles. A guard sergeant in a red-trimmed blue jacket, armed with a revolver, met them with a salute, which Kiro Soran returned; he unfastened the gate and motioned four or five riflemen into positions from which they could fire in between the poles in case the slaves turned on their new owners.

There seemed little danger of that, though Kiro Soran kept his hand close to the butt of his revolver. The slaves, an even hundred of them, squatted under awnings out of the sun, or stood in line to drink at the water-butt. They furtively watched the two men who had entered among them, as though expecting blows or kicks; when none were forthcoming, they relaxed slightly. As the labor foreman had said, they were clean and looked healthy. They were all nearly naked; there were about as many women as men, but no children or old people.

"Radd's right," the captain told the new manager. "They're not local. Much darker skins, and different face-structure; faces wedge-shaped instead of oval, and differently shaped noses, and brown eyes instead of black. I've seen people like that somewhere, but—"

He fell silent. A suspicion, utterly fantastic, had begun to form in his mind, and he stepped closer to a group of a dozen-odd, the manager following him. One or two had been unmercifully lashed, not long ago, and all bore a few lash-marks. Odd sort of marks, more like burn-blisters than welts. He'd have to have the Company doctor look at them. Then he caught their speech, and the suspicion was converted to certainty.

"These are not like the others; they wear fine garments, and walk proudly. They look stern, but not cruel. They are the real masters here; the others are but servants."

He grasped the manager's arm and drew him aside.

"You know that language?" he asked. When the man called Dosu Golan shook his head, he continued: "That's Kharanda; it's a dialect spoken by a people in the Ganges Valley, in India, on the Kholghoor Sector of the Fourth Level."

Dosu Golan blinked, and his face went blank for a moment.

"You mean they're from outtime?" he demanded. "Are you sure?"

"I did two years on Fourth Level Kholghoor with the Paratime Police, before I took this job," the man called Kiro Soran replied. "And another thing. Those lash-marks were made with some kind of an electric whip. Not these rawhide quirts the Caleras use."

It took the plantation manager all of five seconds to add that up. The answer frightened him.

"Kirv, this is going to make a simply hideous uproar, all the way to Home Time-Line main office," he said. "I don't know what I'm going to do—"

"Well, I know what I have to do." The captain raised his voice, using the local language: "Sergeant! Run to the guardhouse, and tell Sergeant Adarada to mount up twenty of his men and take off after those Caleras who sold us these slaves. They're headed down the road toward the river. Tell him to bring them all back, and especially their chief, Coru-hin-Irigod, and him I want alive and able to answer questions. And then get the white-cloak lord Urado Alatena, and come back here."

"Yes, captain." The guards were all Yarana people; they disliked Caleras intensely. The sergeant threw a salute, turned, and ran.

NEXT, we'll have to isolate these slaves," Kiro Soran said. "You'd better make a full report to the Company as soon as possible. I'm going to transpose to Police Terminal Time-Line and make my report to the Sector-Regional Subchief. Then—"

"Now wait a moment, Kirv," Dosu Golan protested. "After all, I'm the manager, even if I am new here. It's up to me to make the decisons—"

Kiro Soran shook his head. "Sorry, Doth. Not this one," he said. "You know the terms under which I was hired by the Company. I'm still a field agent of the Paratime Police, and I'm reporting back on duty as soon as I can transpose to Police Terminal. Look; here are a hundred men and women who have been shifted from one time-line, on one paratemporal sector of probability, to another. Why, the world from which these people came doesn't even exist in this space-time continuum. There's only one way they could have gotten here, and that's the way we did—in a Ghaldron-Hesthor paratemporal transposition field. You can carry it on from there as far as you like, but the only thing it adds up to is a case for the Paratime Police. You had better include in your report mention that I've reverted to police status; my Company pay ought to be stopped as of now. And until somebody who outranks me is sent here, I'm in complete charge. Paratime Transportation Code, Section XVII, Article 238."

The plantation manager nodded. Kiro Soran knew how he must feel; he laid a hand gently on the younger man's shoulder.

"You understand how it is, Doth; this is the only thing I can do."

"I understand, Kirv. Count on me for absolutely anything." He looked at the brown-skinned slaves, and lines of horror and loathing appeared around his mouth. "To think that some of our own people would do a thing like this! I hope you can catch the devils! Are you transposing out, now?"

"In a few minutes. While I'm gone, have the doctor look at those whip-injuries. Those things could get infected. Fortunately, he's one of our own people."

"Yes, of course. And I'll have these slaves isolated, and if Adarada brings back Coru-hin-Irigod and his gang before you get back, I'll have them locked up and waiting for you. I suppose you want to narco-hypnotize and question the whole lot, slaves and slavers?"

The labor foreman, known locally as Urado Alatena, entered the stockade.

"What's wrong, Kirv?" he asked.

The Paratime Police agent told him, briefly. The labor foreman whistled, threw a quick glance at the nearest slaves, and nodded.

"I knew there was something funny about them," he said. "Doth, what a simply beastly thing to happen, two days after you take charge here!"

"Not his fault," the Paratime Police agent said. "I'm the one the Company'll be sore at, but I'd rather have them down on me rather than old Tortha Karf. Well, sit on the lid till I get back," he told both of them. "We'll need some kind of a story for the locals. Let's see—Explain to the guards, in the hearing of some of the more talkative slaves, that these slaves are from the Asian mainland, that they are of a people friendly to our people, and that they were kidnaped by pirates, our enemies. That ought to explain everything satisfactorily."

On his way back to the plantation house, he saw a clump of local slaves staring curiously at the stockade, and noticed that the guards had unslung their rifles and fixed their bayonets. None of them had any idea, of course, of what had happened, but they all seemed to know, by some sort of ESP, that something was seriously wrong. It was going to get worse, too, when strangers began arriving, apparently from nowhere, at the plantation.

VERKAN Vall waited until the small, dark-eyed woman across the circular table had helped herself from one of the bowls on the revolving disk in the middle, then rotated it to bring the platter of cold boar-ham around to himself.

"Want some of this, Dalla?" he asked, transferring a slice of ham and a spoonful of wine sauce to his plate.

"No, I'll have some of the venison," the black-haired girl beside him said. "And some of the pickled beans. We'll be getting our fill of pork, for the next month."

"I thought the Dwarma Sector people were vegetarians," Jandar Jard, the theatrical designer, said. "Most nonviolent peoples are, aren't they?"

"Well, the Dwarma people haven't any specific taboo against taking life," Bronnath Zara, the dark-eyed woman in the brightly colored gown, told him. "They're just utterly noncombative, nonaggressive. When I was on the Dwarma Sector, there was a horrible scandal at the village where I was staying. It seems that a farmer and a meat butcher fought over the price of a pig. They actually raised their voices and shouted contradictions at each other. That happened two years before, and people were still talking about it."

"I didn't think they had any money, either," Verkan Vall's wife, Hadron Dalla, said.

"They don't," Zara said. "It's all barter and trade. What are you and Vall going to use for a visible means of support while you're there?"

"Oh, I have my mandolin, and I've learned all the traditional Dwarma songs by hypno-mech," Dalla said. "And Transtime Tours is fitting Vall out with a bag of tools; he's going to do repair work and carpentry."

"Oh, good; you'll be welcome anywhere," Zara, the sculptress, said. "They're always glad to entertain a singer, and for people who do the fine decorative work they do, they're the most incompetent practical mechanics I've ever seen or heard of. You're going to travel from village to village?"

"Yes. The cover-story is that we're lovers who have left our village in order not to make Vall's former wife unhappy by our presence," Dalla said.

"Oh, good! That's entirely in the Dwarma romantic tradition," Bronnath Zara approved. "Ordinarily, you know, they don't like to travel. They have a saying: 'Happy are the trees, they abide in their own place; sad are the winds, forever they wander.' But that'll be a fine explanation."

Thalvan Dras, the big man with the black beard and the long red coat and cloth-of-gold sash who lounged in the host's seat, laughed.

"I can just see Vall mending pots, and Dalla playing that mandolin and singing," he said. "At least you'll be getting away from police work. I don't suppose they have anything like police on the Dwarma Sector?"

"Oh, no; they don't even have any such concept," Bronnath Zara said. "When somebody does something wrong, his neighbors all come and talk to him about it till he gets ashamed, then they all forgive him and have a feast. They're lovely people, so kind and gentle. but you'll get awfully tired of them in about a month. They have absolutely no respect for anybody's privacy. In fact, it seems slightly indecent to them for anybody to want privacy."

One of Thalvan Dras's human servants came into the room, coughed apologetically, and said:

"A visiphone-call for His Valor, the Mavrad of Nerros."

Vall went on nibbling ham and wine sauce; the servant repeated the announcement a trifle more loudly.

"Vall, you're being paged!" Thalvan Dras told him, with a touch of impatience.

Verkan Vall looked blank for an instant, then grinned. It had been so long since he had even bothered to think about that antiquated title of nobility.

"Vall's probably forgotten that he has a title," a girl across the table, wearing an almost transparent gown and nothing else, laughed.

"That's something the Mavrad of Mnirna and Thalvabar never forgets," Jandar Jard drawled, with what, in a woman, would have been cattishness.

Thalvan Dras gave him a hastily repressed look of venomous anger, then said something, more to Verkan Vall than to Jandar Jard, about titles of nobility being the marks of social position and responsibility which their bearers should never forget. That jab, Vall thought, following the servant out of the room, had been a mistake on Jard's part. A music-drama, for which he had designed the settings, was due to open here in Dhergabar in another ten days.

Thalvan Dras would cherish spite, and a word from the Mavrad of Mnirna and Thalvabar would set a dozen critics to disparaging Jandar's work. On the other hand, maybe it had been smart of Jandar Jard to antagonize Thalvan Dras; for every critic who bowed slavishly to the wealthy nobleman, there were at least two more who detested him unutterably. and they would rush to Jandar Jard's defense, and in the ensuing uproar, the settings would get more publicity than the drama itself.

IN the visiphone booth, Vall found a girl in a green blouse, with the Paratime Police insignia on her shoulder, looking out of the screen. The wall behind her was pale green striped in gold and black.

"Hello, Eldra," he greeted her.

"Hello, Chief's Assistant; I'm sorry to bother you, but the Chief wants to talk to you. Just a moment, please."

The screen exploded into a kaleidoscopic flash of lights and colors, then cleared again. This time, a man looked out of it. He was well into middle age; close to his three hundredth year. His hair, a uniform iron-gray, was beginning to thin in front, and he was acquiring the beginnings of a double chin. His name was Tortha Karf, and he was Chief of Paratime Police, and Verkan Vall's superior.

"Hello, Vall. Glad I was able to locate you. When are you and Dalla leaving?"

"As soon as we can get away from this luncheon, here. Oh, say an hour. We're taking a rocket to Zarabar, and transposing from there to Passenger Terminal Sixteen, and from there to the Dwarma Sector."

"Well, Vall, I hate to bother you like this," Tortha Karf said, "but I wish you'd stop by Headquarters on your way to the rocketport. Something's come up—it may be a very nasty business—and I'd like to talk to you about it."

"Well, Chief, let me remind you that this vacation, which I've had to postpone four times already, has been overdue for four years," Vall said.

"Yes, Vall, I know. You've been working very hard, and you and Dalla are entitled to a little time together. I just want you to look into something, before you leave."

"It'll have to take some fast looking. Our rocket blasts off in two hours."

"It may take a little longer; if it does, you and Dalla can transpose to Police Terminal and take a rocket for Zarabar Equivalent, and transpose from there to Passenger Sixteen. It would save time if you brought Dalla with you to Headquarters."

"Dalla won't like this," Vall understated.

"No. I'm afraid not." Tortha Karf looked around apprehensively, as though estimating the damage an enraged Hadron Dalla could do to his office furnishings. "Well, try to get here as soon as you can."

THALVAN Dras was holding forth, when Vall returned, on one of his favorite preoccupations.

". . . Reason I'm taking such an especially active interest in this year's Arts Exhibitions; I've become disturbed at the extent to which so many of our artists have been content to derive their motifs, even their techniques, from outtime art." He was using his vocowriter, rather than his conversational, voice. "I yield to no one in my appreciation of outtime art—you all know how devotedly I collect objects of art from all over paratime—but our own artists should endeavor to express their artistic values in our own artistic idioms."

Vall bent over his wife's shoulder.

"We have to leave, right away," he whispered.

"But our rocket doesn't blast off for two hours—"

Thalvan Dras had stopped talking and was looking at them in annoyance.

"I have to go to Headquarters before we leave. It'll save time if you come along."

"Oh, no, Vall!" She looked at him in consternation. "Was that Tortha Karf calling?" She replaced her plate on the table and got to her feet.

"I'm dreadfully sorry, Dras," he addressed their host. "I just had a call from Tortha Karf. A few minor details that must be cleared up before I leave Home Time-Line. If you'll accept our thanks for a wonderful luncheon—"

"Why, certainly, Vall. Brogoth, will you call—" He gave a slight chuckle. "I'm so used to having Brogoth Zaln at my elbow that I'd forgotten he wasn't here. Wait, I'll call one of the servants to have a car for you."

"Don't bother; we'll take an aircab," Vall told him.

"But you simply can't take a public cab!" The black-bearded nobleman was shocked at such an obscene idea. "I will have a car ready for you in a few minutes."

"Sorry, Dras; we have to hurry. We'll get a cab on the roof. Good-by, everybody; sorry to have to break away like this. See you all when we get back."

HADRON Dalla watched dejectedly as the green crags and escarpments of the Paratime Building loomed above the city in front of them, and began slipping under the aircab. She felt like a prisoner recaptured at the moment when attempted escape was about to succeed.

"I knew it," she said. "I knew he'd find something. He's trying to break things up between us, the way he did twenty years ago."

Vall crushed out his cigarette and said nothing. That hadn't been true, and she knew it as well as he did. There had been many other factors involved in the disintegration of their previous marriage, most of them of her own contribution. But that had been twenty years ago, she told herself. This time it would be different, if only—

"Really, Vall, he's never liked me," she went on. "He's jealous of me, I think. You're to be his successor, when he retires, and he thinks I'm not a good influence—"

"Oh, rubbish, Dalla! The Chief has always liked you," Vall replied. "If he didn't, do you think he'd always be inviting us to that farm of his, on Fifth Level Sicily? It's just that this job of ours has no end; something's always turning up, out-time."

The music that the cab had been playing died away. "Paratime Building, just below," it said, in a light feminine voice. "Which landing stage, please?" Vall leaned forward and punched at the buttons in front of him. Something in the cab's electronic brain gave a rapid series of clicks as it shifted from the general Paratime Building beam to the beam of the Paratime Police landing stage, then it said, "Thank you." The building below seemed to rotate upward toward them as it settled down. Then the antigrav-field snapped off, the cab door popped open, and the cab said: "Good-by, now. Ride with me again some time."

They crossed the landing stage, entered the antigrav shaft, and floated downward; at the end of a hallway below, Vall opened the door of Tortha Karf's office and ushered her through ahead of him.

Tortha Karf, inside the semicircle of his desk, was speaking into a recording phone as they approached. He shut off the machine and waved, a cigarette in his hand.

"Come on back and sit down," he invited. "Be with you in a moment." Then he switched on the phone again and went on talking—something about prompter evaluation and transmission of reports and less reliance on robot equipment. "Sign that up, my personal order, and see it's transmitted to everybody down to and including Sector Regional Subchief level," he finished, then hung up the phone and turned to them.

"Sorry about this," he said. "Sit down, if you please. Cigarettes?"

Dalla shook her head and sat down in one of the chairs behind the desk; she started to relax and then caught herself and sat erect, her hands on her lap.

"This won't interfere with your vacation, Vall," Tortha Karf was saying. "I just need a little help before you transpose out."

"We have to catch the rocket for Zarabar in an hour and a half," Dalla reminded him.

"Don't worry about that; if you miss the commercial rocket, our police rockets can give it an hour's start and pass it before it gets to Zarabar," Tortha Karf said. Then he turned to Vall.

HERE'S what's happened," he said. "One of our field agents on detached duty as guard captain for Consolidated Outtime Foodstuffs on a fruit plantation in western North America, Third Level Esaron Sector, was looking over a lot of slaves who had been sold to the plantation by a local slave dealer. He heard them talking among themselves—in Kharanda."

Dalla caught the significance of that before Vall did. At first, she was puzzled; then, in spite of herself, she was horrified and angry. Tortha Karf was explaining to Vall just where and on what paratemporal sector Kharanda was spoken.

"No possibility that this agent, Skordran Kirv, could have been mistaken. He worked for a while on Kholghoor Sector, himself; knew the language by hypno-mech and by two years' use," Tortha Karf was saying. "So he ordered himself back on duty, had the slaves isolated and the slave dealers arrested, and then transposed to Police Terminal to report. The SecReg Subchief, old Vulthor Tharn, confirmed him in charge at this Esaron Sector plantation, and assigned him a couple of detectives and a psychist."

"When was this?" Vall asked.

"Yesterday. One-Five-Nine Day. About fifteen hundred local time."

"Twenty-three hundred Dhergabar time," Vall commented.

"Yes. And I just found out about it. Came in in the late morning generalized report-digest; very inconspicuous item, no special urgency symbol or anything. Fortunately, one of the report editors spotted it and messaged Police Terminal for a copy of the original report."

"It's been a long time since we had anything like that," Vall said, studying the glowing tip of his cigarette, his face wearing the curiously with-drawn expression of a conscious memory recall. "Fifty years ago; the time that gang kidnaped some girls from Second Level Triplanetary Empire Sector and sold them into the harem of some Fourth Level Indo-Turanian sultan."

"Yes. That was your first independent case, Vall. That was when I began to think you'd really make a cop. One renegade First Level citizen and four or five ServSec Prole hoodlums, with a stolen fifty-foot conveyer. This looks like a rather more ambitious operation."

DALLA got one of her own cigarettes out and lit it. Vall and Tortha Karf were talking cop talk about method of operation and possible size of the gang involved, and why the slaves had been shipped all the way from India to the west coast of North America.

"Always ready sale for slaves on the Esaron Sector," Vall was saying. "And so many small independent states, and different languages, that out-timers wouldn't be particularly conspicuous."

"And with this barbarian invasion going on on the Kholghoor Sector, slaves could be picked up cheaply," Tortha Karf added.

In spite of her determination to boycott the conversation, curiosity began to get the better of her. She had spent a year and a half on the Kholghoor Sec-tor, investigating alleged psychic powers of the local priests. There'd been nothing to it—the prophecies weren't precognition, they were shrewd infer-ences, and the miracles weren't psychokinesis, they were sleight-of-hand. She found herself asking:

"What barbarian invasion's this?"

"Oh, Central Asian nomadic people, the Croutha," Tortha Karf told her. "They came down through Khyber Pass about three months ago, turned east, and hit the headwaters of the Ganges. Without punching a lot of buttons to find out exactly, I'd say they're halfway to the delta country by now. Leader seems to be a chieftain called Llamh Droogh the Red. A lot of paratime trad-ing companies are yelling for permits to introduce firearms in the Kholghoor Sector to protect their holdings there."

She nodded. The Fourth Level Kholghoor Sector belonged to what was known as Indus-Ganges-Irriwady Basic Sector-Grouping—probability of civi-lization having developed late on the Indian subcontinent, with the rest of the world, including Europe, in Stone Age savagery or early Bronze Age barbarism. The Kharandas, the people among whom she had once done field-research work, had developed pre-mechanical, animal-power, handcraft, edge-weapon culture. She could imagine the roads jammed with fugitives from the barbarian invaders, the conveyer hidden among the trees, the lurking slavers—

Watch it, Dalla! Don't let the old scoundrel play on your feelings!

WELL, what do you want me to do, Chief?" Vall was asking.

"Well, I have to know just what this situation's likely to develop into, and I want to know why Vulthor Tharn's been sitting on this ever since Skordran Kirv reported it to him—"

"I can answer the second one now," Vall replied. "Vulthor Tharn is due to retire in a few years. He has a negatively good, undistinguished record. He's trying to play it safe."

Tortha Karf nodded. "That's what I thought. Look, Vall; suppose you and Dalla transpose from here to Police Terminal, and go to Novilan Equivalent, and give this a quick look-over and report to me, and then rocket to Zarabar Equivalent and go on with your trip to the Dwarma Sector. It may delay you eight or ten hours, but—"

"Closer to twenty-four," Vall said. "I'd have to transpose to this plantation, on the Esaron Sector. How about it, Dalla? Would you want to do that?"

She hesitated for a moment, angry with him. He didn't want to refuse, and he was trying to make her do it for him.

"I know it's a confounded imposition, Dalla," Tortha Karf told her. "But it's important that I get a prompt and full estimate of the situation. This may be something very serious. If it's an isolated incident, it can be handled in a routine manner, but I'm afraid it's not. It has all the marks of a large-scale operation, and if this is a matter of mass kidnapings from one sector and transpositions to another, you can see what a threat this is to the Paratime Secret."

"Moral considerations entirely aside," Vall said. "We don't need to discuss them; they're too obvious."

She nodded. For over twelve millennia, the people of her race and Vall's and Tortha Karf's had been existing as parasites on all the innumerable other worlds of alternate probability on the lateral dimension of time. Smart parasites never injure their hosts, and try never to reveal their existence.

"We could do that, couldn't we, Vall?" she asked, angry at herself now for giving in. "And if you want to question these slaves, I speak Kharanda, and I know how they think. And I'm a qualified and licensed narco-hypnotic technician."

"Well, that's splendid, Dalla!" Tortha Karf enthused. "Wait a moment; I'll message Police Terminal to have a rocket ready for you."

"I'll need a hypno-mech for Kharanda, myself," Vall said. "Dalla, do you know Acalan?" When she shook her head, he turned back to Tortha Karf. "Look; it's about a four-hour rocket hop to Novilan Equivalent. Say we have the hypno-mech machines installed in the rocket; Dalla and I can take our language lessons on the way, and be ready to go to work as soon as we land."

"Good idea," Tortha Karf approved. "I'll order that done right away. Now—"

Oddly enough, she wasn't feeling so angry, now that she had committed herself and Vall. Come to think of it, she had never been on Police Terminal Time Line; very few people, outside the Paratime Police, ever had. And, she had always wanted to learn more about Vall's work, and participate in it with him. And if she'd made him refuse, it would have been something ugly between them all the time they would be on the Dwarma Sector. But this way—

THE big circular conveyer room was crowded, as it had been every minute of every day for the past ten thousand years. At the great circular desk in the center, departing or returning police officers were checking in or out with the flat-topped cylindrical robot clerks, or talking to human attendants. Some were in the regulation green uniform; others, like himself, were in civilian clothes; more were in out-time costumes from all over paratime. Fringed robes and cloth-of-gold sashes and conical caps from the Second Level Khiftan Sector; Fourth Level Proto-Aryan mail and helmets; the short tunics and kilts of Fourth Level Alexandrian-Roman Sector; the Zarkantha loincloth and felt cap and daggers; there were priestly vestments stiff with gold, and military uniforms; there were trousers and jackboots and bare legs; blasters, and swords, and pistols, and bows and quivers, and spears. And the place was loud with a babel of voices and the clatter of tele-printers.

Dalla was looking about her in surprised delight; for her, the vacation had already begun. He was glad; for a while, he had been afraid that she would be unhappy about it. He guided her through the crowd to the desk, spoke for a while to one of the human attendants, and found out which was their conveyer. It was a fixed-destination shuttler, operative only between Home Time-Line and Police Terminal, from which most of the Paratime Police operations were routed. He put Dalla in through the sliding door, followed, and closed it behind him, locking it. Then, before he closed the starting switch, he drew a pistol-like weapon and checked it.

In theory, the Ghaldron-Hesthor paratemporal transposition field was un-influenced by material objects outside it. In practice, however, such objects occasionally intruded, and sometimes they were alive and hostile. The last time he had been in this conveyer room, he had seen a quartet of returning of-ficers emerge from a conveyer dome dragging a dead lion by the tail. The sigma-ray needler, which he carried, was the only weapon which could be used, under the circumstances. It had no effect whatever on any material structure and could be used inside an activated conveyer without deranging the conductor-mesh, as, say, a bullet or the vibration of an ultra-sonic para-lyzer would do, and it was instantly fatal to anything having a central nervous system. It was a good weapon to use out-time for that reason, also; even on the most civilized time-line, the most elaborate autopsy would reveal no spe-cific cause of death.

"What's the Esaron Sector like?" Dalla asked, as the conveyer dome around them coruscated with shifting light and vanished.

"Third Level; probability of abortive attempt to colonize this planet from Mars about a hundred thousand years ago," he said. "A few survivors—a shipload or so—were left to shift for themselves while the parent civilization on Mars died out. They lost all vestiges of their Martian culture, even mem-ory of their extraterrestrial origin. About fifteen hundred to two thousand years ago, a reasonably high electrochemical civilization developed and they began working with nuclear energy and developed reaction-drive spaceships. But they'd concentrated so on the inorganic sciences, and so far neglected the bio-sciences, that when they launched their first ship for Venus, they hadn't yet developed a germ theory of disease."

"What happened when they ran into the green-vomit fever?" Dalla asked.

"About what you could expect. The first—and only—ship to return brought it back to Terra. Of course, nobody knew what it was, and before the epidemic ended, it had almost de-populated this planet. Since the survivors knew nothing about germs, they blamed it on the anger of the gods—the old story of recourse to supernaturalism in the absence of a known explanation—and a fanatically anti-scientific cult got control. Of course, space travel was taboo; so was nuclear and even electric power. For some reason, steam power and gunpowder weren't offensive to the gods. They went back to a low-order steampower, black-powder, culture, and haven't gotten beyond that to this day. The relatively civilized regions are on the east coast of Asia and the west coast of North America; civilized race more or less Caucasian. Political organization just barely above the tribal level—thousands of petty kingdoms and republics and principalities and feudal holdings and robbers' roosts. The principal industries are brigandage, piracy, slave-raiding, cattle-rustling and inter-communal warfare. They have a few ramshackle steam railways, and some steamboats on the rivers. We sell them coal and manufactured goods, mostly in exchange for foodstuffs and tobacco. Consolidated Outtime Foodstuffs has the sector franchise. That's one of the companies Thalvan Dras gets his money from."

They had run down through the civilized Second and Third Levels and were leaving the Fourth behind and entering the Fifth, existing in the probability of a world without human population. Once in a while, around them, they caught brief flashes of buildings and rocketports and spaceports and landing stages, as the conveyer took them through narrow paratime belts on which their own civilization had established outposts—Fifth Level Commercial, Fifth Level Passenger, Industrial Sector, Service Sector.

Finally the conveyer dome around them shimmered into visibility and materialized; when they emerged, there were policemen in green uniforms who entered to search the dome with drawn needlers to make sure they had picked up nothing dangerous on the way. The room outside was similar to the one they had left on Home Time-Line, even to the shifting, noisy crowd in incongruously mixed costumes.

THE rocketport was a ten minutes' trip by aircar from the conveyer head; when they boarded the stubby-winged strato-rocket, Vall saw that two of the passenger-seats had square metal cabinets bolted in place behind them and blue plastic helmets on swinging arms mounted above them.

"Everything's set up," the pilot told them. "Dr. Hadron, you sit on the left; that cabinet's loaded with language tape for Acalan. Yours is loaded with a tape of Kharanda; that's the Fourth Level Kholghoor language you wanted, Chief's Assistant. Shall I help you get fixed in your seats?"

"Yes, if you please. Here, Dalla, I'll fix that for you."

Dalla was already asleep when the pilot was adjusting his helmet and giving him his injection. He never felt the rocket tilt into firing position, and while he slept, the Kharanda language, with all its vocabulary and grammar, became part of his subconscious knowledge, needing only the mental pronunciation of a trigger-symbol to bring it into consciousness. The pilot was already unfastening and raising his helmet when he opened his eyes. Dalla, beside him, was sipping a cup of spiced wine.

On the landing stage of the Sector-Regional Headquarters at Novilan Equivalent, four or five people were waiting for them. Vall recognized the subchief, Vulthor Tharn, who introduced another man, in riding boots and a white cloak, as Skordran Kirv. Vall clasped hands with him warmly.

"Good work, Agent Skordran. You got onto this promptly."

"I tried to, sir. Do you want the dope now? We have half an hour's flight to our spatial equivalent, and another half an hour in transposition."

"Give it to me on the way," he said, and turned to Vulthor Tharn. "Our Esaron costumes ready?"

"Yes. Over there in the control tower. We have a temporary conveyer head set up about two hundred miles south of here, which will take you straight through to the plantation."

"Suppose you change now, Dalla," he said. "Subchief, I'd like a word with you privately."

He and Vulthor Tharn excused themselves and walked over to the edge of the landing stage. The SecReg subchief was outwardly composed, but Vall sensed that he was worried and embarrassed.

"Now, what's been done since you got Agent Skordran's report?" Vall asked.

"Well, sir, it seems that this is more serious than we had anticipated. Field Agent Skordran, who will give you the particulars, says that there is every indication that a large and well-organized gang of paratemporal criminals, our own people, are at work. He says that he's found evidence of activities on Fourth Level Kholghoor that don't agree with any information we have about conditions on that sector."

"Besides transmitting Agent Skordran's report to Dhergabar through the robot report-system, what have you done about it?"

"I confirmed Agent Skordran in charge of the local investigation, and gave him two detectives and a psychist, sir. As soon as we could furnish hypno-mech indoctrination in Kharanda to other psychists, I sent them along. He now has four of them, and eight detectives. By that time, we had a conveyer head right at this Consolidated Outtime Foodstuffs plantation."

"Why didn't you just borrow psychists from SecReg for Kholghoor, Eastern India?" Vall asked. "Subchief Ranthar would have loaned you a few."

"Oh, I couldn't call on another SecReg for men without higher-echelon authorization. Especially not from another Sector Organization, even another Level Authority," Vulthor Tharn said. "Besides, it would have taken longer to bring them here than hypno-mech our own personnel."

He was right about the second point, Vall agreed mentally; however, his real reason was procedural.

"Did you alert Ranthar Jard to what was going on in his SecReg?" he asked.

"Gracious, no!" Vulthor Tharn was scandalized. "I have no authority to tell people of equal echelon in other Sector and Level organizations what to do. I put my report through regular channels; it wasn't my place to go outside my own jurisdiction."

And his report had crawled through channels for fourteen hours, Vall thought.

"Well, on my authority, and in the name of Chief Tortha, you message Ranthar Jard at once; send him every scrap of information you have on the subject, and forward additional information as it comes in to you. I doubt he'll find anything on any time-line that's being exploited by any legitimate paratimers. This gang probably works exclusively on unpenetrated time-lines; this business Skordran Kirv came across was a bad blunder on some underling's part." He saw Dalla emerge from the control tower in breeches and boots and a white cloak, buckling on a heavy revolver. "I'll go change, now; you get busy calling Ranthar Jard. I'll see you when I get back."

ARE you taking over, Chief's Assistant?" Skordran Kirv asked, as the aircar lifted from the landing stage.

"Not at all. My wife and I are starting on our vacation, as soon as I find out what's been happening here, and report to Chief Tortha. Did your native troopers catch those slavers?"

"Yes, they got them yesterday afternoon; we've had them ever since. Do you want the whole thing just as it happened, Assistant Verkan, or just a condensation?"

"Give me what you think it indicates, remembering that you're probably trying to analyze a large situation from a very small sample."

"It's big, all right," Skordran Kirv said. "This gang can't number less than a hundred men, maybe several hundred. They must have at least two two-hundred-foot conveyers and several small ones, and bases on what sounds like some Fifth Level time-line, and at least one air freighter of around five thousand tons. They are operating on a number of Kholghoor and Esaron time-lines."

Verkan Vall nodded. "I didn't think it was any petty larceny," he said.

"Wait till you hear the rest of it. On the Kholghoor Sector, this gang is known as the Wizard Traders; we've been using that as a convenience label. They pose as sorcerers—black robes and hood-masks covered with luminous symbols, voice-amplifiers, cold-light auras, energy-weapons, mechanical magic tricks, that sort of thing. They have all the Croutha scared witless. Their procedure is to establish camps in the forest near recently conquered Kharanda cities; then they appear to the Croutha, impress them with their magical powers, and trade manufactured goods for Kharanda captives. They mainly trade firearms, apparently some kind of flintlocks, and powder."

Then they were confining their operations to unpenetrated time-lines; there had been no reports of firearms in the hands of the Croutha invaders.

"After they buy a batch of slaves," Skordran Kirv continued, "they transpose them to this presumably Fifth Level base, where they have concentration camps. The slaves we questioned had been airlifted to North America, where there's another concentration camp, and from there transposed to this Esaron Sector time-line where I found them. They say that there are at least two to three thousand slaves in this North American concentration camp and that they are being transposed out in small batches and replaced by others airlifted in from India. This lot was sold to a Calera named Nebu-hin-Abenoz, the chieftain of a hill town, Careba, about fifty miles southwest of the plantation. There were two hundred and fifty in this batch; this Coru-hin-Irigod only bought the batch he sold at the plantation."

THE aircar lost speed and altitude; below, the countryside was dotted with conveyer heads, each spatially co-existent with some out-time police post or operation. There were a great many of them; the western coast of North America was a center of civilization on many paratemporal sectors, and while the conveyer heads of the commercial and passenger companies were scattered over hundreds of Fifth Level time-lines, those of the Paratime Police were concentrated upon one. The antigrav-car circled around a three-hundred-foot steel tower that supported a conveyer head partially coexistent with one on a top floor of some out-time tall building, and let down in front of a low prefabricated steel shed. A man in police uniform came out to meet them. There was a fifty-foot conveyer dome inside, and a fifty-foot redlined circle that marked the transposition point of an out-time conveyer. They all entered the dome, and the operator put on the transposition field.

"You haven't heard the worst of it yet," Skordran Kirv was saying. "On this time-line, we have reason to think that the native, Nebu-hin-Abenoz, who bought the slaves, actually saw the slavers' conveyer. Maybe even saw it activated."

"If he did, we'll either have to capture him and give him a memory-obliteration, or kill him," Vall said. "What do you know about him?"

"Well, this Careba, the town he bosses, is a little walled town up in the hills. Everybody there is related to everybody else; this man we have, Coru-hin-Irigod, is the son of a sister of Nebu-hin-Abenoz's wife. They're all bandits and slavers and cattle rustlers and what have you. For the last ten years, Nebu-hin-Abenoz has been buying slaves from some secret source. Before the Kholghoor Sector, people began coming in, they were mostly white, with a few brown people who might have been Polynesians. No Negroes—there's no black race on this sector, and I suppose the paratime slavers didn't want too many questions asked. Coru-hin-Irigod, under narco-hypnosis, said that they were all outlanders, speaking strange languages."

"Ten years! And this is the first hint we've had of it," Vall said. "That's not a bright mark for any of us. I'll bet the slave population on some of these Esaron time-lines is an anthropologist's nightmare."

"Why, if this has been going on for ten years, there must have been millions upon millions of people dragged from their own time-lines into slavery!" Dalla said in a shocked voice.

"Ten years may not be all of it," Vall said. "This Nebu-hin-Abenoz looks like the only tangible lead we have, at present. How does he operate?"

"About once every ten days, he'll take ten or fifteen men and go a day's ride—that may be as much as fifty miles; these Caleras have good horses and they're hard riders—into the hills. He'll take a big bag of money, all gold. After dark, when he has made camp, a couple of strangers in Calera dress will come in. He'll go off with them, and after about an hour, he'll come back with eight or ten of these strangers and a couple of hundred slaves, always chained in batches of ten. Nebu-hin-Abenoz pays for them, makes arrangements for the next meeting, and the next morning he and his party start marching the slaves to Careba. I might add that, until now, these slaves have been sold to the mines east of Careba; these are the first that have gotten into the coastal country."

"That's why this hasn't come to light before, then. The conveyer comes in every ten days, at about the same place?"

"Yes. I've been thinking of a way we might trap them," Skordran Kirv said. "I'll need more men, and equipment."

"Order them from Regional or General Reserve," Vall told him. "This thing's going to have overtop priority till it's cleared up."

He was mentally cursing Vulthor Tharn's procedure-bound timidity as the conveyer flickered and solidified around them and the overhead red light turned green.

THEY emerged into the interior of a long shed, adobe-walled and thatch-roofed, with small barred windows set high above the earth floor. It was cool and shadowy, and the air was heavy with the fragrance of citrus fruits. There were bins along the walls, some partly full of oranges, and piles of wicker baskets. Another conveyer dome stood beside the one in which they had arrived; two men in white cloaks and riding boots sat on the edge of one of the bins, smoking and talking.

Skordran Kirv introduced them—Gathon Dard and Krador Arv, special detectives—and asked if anything new had come up. Krador Arv shook his head.

"We still have about forty to go," he said. "Nothing new in their stories; still the same two time-lines."

"These people," Skordran Kirv explained, "were all peons on the estate of a Kharanda noble just above the big bend of the Ganges. The Croutha hit their master's estate about a ten-days ago, elapsed time. In telling about their capture, most of them say that their master's wife killed herself with a dagger after the Croutha killed her husband, but about one out of ten say that she was kidnaped by the Croutha. Two different time-lines, of course. The ones who tell the suicide story saw no firearms among the Croutha; the ones who tell the kidnap story say that they all had some kind of muskets and pistols. We're making synthetic summaries of the two stories."

"We're having trouble with the locals about all these strangers coming in," Gathon Dard added. "They're getting curious."

"We'll have to take a chance on that," Vall said. "Are the interrogations still going on? Then let's have a look-in at them."

The big double doors at the end of the shed were barred on the inside. Krador Arv unlocked a small side door, letting Vall, Dalla and Gathon Dard out. In the yard outside, a gang of slaves were unloading a big wagon of oranges and packing them into hampers; they were guarded by a couple of native riflemen who seemed mostly concerned with keeping them away from the shed, and a man in a white cloak was watching the guards for the same purpose. He walked over and introduced himself to Vall.

"Golzan Doth, local alias Dosu Golan. I'm Consolidated Outtime Foodstuffs' manager here."

"Nasty business for you people," Vall sympathized. "If it's any consolation, it's a bigger headache for us."

"Have you any idea what's going to be done about these slaves?" Golzan Doth asked. "I have to remember that the company has forty thousand Paratemporal Exchange Units invested in them. The top office was very specific in requesting information about that."

Vall shook his head. "That's over my echelon," he said. "Have to be decided by the Paratime Commission. I doubt if your company'll suffer. You bought them innocently, in conformity with local custom. Ever buy slaves from this Coru-hin-Irigod before?"

"I'm new here. The man I'm replacing broke his neck when his horse put a foot in a gopher hole about two ten-days ago."

Beside him, Vall could see Dalla nod as though making a mental note. When she got back to Home Time-Line, she'd put a crew of mediums to work trying to contact the discarnate former plantation manager; at Rhogom Institute, she had been working on the problem of return of a discarnate personality from out-time.

"A few times," Skordran Kirv said. "Nothing suspicious; all local stuff. We questioned Coru-hin-Irigod pretty closely on that point, and he says that this is the first time he ever brought a batch of Nebu-hin-Abenoz's outlanders this far west."

THE interrogations were being conducted inside the plantation house, in the secret central rooms where the paratimers lived. Skordran Kirv used a door-activator to slide open a hidden door.

"I suppose I don't have to warn either of you that any positive statement made in the hearing of a narco-hypnotized subject—" he began.

"Has the effect of hypnotic suggestion—" Vall picked up after him.

"And should be avoided unless such suggestion is intended," Dalla finished.

Skordran Kirv laughed, opening another, inner door, and stood aside. In what had been the paratimers' recreation room, most of the furniture had been shoved into the corners. Four small tables had been set up, widely spaced and with screens between; across each of them, with an electric recorder between, an almost naked Kharanda slave faced a Paratime Police psychist. At a long table at the far side of the room, four men and two girls were working over stacks of cards and two big charts.

"Phrakor Vuln," the man who was working on the charts introduced himself. "Synthesist." He introduced the others.

Vall made a point of the fact that Dalla was his wife, in case any of the cops began to get ideas, and mentioned that she spoke Kharanda, had spent some time on the Fourth Level Kholghoor, and was a qualified psychist.

"What have you got so far?" he asked.

"Two different time-lines, and two different gangs of Wizard Traders," Phrakor Vuln said. "We've established the latter from physical descriptions and because both batches were sold by the Croutha at equivalent periods of elapsed time."

Vall picked up one of the kidnap-story cards and glanced at it.

"I notice there's a fair verbal description of these firearms, and mention of electric whips," he said. "I'm curious about where they came from."

"Well, this is how we reconstructed them, Chief's Assistant," one of the girls said, handing him a couple of sheets of white drawing paper.

The sketches had been done with soft pencil; they bore repeated erasures and corrections. That of the whip showed a cylindrical handle, indicated as twelve inches in length and one in diameter, fitted with a thumb-switch.

"That's definitely Second Level Khiftan," Vall said, handing it back. "Made of braided copper or silver wire and powered with a little nuclear-conversion battery in the grip. They heat up to about two hundred centigrade; produce really painful burns."

"Why, that's beastly!" Dalla exclaimed.

"Anything on the Khiftan Sector is." Skordran Kirv looked at the four slaves at the tables. "We don't have a really bad case here now. A few of these people were lash-burned horribly, though."

Vall was looking at the other sketches. One was a musket, with a wide butt and a band-fastened stock; the lock-mechanism, vaguely flintlock, had been dotted in tentatively. The other was a long pistol, similarly definite in outline and vague in mechanical detail; it was merely a knob-butted miniature of the musket.

"I've seen firearms like these; have a lot of them in my collection," he said, handing back the sketches. "Low-order mechanical or high-order pre-mechanical cultures. Fact is, things like those could have been made on the Kholghoor Sector, if the Kharandas had learned to combine sulfur, carbon and nitrates to make powder."

The interrogator at one of the tables had evidently heard all his subject could tell him. He rose, motioning the slave to stand.

"Now, go with that man," he said in Kharanda, motioning to one of the detectives in native guard uniform. "You will trust him; he is your friend and will not harm you. When you have left this room, you will forget everything that has happened here, except that you were kindly treated and that you were given wine to drink and your hurts were anointed. You will tell the others that we are their friends and that they have nothing to fear from us. And you will not try to remove the mark from the back of your left hand."

As the detective led the slave out a door at the other side of the room, the psychist came over to the long table, handing over a card and lighting a cigarette.

"Suicide story," he said to one of the girls, who took the card.

"Anything new?"

"Some minor details about the sale to the Caleras on this time-line. I think we've about scraped bottom."

"You can't say that," Phrakor Vuln objected. "The very last one may give us something nobody else had noticed."

Another subject was sent out. The interrogator came over to the table.

"One of the kidnap-story crowd," he said. "This one was right beside that Croutha who took the shot at the wild pig or whatever it was on the way to the Wizard Traders' camp. Best description of the guns we've gotten so far. No questions that they're flintlocks." He saw Verkan Vall. "Oh, hello, Assistant Verkan. What do you make of them? You're an authority on out-time weapons, I understand."

"I'd have to see them. These people simply don't think mechanically enough to give a good description. A lot of peoples make flintlock firearms."

He started running over, in his mind, the paratemporal areas in which gunpowder but not the percussion-cap was known. Expanding cultures, which had progressed as far as the former but not the latter. Static cultures, in which an accidental discovery of gunpowder had never been followed up by further research. Post-debacle cultures, in which a few stray bits of ancient knowledge had survived.

Another interrogator came over, and then the fourth. For a while they sat and talked and drank coffee, and then the next quartet of slaves, two men and two women, were brought in. One of the women had been badly blistered by the electric whips of the Wizard Traders; in spite of reassurances, all were visibly apprehensive.

"We will not harm you," one of the psychists told them. "Here; here is medicine for your hurts. At first, it will sting, as good medicines will, but soon it will take away all pain. And here is wine for you to drink."

A couple of detectives approached, making a great show of pouring wine and applying ointment; under cover of the medication, they jabbed each slave with a hypodermic needle, and then guided them to seats at the four tables. Vall and Dalla went over and stood behind one of the psychists, who had a small flashlight in his hand.

"Now, rest for a while," the psychist was saying. "Rest and let the good medicine do its work. You are tired and sleepy. Look at this magic light, which brings comfort to the troubled. Look at the light. Look . . . at . . . the . . . light."

They moved to the next table.

"Did you have a hand in the fighting?"

"No, lord. We were peasant folk, not fighting people. We had no weapons, nor weapon-skill. Those who fought were all killed; we held up empty hands, and were spared to be captives of the Croutha."

"What happened to your master, the Lord Ghromdour, and to his lady?"

"One of the Croutha threw a hatchet and killed our master, and then his lady drew a dagger and killed herself."

The psychist made a red mark on the card in front of him, and circled the number on the back of the slave's hand with red indelible crayon. Vall and Dalla went to the third table.

"They had the common weapons of the Croutha, lord, and they also had the weapons of the Wizard Traders. Of these, they carried the long weapons slung across their backs, and the short weapons thrust through their belts."

A blue mark on the card; a blue circle on the back of the slave's hand.

They listened to both versions of what had happened at the sack of the Lord Ghromdour's estate, and the march into the captured city of Jhirda, and the second march into the forest to the camp of the Wizard Traders.

"The servants of the Wizard Traders did not appear until after the Croutha had gone away; they wore different garb. They wore short jackets, and trousers, and short boots, and they carried small weapons on their belts—"

"They had whips of great cruelty that burned like fire; we were all lashed with these whips, as you may see, lord—"

"The Croutha had bound us two and two, with neck-yokes; these the servants of the Wizard Traders took off from us, and they chained us together by tens, with the chains we still wore when we came to this place—"

"They killed my child, my little Zhouzha!" the woman with the horribly blistered back was wailing. "They tore her out of my arms, and one of the servants of the Wizard Traders—may Khokhaat devour his soul forever!— dashed out her brains. And when I struggled to save her, I was thrown on the ground, and beaten with the fire-whips until I fainted. Then I was dragged into the forest, along with the others who were chained with me." She buried her head in her arms, sobbing bitterly.

Dalla stepped forward, taking the flashlight from the interrogator with one hand and lifting the woman's head with the other. She flashed the light quickly in the woman's eyes.

"You will grieve no more for your child," she said. "Already, you are forgetting what happened at the Wizard Traders' camp, and remembering only that your child is safe from harm. Soon you will remember her only as a dream of the child you hope to have, some day." She flashed the light again, then handed it back to the psychist. "Now, tell us what happened when you were taken into the forest; what did you see there?"

The psychist nodded approvingly, made a note on the card, and listened while the woman spoke. She had stopped sobbing, now, and her voice was clear and cheerful.

VALL went over to the long table.

"Those slaves were still chained with the Wizard Traders' chains when they were delivered here. Where are the chains?" he asked Skordran Kirv.

"In the permanent conveyer room," Skordran Kirv said. "You can look at them there; we didn't want to bring them in here, for fear these poor devils would think we were going to chain them again. They're very light, very strong; some kind of alloy steel. Files and power saws only polish them; it takes fifteen seconds to cut a link with an atomic torch. One long chain, and short lengths, fifteen inches long, staggered, every three feet, with a single hinge-shackle for the ankle. The shackles were riveted with soft wrought-iron rivets, evidently made with some sort of a power riveting-machine. We cut them easily with a cold chisel."

"They ought to be sent to Dhergabar Equivalent, Police Terminal, for study of material and workmanship. Now, you mentioned some scheme you had for capturing this conveyer that brings in the salves for Nebu-hin-Abenoz. What have you in mind?"

"We still have Coru-hin-Irigod and all his gang, under hypno. I'd thought of giving them hypnotic conditioning, and sending them back to Careba with orders to put out some kind of signal the next time Nebu-hin-Abenoz starts out on a buying trip. We could have a couple of men posted in the hills overlooking Careba, and they could send a message-ball through to Police Terminal. Then, a party could be sent with a mobile conveyer to ambush Nebu-hin-Abenoz on the way, and wipe out his party. Our people could take their horses and clothing and go on to take the conveyer by surprise."

"I'd suggest one change. Instead of relying on visual signals by the hypno-conditioned Coru-hin-Irigod, send a couple of our men to Careba with midget radios."

Skordran Kirv nodded. "Sure. We can condition Coru-hin-Irigod to accept them as friends and vouch for them at Careba. Our boys can be traders and slave buyers. Careba's a market town; traders are always welcome. They can have firearms to sell—revolvers and repeating rifles. Any Calera'll buy any firearm that's better than the one he's carrying; they'll always buy revolvers and repeaters. We can get what we want from Commercial Four-Oh-Seven; we can get riding and pack horses here."

Vall nodded. "And the post overlooking or in radio range of Careba on this time-line, and another on PolTerm. For the ambush of Nebu-hin-Abenoz's gang and the capture of the conveyer, use anything you want to—sleep-gas, paralyzers, energy-weapons, antigrav-equipment, anything. As far as regulations about using only equipment appropriate to local culture-levels, forget them entirely. But take that conveyer intact. You can locate the base time-line from the settings of the instrument panel, and that's what we want most of all."

DALLA and the police psychist, having finished with and dismissed their subject, came over to the long table.

". . . That poor creature," Dalla was saying. "What sort of fiends are they?"

"If that made you sick, remember we've been listening to things like that for the last eight hours. Some of the stories were even worse than that one."

"Well, I'd like to use a heat-gun on the whole lot of them, turned down to where it'd just fry them medium-rare," Dalla said. "And for whoever's back of this, take him to Second Level Khiftan and sell him to the priests of Fasif."

"Too bad you're not coming back from your vacation, instead of starting out, Chief Assistant Verkan," Skordran Kirv said. "This is too big for me to handle alone, and I'd sooner work under you than anybody else Chief Tortha sends in."

"Vall!" Dalla cried in indignation. "You're not going to just report on this and then walk away from it, are you?"

"But, darling," Vall replied, in what he hoped was a convincing show of surprise. "You don't want our vacation postponed again, do you? If I get mixed up in this, there's no telling when I can get away, and by the time I'm free, something may come up at Rhogom Institute that you won't want to drop—"

"Vall, you know perfectly well that I wouldn't be happy for an instant on the Dwarma Sector, thinking about this—"

"All right, then; let's forget about the vacation. You want to stay on for a while and help me with this? It'll be a lot of hard work, but we'll be together."

"Yes, of course. I want to do something to smash those devils. Vall, if you'd heard some of the things they did to those poor people—"

"Well, I'll have to go back to PolTerm, as soon as I'm reasonably well filled in on this, and report to Tortha Karf and tell him I've taken charge. You can stay here and help with these interrogations; I'll be back in about ten hours. Then, we can go to Kholghoor East India SecReg HQ to talk to Ranthar Jard. We may be able to get something that'll help us on that end—"

"You may be able to have your vacation before too long, Dr. Hadron," Skordran Kirv told her. "Once we capture one of their conveyers, the instrument panel'll tell us what time-line they're working from, and then we'll have them."

"There's an Indo-Turanian Sector parable about a snake charmer who thought he was picking up his snake and found that he had hold of an elephant's tail," Vall said. "That might be a good thing to bear in mind, till we find out just what we have picked up."

COMING down a hallway on the hundred and seventh floor of the Management wing of the Paratime Building, Yandar Yadd paused to admire, in the green mirror of the glassoid wall, the jaunty angle of his silver-feathered cap, the fit of his short jacket, and the way his weapon hung at his side. This last was not instantly recognizable as a weapon; it looked more like a portable radio, which indeed it was. It was, nonetheless, a potent weapon. One flick of his finger could connect that radio with one at Tri-Planet News Service, and within the hour anything he said into it would be heard by all Terra, Mars and Venus. In consequence, there existed around the Paratime Building a marked and understandable reluctance to antagonize Yandar Yadd.

He glanced at his watch. It was twenty minutes short of 1000, when he had an appointment with Baltan Vrath, the comptroller general. Glancing about, he saw that he was directly in front of the doorway of the Outtime Claims Bureau, and he strolled in, walking through the waiting room and into the claims-presentation office. At once, he stiffened like a bird dog at point.

Sphabron Larv, one of his young legmen, was in an altercation across the counter-desk with Varkar Klav, the Deputy Claims Agent on duty at the time. Varkar was trying to be icily dignified; Sphabron Larv's black hair was in disarray and his face was suffused with anger. He was pounding with his fist on the plastic counter-top.

"You have to!" he was yelling in the older man's face. "That's a public document, and I have a right to see it. You want me to go into Tribunes' Court and get an order? If I do, there'll be a Question in Council about why I had to before the day's out!"

"What's the matter, Larv?" Yandar Yadd asked lazily. "He trying to hold something out on you?"

Sphabron Larv turned; his eyes lit happily when he saw his boss, and then his anger returned.

"I want to see a copy of an indemnity claim that was filed this morning," he said. "Varkar, here, won't show it to me. What does he think this is, a Fourth Level dictatorship?"

"What kind of a claim, now?" Yandar Yadd addressed Larv, ignoring Varkar Klav.

"Consolidated Outtime Foodstuffs—one of the Thalvan Interests companies—just claimed forty thousand P.E.U. for a hundred slaves bought by one of their plantation managers on Third Level Esaron from a local slave dealer. The Paratime Police impounded the slaves for narco-hypnotic interrogation, and then transposed the lot of them to Police Terminal."

Yandar Yadd still held his affectation of sleepy indolence.

"Now why would the Paracops do that, I wonder? Slavery's an established local practice on Esaron Sector; our people have to buy slaves if they want to run a plantation."

"I know that," Sphabron Larv replied. "That's what I want to find out. There must be something wrong, either with the slaves, or the treatment our people were giving them, or the Paratime Police, and I want to find out which."

"To tell the truth, Larv, so do I," Yandar Yadd said. He turned to the man behind the counter. "Varkar, do we see that claim, or do I make a story out of your refusal to show it?" he asked.

"The Paratime Police asked me to keep this confidential," Varkar Klav said. "Publicity would seriously hamper an important police investigation."

Yander Yadd made an impolite noise. "How do I know that all it would do would be to reveal police incompetence?" he retorted. "Look, Varkar; you and the Paratime Police and the Paratime Commission and the Home Time Line Management are all hired employees of the Home Time Line public. The public has a right to know what its employees are doing, and it's my business to see that they're informed. Now, for the last time—will you show us a copy of that claim?"

"Well, let me explain, off the record—" the official begged.

"Huh-uh! Huh-uh! I had that off-the-record gag worked on me when I was about Larv's age, fifty years ago. Anything I get, I put on the air or not at my own discretion."

"All right," Varkar Klav surrendered, pointing to a reading screen and twiddling a knob. "But when you read it, I hope you have enough discretion to keep quiet about it."

The screen lit, and Yandar Yadd automatically pressed a button for a photo-copy. The two newsmen stared for a moment, and then even Yandar Yadd's shell of drowsy negligence cracked and fell from him. His hand brushed the switch as he snatched the hand-phone from his belt.

"Marva!" he barked, before the girl at the news office could more than acknowledge. "Get this recorded for immediate telecast! . . . Ready? Beginning: The existence of a huge paratemporal slave trade came to light on the afternoon of One-Five-Nine Day, on a time-line of the Third Level Esaron Sector, when Field Agent Skordran Kirv, Paratime Police, discovered, at an orange plantation of Consolidated Outtime Footstuffs—"

Salgath Trod sat alone in his private office, his half-finished lunch growing cold on the desk in front of him as he watched the teleview screen across the room, tuned to a pickup behind the Speaker's chair in the Executive Council Chamber ten stories below. The two thousand seats had been almost all empty at 1000, when Council had convened. Fifteen minutes later, the news had broken; now, at 1430, a good three quarters of the seats were occupied. He could see, in the aisles, the gold-plated robot pages gliding back and forth, receiving and delivering messages. One had just slid up to the seat of Councilman Hasthor Flan, and Hasthor was speaking urgently into the recorder mouthpiece. Another message for him, he supposed; he'd gotten at least a score of such calls since the crisis had developed.

People were going to start wondering, he thought. This situation should have been perfect for his purposes; as leader of the Opposition he could easily make himself the next General Manager, if he exploited this scandal properly. He listened for a while to the Centrist-Management member who was speaking; he could rip that fellow's arguments to shreds in a hundred words— but he didn't dare. The Management was taking exactly the line Salgath Trod wanted the whole Council to take; treat this affair as an isolated and extraordinary occurrence, find a couple of convenient scapegoats, cobble up some explanation acceptable to the public, and forget it. He wondered what had happened to the imbecile who had transposed those Kholghoor Sector slaves onto an exploited time-line. Ought to be shanghaied to the Khiftan Sector and sold to the priests of Fasif!

A buzzer sounded, and for an instant he thought it would be the message he had seen Hasthor Flan recording. Then he realized that it was the buzzer for the private door, which could only be operated by someone with a special identity sigil. He pressed a button and unlocked the door.

The young man in the loose wrap-around tunic who entered was a stranger. At least, his face and his voice were strange, but voices could be mechanically altered, and a skilled cosmetician could render any face unrecognizable. He looked like a student, or a minor commercial executive, or an engineer, or something like that. Of course, his tunic bulged slightly under the left armpit, but even the most respectable tunics showed occasional weapon-bulges.

"Good afternoon, councilman," the newcomer said, sitting down across the desk from Salgath Trod. "I was just talking to . . . somebody we both know."

Salgath Trod offered cigarettes, lighted his visitor's and then his own.

"What does Our Mutual Friend think about all this?" he asked, gesturing toward the screen.

"Our Mutual Friend isn't at all happy about it."

"You think, perhaps, that I'm bursting into wild huzzas?" Salgath Trod asked. "If I were to act as everybody expects me to, I'd be down there on the floor now, clawing into the Management tooth and nail. All my adherents are wondering why I'm not. So are all my opponents, and before long one of them is going to guess the reason."

"Well, why not go down?" the stranger asked. "Our Mutual Friend thinks it would be an excellent idea. The leak couldn't be stopped, and it's gone so far already that the Management will never be able to play it down. So the next best thing is to try to exploit it."

Salgath Trod smiled mirthlessly. "So I am to get in front of it, and lead it in the right direction? Fine . . . as long as I don't stumble over something. If I do, it'll go over me like a Fifth Level bison-herd."

"Don't worry about that," the stranger laughed reassuringly. "There are others on the floor who are also friends of Our Mutual Friend. Here; what you'd better do is attack the Paratime Police, especially Tortha Karf and Verkan Vall. Accuse them of negligence and incompetence, and, by implication, of collusion, and demand a special committee to investigate. And try to get a motion for a confidence vote passed. A motion to censure the Management, say—"

Salgath Trod nodded. "It would delay things, at least. And if Our Mutual Friend can keep properly covered, I might be able to overturn the Management." He looked at the screen again. "That old fool of a Nanthav is just getting started; it'll be an hour before I could get recognized. Plenty of time to get a speech together. Something short and vicious—"

"You'll have to be careful. It won't do, with your political record, to try to play down these stories of a gigantic criminal conspiracy. That's too close to the Management line. And at the same time, you want to avoid saying anything that would get Verkan Vall and Tortha Karf started off on any new lines of investigation."

Salgath Trod nodded. "Just depend on me; I'll handle it."

After the stranger had gone, he shut off the sound reception, relying on visual dumb-show to keep him informed of what was going on on the Council floor. He didn't like the situation. It was too easy to say the wrong thing. If only he knew more about the shadowy figures whose messengers used his private door—

CORU-HIN-IRIGOD held his aching head in both hands, as though he were afraid it would fall apart, and blinked in the sunlight from the window. Lord Safar, how much of that sweet brandy had he drunk last night? He sat on the edge of the bed for a moment, trying to think. Then, suddenly apprehensive, he thrust his hand under his pillow. The heavy four-barreled pistols were there, all right, but—*the money!*

He rummaged frantically among the bedding and among his clothes, piled on the floor, but the leather bag was nowhere to be found. Two thousand gold *obus,* the price of a hundred slaves. He snatched up one of the pistols, his headache forgotten. Then he laughed and tossed the pistol down again. Of course! He'd given the bag to the plantation manager, what was his outlandish name, Dosu Golan, to keep for him before the drinking bout had begun. It was safely waiting for him in the plantation strongbox. Well, nothing like a good scare to make a man forget a brandy head, anyhow. And there was something else, something very nice—

Oh, yes, there it was, beside the bed. He picked up the beautiful gleaming repeater, pulled down the lever far enough to draw the cartridge halfway out of the chamber, and closed it again, lowering the hammer. Those two Jeseru traders from the North, what were their names? Ganadara and Atarazola. That was a stroke of luck, meeting them here. They'd given him this lovely rifle, and they were going to accompany him and his men back to Careba; they had a hundred such rifles, and two hundred six-shot revolvers, and they wanted to trade for slaves. The Lord Safar bless them both, wouldn't they be welcome at Careba!

He looked at the sunlight falling through the window on the still recumbent form of his companion, Faru-hin-Obaran. Outside, he could hear the sounds of the plantation coming to life—an ax thudding on wood, the clatter of pans from the kitchens. Crossing to Faru-hin-Obaran's bed, he grasped the sleeper by the ankle, tugging.

"Waken, Faru!" he shouted. "Get up and clear the fumes from your head! We start back to Careba today!"

Faru swore groggily and pushed himself into a sitting position, fumbling on the floor for his trousers.

"What day's this?" he asked.

"The day after we went to bed, ninny!" Then Coru-hin-Irigod wrinkled his brow. He could remember, clearly enough, the sale of the slaves, but after that—oh, well, he'd been drinking; it would all come back to him after a while.

VERKAN Vall rubbed his hand over his face wearily, started to light another cigarette, and threw it across the room in disgust. What he needed was a drink—a long drink of cool, tart white wine, laced with brandy—and then he needed to sleep.

"We're absolutely nowhere!" Ranthar Jard said. "Of course they're operating on time-lines we've never penetrated. The fact that they're supplying the Croutha with guns proves that; there isn't a firearm on any of the time-lines our people are legitimately exploiting. And there are only about three billion time-lines on this belt of the Croutha invasion—"

"If we could think of a way to reduce it to some specific area of paratime—" one of Ranthar Jard's deputies began.

"That's precisely what we've been trying to do, Klav," Vall said. "We haven't done it."

Dalla, who had withdrawn from the discussion and was on a couch at the side of the room, surrounded by reports and abstracts and summaries, looked up.

"I took hours and hours of hypno-mech on Kholghoor Sector religions before I went out on that wild-goose chase for psychokinesis and precognition data," she said. "About six or eight hundred years ago, there were religious wars and heresies and religious schisms all over the Kharanda country. No matter how uniform the Kholghoor Sector may be otherwise, there are dozens and dozens of small belts and subsectors of different religions or sects or god-cults."

"That's right," Ranthar Jard agreed, brightening. "We have hagiologists who know all that stuff; we'll have a couple of them interrogate those slaves. I don't know how much they can get out of them—lot of peasants, won't be up on the theological niceties—but a synthesis of what we get from the lot of them—"

"That's an idea," Vall agreed. "About the first idea we've had here—oh, how about politics, too? Check on who's the king, what the stories about the royal family are, that sort of thing."

Ranthar Jard looked at the map on the wall. "The Croutha have only gotten halfway to Nharkan, here. Say we transpose detectives in at night on some of these time-lines we think are promising, and check up at the tax-collection offices on a big landowner north of Jhirda named Ghromdour? That might get us something."

"Well, I don't want you to think we're trying to get out of work, Chief's Assistant," one of the deputies said, "but is there any real necessity for our trying to locate the Wizard Trader time-lines? If you can get them from the Esaron Sector, it'll be the same, won't it?"

"Marv, in this business you never depend on just one lead," Ranthar Jard told him. "And besides, when Skordran Kirv's gang hits the base of operations in North America, there's no guarantee that they may not have time to send off a radio warning to the crowd at the base here in India. We have to hit both places at once."

"Well, that, too," Vall said. "But the main thing is to get these Wizard Trader camps on the Kholghoor Sector cleaned out. How are you fixed for men and equipment for a big raid, Jard?"

Ranthar Jard shrugged. "I can get about five hundred men with conveyers, including a couple of two-hundred-footers to carry airboats," he said.

"Not enough. Skordran Kirv has one complete armored brigade, one airborne infantry brigade, and an air cavalry regiment, with Ghaldron-Hesthor equipment for a simultaneous transposition," Vall said.

"Where in blazes did he get them all?" Ranthar Jard demanded.

"They're guard troops from Service Sector and Industrial Sector. We'll get you the same sort of a force. I only hope we don't have another Prole insurrection while they're away—"

"Well, don't think I'm trying to argue policy with you," Ranthar Jard said, "but that could raise a dreadful stink on Home Time-Line. Especially on top of this news-break about the slave trade."

"We'll have to take a chance on that," Vall said. "If you're worried about what the book says, forget it. We're throwing the book away on this operation. Do you realize that this thing is a threat to the whole Paratime Civilization?"

"Of course I do," Ranthar Jard said. "I know the doctrine of Paratime Security as well as you or anybody else. The question is, does the public realize it?"

A buzzer sounded. Ranthar Jard pressed a switch on the intercom-box in front of him and said: "Ranthar here. Well?"

"Visiphone call, top urgency, just came in for Chief's Assistant Verkan, from Novilan Equivalent. Where can I put it through, sir?"

"Here; booth seven." Ranthar Jard pointed across the room, nodding to Vall. "In just a moment."

GATHON Dard and Antrath Alv—temporary local aliases Ganadara and Atarazola—sat relaxed in their saddles, swaying to the motion of their horses. They wore the rust-brown hooded cloaks of the northern Jeseru people, in sober contrast to the red and yellow and blue striped robes and sun-bonnets of the Caleras in whose company they rode. They carried short repeating carbines in saddle scabbards, and heavy revolvers and long knives on their belts, and each led six heavily laden pack-horses.

Coru-hin-Irigod, riding beside Ganadara, pointed up the trail ahead.

"From up there," he said, speaking in Acalan, the lingua franca of the North American West Coast on that sector, "we can see across the valley to Careba. It will be an hour, as we ride, with the pack-horses. Then we will rest, and drink wine, and feast."

Ganadara nodded. "It was the guidance of our gods—and yours, Coru-hin-Irigod—that we met. Such slaves as you sold at the outlanders' plantation would bring a fine price in the North. The men are strong, and have the look of good field-workers; the women are comely and well-formed. Though I fear that my wife would little relish it did I bring home such handmaidens."

Coru-hin-Irigod laughed. "For your wife, I will give you one of our riding whips." He leaned to the side, slashing at a cactus with his quirt. "We in Careba have no trouble with our wives, about handmaidens or anything else."

"By Safar, if you doubt your welcome at Careba, wait till you show your wares," another Calera said. "Rifles and revolvers like those come to our country seldom, and then old and battered, sold or stolen many times before we see them. Rifles that fire seven times without taking butt from shoulder!" He invoked the name of the Great Lord Safar again.

The trail widened and leveled; they all came up abreast, with the pack-horses strung out behind, and sat looking across the valley to the adobe walls of the town that perched on the opposite ridge. After a while, riders began dismounting and checking and tightening saddle-girths; a couple of Caleras helped Ganadara and Atarazola inspect their pack-horses. When they remounted, Atarazola bowed his head, lifting his left sleeve to cover his mouth, and muttered into it at some length. The Caleras looked at him curiously, and Coru-hin-Irigod inquired of Ganadara what he did.

"He prays," Ganadara said. "He thanks our gods that we have lived to see your town, and asks that we be spared to bring many more trains of rifles and ammunition up this trail."

The slaver nodded understandingly. The Caleras were a pious people, too, who believed in keeping on friendly terms with the gods.

"May Safar's hand work with the hands of your gods for it," he said, making what, to a non-Calera, would have been an extremely ribald sign.

"The gods watch over us," Atarazola said, lifting his head. "They are near us even now; they have spoken words of comfort in my ear."

Ganadara nodded. The gods to whom his partner prayed were a couple of paratime policemen, crouching over a radio a mile or so down the ridge.

"My brother," he told Coru-hin-Irigod, "is much favored by our gods. Many people come to him to pray for them."

"Yes. So you told me, now that I think on it." That detail had been included in the pseudo-memories he had been given under hypnosis. "I serve Safar, as do all Caleras, but I have heard that the Jeserus' gods are good gods, dealing honestly with their servants."

An hour later, under the walls of the town, Coru-hin-Irigod drew one of his pistols and fired all four barrels in rapid succession into the air, shouting, "Open! Open for Coru-hin-Irigod, and for the Jeseru traders, Ganadara and Atarazola, who are with him!"

A head, black-bearded and sun-bonneted, appeared between the brick merlons of the wall above the gate, shouted down a welcome, and then turned away to bawl orders. The gate slid aside, and after the caravan had passed through, naked slaves pushed the massive thing shut again. Although they were familiar with the interior of the town from photographs taken with boomerang-balls—automatic-return transposition spheres like message-balls—they looked around curiously. The central square was thronged—Caleras in striped robes, people from the south and east in baggy trousers and embroidered shirts, mountaineers in deerskins. A slave market was in progress, and some hundred-odd items of human merchandise were assembled in little groups, guarded by their owners and inspected by prospective buyers. They seemed to be all natives of that geographic and paratemporal area.

"Don't even look at those," Coru-hin-Irigod advised. "They are but culls; the market is almost over. We'll go to the house of Nebu-hin-Abenoz, where all the considerable men gather, and you will find those who will be able to trade slaves worthy of the goods you have with you. Meanwhile, let my people take your horses and packs to my house; you shall be my guests while you stay in Careba."

It was perfectly safe to trust Coru-hin-Irigod. He was a murderer and a brigand and a slaver, but he would never incur the scorn of men and the curse of the gods by dealing foully with a guest. The horses and packs were led away by his retainers; Ganadara and Atarazola pushed their horses after his and Faru-hin-Obaran's through the crowd.

The house of Nebu-hin-Abenoz, like every other building in Careba, was flat-roofed, adobe-walled and windowless except for narrow rifle-slits. The wide double-gate stood open, and five or six heavily armed Caleras lounged just inside. They greeted Coru and Faru by name, and the strangers by their assumed nationality. The four rode through, into what appeared to be the stables, turning their horses over to slaves, who took them away. There were between fifty and sixty other horses in the place.

Divesting themselves of their weapons in an anteroom at the head of a flight of steps, they passed under an arch and into a wide, shady patio, where thirty or forty men stood about or squatted on piles of cushions, smoking cheroots, drinking from silver cups, talking in a continuous babel. Most of them were in Calera dress, though there were men of other communities and nations, in other garb. As they moved across the patio, Gathon Dard caught snatches of conversations about deals in slaves and horse trades, about bandit raids and blood feuds, about women and horses and weapons.

An old man with a white beard and an unusually clean robe came over to intercept them.

"Ha, lord of my daughter, you're back at last. We had begun to fear for you," he said.

"Nothing to fear, father of my wife," Coru-hin-Irigod replied. "We sold the slaves for a good price, and tarried the night feasting in good company. Such good company that we brought some of it with us—Atarazola and Ganadara, men of the Jeseru; Cavu-hin-Avoran, whose daughter mothered my sons." He took his father-in-law by the sleeve and pulled him aside, motioning Gathon Dard and Antrath Alv to follow.

"They brought weapons; they want outland slaves, of the sort I took to sell in the Big Valley country," he whispered. "The weapons are repeating rifles from across the ocean, and six-shot revolvers. They also have much ammunition."

"Oh, Safar bless you!" the white-beard cried, his eyes brightening. "Name your own price; satisfy yourselves that we have dealt fairly with you; go, and return often again! Come, lord of my daughter; let us make them known to Nebu-hin-Abenoz. But not a word about the kind of weapons you have, strangers, until we can speak privately. Say only that you have rifles to trade."

Gathon Dard nodded. Evidently there was some sort of power-struggle going on in Careba; Coru-hin-Irigod and his wife's father were of the party of Nebu-hin-Abenoz, and wanted the repeaters and six-shooters for themselves.

NEBU-HIN-ABENOZ, swarthy, hook-nosed, with a square-cut graying beard, lounged in a low chair across the patio; near him four or five other

Caleras sat or squatted or reclined, all smoking the rank black tobacco of the country and drinking wine or brandy. Their conversation ceased as Cavu-hin-Avoran and the others approached. The chief of Careba listened to the introduction, then heaved himself to his feet and clapped the newcomers on the shoulders.

"Good, good!" he said. "We know you Jeseru people; you're honest traders. You come this far into our mountains too seldom. We can trade with you. We need weapons. As for the sort of slaves you want, we have none too many now, but in eight days we will have plenty. If you stay with us that long—"

"Careba is a pleasant place to be," Ganadara said. "We can wait."

"What sort of weapons have you?" the chief asked.

"Pistols and rifles, lord of my father's sister," Coru-hin-Irigod answered for them. "The packs have been taken to my house, where our friends will stay. We can bring a few to show you, the hour after evening prayers."

Nebu-hin-Abenoz shot a keen glance at his brother-in-law's son and nodded. "Or, better, I will come to your house then; thus I can see the whole load. How will that be?"

"Better; I will be there, too," Cavu-hin-Avoran said, then turned to Gathon Dard and Antrath Alv. "You have been long on the road; come, let us drink cool wine, and then we will eat," he said. "Until this evening, Nebu-hin-Abenoz."

He led his son-in-law and the traders to one side, where several kegs stood on trestles with cups and flagons beside them. They filled a flagon, took a cup apiece, and went over to a pile of cushions at one side.

As they did, three men came pushing through the crowd toward Nebu-hin-Abenoz's seat. They wore a costume unfamiliar to Gathon Dard—little round caps with red and green streamers behind, and long, wide-sleeved white gowns—and one of them had gold rings in his ears.

"Nebu-hin-Abenoz?" one of them said, bowing. "We are three men of the Usasu cities. We have gold *obus* to spend; we seek a beautiful girl, to be first concubine to our king's son, who is now come to the estate of manhood."

Nebu-hin-Abenoz picked up the silver-mounted pipe he had laid aside, and re-lighted it, frowning.

"Men of the Usasu, you have a heavy responsibility," he said. "You have the responsibility for the future of your kingdom, for a boy's character is more shaped by his first concubine than by his teachers. How old is the boy?"

"Sixteen, Nebu-hin-Abenoz; the age of manhood among us."

"Then you want a girl older, but not much older. She should be versed in the arts of love, but innocent of heart. She should be wise, but teachable; gentle and loving, but with a will of her own—"

The three men in white gowns were fidgeting. Then, suddenly, like three marionettes on a single string, they put their right hands to their mouths and then plunged them into the left sleeves of their gowns, whipping out knives and then sprang as one upon Nebu-hin-Abenoz, slashing and stabbing.

Gathon Dard was on his feet at once; he hurled the wine flagon at the three murderers and leaped across the room. Antrath Alv went bounding after him, and by this time three or four of the group around Nebu-hin-Abenoz's chair had recovered their wits and jumped to their feet. One of the three assailants turned and slashed with his knife, almost disemboweling a Calera who had tried to grapple with him. Before he could free the blade, another Calera brought a brandy bottle down on his head. Gathon Dard sprang upon the back of a second assassin, hooking his left elbow under the fellow's chin and grabbing the wrist of his knife-hand with his right; the man struggled for an instant, then went limp and fell forward. The third of the trio of murderers was still slashing at the fallen chieftain when Antrath Alv chopped him along the side of the neck with the edge of his hand; he simply dropped and lay still.

NEBU-HIN-ABENOZ was dead. He had been slashed and cut and stabbed in twenty places; his throat had been cut at least three times, and he had almost been decapitated. The wounded Calera wasn't dead yet; however, even if he had been at the moment on the operating table of a First Level Home Time Line hospital, it was doubtful if he could have been saved, and under the circumstances, his life-expectancy could be measured in seconds. Some cushions were placed under his head, and women called to attend him, but he died before they arrived.

The three assassins were also dead. Except for a few cuts on the scalp of the one who had been felled with the bottle, there was not a mark on any of them. Cavu-hin-Avoran kicked one of them in the face and cursed.

"We killed the skunks too quickly," he cried. "We should have overcome them alive, and then taken our time about dealing with them as they deserved." He went on to specify the nature of their deserts. "Such infamy!"

"Well, I'll swear I didn't think a little tap like I gave that one would kill him," the bottle-wielder excused himself. "Of course, I was thinking only of Nebu-hin-Abenoz, Safar receive him—"

Antrath Alv bent over the one he had hand-chopped.

"I didn't kill this one," he said. "The way I hit him, if I had, his neck would be broken, and it's not. See?" He twisted at the dead man's neck. "I think they took poison before they drew their knives."

"I saw all of them put their hands to their mouths!" a Calera exclaimed. "And look; see how their jaws are clenched." He picked up one of the knives and used it to pry the dead man's jaws apart, sniffing at his lips and looking into his mouth. "Look, his teeth and his tongue are discolored; there is a strange smell, too."

Antrath Alv sniffed, then turned to his partner. "Halatane," he whispered. Gathon Dard nodded. That was a First Level poison; paratimers often carried halatane capsules on the more barbaric time-lines, as a last insurance against torture.

"But, Holy Name of Safar, what manner of men were these?" Coru-hin-Irigod demanded. "There are those I would risk my life to kill, but I would not throw it away thus."

"They came knowing that we would kill them, and took the poison that they might die quickly and without pain," a Calera said.

"Or that your tortures would not wring from them the names and nation of those who sent them," an elderly man in the dress of a rancher from the southeast added. "If I were you, I would try to find out who these enemies are, and the sooner the better."

Gathon Dard was examining one of the knives—a folding knife with a broad single-edged blade, locked open with a spring; the handle was of tortoise shell, bolstered with brass.

"In all my travels," he said, "I never saw a knife of this workmanship before. Tell me, Coru-hin-Irigod, do you know from what country these outland slaves of Nebu-hin-Abenoz's come?"

"You think that might have something to do with it?" the Calera asked.

"It could. I think that these people might not have been born slaves, but people taken captive. Suppose, at some time, there had been sold to Nebu-hin-Abenoz, and sold elsewhere by him, one who was a person of consequence—the son of a king, or the priest of some god," Gathon Dard suggested.

"By Safar, yes! And now that nation, wherever it is, is at blood-feud with us," Cavu-hin-Avoran said. "This must be thought about; it is an ill thing to have unknown enemies."

"Look!" a Calera who had begun to strip the three dead men cried.

"These are not of the Usasu cities, or any other people of this land. See, they are uncircumcised!"

"Many of the slaves whom Nebu-hin-Abenoz brought to Careba from the hills have been uncircumcized," Coru-hin-Irigod said. "Jeseru, I think you have your sights on the heart of it." He frowned. "Now, think you, will those who had this done be satisfied, or will they carry on their hatred against all of us?"

"A hard question," Antrath Alv said. "You Caleras do not serve our gods, but you are our friends. Suffer me to go apart and pray; I would take counsel with the gods, that they may aid us all in this."

II

It was full daylight, but the sun was hidden; a thin rain fell on the landing ground at Police Terminal Dhergabar Equivalent when Vall and Dalla left the rocket. Across the black lavalike pavement, they could see the bulky form of Tortha Karf, hunched under a long cloak, with his flat cap pulled down over his brow. He shook hands with Vall and kissed cheeks with Dalla when they joined him.

"Car's over here," he said, nodding toward the waiting vehicle. "Yesterday wasn't one of our better days, was it?"

"No, it wasn't," Vall agreed. They climbed into the car, and the driver lifted straight up to two thousand feet and turned, soaring down to land on the Chief's Headquarters Building, a mile away. "We're not completely stopped, sir. Ranthar Jard is working on a few ideas that may lead him to the Kholghoor time-lines where the Wizard Traders are operating. If we can't get them through their output, we may nail them at the intake."

"Unless they've gotten the wind up and closed down all their operations," Tortha Karf said.

"I doubt if they've done that, Chief," Vall replied. "We don't know who these people are, of course, and it's hard to judge their reactions, but they're willing to take chances for big gains. I believe they think they're safe, now that they've closed out the compromised time-line and killed the only witness against them."

"Well, what's Ranthar Jard doing?"

"Trying to locate the subsector and probability belt from what the slaves can tell him about their religious beliefs, about the local king and the prince of Jhirda, and the noble families of the neighborhood," Vall said. "When he has it localized as closely as he can, he's going to start pelting the whole paratemporal area with photographic auto-return balls dropped from aircars on Police Terminal over the spatial equivalents of a couple of Croutha-conquered cities. As soon as he gets a photo that shows Croutha with firearms, he'll have a Wizard Trader time-line."

"Sounds simple," the Chief said. The car landed, and he helped Dalla out. "I suppose both you and he know how many chances against one he has of finding anything." They went over to an antigrav-shaft and floated down to the floor on which Tortha Karf had a duplicate of the office in the Paratime Building on Home Time Line. "It's the only chance we have, though."

"There's one thing that bothers me," Dalla said, as they entered the office and went back behind the horse-shoe-shaped desk. "I understand that the news about this didn't break on Home Time-Line till the late morning of One-Six-One Day. Nebu-hin-Abenoz was murdered at about 1700 local time, which would be 0100 this morning Dhergabar time. That would give this gang fourteen hours to hear the news, transmit it to their base, and get these three men hypno-conditioned, disguised, transposed to this Esaron Sector time-line, and into Careba." She shook her head. "That's pretty fast work."

Tortha Karf looked sidewise at Verkan Vall. "Your girl has the makings of a cop, Vall," he commented.

"She's been a big help on Esaron and Kholghoor Sectors," Vall said. "She wants to stay with it and help me; I'll be very glad to have her with me."

Tortha Karf nodded. He knew, too, that Dalla wouldn't want to have to go back to Home Time-Line and wait the long investigation out.

"Of course; we can use all the help we can get. I think we can get a lot from Dalla. Fix her up with some kind of a title and police status—technical-expert assistant, or something like that." He clasped hands, man-fashion, with her. "Glad to have you on the cops with us, Dalla," he said. Then he turned to Vall. "There was almost twenty-four hours between the time I heard about this and when this blasted Yandar Yadd got hold of the story. Of all the infernal, irresponsible—" He almost choked with indignation. "And it was another fourteen hours between the time Skordran sent in his report and I heard about it."

"Golzan Doth sent in a report to his company about the same time Skordran Kirv made his first report to his Sector-Regional Subchief," Vall mentioned.

"That might be it," Tortha Karf considered. "I wish there were another explanation, because that implies a very extensive intelligence network, which means a big organization. But I'm afraid that's it. I wish I could pull in everybody in Consolidated Outtime Foodstuffs who handled that report, and nacro-hypnotize them. Of course, we can't do things like that on Home Time Line, and with the political situation what it is now—"

"Why, what's been happening, Chief?"

TORTHA Karf swore with weary bitterness. "Salgath Trod's what's been happening. At first, after Yandar Yadd broke the story on the air, there was just a lot of unorganized Opposition sniping in Council; Salgath waited till the middle of the afternoon, when the Management members were beginning to rally, and took the floor. The Centrists and Right Moderates were trying the appeal-to-reason approach; that did as much good as trying to put out a Fifth Level forest fire with a hand-extinguisher. Finally, Salgath got a motion of censure against the Management recognized. That means a confidence vote in ten days. Salgath has a rabble of Leftists and dissident Centrists with him; I doubt if he can muster enough votes to overturn the Management, but it's going to make things rough for us."

"Which may be just the reason Salgath started this uproar," Vall suggested.

"That," Tortha Karf said, "is being considered; there is a discreet inquiry made into Salgath Trod's associates, his sources of income, and so on. Nothing has turned up as yet, but we have hopes."

"I believe," Vall said, "that we have a better chance right on Home Time-Line than outtime."

Tortha Karf looked up sharply. "So?" he asked.

Vall was stuffing tobacco into a pipe. "Yes, Chief. We have a big criminal organization—let's call it the Slave Trust, for a convenience-label. The people who run it aren't stupid. The fact that they've been shipping slaves to the Esaron Sector for ten years before we found out about it proves that. So does the speed with which they got rid of this Nebu-hin-Abenoz, right in front of a pair of our detectives. For that matter, so does the speed with which they moved in to exploit this Croutha invasion of Kholghoor Sector India.

"Well, I've studied illegal and subversive organizations all over paratime, and among the really successful ones, there are a few uniform principles. One is cellular organization—small groups, acting in isolation from one another, cooperating with other cells but ignorant of their composition. Another is the principle of no upward contact—leaders contacting their subordinates through contact-blocks and ignorant intermediaries. And another is a willingness to kill off anybody who looks like a potential betrayer or forced witness. The late Nebu-hin-Abenoz, for instance.

"I'll be willing to bet that if we pick up some of these Wizard Traders, say, or a gang that's selling slaves to some Nebu-hin-Abenoz personality on some other time-line, and narco-hypnotize them, all they'll be able to do will be name a few immediate associates, and the group leader will know that he's contacted from time to time by some stranger with orders, and that he can make emergency contacts only through some blind accommodation-address. The men who are running this are right on Home Time Line, many of them in positions of prominence, and if we can catch one of them and narco-hyp him, we can start a chain reaction of disclosures all through this Slave Trust."

"How are we going to get at these top men?" Tortha Karf wanted to know. "Advertise for them on telecast?"

"They'll leave traces; they won't be able to avoid it. I think, right now, that Salgath Trod is one of them. I think there are other prominent politicians and businesspeople. Look for irregularities and peculiarities in outtime currency-exchange transactions. For instance, to sections in Esaron Sector *obus*. Or big gold bullion transactions."

"Yes. And if they have any really elaborate outtime bases, they'll need equipment that can only be gotten on Home Time Line," Tortha Karf added. "Paratemporal conveyer parts and field-conductor mesh. You can't just walk into a hardware store and buy that sort of thing."

Dalla leaned forward to drop her cigarette ash into a tray.

"Try looking into the Bureau of Psychological Hygiene," she suggested. "That's where you'll really strike it rich."

Vall and Tortha Karf both turned abruptly and looked at her for an instant.

"Go on," Tortha Karf encouraged. "This sounds interesting."

THE people back of this," Dalla said, "are definitely classifiable as criminals. They may never perform a criminal act themselves, but they give orders for and profit from such acts, and they must possess the motivation and psychology of criminals. We define people as criminals when they suffer from psychological aberrations of an antisocial character, usually paranoid—excessive egoism, disregard for the rights of others, inability to recognize the social necessity for mutual cooperation and confidence. On Home Time Line, we have universal psychological testing, for the purpose of detecting and eliminating such characteristics."

"It seems to have failed in this case," Tortha Karf began, then snapped his fingers. "Of course! How blasted silly can I get when I'm not trying?"

"Yes, of course," Verkan Vall agreed. "Find out how these people missed being spotted by psychotesting; that'll lead us to *who* missed being tested adequately, and also who got into the Bureau of Psychological Hygiene who didn't belong there."

"I think you ought to give an investigation of the whole BuPsychHyg setup very high priority," Dalla said. "A psychotest is only as good as the people who give it, and if we have criminals administering these tests—"

"We have our friends on Executive Council," Tortha Karf said. "I'll see that that point is raised when Council reconvenes." He looked at the clock. "That'll be in three hours, by the way. If it doesn't accomplish another thing, it'll put Salgath Trod in the middle. He can't demand an investigation of the Paratime Police out of one side of his mouth and oppose an investigation of Psychological Hygiene out of the other. Now what else have we to talk about?"

"Those hundred slaves we got off the Esaron Sector," Vall said. "What are we going to do with them? And if we locate the time-line the slavers have their bases on, we'll have hundreds, probably thousands, more."

"We can't sort them out and send them back to their own time-lines, even if that would be desirable," Tortha Karf decided. "Why, settle them somewhere on the Service Sector. I know, the Paratime Transposition Code limits the Service Sector to natives of time-lines below second-order barbarism, but the Paratime Transposition Code has been so badly battered by this business that a few more minor literal infractions here and there won't make any difference. Where are they now?"

"Police Terminal, Nharkan Equivalent."

"Better hold them there for the time being. We may have to open a new Serve Sec time-line to take care of all the slaves we find, if we can locate the outtime base lien these people are using—Vall, this thing's too big to handle as a routine operation, along with our other work. You take charge of it. Set up your headquarters here, and help yourself to anything in the way of personnel and equipment you need. And bear in mind that this confidence vote is coming up in ten days—on the morning of One-Seven-Two Day. I'm not asking for any miracles, but if we don't get this thing cleared up by then, we're in for trouble."

"I realize that, sir. Dalla, you'd better go back to Home Time Line with the Chief," he said. "There's nothing you can do to help me here, at present.

Get some rest, and then try to wangle an invitation for the two of us to dinner at Thalvan Dras's apartment this evening." He turned back to Tortha Karf. "Even if he never pays any attention to business, Dras still owns Consolidated Outtime Foodstuffs," he said. "He might be able to find out, or help us find out, how the story about those slaves leaked out of his company."

"Well, that won't take much doing," Dalla said. "If there's as much excitement on Home Time Line as I think, Dras would turn somersaults and jump through hoops to get us to one of his dinners right now."

SALGATH Trod pushed the litter of papers and record-tape spools to one side impatiently.

"Well, what else did you expect?" he demanded. "This was the logical next move. BuPsychHyg is supposed to detect anybody who believes in looking out for his own interests first, and condition him into a pious law-abiding sucker. Well, the sacred Bureau of Sucker-Makers slipped up on a lot of us. It's a natural alibi for Tortha Karf."

"It's also a lot of grief for all of us," the young man in the wrap-around tunic added. "I don't want my psychotests reviewed by some duty-struck bigot who can't be reasoned with, and neither do you."

"I'm getting something organized to counter that," Salgath Trod said. "I'm going to attack the whole scientific basis of psychotesting. There's Dr. Frasthor Klav; he's always contended that what are called criminal tendencies are the result of the individual's total environment, and that psychotesting and personality-analysis are valueless, because the total environment changes from day to day, even from hour to hour—"

"That won't do," the nameless young man who was the messenger of somebody equally nameless retorted. "Frasthor's a crackpot; no reputable psychologist or psychist gives his opinions a moment's consideration. And besides, we don't want to attack Psychological Hygiene. The people in it with whom we can do business are our safeguard; they've given all of us a clean bill of mental health, and we have papers to prove it. What we have to do is to make it appear that that incident on the Esaron Sector is all there is to this, and also involve the Paratime Police themselves. The slavers are all paracops. It isn't the fault of BuPsychHyg, because the Paratime Police have their own psychotesting staff. That's where the trouble is; the paracops haven't been adequately testing their own personnel."

"Now how are you going to do that?" Salgath Trod asked disdainfully.

"You'll take the floor, the first thing tomorrow, and utilize these new revelations about the Wizard Traders. You'll accuse the Paratime Police of being the Wizard Traders themselves. Why not? They have their own paratemporal transposition equipment shops on Police Terminal, they have facilities for manufacturing duplicates of any kind of outtime items, like the firearms, for instance, and they know which time-lines on which sectors are being exploited by legitimate paratime traders and which aren't. What's to prevent a gang of unscrupulous paracops from moving in on a few unexpected Kholghoor time-lines, buying captives from the Croutha, and shipping them to the Esaron Sector?"

"They why would they let a thing like this get out?" Salgath Trod inquired.

"Somebody slipped up and removed a lot of slaves onto an exploited Esaron time-line. Or, rather, Consolidated Outtime Foodstuffs established a plantation on a time-line they were shipping slaves to. Parenthetically, that's what really did happen; the mistake our people made was in not closing out that time-line as soon as Consolidated Foodstuffs moved in," the young man said.

"So, this Skordran Kirv, who is a dumb boy who doesn't know what the score is, found these slaves and blatted about it to this Golzan Doth, and Golzan reported it to his company, and it couldn't be hushed up, so now Tortha Karf is trying to scare the public with ghost stories about a gigantic paratemporal conspiracy, to get more appropriations and more power."

How long do you think I'd get away with that?" Salgath Trod demanded. "I can only stretch parliamentary immunity so far. Sooner or later, I'd have to make formal charges to a special judicial committee, and that would mean narco-hypnosis, and then it would all come out."

"You'll have proof," the young man said. "We'll produce a couple of these Kharandas whom Verkan Vall didn't get hold of. Under narco-hypnosis, they'll testify that they saw a couple of Wizard Traders take their robes off. Under the robes were Paratime Police uniforms. Do you follow me?"

Salgath Trod made a noise of angry disgust.

"That's ridiculous! I suppose these Kharandas will be given what is deludedly known as memory obliteration, and a set of pseudo-memories; how long do you think that would last? About three ten-days. There is no such thing as memory obliteration; there's memory-suppression, and pseudo-memory overlay. You can't get behind that with any quickie narco-hypnosis in the back room of any police post, I'll admit that," he said. "But a skilled psychist can discover, inside of five minutes, when a narco-hypnotized subject is carrying a load of false memories and, in time, and not too much time, all that top layer of false memories and blockages can be peeled off. And then where would we be?"

"Now wait a minute, Councilman. This isn't just something I dreamed up," the visitor said. "This was decided upon at the top. At the very top."

"I don't care whose idea it was," Salgath Trod snapped. "The whole thing is idiotic, and I won't have anything to do with it."

The visitor's face froze. All the respect vanished from his manner and tone; his voice was like ice cakes grating together in a winter river.

"Look, Salgath; this is an Organization order," he said. "You don't refuse to obey Organization orders and you don't quit the Organization. Now get smart, big boy; do what you're told to." He took a spool of record tape from his pocket and laid it on the desk. "Outline for your speech; put it in your own words, but follow it exactly." He stood watching Salgath Trod for a moment. "I won't bother telling you what'll happen to you if you don't," he added. "You can figure that out for yourself."

With that, he turned and went out the private door. For a while, Salgath Trod sat staring after him. Once he put his hand out toward the spool, then jerked it back as though the thing were radioactive. Once he looked at the clock; it was just 1600.

THE green aircar settled onto the landing stage; Verkan Vall, on the front seat beside the driver, opened the door.

"Want me to call for you later, Assistant Verkan?" the driver asked.

"No thank you, Drenth. My wife and I are going to a dinner-party, and we'll probably go night-clubbing afterward. Tomorrow morning, all the anti-Management commentators will be yakking about my carousing around when I ought to be battling the Slave Trust. No use advertising myself with an official car, and giving them a chance to add, 'at public expense.'"

"Well, have some fun while you can," the driver advised, reaching for the car-radio phone. "Want me to check you in here, sir?"

"Yes, if you will. Thank you, Drenth."

Kandagro, his human servant, admitted him to the apartment six floors down.

"Mistress Dalla is dressing," he said. "She asked me to tell you that you are invited to dinner, this evening, with Thavan Dras at his apartment."

Vall nodded. "I'll talk to her about it now," he said. "Lay out my dress uniform, short jacket, boots and breeches, and needler."

"Yes, master; I'll go lay out your things and get your bath ready."

The servant turned and went into the alcove which gave access to the dressing rooms, turning right into Vall's. Vall followed him, turning left into his wife's.

"Oh, Dalla!" he called.

"In here!" her voice came out of her bathroom.

He passed through the dressing room to find her stretched on a plastic-sheeted couch, while her maid, Rendarra, was rubbing her body vigorously with some pungent-smelling stuff about the consistency of machine-grease. Her face was masked in the stuff, and her hair was covered with an elastic cap. He had always suspected that beauty was the real feminine religion, from the willingness of its devotees to submit to martyrdom for it. She wiggled a hand at him in greeting.

"How did it go?" she asked.

"So-so. I organized myself a sort of miniature police force within a police force and I have liaison officers in every organization down to Sector Regional so that I can be informed promptly in case anything new turns up anywhere. What's been happening on Home Time-Line? I picked up a news-summary at Paratime Police Headquarters; it seems that a lot more stuff has leaked out. Kholghoor Sector, Wizard Traders and all. How'd it happen?"

Dalla rolled over to allow Rendarra to rub the blue-green grease on her back.

"Consolidated Outtime Foodstuffs let a gang of reporters in today. I think they're afraid somebody will accuse them of complicity, and they want to get their side of it before the public. All our crowd are off that time-line except a couple of detectives at the plantation."

"I know." He smiled; Dalla was thinking of the Paratime Police as "our crowd" now. "How about this dinner at Dras's place?"

"Oh, that was easy." She shifted position again. "I just called Dras up and told him that our vacation was off, and he invited us before I could begin hinting. What are you going to wear?"

"Short-jacket greens; I can carry a needler with that uniform, even wear it at the table. I don't think it's smart for me to run around unarmed, even on

Home Time-Line. Especially on Home Time-Line," he amended. "When's this affair going to start, and how long will Rendarra take to get that goo off you?"

SALGATH Trod left his aircar at the top landing stage of his apartment building and sent it away to the hangars under robot control; he glanced about him as he went toward the antigrav shaft. There were a dozen vehicles in the air above; any of them might have followed him from the Paratime Building. He had no doubt that he had been under constant surveillance from the moment the nameless messenger had delivered the Organization's ultimatum. Until he delivered that speech the next morning, or manifested an intention of refusing to do so, however, he would be safe. After that—

Alone in his office, he had reviewed the situation point by point, and then gone back and reviewed it again; the conclusion was inescapable. The Organization had ordered him to make an accusation which he himself knew to be false; that was the first premise. The conclusion was that he would be killed as soon as he had made it. That was the trouble with being mixed up with that kind of people—you were expendable, and sooner or later, they would decide that they would have to expend you. And what could you do?

To begin with, an accusation of criminal malfeasance made against a Management or Paratime Commission agency on the floor of Executive Council was tantamount to an accusation made in court; automatically, the accuser became a criminal prosecutor, and would have to repeat his accusation under narco-hypnosis. Then the whole story would come out, bit by bit, back to its beginning in that first illegal deal in Indo-Turanian opium, diverted from trade with the Khiftan Sector and sold on Second Level Luvarian Empire Sector, and the deals in radioactive poisons, and the slave trade. He would be able to name few names—the Organization kept its activities too well compartmented for that—but he could talk of things that had happened, and when, and where, and on what paratemporal areas.

No. The Organization wouldn't let that happen, and the only way it could be prevented would be by the death of Salgath Trod, as soon as he had made his speech. All the talk of providing him with corroborative evidence was silly; it had been intended to lead him more trustingly to the slaughter. They'd kill him, of course, in some way that would be calculated to substantiate the story he would no longer be able to repudiate. The killer, who would be promptly rayed dead by somebody else, would wear a Paratime Police uniform, or something like that. That was of no importance, however; by then, he'd be beyond caring.

ONE of his three ServSec Prole servants—the slim brown girl who was his housekeeper and hostess, and also his mistress—admitted him to the apartment. He kissed her perfunctorily and closed the door behind him.

"You're tired," she said. "Let me call Nindrandigro and have him bring you chilled wine; lie down and rest until dinner."

"No, no; I want brandy." He went to a cellaret and got out a decanter and goblet, pouring himself a drink. "How soon will dinner be ready?"

The brown girl squeezed a little golden globe that hung on a chain around her neck; a tiny voice inside it repeated: "Eighteen twenty-three ten, eighteen twenty-three eleven, eighteen twenty-three twelve—"

"In half an hour. It's still in the robi-chef," she told him.

He downed half the goblet-full, set it down, and went to a painting, a brutal scarlet and apple-green abstraction, that hung on the wall. Swinging it aside and revealing the safe behind it, he used his identity-sigil, took out a wad of Paratemporal Exchange Bank notes and gave them to the girl.

"Here, Zinganna; take these, and take Nindrandigro and Calilla out for the evening. Go where you can all have a good time, and don't come back till after midnight. There will be some business transacted here, and I want them out of this. Get them out of here as soon as you can; I'll see to the dinner myself. Spend all of that you want to."

The girl riffled through the wad of banknotes. "Why, *thank* you, Trod!" She threw her arms around his neck and kissed him enthusiastically. "I'll go tell them at once."

"And have a good time, Zinganna; have the best time you possibly can," he told her, embracing and kissing her. "Now, get out of here; I have to keep my mind on business."

When she had gone, he finished his drink and poured another. He drew and checked his needler. Then, after checking the window-shielding and activating the outside viewscreens, he lit a cheroot and sat down at the desk, his goblet and his needler in front of him, to wait until the servants were gone.

There was only one way out alive. He knew that, and yet he needed brandy, and a great deal of mental effort, to steel himself for it. Psychorehabilitation was a dreadful thing to face. There would be almost a year of unremitting agony, physical and mental, worse than a Khiftan torture rack.

There would be the shame of having his innermost secrets poured out of him by the psychotherapists, and at the end, there would emerge someone who would not be Salgath Trod, or anybody like Salgath Trod, and he would have to learn to know this stranger and build a new life for him.

In one of the viewscreens, he saw the door to the service hallway open. Zinganna, in a black evening gown and a black velvet cloak, and Calilla, the housemaid, in what she believed to be a reasonable facsimile of fashionable First Level dress, and Nindrandigro, in one of his master's evening suits, emerged. Salgath Trod waited until they had gone down the hall to the anti-grav shaft, and then he turned on the visiphone, checked the security, set it for sealed beam communication, and punched out a combination.

A girl in a green tunic looked out of the screen.

"Paratime Police," she said. "Office of Chief Tortha."

"I am Executive Councilman Salgath Trod," he told her. "I am, and for the past fifteen years have been, criminally involved with the organization responsible for the slave trade which recently came to light on Third Level Esaron. I give myself up unconditionally; I am willing to make full confession under narco-hypnosis, and will accept whatever disposition of my case is lawfully judged fit. You'll have to send an escort for me; I might start from my apartment alone, but I'd be killed before I got to your headquarters—"

The girl, who had begun to listen in the bored manner of public-servant phone girls, was staring wide-eyed.

"Just a moment, Councilman Salgath; I'll put you through to Chief Tortha."

THE dinner lacked a half hour of being served; Thalvan Dras's guests loitered about the drawing room, sampling appetizers and chilled drinks and chatting in groups. It wasn't the artistic crowd usual at Thalvan Dras's dinners; most of the guests seemed to be business or political people. Thalvan Dras had gotten Vall and Dalla into the small group around him, along with pudgy, infantile-faced Brogoth Zaln, his confidential secretary, and Javrath Brend, his financial attorney.

"I don't see why they're making such a fuss about it," one of the Banking Cartel people was saying. "Causing a lot of public excitement all out of proportion to the importance of the affair. After all, those people were slaves on their own time line, and if anything, they're much better off on the Esaron Sector than they would be as captives of the Croutha. As far as that goes, what's the difference between that and the way we drag these Fourth Level Primitive Sector-Complex people off to Fifth Level Service Sector to work for us?"

"Oh, there's a big difference, Farn," Javrath Brend said. "We recruit those Fourth Level Primitives out of probability worlds of Stone Age savagery, and transpose them to our own Fifth Level time-lines, practically outtime extensions of the Home Time-Line. There's absolutely no question of the Paratime Secret being compromised."

"Besides, we need a certain amount of human labor, for tasks requiring original thought and decision that are beyond the ability of robots, and most of it is work our Citizens simply wouldn't perform," Thalvan Dras added.

"Well, from a moral standpoint, wouldn't these Esaron Sector people who buy the slaves justify slavery in the same terms?" a woman whom Vall had identified as a Left Moderate Council Member asked.

"There's still a big difference," Dalla told her. "The ServSec Proles aren't beaten or tortured or chained; we don't break up families or separate friends. When we recruit Fourth Level Primitives, we take whole tribes, and they come willingly. And—"

One of Thalvan Dras's black-liveried human servants, out of the class under discussion, approached Vall.

"A visiphone call for your lordship," he whispered. "Chief Tortha Karf calling. If your lordship will come this way—"

In a screen-booth outside, Vall found Tortha Karf looking out of the screen; he was seated at his desk, fiddling with a gold multicolor pen.

"Oh, Vall; something interesting has just come up." He spoke in a voice of forced calmness. "I can't go into it now, but you'll want to hear about it. I'm sending a car for you. Better bring Dalla along; she'll want in on it, too."

"Right; we'll be on the top southwest landing stage in a few minutes."

Dalla was still heatedly repudiating any resemblance between the normal First Level methods of labor-recruitment and the activities of the Wizard Traders; she had just finished the story of the woman whose child had been brained when Vall rejoined the group.

"Dras, I'm awfully sorry," he said. "This is the second time in succession that Dalla and I have had to bolt away from here, but policemen are like doctors—always on call, and consequently unreliable guests. While you're feasting, think commiseratingly of Dalla and me; we'll probably be having a sandwich and a cup of coffee somewhere."

"I'm terribly sorry," Thalvan Dras replied. "We had all been looking forward—Well! Brogoth, have a car called for Vall and Dalla."

"Police car coming for us; it's probably on the landing stage now," Vall said. "Well, good-by, everybody. Coming, Dalla?"

THEY had a few minutes to wait, under the marquee, before the green police aircar landed and came rolling across the rain-wet surface of the landing stage. Crossing to it and opening the rear door, he put Dalla in and climbed in after her, slamming the door. It was only then that he saw Tortha Karf hunched down in the rear seat. He motioned them to silence, and did not speak until the car was rising above the building.

"I wanted to fill you in on this, as soon as possible," he said. "Your hunch about Salgath Trod was good; just a few minutes before I called you, he called me. He says this slave trade is the work of something he calls the Organization; says he's been taking orders from them for years. His attack on the Management and motion for a censure-vote were dictated from Organization top echelon. Now he's convinced that they're going to force him to make false accusations against the Paratime Police and then kill him before he's compelled to repeat his charges under narco-hypnosis. So he's offered to surrender and trade information for protection."

"How much does he know?" Vall asked.

Tortha Karf shook his head. "Not as much as he claims to, I suppose; he wouldn't want to reduce his own trade-in value. But he's been involved in this thing for the last fifteen years, and with his political prominence, he'd know quite a lot."

"We can protect him from his own gang; can we protect him from psycho-rehabilitation?"

"No, and he knows it. He's willing to accept that. He seems to think that death at the hands of his own associates is the only other alternative. Probably right, too."

The floodlighted green towers of the Paratime Building were wheeling under them as they circled down.

"Why would they sacrifice a valuable accomplice like Salgath Trod, in order to make a transparently false accusation against us?" Vall wondered.

"Ha, that's our new rookie cop's idea!" Tortha Karf chuckled, nodding toward Dalla. "We got Zortan Harn to introduce an urgent-business motion to appoint a committee to investigate BuPsychHyg this morning. The motion passed, and this is the reaction to it. The Organization's scared. Just as Dalla predicted, they don't want us finding out how people with potentially criminal characteristics missed being spotted by psychotesting. Salgath Trod is being sacrificed to block or delay that."

Vall nodded as the wheels bumped on the landing stage and the antigrav field went off. That was the sort of thing that happened when you started on a really fruitful line of investigation. They got out and hurried over under the marquee, the car lifting and moving off toward the hangars. This was the real break; no matter how this Organization might be compartmented, a man like Salgath Trod would know a great deal. He would name names, and the bearers of those names, arrested and narco-hypnotized, would name other names, in a perfect chain reaction of confessions and betrayals.

Another police car had landed just ahead of them, and three men were climbing out; two were in Paratime Police green, and the third, handcuffed, was in Service Sector Proletarian garb. At first, Vall thought that Salgath Trod had been brought in disguised as a Prole prisoner, and then he saw that the prisoner was short and stocky, not at all like the slender and elegant politician. The two officers who had brought him in were talking to a lieutenant, Sothran Barth, outside the antigrav shaft kiosk. As Vall and Tortha Karf and Dalla walked over, the car which had brought them lifted out.

"Something that just came in from Industrial Twenty-four, Chief," Lieutenant Sothran said in answer to Tortha Karf's question. "May be for Assistant Verkan's desk."

"He's a Prole named Yandragno, sir," one of the policemen said. "Industrial Sector Constabulary grabbed him peddling Martian hellweed cigarettes to the girls in a textile mill at Kangabar Equivalent. Captain Jamzar thinks he may have gotten them from somebody in the Organization."

A LITTLE warning bell began ringing in the back of Verkan Vall's mind, but at first he could not consciously identify the cause of his suspicions. He looked the two policemen and their prisoner over carefully, but could see nothing visibly wrong with them. Then another car came in for a landing and rolled over under the marquee; the door opened, and a police officer got out, followed by an elegantly dressed civilian whom he recognized at once as Salgath Trod. A second policeman was emerging from the car when Vall suddenly realized what it was that had disturbed him.

It had been Salgath Trod, himself, less than half an hour ago, who had introduced the term "the Organization" to the Paratime Police. At that time, if these people were what they claimed to be, they would have been in transposition from Industrial Twenty-four, on the Fifth Level. Immediately, he reached for his needler. He was clearing it for the holster when things began happening.

The handcuffs fell from the "prisoner's" wrists; he jerked a neutron-disruption blaster from under his jacket. Vall, his needler already drawn, rayed the fellow dead before he could aim it, then saw that the two pseudo-policemen had drawn their needlers and were aiming in the direction of Salgath Trod. There were no flashes or reports; only the spot of light that had winked on and off under Vall's rear sight had told him that his weapon had been activated. He saw it appear again as the sights centered on one of the "policemen." Then he saw the other imposter's needler aimed at himself. That was the last thing he expected ever to see, in that life; he tried to shift his own weapon, and time seemed frozen, with his arm barely moving. Then there was a white blur as Dalla's cloak moved in front of him, and the needler dropped from the fingers of the disguised murderer. Time went back to normal for him; he safetied his own weapon and dropped it, jumping forward.

He grabbed the fellow in the green uniform by the nose with his left hand, and punched him hard in the pit of the stomach with his right fist. The man's mouth flew open, and a green capsule, the size and shape of a small bean, flew out. Pushing Dalla aside before she would step on it, he kicked the murderer in the stomach, doubling him over, and chopped him on the base of the skull with the edge of his hand. The pseudo-policeman dropped senseless.

With a handful of handkerchief-tissue from his pocket, he picked up the disgorged capsule, wrapping it carefully after making sure that it was unbroken. Then he looked around. The other two assassins were dead. Tortha Karf, who had been looking at the man in Proletarian dress whom Vall had killed first, turned, looked in another direction, and then cursed. Vall followed his eyes and cursed also. One of the two policemen who had gotten out of the aircar was dead, too, and so was the all-important witness, Salgath Trod—as dead as Nebu-hin-Abenoz, a hundred thousand parayears away.

THE whole thing had ended within thirty seconds; for about half as long, everybody waited, poised in a sort of action-vacuum, for something else to happen. Dalla had dropped the shoulder-bag with which she had clubbed the prisoner's needler out of his hand, and caught up the fallen weapon. When she saw that the man was down and motionless, she laid it aside and began picking up the glittering or silken trifles that had spilled from the burst bag. Vall retrieved his own weapon, glanced over it, and holstered it. Sothran Barth, the lieutenant in charge of the landing stage, was bawling orders, and men were coming out of the ready-room and piling into vehicles to pursue the aircar which had brought the assassins.

"Barth!" Vall called. "Have you a hypodermic and a sleep-drug ampoule? Well, give this boy a shot; he's only impact-stunned. Be careful of him; he's important." He glanced around the landing stage. "Fact is, he's all we have to show for this business."

Then he stopped to help Dalla gather her things, picking up a few of them—a lighter, a tiny crystal perfume flask, miraculously unbroken, a face-powder box which had sprung open and spilled half its contents. He handed them to her, while Sothran Barth bent over the prisoner and gave him an injection, then went to the body of the other pseudo-policeman, forcing open his mouth. In his cheek, still unbroken, was a second capsule, which he added to the first. Tortha Karf was watching him.

"Same gang that killed that Calera slaver on Esaron Sector?" he asked. "Of course, exactly the same general procedure. Let's have a look at the other one."

The man in Proletarian dress must have had his capsule between his molars when he had been killed; it was broken, and there was a brownish discoloration and chemical odor in his mouth.

"Second time we've had a witness killed off under our noses," Tortha Karf said. "We're going to have to smarten up in a hurry."

"Here's one of us who doesn't have to, much," Vall said, nodding toward Dalla. "She knocked a needler out of one man's hand, and we took him alive. The Force owes her a new shoulder-bag; she spoiled that one using it for a club."

"Best shoulder-bag we can find you, Dalla," Tortha Karf promised. "You're promoted, herewith, to Special Chief's Assistant's Special Assistant—You know, this Organization murder-section is good; they could kill anybody. It won't be long before they assign a squad to us. Blast it, I don't want to have to go around bodyguarded like a Fourth Level dictator, but—"

A detective came out of the control room and approached.

"Screen call for you, sir," he told Tortha Karf. "One of the news services wants a comment on a story they've just picked up that we've illegally arrested Councilman Salgath and are holding him incommunicado and searching his apartment."

"That's the Organization," Vall said. "They don't know how their boys made out; they're hoping we'll tell them."

"No comment," Tortha Karf said. "Call the girl on my switchboard and tell her to answer any other news-service calls. We have nothing to say at this time, but there will be a public statement at . . . at 2330," he decided after a glance at his watch. "That'll give us time to agree on a publicity line to adopt. Lieutenant Sothran! Take charge up here. Get all these bodies out of sight somewhere, including those of Councilman Salgath and Detective Malthor. Don't let anybody talk about this; put a blackout on the whole story. Vall, you and Dalla and . . . oh, you, over there; take the prisoner down to my office. Sothran, any reports from any of the cars that were chasing that fake police car?"

Verkan Vall and Dalla were sitting behind Tortha Karf's desk; Vall was issuing orders over the intercom and talking to the detectives who had remained at Salgath Trod's apartment by visiscreen; Dalla was sorting over the things she had spilled when her bag had burst. They both looked up as Tortha Karf came in and joined them.

"The prisoner's still under the drug," the Chief said. "He'll be out for a couple of hours; the psych-techs want to let him out of it naturally and sleep naturally for a while before they give him a hypno. He's not a ServSec Prole; uncircumcised, never had any syntho-enzyme shots or immunizations, and none of the longevity operations or grafts. Same thing for the two stiffs. And no identity records on any of the three."

"The men at Salgath's apartment say that his housekeeper and his two servants checked out through the house conveyer for ServSec One-Six-Five, at about 1830," Vall said. "There's a Prole entertainment center on that time line. I suppose Salgath gave them the evening off before he called you."

Tortha Karf nodded. "I suppose you ordered them picked up. The news services are going wild about this. I had to make a preliminary statement, to the effect that Salgath Trod was not arrested, came to Headquarters of his own volition, and is under no restraint whatever."

"Except, of course, a slight case of rigor mortis," Dalla added. "Did you mention that, Chief?"

"No, I didn't." Tortha Karf looked as though he had quinine in his mouth. "Vall, how in blazes are we going to handle this?"

"We ought to keep Salgath's death hushed up as long as we can," Vall said. "The Organization doesn't know positively what happened here; that's why they're handing out tips to the news services. Let's try to make them believe he's still alive and talking."

"How can we do it?"

"There ought to be somebody on the Force close enough to Salgath Trod's anthropometric specifications that our cosmeticians could work him over into a passable impersonation. Our story is that Salgath is on PolTerm, undergoing narco-hypnosis. We will produce an audio-visual of him as soon as he is out of narco-hyp. That will give us time to fix up an impersonator. We'll need a lot of sound-recordings of Salgath Trod's voice, of course—"

"I'll take care of the Home Time-Line end of it; as soon as we get you an impersonator, you go to work with him. Now, let's see whom we can depend on to help us with this. Lovranth Rolk, of course; Home Time-Line section of the Paratime Code Enforcement Division. And—"

VERKAN Vall and Dalla and Tortha Karf and four or five others looked across the desk and to the end of the room as the telecast screen broke into a shifting light-pattern and then cleared. The face of the announcer appeared; a young woman.

"And now, we bring you the statement which Chief Tortha, of the Paratime Police, has promised for this time. This portion of the program was audio-visually recorded at Paratime Police Headquarters earlier this evening."

Tortha Karf's face appeared on the screen. His voice began an announcement of how Executive Councilman Salgath Trod had called him by visiphone, admitting to complicity in the recently discovered paratemporal slave trade.

"Here is a recording of Councilman Salgath's call to me from his apartment to my office, at 1945 this evening."

The screen-image shattered into light-shards and rebuilt itself; Salgath Trod, at his desk in the library of his apartment, the brandy goblet and the needler within reach, appeared. He began to speak; from time to time the voice of Tortha Karf interrupted, questioning or prompting him.

"You understand that this confession renders you liable to psycho-rehabilitation?" Tortha Karf asked.

Yes, Councilman Salgath understood that.

"And you agree to come voluntarily to Paratime Police Headquarters, and you will voluntarily undergo narco-hypnotic interrogation?"

Yes, Salgath Trod agreed to that.

"I am now terminating the playback of Councilman Salgath's call to me," Tortha Karf said, re-appearing on the screen. "At this point Councilman Salgath began making a statement about his criminal activities, which we have on record. Because he named a number of his criminal associates, whom we have no intention of warning, this portion of Councilman Salgath's call cannot at this time be made public. We have no intention of having any of these suspects escape, or of giving their associates an opportunity to murder them to prevent their furnishing us with additional information. Incidentally, there was an attempt, made on the landing stage of Paratime Police Headquarters, to murder Councilman Salgath when he was brought here guarded by Paratime Police officers—"

He went on to give a colorful and, as far as possible, truthful, account of the attack by the two pseudo-policemen and their pseudo-prisoner. As he told it, however, all three had been killed before they could accomplish their purpose, one of them by Salgath Trod himself.

The image of Tortha Karf was replaced by a view of the three assassins lying on the landing stage. They all looked dead, even the one who wasn't; there was nothing to indicate that he was merely drugged. Then, one after another, their faces were shown in closeup, while Tortha Karf asked for close attention and memorization.

"We believe that these men were Fifth Level Proles; we think that they were under hypnotic influence or obeying post-hypnotic commands when they made their suicidal attack. If any of you have ever seen any of these men before, it is your duty to inform the Paratime Police."

THAT ended it. Tortha Karf pressed a button in front of him and the screen went dark. The spectators relaxed.

"Well! Nothing like being sincere with the public, is there?" Dalla commented. "I'll remember this the next time I tune in a Management public statement."

"In about five minutes," one of the bureau-chiefs said, "all hell is going to break loose. I think the whole thing is crazy!"

"I hope you have somebody who can give a convincing impersonation," Lovranth Rolk said.

"Yes. A field agent named Kostran Galth," Tortha Karf said. "We ran the personal description cards for the whole Force through the machine; Kostran checked to within one-twentieth of one percent; he's on Police Terminal now, coming by rocket from Ravvanan Equivalent. We ought to have the whole thing ready for telecast by 1730 tomorrow."

"He can't learn to imitate Salgath's voice convincingly in that time, with all the work the cosmeticians'll have to be doing on him," Dalla said.

"Make up a tape of Salgath's own voice, out of that pile of recordings we got at his apartment and what we can get out of the news file," Vall said. "We have phoneticists who can split syllables and splice them together. Kostran will deliver his speech in dumb-show, and we'll dub the sound in and telecast them as one. I've messaged PolTerm to get to work on that; they can start as soon as we have the speech written."

"The more it succeeds now, the worse the blow-up will be when we finally have to admit that Salgath was killed here tonight," the Chief Interoffice Coordinator, Zostha Olv, said. "We'd better have something to show the public to justify that."

"Yes, we had," Tortha Karf agreed. "Vall, how about the Kholghoor Sector operation. How far's Ranthar Jard gotten toward locating one of those Wizard Trader time lines?"

"Not very far," Vall admitted. "He has it pinned down to the sub-sector, but the belt seems to be one we haven't any information at all for. Never been any legitimate penetration by paratimers. He has his own hagiologists, and a couple borrowed from Outtime Religious Institute; they've gotten everything the slaves can give them on that. About the only thing to do is start random observation with boomerang-balls."

"Over about a hundred thousand time-lines," Zostha Olv scoffed. He was an old man, even for his long-lived race; he had a thin nose and a narrow, bitter mouth. "And what will he look for?"

"Croutha with guns," Tortha Karf told him, then turned to Vall. "Can't he narrow it more than that? What have his experts been getting out of those slaves?"

"That I don't know, to date." Vall looked at the clock. "I'll find out, though; I'll transpose to Police Terminal and call him up. And Skordran Kirv. No, Vulthor Tharn; it'd hurt the old fellow's feelings if I bypassed him and went to one of his subordinates. Half an hour each way, and at most another hour talking to Ranthar and Vulthor; there won't be anything doing here for two hours." He rose. "See you when I get back."

Dalla had turned on the telescreen again; after tuning out a dance orchestra and a comedy show, she got the image of an angry-faced man in evening clothes.

". . . And I'm going to demand a full investigation, as soon as Council convenes tomorrow morning!" he was shouting. "This whole story is a preposterous insult to the integrity of the entire Executive Council, your elected representatives, and it shows the criminal lengths to which this would-be dictator, Tortha Karf, and his jackal Verkan Vall will go—"

"So long, jackal," Dalla called to him as he went out.

He spent the half-hour transposition to Police Terminal sleeping. Paratime transpositions and rocket-flights seemed to be his only chance to get any sleep. He was still sleepy when he sat down in front of the radio telescreen behind his duplicate of Tortha Karf's desk and put through a call to Nharkan Equivalent. It was 0600 in India; the Sector Regional Deputy Subchief who was holding down Ranthar Jard's desk looked equally sleepy; he had a mug of coffee in front of him, and a brown-paper cigarette in his mouth.

"Oh, hello, Assistant Verkan. Want me to call Subchief Ranthar?"

"Is he sleeping? Then for mercy's sake don't. What's the present status of the investigation?"

"Well, we were dropping boomerang-balls yesterday, while we had sun to mask the return-flashes. Nothing. The Croutha have taken the city of Sohram, just below the big bend of the river. Tomorrow, when we have sunlight, we're going to start boomerang-balling the central square. We may get something."

"The Wizard Traders'll be moving in near there, about now," Vall said. "The Croutha ought to have plenty of merchandise for them. Have you gotten anything more done on narrowing down the possible area?"

The deputy bit back a yawn and reached for his coffee mug.

"The experts have just about pumped these slaves empty," he said. "The local religion is a mess. Seems to have started out as a Great Mother cult; then it picked up a lot of gods borrowed from other peoples; then it turned into a dualistic monotheism; then it picked up a lot of minor gods and devils—new devils, usually gods of the older pantheon. And we got a lot of gossip about the feudal wars and faction-fights among the nobility, and so on, all garbled, because these people are peasants who only knew what went on on the estate of their own lord."

"What did go on there?" Vall asked. "Ask them about recent improvements, new buildings, new fields cleared, new paddies flooded, that sort of thing. And pick out a few of the highest IQ's from both time lines, and have them locate this estate on a large-scale map, and draw plans showing the location of buildings, fields and other visible features. If you have to, teach them mapping and sketching by hypno-mech. And then drop about five hundred to a thousand boomerang-balls, at regular intervals, over the whole paratemporal area. When you locate a time line that gives you a picture to correspond to their description, boomerang the main square in Sohram over the whole belt around it to find Croutha with firearms."

The deputy looked at him for a moment, then gulped more coffee.

"Can do, Assistant Verkan. I think I'll send somebody to wake up Subchief Ranthar right now. Want to talk to him?"

"Won't be necessary. You're recording this call, of course? Then play it back to him. And get cracking with the slaves; you want enough information out of them to enable you to start boomerang-balling as soon as the sun's high enough."

He broke off the connection and sent out for coffee for himself. Then he put through a call to Novilan Equivalent, in western North America.

It was 1530 there, when he got Vulthor Tharn on the screen.

"Good afternoon, Assistant Verkan. I suppose you're calling about the slave business. I've turned the entire matter over to Field Agent Skordran; gave him a temporary rank of Deputy Subchief. That's subject to your approval and Chief Tortha's, of course—"

"Make the appointment permanent," Vall said. "I'll have a confirmation along from Chief Tortha directly. And let me talk to him now, if you please, Subchief Vulthor."

"Yes, sir. Switching you over now." The screen went into a beautiful burst of abstract art, and cleared, after a while, with Skordran Kirv looking out of it.

Hello, Deputy Skordran, and congratulations. What's come up since we had Nebu-hin-Abenoz cut out from under us?"

"We went in on that time-line that same night, with an airboat, and made a recon in the hills back of Careba. Scared the fear of Safar into a party of Caleras while we were working at low altitude, by the way. We found the conveyer-head site; hundred-foot circle with all the grass and loose dirt transposed off it, and a pole pen, very unsanitary, where about two-three hundred slaves would be kept at a time. No indications of use in the last ten days. We did some pretty thorough boomeranging on that spatial equivalent over a couple of thousand time-lines and found thirty more of them. I believe the slavers have closed out the whole Esaron Sector operation, at least temporarily."

That was what he'd been afraid of; he hoped they wouldn't do the same thing on the Kholghoor Sector.

"Let me have the designations of the time-lines on which you found conveyer heads," he said.

"Just a moment, Chief's Assistant; I'll photoprint them to you. Set for reception?"

Vall opened a slide under the screen and saw that the photoprint film was in place, then closed it again, nodding. Skordran Kirv fed a sheet of paper into his screen cabinet and his arm moved forward out of the picture.

"On, sir," he said. He and Vall counted ten seconds together, and then Skordran Kirv said: "Through to you." Vall pressed a lever under his screen, and a rectangle of microcopy print popped out.

"That's about all I have, sir. Want me to keep my troops ready here, or shall I send them somewhere else?"

"Keep them ready, Kirv," Vall told him. "You may need them before long. Call you later."

He put the microcopy in an enlarger, and carried the enlarged print with him to the conveyer room. There was something odd about the list of time-line designations. They were expressed numerically, in First Level notation; extremely short groups of symbols capable of exact expression of almost inconceivably enormous numbers. Vall had only a general-education smattering of mathematics—enough to qualify him for the chair of Higher Mathematics at any university on, say, the Fourth Level Europo-American Sector—and he could not identify the peculiarity, but he could recognize that there existed some sort of pattern. Shoving in the starting lever, he relaxed in one of the chairs, waiting for the transposition field to build up around him, and fell asleep before the mesh dome of the conveyer had vanished. He woke, the list of time-line designations in his hand, when the conveyor rematerialized on Home Time-Line. Putting it in his pocket, he hurried to an antigrav shaft and floated up to the floor on which Tortha Karf's office was.

TORTHA Karf was asleep in his chair; Dalla was eating a dinner that had been brought in for her—something better than the sandwich and mug of coffee Vall had mentioned to Thalvan Dras. Several of the bureau chiefs who had been there when he had gone out had left, and the psychist who had taken charge of the prisoner was there.

"I think he's coming out of the drug now," he reported. "Still asleep, though. We want him to waken naturally before we start on him. They'll call me as soon as he shows signs of stirring."

"The Opposition's claiming now that we drugged and hypnotized Salgath into making that visiscreen confession," Dalla said. "Can you think of any way you could do that without making the subject incapable of lying?"

"Pseudo-memories," the psychist said. "It would take about three times as long as the time between Salgath Trod's departure from his apartment and the time of the telecast, though—"

"You know much higher math?" Vall asked the psychist.

"Well, enough to handle my job. Neuron-synapse inter-relations, memory-and-association patterns, that kind of thing, all have to be expressed mathematically."

Vall nodded and handed him the time-line designation list.

"See any kind of pattern there?" he asked.

The psychist looked at the paper and blanked his face as he drew on hypnotically acquired information.

"Yes. I'd say that all the numbers are related in some kind of a series to some other number. Simplified down to kindergarten level, say the difference between A and B is, maybe, one-decillionth of the difference between X and A, and the difference between B and C is one-decillionth of the difference between X and B, and so on—"

A VOICE came out of one of the communication boxes:

"Dr. Nentrov; the patient's out of the drug, and he's beginning to stir about."

"That's it," the psychist said. "I have to run." He handed the sheet back to Vall, took a last drink from his coffee cup, and bolted out of the room.

Dalla picked up the sheet of paper and looked at it. Vall told her what it was.

"If those time lines are in regular series, they relate to the base line of operations," she said. "Maybe you can have that worked out. I can see how it would be; a stated interval between the Esaron Sector lines, to simplify transposition control settings."

"That was what I was thinking. It's not quite as simple as Dr. Nentrov expressed it, but that could be the general idea. We might be able to work out the location of the base line from that. There seems to be a break in the number sequence in here; that would be the time line Skordran Kirv found those slaves on." He reached for the pipe he had left on the desk when he had gone to Police Terminal and began filling it.

A little later, a buzzer sounded and a light came on on one of the communication boxes. He flipped the switch and said, "Verkan Vall here." Sothran Barth's voice came out of the box.

"They've just brought in Salgath Trod's servants. Picked them up as they came out of the house conveyer at the apartment building. I don't believe they know what's happened."

Vall flipped a switch and twiddled a dial; a viewscreen lit up, showing the landing stage. The police car had just landed; one detective had gotten out, and was helping the girl, Zinganna, who had been Salgath Trod's housekeeper and mistress, to descend. She was really beautiful, Vall thought; rather tall, slender, with dark eyes and a creamy light-brown skin. She wore a black cloak and, under it, a black and silver evening gown. A single jewel twinkled in her black hair. She could have very easily passed for a woman of his own race.

The housemaid and the butler were a couple of entirely different articles. Both were about four or five generations from Fourth Level Primitive savagery. The maid, in garishly cheap finery, was big-boned and heavy-bodied, with red-brown hair; she looked like a member of one of the northern European reindeer-herding peoples who had barely managed to progress as far as the bow and arrow. The butler was probably a mixture of half a dozen primitive races; he was wearing one of his late master's evening suits, a bright mellow-pink, which was distinctly unflattering to his complexion.

The sound-pickup was too far away to give him what they were saying, but the butler and maid were waving their arms and protesting vehemently. One of the detectives took the woman by the arm; she jerked it loose and aimed a backhand slap at him. He blocked it on his forearm. Immediately, the girl in black turned and said something to her, and she subsided. Vall said, into the box:

"Barth, have the girl in the black cloak brought down to Number Four Interview Room. Put the other two in separate detention cubicles; we'll talk to them later." He broke the connection and got to his feet. "Come on, Dalla. I want you to help me with the girl."

"Just try and stop me," Dalla told him. "Any interviews you have with that little item, I want to sit in on."

THE Proletarian girl, still guarded by a detective, had already been placed in the interview room. The detective nodded to Vall, tried to suppress a grin when he saw Dalla behind him, and went out. Vall saw his wife and the prisoner seated, and produced his cigarette case, handing it around.

"You're Zinganna; you're of the household of Councilman Salgath Trod, aren't you?" he asked.

"Housekeeper and hostess," the girl replied. "I am also his mistress."

Vall nodded, smiling. "Which confirms my long-standing respect for Councilman Salgath's exquisite taste."

"Why, thank you," she said. "But I doubt if I was brought here to receive compliments. Or was I?"

"No, I'm afraid not. Have you heard the newscasts of the past few hours concerning Councilman Salgath?"

She straightened in her seat, looking at him seriously.

"No. I and Nindrandigro and Calilla spent the evening on ServSec One-Six-Five. Councilman Salgath told me that he had some business and wanted them out of the apartment, and wanted me to keep an eye on them. We didn't hear any news at all." She hesitated. "Has anything . . . serious . . . happened?"

Vall studied her for a moment, then glanced at Dalla. There existed between himself and his wife a sort of vague, semitelepathic, rapport; they had never been able to transmit definite and exact thoughts, but they could clearly comprehend one another's feelings and emotions. He was conscious, now, of Dalla's sympathy for the Proletarian girl.

"Zinganna, I'm going to tell you something that is being kept from the public," he said. "By doing so, I will make it necessary for us to detain you, at least for a few days. I hope you will forgive me, but I think you would forgive me less if I didn't tell you."

"Something's happened to him," she said, her eyes widening and her body tensing.

"Yes, Zinganna. At about 2010 this evening," he said, "Councilman Salgath was murdered."

"Oh!" She leaned back in the chair, closing her eyes. "He's dead?" Then, again, statement instead of question: "He's dead!"

For a long moment, she lay back in the chair, as though trying to re-orient her mind to the fact of Salgath Trod's death, while Vall and Dalla sat watching her. Then she stirred, opened her eyes, looked at the cigarette in her fingers as though she had never seen it before, and leaned forward to stuff it into an ash receiver.

"Who did it?" she asked, the Stone Age savage who had been her ancestor not ten generations ago peeping out of her eyes.

"The men who actually used the needlers are dead," Vall told her. "I killed a couple of them myself. We still have to find the men who planned it. I'd hoped you'd want to help us do that, Zinganna."

He side-glanced to Dalla again; she nodded. The relationship between Zinganna and Salgath Trod hadn't been purely business with her; there had been some real affection. He told her what had happened, and when he reached the point at which Salgath Trod had called Tortha Karf to confess complicity in the slave trade, her lips tightened and she nodded.

"I was afraid it was something like that," she said. "For the last few days, well, ever since the news about the slave trade got out, he's been worried about something. I've always thought somebody had some kind of a hold over him. Different times in the past, he's done things so far against his own political best interests that I've had to believe he was being forced into them. Well, this time they tried to force him too far. What then?"

Vall continued the story. "So we're keeping this hushed up, for a while. The way we're letting it out, Salgath Trod is still alive, on Police Terminal, talking under narco-hypnosis."

She smiled savagely. "And they'll get frightened, and frightened men do foolish things," she finished. She hadn't been a politician's mistress for nothing. "What can I do to help?"

"Tell us everything you can," he said. "Maybe we can be able to take such actions as we would have taken if Salgath Trod had lived to talk to us."

"Yes, of course." She got another cigarette from the case Vall had laid on the table. "I think, though, that you'd better give me a narco-hypnosis. You want to be able to depend on what I'm going to tell you, and I want to be able to remember things exactly."

Vall nodded approvingly and turned to Dalla.

"Can you handle this yourself?" he asked. "There's an audio-visual recorder on now; here's everything you need." He opened the drawers in the table to show her the narco-hypnotic equipment. "And the phone has a whisper mouth-piece; you can call out without worrying about your message getting into Zinganna's subconscious. Well, I'll see you when you're through; you bring Zinganna to Police Terminal; I'll probably be there."

He went out, closing the door behind him, and went down the hall, meeting the officer who had taken charge of the butler and housemaid.

WE'RE having trouble with them, sir," he said. "Hostile. Yelling about their rights, and demanding to see a representative of the Proletarian Protective League."

Vall mentioned the Proletarian Protective League with unflattering vulgarity.

"If they don't cooperate, drag them out and inject them and question them anyhow," he said.

The detective-lieutenant looked worried. "We've been taking a pretty high hand with them as it is," he protested. "It's safer to kill a Citizen than bloody a Prole's nose; they have all sorts of laws to protect them."

"There are all sorts of laws to protect the Paratime Secret," Vall replied. "And I think there are one or two laws against murdering members of the Executive Council. In case P.P.L. makes any trouble, they aren't here; they have faithfully joined their beloved master in his refuge on PolTerm. But one or both of them work for the Organization."

"You're sure of that?"

"The Organization is too thorough not to have had a spy in Salgath's household. It wasn't Zinganna, because she's volunteered to talk to us under narco-hyp. So who does that leave?"

"Well, that's different; that makes them suspects." The lieutenant seemed relieved. "We'll pump that pair out right away."

When he got back to Tortha Karf's office, the Chief was awake, and doodling on his notepad with his multicolor pen. Vall looked at the pad and winced; the Chief was doodling bugs again—red ants with black legs, and blue-and-green beetles. Then he saw that the psychist, Nentrov Dard, was drinking straight 150-proof palm-rum.

"Well, tell me the worst," he said.

"Our boy's memory-obliterated," Nentrov Dard said, draining his glass and filling it again. "And he's plastered with pseudo-memories a foot thick. It'll be five or six ten-days before we can get all that stuff peeled off and get him unblocked. I put him to sleep and had him transposed to Police Terminal. I'm going there myself tomorrow morning, after I've had some sleep, and get to work on him. If you're hoping to get anything useful out of him in time to head off this Council crisis that's building up, just forget it."

"And that leaves us right back with our old friends, the Wizard Traders," Tortha Karf added. "And if they've decided to suspend activities on the Kholghoor Sector, too—" He began drawing a big blue and black spider in the middle of the pad.

Nentrov Dard crushed out his cigar, drank his rum, and got to his feet.

"Well, good night, Chief; Vall. If you decide to wake me up before 1000, send somebody you want to get rid of in a hurry." He walked around the deck and out the side door.

"I hope they don't," Vall said to Tortha Karf. "Really, though, I doubt if they do. This is their chance to pick up a lot of slaves cheaply; the Croutha are too busy to bother haggling. I'm going through to PolTerm, now; when Dalla and Zinganna get through, tell them to join me there."

On Police Terminal, he found Kostran Galth, the agent who had been selected to impersonate Salgath Trod. After calling Zulthran Torv, the mathematician in charge of the Computer Office, and giving him the Esaron time-line designations and Nentrov Dard's ideas about them, he spent about an hour briefing Kostran Galth on the role he was to play. Finally, he undressed and went to bed on a couch in the rest room behind the office.

It was noon when he woke. After showering, shaving and dressing hastily, he went out to the desk for breakfast, which arrived while he was putting a call through to Ranthar Jard, at Nharkan Equivalent.

"Your idea paid off, Chief's Assistant," the Kholghoor SecReg Subchief told him. "The slaves gave us a lot of physical description data on the estate, and told us about new fields that had been cleared, and a dam this Lord Ghromdour was building to flood some new rice-paddies. We located a belt of about five parayears where these improvements had been made; we started boomeranging the whole belt, time-line by time-line. So far, we have ten or fifteen pictures of the main square at Sohram showing Croutha with firearms, and pictures of Wizard Trader camps and conveyer heads on the same time-lines. Here, let me show you; this is from an airboat over the forest outside the equivalent of Sohram."

There was no jungle visible when the view changed; nothing but clusters of steel towers and platforms and buildings that marked conveyer heads, and a large rectangle of red-and-white antigrav-buoys moored to warn air traffic out of the area being boomeranged. The pickup seemed to be pointed downward from the bow of an airboat circling at about ten thousand feet.

"Balls ready to go," a voice called, and then repeated a string of time-line designations. "Estimated return, 1820, give or take four minutes."

"Varth," Ranthar Jard said, evidently out of the boat's radio. "Your telecast is being beamed on Dhergabar Equivalent; Chief's Assistant Verkan is watching. When do you estimate your next return?"

"Any moment, now, sir; we're holding this drop till they rematerialize."

Vall watched unblinkingly, his fork poised halfway to his mouth. Suddenly, about a thousand feet below the eye of the pickup, there was a series of blue flashes and, an instant later, a blossoming of red-and-white parachutes, ejected from the photo-reconnaissance balls that had returned from the Kholghoor Sector.

"All right; drop away," the boat captain called. There was a gush, from underneath, of eight-inch spheres, their conductor-mesh twinkling golden-bright in the sunlight. They dropped in a tight cluster for a thousand or so feet and then flashed and vanished. From the ground, six or eight aircars rose to meet the descending parachutes and catch them.

THE screen went cubist for a moment, and then Ranthar Jard's swarthy, wide-jawed face looked out of it again. He took his pipe from his mouth.

"We'll probably get a positive out of the batch you just saw coming in," he said. "We get one out of about every two drops."

"Message a list of the time-line designations you've gotten so far to Zulthran Torv, at the Computer Office here," Vall said. "He's working on the Esaron Sector dope; we think a pattern can be established. I'll be seeing you in about five hours; I'm rocketing out of here as soon as I get a few more things cleared up."

Zulthran Torv, normally cautious to the degree of pessimism, was jubilant when Vall called him.

"We have something, Vall," he said. "It is, roughly, what Dr. Nentrov suggested—each of the intervals between the designations is a very minute but very exact fraction of the difference between the lesser designation and the base-line designation."

"You have the base-line designation?" Vall demanded.

"Oh, yes. That's what I was telling you. We worked that out from the designations you gave me." He recited it. "And the designations you gave me are—"

Vall wasn't listening to him. He frowned in puzzlement.

"That's not a Fifth Level designation," he said. "That's First Level!"

"That's correct. First Level Abzar Sector."

"Now why in blazes didn't anybody think of that before?" he marveled, and as he did, he knew the answer. Nobody ever thought of the Abzar Sector.

Twelve millennia ago, the world of the First Level had been exhausted; having used up the resources of their home planet, Mars, a hundred thousand years before, the descendants of the population that had migrated across space had repeated on the third planet the devastation of the fourth. The ancestors of Verkan Vall's people had discovered the principle of paratime transposition and had begun to exploit an infinity of worlds on other lines of probability. The people of the First Level Dwarma Sector, reduced by sheer starvation to a tiny handful, had abandoned their cities and renounced their technologies and created for themselves a farm-and-village culture without progress or change or curiosity or struggle or ambition, and a way of life in which every day was like every other day that had been or that would come.

The Abzar people had done neither. They had wasted their resources to the last, fighting bitterly over the ultimate crumbs with fission bombs, and with muskets, and with swords, and with spears and clubs, and finally they had died out, leaving a planet of almost uniform desert dotted with vast empty cities, which even twelve thousand years had hardly begun to obliterate.

So nobody on the Paratime Sector went to the Abzar Sector. There was nothing there—except a hiding-place.

"Well, message that to Subchief Ranthar Jard, Kholghoor Sector at Nharkan Equivalent, and to Subchief Vulthor, Esaron Sector, Novilan Equivalent," Vall said. "And be sure to mark what you send Vulthor 'Immediate attention Deputy Subchief Skordran.'"

That reminded him of something; as soon as he was through with Zulthran, he got out an order in the name of Tortha Karf authorizing Skordran Kirv's promotion on a permanent basis and messaged it out. Something was going to have to be done with Vulthor Tharn, too. A promotion of course—say Deputy Bureau Chief. Hypno-Mech Tape Library at Dhergabar Home Time-Line; there Vulthor's passion for procedure and his caution would be assets instead of liabilities. He called Vlasthor Arph, the Chief's Deputy assigned to him as adjutant.

"I want more troops from ServSec and IndSec," he said. "Go over the TO's and see what can be spared from where; don't strip any time-line, but get a force of the order of about three divisions. And locate all the big antigrav-equipped ship transposition docks on Commercial and Passenger Sectors, and a list of freighters and passenger ships that can be commandeered in a hurry. We think we've spotted the time-line the Organization's using as a base. As soon as we raid a couple of places near Nharkan and Novilan Equivalents, we're going to move in for a planet-wide cleanup."

"I get it, Chief's Assistant. I do everything I can to get ready for a big move, without letting anything leak out. After you strike the first blow, there won't be any security problem, and the lid will be off. In the meantime, I make up a general plan, and alert all our own people. Right?"

"Right. And for your information, the base isn't Fifth Level; it's First Level Abzar." He gave the designation.

Vlasthor Arph chuckled. "Well, think of that! I'd even forgotten there was an Abzar Sector. Shall I tell the reporters that?"

"Fangs of Fasif, no!" Vall fairly howled. Then, curiously: "What reporters? How'd they get onto PolTerm?"

"About fifty or sixty news-service people Chief Tortha sent down here this morning, with orders to prevent them from filing any stories from here but to let them cover the raids, when they come off. We were instructed to furnish them weapons and audio-visual equipment and vocowriters and anything else they needed, and—"

Vall grinned. "That was one I'd never thought of," he admitted. "The old fox is still the old fox. No, tell them nothing; we'll just take them along and show them. Oh, and where are Dr. Hadron Dalla and that girl of Salgath Trod's?"

"They're sleeping, now. Rest Room Eighteen."

DALLA and Zinganna were asleep on a big mound of silk cushions in one corner, their glossy black heads close together and Zinganna's brown arm around Dalla's white shoulder. Their faces were calmly beautiful in repose, and they smiled slightly, as though they were wandering through a happy dream. For a little while, Vall stood looking at them, then he began whistling softly. On the third or fourth bar, Dalla woke and sat up, waking Zinganna, and blinked at him perplexedly.

"What time is it?" she asked.

"About 1245," he told her.

"Ohhh! We just got to sleep," she said. "We're both bushed!"

"You had a hard time. Feel all right after your narco-hyp, Zinganna?"

"It wasn't so bad, and I had a nice sleep. And Dalla . . . Dr. Hadron, I mean—"

"Dalla," Vall's wife corrected. "Remember what I told you?"

"Dalla, then," Zinganna smiled. "Dalla gave me some hypno-treatment, too. I don't feel so badly about Trod, any more."

"Well, look, Zinganna. We're going to have a man impersonate Councilman Salgath on a telecast. The cosmeticians are making him over now. Would you find it too painful to meet him, and talk to him?"

"No, I wouldn't mind. I can criticize the impersonation; remember, I knew Trod very well. You know, I was his hostess, too. I met many of the people with whom he was associated, and they know me. Would things look more convincing if I appeared on the telecast with your man?"

"It certainly would; it would be a great help!" he told her enthusiastically. "Maybe you girls ought to get up now. The telecast isn't till 1930, but there's a lot to be done getting ready."

Dalla yawned. "What I get, trying to be a cop," she said, then caught the other girl's hands and rose, pulling her up. "Come on, Zinna; we have to get to work!"

VALL rose from behind the reading-screen in Ranthar Jard's office, stretching his arms over his head. For almost an hour, he had sat there pushing buttons and twiddling selector and magnification-adjustment knobs, looking at the pictures the Kholghoor-Nharkan cops had taken with auto-return balls dropped over the spatial equivalent of Sohram. One set of pictures, taken at two thousand feet, showed the central square of the city. The effects of the Croutha sack were plainly visible; so were the captives herded together under guard like cattle. By increasing magnification, he looked at groups of the barbarian conquerers, big men with blond or reddish-brown hair, in loose shirts and baggy trousers and rough cowhide buskins. Many of them wore bowl-shaped helmets, some had shirts of ring-mail, all of them carried long straight swords with cross-hilts, and about half of them had pistols thrust through their belts or muskets slung from their shoulders.

The other set of pictures showed the Wizard Trader camps and conveyer heads. In each case, a wide oval had been burned out in the jungle, probably with heavy-duty heat guns. The camps were surrounded with stout wire-mesh fence; in each there were a number of metal prefab-huts, and an inner fenced slave-pen. A trail had been cut from each to a similarly cleared circle farther back in the forest, and in the centers of one or two of these circles he saw the actual conveyer domes. There was a great deal of activity in all of them, and he screwed the magnification-adjustment to the limit to scrutinize each human figure in turn. A few of the men, he was sure, were First Level Citizens; more were either Proles or outtimers. Quite a few of them were of a dark, heavy-featured, black-bearded type.

"Some of these fellows look like Second Level Khiftans," he said. "Rush an individual picture of each one, maximum magnification consistent with clarity, to Dhergabar Equivalent to the transposed to Home Time-Line. You get all the dope from Zulthran Torv?"

"Yes; Abzar Sector," Ranthar Jard said. "I'd never have thought of that. Wonder why they used that series system, though. I'd have tried to spot my operations as completely at random as possible."

"Only thing they could have done," Vall said. "When we get hold of one of their conveyers, we're going to find the control panel's just a mess of arbitrary symbols, and there'll be something like a computer-machine built into the control cabinet, to select the right time line whenever a dial's set or a button pushed, and the only way that could be done would be by establishing some kind of a numerical series. And we were trustingly expecting to locate their base from one of their conveyers! Why, if we give all those people in the pictures narco-hyps, we won't learn the base-line designation; none of them will know it. They just go where the conveyers take them."

"Well, we're all set now," Ranthar Jard said. "I have a plan of attack worked out; subject to your approval, I'm ready to start implementing it now." He glanced at his watch. "The Salgath telecast is over, on Home Time-Line, and in a little while, a transcript will be on this time-line. Want to watch it here, sir?"

THE telecast screen in the living room of Tortha Karf's town apartment was still on; in it, a girl with bright red hair danced slowly to soft music against a background of shifting color. The four men who sat in a semicircle facing it sipped their drinks and watched idly.

"Ought to be getting some sort of public reaction soon," Tortha Karf said, glancing at his watch.

"Well, I'll have to admit, it was done convincingly," Zostha Olv, the Chief Interoffice Coordinator, admitted grudgingly. "I'd have believed it, if I hadn't known the real facts."

"Shooting it against the background of those wide windows was smart," Lovranth Rolk said. "Every schoolchild would recognize that view of the rocketport as being on Police Terminal. And including that girl Zinganna; that was a real masterpiece!"

"I've met her a few times," Elbraz Vark, the Political Liaison Assistant, said. "Isn't she lovely!"

"Good actress, too," Tortha Karf said. "It's not easy to impersonate yourself."

"Well, Kostran Galth did a fine job of acting, too," Lovranth Rolk said. "That was done to perfection—the distinguished politician, supported by his loyal mistress, bravely facing the disgraceful end of his public career."

"You know, I believe I could get that girl a booking with one of the big theatrical companies. Now that Salgath's dead, she'll need somebody to look after her."

"What sharp, furry ears you have, Mr. Elbraz!" Zostha Olv grunted.

The music stopped as though cut off with a knife, and the slim girl with the red hair vanished in a shatter of many colors. When the screen cleared, one of the announcers was looking out of it.

"We interrupt the program for an important newscast of a sensational development in the Salgath affair," he said. "Your next speaker will be Yandar Yadd—"

"I thought you'd managed to get that blabbermouth transposed to PolTerm," Zostha said.

"He wouldn't go," Tortha Karf replied. "Said it was just a trick to get him off Home Time-Line during the Council crisis."

Yandar Yadd had appeared on the screen as the pickup swung about.

". . . Recording ostensibly made by Councilman Salgath on Police Terminal Time-Line, and telecast on Home Time-Line an hour ago. Well, I don't know who he was, but I now have positive proof that he definitely was not Salgath Trod!"

"We're sunk!" Zostha Olv grunted. "He'd never make a statement like that unless he could prove it."

". . . Something suspicious about the whole thing from the beginning," the newsman was saying. "So I checked. If you recall, the actor impersonating Salgath gestured rather freely with his hands, in imitation of a well-known mannerism of the real Salgath Trod; at one point, the ball of his right thumb was presented directly to the pickup. Here's a still of that scene."

He stepped aside, revealing a viewscreen behind him; when he pressed a button, the screen lighted; on it was a stationary picture of Kostran Galth as Salgath Trod, his right hand raised in front of him.

"Now watch this. I'm going to step up the magnification, slowly, so that you can be sure there's no substitution. Camera a little closer, Trath!"

The screen in the background seemed to advance, until it filled the entire screen. Yandar Yadd was still talking, out of the picture; a metal-tipped pointer came into the picture, touching the right thumb, which grew larger and larger until it was the only thing visible.

"Now here," Yandar Yadd's voice continued. "Any of you who are familiar with the ancient science of dactyloscopy will recognize this thumb as having the ridge-pattern known as a twin loop. Even with the high degree of magnification possible with the microgrid screen, we can't bring out the individual ridges, but the pattern is unmistakable. I ask you to memorize that image, while I show you another right thumb print, this time a certified photocopy of the thumb print of the real Salgath Trod." The magnification was reduced a little, a card was moved into the picture, and it was stepped up again. "See, this thumb print is of the type known as a tented arch. Observe the difference."

"That does it!" Zostha Olv cried. "Karf, for the first and last time, let me remind you that I opposed this lunacy from the beginning. Now, what are we going to do next?"

"I suggest that we get to Headquarters as soon as we can," Tortha Karf said. "If we wait too long, we may not be able to get in."

Yandar Yadd was back on the screen, denouncing Tortha Karf passionately. Tortha went over and snapped it off.

"I suggest we transpose to PolTerm," Lovranth Rolk said. "It won't be so easy for them to serve a summons on us there."

"You can go to PolTerm if you want to," Tortha Karf retorted. "I'm going to stay here and fight back, and if they try to serve me with a summons, they'd better send a robot for a process server."

"Fight back!" Zostha Olv echoed. "You can't fight the Council and the whole Management! They'll tear you into inch bits!"

"I can hold them off till Vall's able to raid those Abzar Sector bases," Tortha Karf said. He thought for a moment. "Maybe this is all for the best, after all. If it distracts the Organization's attention—"

I WISH we could have made a boomerang-ball reconnaissance," Ranthar Jard was saying, watching one of the viewscreens in which a film, taken from an airboat transposed to an adjoining Abzar Sector time-line, was being shown. The boat had circled over the Ganges, a mere trickle between wide, deeply cut banks, and was crossing a gullied plain, sparsely grown with thornbush. "The base ought to be about there, but we have no idea what sort of changes this gang has made."

"Well, we couldn't; we didn't dare take the chance of it being spotted. This has to be a complete surprise. It'll be about like the other place, the one the slaves described. There won't be any permanent buildings. This operation only started a few months ago, with the Croutha invasion; it may go on for four or five months, till the Croutha have all their surplus captives sold off. That country," he added, gesturing at the screen, "will be flooded out when the rains come. See how it's suffered from flood-erosion. There won't be a thing there that can't be knocked down and transposed out in a day or so."

"I wish you'd let me go along," Ranthar Jard worried.

"We can't do that, either," Vall said. "Somebody's got to be in charge here, and you know your own people better than I do. Besides, this won't be the last operation like this. Next time, I'll have to stay on Police Terminal and command from a desk; I want first-hand experience with the outtime end of the job, and this is the way I can get it."

He watched the four police girls who were working at the big terrain board showing the area of the Police Terminal time-line around them. They had covered the miniature buildings and platforms and towers with a fine mesh, at a scale-equivalent of fifty feet; each intersection marked the location of a three-foot conveyer ball, loaded with a sleep-gas bomb and rigged with an automatic detonator which would explode it and release the gas as soon as it rematerialized on the Abzar Sector. Higher, on stiff wires that raised them to what represented three thousand feet, were the disks that stood for ten hundred-foot conveyers; they would carry squads of Paratime Police in air-cars and thirty-foot airboats. There was a ring of big two-hundred-foot conveyers a mile out; they would carry the armor and the airborne infantry and the little two-man scooters of the air-cavalry, from the Service and Industrial Sectors. Directly over the spatial equivalent of the Kholghoor Sector Wizard Traders' conveyers was the single disk of Verkan Vall's command conveyer, at a represented five thousand feet, and in a half-mile circle around it were the five news-service conveyers.

"Where's the ship-conveyer?" he asked.

"Actually, it's on antigrav about five miles north of here," one of the girls said. "Representationally, about where Subchief Ranthar's standing."

Another girl added a few more bits to the network that represented the sleep-gas bombs and stepped back, taking off her earphones.

"Everything's in place now, Assistant Verkan," she told him.

"Good. I'm going aboard now," he said. "You can have it, Jard."

He shook hands with Ranthar Jard, who moved to the switch which would activate all the conveyers simultaneously, and accepted the good wishes of the girls at the terrain board. Then he walked to the mesh-covered dome of the hundred-foot conveyer, with the five news-service conveyers surrounding it in as regular a circle as the buildings and towers of the regular conveyer heads would permit. The members of his own detail, smoking and chatting outside, saw him and started moving inside; so did the news people. A public-address speaker began yelping in a hundred voices all over the area, warning those who were going with the conveyers to get aboard. He went in through a door, between two aircars, and on to the central control-desks, going up to a visi-screen over which somebody had crayoned "Novilan EQ." It gave him a view, over the shoulder of a man in the uniform of a field agent third class, of the interior of a conveyer like his own.

HELLO, Assistant Verkan," a voice came out of the speaker under the screen, as the man moved his lips. "Deputy Skordran! Here's Chief's Assistant Verkan, now!"

Skordran Kirv moved in front of the screen as the operator got up from his stool.

"Hello, Vall; we're all set to move out as soon as you give the word," he said. "We're all in position on antigrav."

"That's smart work. We've just finished our gas-bomb net," Vall said. "Going on antigrav now," he added, as he felt the dome lift. "I hope you won't be too disappointed if you draw a blank on your end."

"We realize that they've closed out the whole Esaron Sector," Skordran Kirv, eight thousand odd miles away, replied. "We're taking in a couple of ships; we're going to make a survey all up the coast. There are a lot of other sectors where slaves can be sold in this area."

In the outside viewscreen, tuned to a slowly rotating pick-up on the top of a tower spatially equivalent with a room in a tall building on Second Level Triplanetary Empire Sector, he could see his own conveyer rising vertically, with the news conveyers following, and the troop conveyers, several miles away, coming into position. Finally, they were all placed; he reported the fact to Skordran Kirv and then picked up a hand-phone.

"Everybody ready for transposition?" he called. "On my count. Thirty seconds . . . Twenty seconds . . . Fifteen seconds . . . Five seconds . . . Four seconds . . . Three seconds . . . Two seconds . . . One second, *out!*"

All the screens went gray. The inside of the dome passed into another space-time continuum, even into another kind of space-time. The transposition would take half an hour; that seemed to be the time needed to build up and collapse the transposition field, regardless of the paratemporal distance covered. The dome above and around them vanished; the bare, tower-forested, building-dotted world of Police Terminal vanished, too, into the uniform green of the uninhabited Fifth Level. A planet could take pretty good care of itself, he thought, if people would only leave it alone. Then he began to see the fields and villages of Fourth Level. Cities appeared and vanished, growing higher and vaster as they went across the more civilized Third Level. One was under air attack—there was almost never a paratemporal transposition which did not run through some scene of battle.

He unbuckled his belt and took off his boots and tunic; all around him, the others were doing the same. Sleep-gas didn't have to be breathed; it could enter the nervous system by any orifice or lesion, even a pore or a scratch. A spacesuit was the only protection. One of the detectives helped him on with his metal and plastic armor; before sealing his gauntlets, he reciprocated the assistance, then checked the needler and blaster and the long batonlike ultra-sonic paralyzer on his belt and made sure that the radio and sound-phones in his helmet were working. He hoped that the frantic efforts to gather several thousand spacesuits onto Police Terminal from the Industrial and Commercial and Interplanetary Sectors hadn't started rumors which had gotten to the ears of some of the Organization's ubiquitous agents.

THE country below was already turning to the parched browns and yellows of the Abzar Sector. There was not another of the conveyers in sight, but electronic and mechanical lag in the individual controls and even the distance-difference between them and the central radio control would have prevented them from going into transposition at the same fractional microsecond. The recon-details began piling into their cars. Then the red light overhead winked to green, and the dome flickered and solidified into cold, inert metal. The screens lighted up again, and Vall could see Skordran Kirv, across Asia and the Pacific, getting into his helmet. A dot of light in the center of the under-view screen widened as the mesh under the conveyer irised open around the pickup.

Below, the Organization base—big rectangles of fenced slave-pens, with metal barracks inside; the huge circle of the Kholghoor Sector conveyer-head building, and a smaller structure that must house conveyers to other Abzar Sector time-lines; the workshops and living quarters and hangars and warehouses and docks—was wreathed in white-green mist. The ring of conveyers at three thousand feet were opening and spewing out aircars and airboats; farther away, the greater ring of heavy conveyers were unloading armored and shielded combat-craft. An aircar which must have been above the reach of the gas was streaking away toward the west, with three police cars after it. As he watched, the air around it fairly sizzled blue with the rays of neutron disruption blasters, and then it blew apart. The three police cars turned and came back more slowly. The three-thousand-ton passenger ship which had been hastily fitted with armament was circling about; the great dock conveyer which had brought it was gone, transposed back to Police Terminal to pick up another ship.

He recorded a message announcing the arrival of the taskforce, pulled out the tape and sealed it in a capsule, and put the capsule in a mesh message ball, attaching it to a couple of wires and flipping a switch. The ball flashed and vanished, leaving the wires cleanly sheared off. When it got back to Police Terminal, half an hour later, it would rematerialize, eject a parachute, and turn on a whistle to call attention to itself. Then he sealed on his helmet, climbed into an aircar, and turned on his helmet-radio to speak to the driver. The car lifted a few inches, floated out an open port, and dived downward.

HE landed at the big conveyer-head building. There were spaces for fifty conveyers around it, and all but eight of them were in place. One must have arrived since the gas bombs burst; it was crammed with senseless Kharanda slaves. A couple of Paratime Police officers were towing a tank of sleep-gas around on an antigrav-lifter, maintaining the proper concentration in case any more came in. At the smaller conveyer building, there were no conveyers, only a number of red-lined fifty-foot circles around a central two-hundred-foot circle. The Organization personnel there had been dragged outside, and a group of paracops were sealing it up, installing robot watchmen, and preparing to flood it with gas. At the slave-pens, a string of two-hundred-foot conveyers, having unloaded soldiers and fighting-gear, were coming in to take on unconscious slaves for transposition to Police Terminal. Aircars and airboats were bringing in gassed slavers; they were being shackled and dumped into the slave barracks; as soon as the gas cleared and they could be brought back to consciousness, they would be narco-hypnotized and questioned.

He had finished a tour of the warehouses, looking at the kegs of gunpowder and the casks of brandy, the piles of pig lead, the stacks of cases containing muskets. These must have all come from some low-order handcraft time line. Then there were swords and hatchets and knives that had been made on Industrial Sector—the Organization must be getting them through some legitimate trading company—and mirrors and perfumes and synthetic fiber textiles and cheap jewelry, of similar provenance. It looked as though this stuff had been brought in by ship from somewhere else on this time-line; the warehouses were too far from the conveyers and right beside the ship dock—

There was a tremendous explosion somewhere. Vall and the men with him ran outside, looking about, the sound-phones of their helmets giving them no idea of the source of the sound. One of the policemen pointed, and Vall's eyes followed his arm. The ship that had been transposed in in the big conveyer was falling, blown in half; as he looked, both sections hit the ground several miles away. A strange ship, a freighter, was coming in fast, and as he watched, a blue spark winked from her bow as a heavy-duty blaster was activated. There was another explosion, overhead; they all ran for shelter as Vall's command-conveyer disintegrated into falling scrap metal. At once, all the other conveyers which were on antigrav began flashing and vanishing. That was the right, the only, thing to do, he knew. But it was leaving him and his men isolated and under attack.

So that was it," Dalgroth Sorn, the Paratime Commissioner for Security said, relieved, when Tortha Karf had finished.

"Yes, and I'll repeat it under narco-hyp, too," Tortha Karf added.

"Oh, don't talk that way, Karf," Dalgroth Sorn scolded. He was at least a century Tortha Karf's senior; he had the face of an elderly and sore-toothed lion. "You wanted to keep this prisoner under wraps till you could mind-pump him, and you wanted the Organization to think Salgath was alive and talking. I approve both. But—"

He gestured to the viewscreen across the room, tuned to a pickup back of the Speaker's chair in the Council Chamber. Tortha Karf turned a knob to bring the sound volume up.

"Well, I'm raising this point," a member from the Management seats in the center was saying, "because these earlier charges of illegal arrest and illegal detention are part and parcel with the charges growing out of the tele-cast last evening."

"Well, that telecast was a fake; that's been established," somebody on the left heckled.

"Councilman Salgath's confession on the evening of One-Six-Two-Day wasn't a fake," the Management supporter, Nanthav Skov, retorted.

"Well, then why was it necessary to fake the second one?"

A light began winking on the big panel in front of the Speaker, Asthar Varn.

"I recognize Councilman Hasthor Flan," Asthar said.

"I believe I can construct a theory that will explain that," Hasthor Flan said. "I suggest that when the Paratime Police were questioning Councilman Salgath under narco-hypnosis, he made statements incriminating either the Paratime Police as a whole or some member of the Paratime Police whom Tortha Karf had to protect—say somebody like Assistant Verkan. So they just killed him, and made up this imposter—"

Tortha Karf began, alphabetically, to blaspheme every god he had ever heard of. He had only gotten as far as a Fourth Level deity named Allah when a red light began flashing in front of Asthar Varn, and the voice of a page-robot, amplified, roared:

"Point of special urgency! Point of special urgency! It has been requested that the news telecast screen be activated at once, with playback to 1107. An important bulletin has just come in from Nagorabar, Home Time-Line, on the Indian subcontinent—"

"You can stop swearing now, Karf," Dalgroth Sorn grinned. "I think this is it."

KOSTRAN Galth sat on the edge of the couch, with one arm around Zin-ganna's waist; on the other side of him, Hadron Dalla lay at full length, her el-bows propped and her chin in her hands. The screen in front of them showed a fading sunset, although it was only a little past noon at Dhergabar Equiva-lent. A dark ship was coming slowly in against the red sky; in the center of a wire-fenced compound a hundred-foot conveyer hung on antigrav twenty feet from the ground, and beyond, a long metal prefab-shed was spilling light from open doors and windows.

"That crowd that was just taken in won't be finished for a couple of hours," a voice was saying. "I don't know how much they'll be able to tell; the psychists say they're all telling about the same stories. What those stories are, of course, I'm not able to repeat. After the trouble caused by a certain news commentator who shall be nameless—he's not connected with this news service, I'm happy to say—we're all leaning over backward to keep from breaking Paratime Police security.

"One thing; shortly after the arrival of the second ship from Police Terminal—and believe me, that ship came in just in the nick of time!—the dead Abzar city which the criminals were using as their main base for this time line, and from which they launched the air attack against us, was located, and now word has come in that it is entirely in the hands of the Paratime Police. Personally, I doubt if a great deal of information has been gotten from any prisoners taken there. The lengths to which this Organization went to keep their own people in ignorance is simply unbelievable."

A man appeared for a moment in the lighted doorway of the shed, then stepped outside.

"Look!" Dalla cried. "There's Vall!"

"There's Assistant Verkan now," the commentator agreed. "Chief's Assistant, would you mind saying a few words, here? I know you're a busy man, sir, but you are also the public hero of Home Time-Line, and everybody will be glad if you say something to them—"

TORTHA Karf sealed the door of the apartment behind them, then activated one of the robot servants and sent it gliding out of the room for drinks. Verkan Vall took off his belt and holster and laid them aside, then dropped into a deep chair with a sigh of relief. Dalla advanced to the middle of the room and stood looking about in surprised delight.

"Didn't expect this, from the mess outside?" Vall asked. "You know, you really are on the paracops, now. Nobody off the Force knows about this hideout of the Chief's."

"You'd better find a place like this, too," Tortha Karf advised. "From now on, you'll have about as much privacy at that apartment in Turquoise Towers as you'd enjoy on the stage of Dhergabar Opera House."

"Just what is my new position?" Vall asked, hunting his cigarette case out of his tunic. "Duplicate Chief of Paratime Police?"

The robot came back with three tall glasses and a refrigerated decanter on its top. It stopped in front of Tortha Karf and slewed around on its treads; he filled a glass and sent it to the chair where Dalla had seated herself; when she got a drink, she sent it to Vall. Vall sent it back to Tortha Karf, who turned it off.

"No; you have the modifier in the wrong place. You're Chief of Duplicate Paratime Police. You take the setup you have now, and expand it; continue the present lines of investigation, and be ready to exploit anything new that comes up. You won't bother with any of this routine flying-saucer-scare stuff; just handle the Organization business. That'll keep you busy for a long time, I'm afraid."

"I notice you slammed down on the first Council member who began shouting about how you'd wiped out the Great Paratemporal Crime-Ring," Vall said.

"Yes. It isn't wiped out, and it won't be wiped out for a long time. I shall be unspeakably delighted if, when I turn my job over to you, you have it wiped out. And even then, there'll be a loose end to pick up every now and then till you retire."

"We have Council and the Management with us now," Vall said. "This was the first secret session of Executive Council in over two thousand years. And I thought I'd drop dead when they passed that motion to submit themselves to narco-hypnosis."

"A few Councilmen are going to drop dead before they can be narco-hypped," Dalla prophesied over the rim of her glass.

"A few have already. I have a list of about a dozen of them who have had fatal accidents or committed suicide, or just died or vanished since the news of your raid broke. Four of them I saw, on the screen, jump up and run out as soon as the news came in, on One-Six-Five Day. And a lot of other people; our friend Yandar Yadd's dropped out of sight, for one. You heard what we got out of those servants of Salgath Trod's?"

"I didn't," Dalla said. "What?"

"Both spies for the Organization. They reported to a woman named Far-illa, who ran a fortune-telling parlor in the Prole district. Her occult powers didn't warn her before we sent a squad of plain-clothes men for her. That was an entirely illegal arrest, by the way, but it netted us a list of about three hundred prominent political, business and social persons whose servants have been reporting to her. She thought she was working for a telecast gossipist."

"That's why we have a new butler, darling," Vall interrupted. "Kandagro was reporting on us."

WHO did she pass the reports on to?" Dalla asked.

Tortha Karf beamed. "She thinks more like a cop every time I talk to her," he told Vall. "You better appoint her your Special Assistant. Why, about 1800 every day, some Prole would come in, give the recognition sign, and get the day's accumulation. We only got one of them, a fourteen-year-old girl. We're having some trouble getting her deconditioned to a point where she can be hypnotized into talking; by the time we do, they'll have everything closed out, I suppose. What's the latest from Abzar Sector? I missed the last report in the rush to get to this Council session."

"All stalled. We're still boomeranging the sector, but it's about five billion time-lines deep, and the pattern for the Kholghoor and Esaron Sectors doesn't seem to apply. I think they have a lot of these Abzar time-lines close together, and they get from one to another via some terminal on Fifth Level."

Tortha Karf nodded. It was impossible to make a transposition of less than ten parayears—a hundred thousand time-lines. It was impossible that the field could build and collapse that soon.

"We also think that this Abzar time-line was only used for the Croutha-Wizard Trader operation. Nothing we found there was more than a couple of months old; nothing since the last rainy season in India, for instance. Everything was cleaned out on Skordran Kirv's end."

"Tell him to try the Mississippi, Missouri and Ohio Valleys," Tortha Karf said. "A lot of those slaves are sure to have been sold to Second Level Khiftan Sector."

"Well, it looks as though our vacation's out the window for a long time," Dalla said resignedly.

"Why don't you and Vall go to my farm, on Fifth Level Sicily," Tortha Karf suggested. "I own the whole island on that time-line, and you can always be reached in a hurry if anything comes up."

"We could have as much fun there as on the Dwarma Sector," Dalla said. "Chief, could we take a couple of friends along?"

"Well, who?"

"Zinganna and Kostran Galth," she replied. "They've gotten interested in one another; they're talking about a tentative marriage."

"It'll have to be mighty tentative," Vall said. "Kostran Galth can't marry a Prole."

"She won't be a Prole very long. I'm going to adopt her as my sister."

Tortha Karf looked at her sharply. "You sure you know what you're doing, Dalla?" he asked.

"Of course I'm sure. I know that girl better than she knows herself. I narco-hypped her, remember. Zinna's the kind of a sister I've always wished I'd had."

"Well, that's all right then. But about this marriage. She was in love with Salgath Trod," Tortha Karf said. "Now, she's identifying Agent Kostran with him—"

"She was in love with the kind of man Salgath could have been if he hadn't gotten into this Organization filth," Dalla replied. "Galth is that kind of a man. They'll get along all right."

"Well, she'll qualify on IQ and general psych rating for Citizenship, I'll say that. And she's the kind of girl I like to see my boys take up with. Like you, Dalla. Yes, of course; take them along with you. Sicily's big enough that two couples won't get in each other's way."

A phone-robot, its slender metal stem topped by a metal globe, slid into the room on its ball-rollers, moving falteringly, like a blind man. It could sense Tortha Karf's electro-encephalic wave-patterns, but it was having trouble locating the source. They all sat motionless, waiting; finally it came over to Tortha Karf's chair and stopped. He unhooked the phone and held a lengthy whispered conversation with somebody before replacing it.

"Now, there," he explained to Dalla. "That's a sample of why we have to set up this duplicate organization. Revolution just broke out at Ftanna, on Third Level Tsorshay Sector; a lot of our people, mostly tourists and students, are cut off from their conveyers by street fighting. Going to be a pretty bloody business getting them out." He finished his drink and got to his feet. "Sit still; I just have to make a few screen-calls. Send the robot for something to eat, Vall. I'll be right back."

Introduction to
"Temple Trouble"

In "Temple Trouble" we get an insider's view of paratime commercial exploitation, and see that sometimes not even a good thing is good enough.

TEMPLE TROUBLE

THROUGH a haze of incense and altar smoke, Yat-Zar looked down from his golden throne at the end of the dusky, many-pillared temple. Yat-Zar was an idol, of gigantic size and extraordinarily good workmanship; he had three eyes, made of turquoises as big as doorknobs, and six arms. In his three right hands, from top to bottom, he held a sword with a flame-shaped blade, a jeweled object of vaguely phallic appearance, and, by the ears, a rabbit, In his left hands were a bronze torch with burnished copper flames, a big goblet, and a pair of scales with an egg in one pan balanced against a skull in the other. He had a long bifurcate beard made of gold wire, feet like a bird's, and other rather startling anatomical features. His throne was set upon a stone plinth about twenty feet high, into the front of which a doorway opened; behind him was a wooden screen, elaborately gilded and painted.

Directly in front of the idol, Ghullam the high priest knelt on a big blue and gold cushion. He wore a gold-fringed robe of dark blue, and a tall conical gold miter, and a bright blue false beard, forked like the idol's golden one; he was intoning a prayer, and holding up, in both hands, for divine inspection and approval, a long curved knife. Behind him, about thirty feet away, stood a square stone altar, around which four of the lesser priests, in light blue robes with less gold fringe and dark-blue false beards, were busy with the preliminaries to the sacrifice. At considerable distance, about halfway down the length of the temple, some two hundred worshipers—a few substantial citizens in gold-fringed tunics, artisans in tunics without gold fringe, soldiers in mail hauberks and plain steel caps, one officer in ornately gilded armor, a number of peasants in nondescript smocks, and women of all classes—were beginning to prostrate themselves on the stone floor.

Ghullam rose to his feet, bowing deeply to Yat-Zar and holding the knife extended in front of him, and backed away toward the altar. As he did, one of the lesser priests reached into a fringed and embroidered sack and pulled out a live rabbit, a big one, obviously of domestic breed, holding it by the ears while one of his fellows took it by the hind legs. A third priest caught up a silver pitcher, while the fourth fanned the altar fire with a sheet-silver fan. As they began chanting antiphonally, Ghullam turned and quickly whipped the edge of his knife across the rabbit's throat. The priest with the pitcher stepped in to catch the blood, and when the rabbit was bled, it was laid on the fire. Ghullam and his four assistants all shouted together, and the congregation shouted in response.

The high priest waited as long as was decently necessary and then, holding the knife in front of him, stepped around the prayer-cushion and went through the door under the idol, into the Holy of Holies. A boy in novice's white robes met him and took the knife, carrying it reverently to a fountain for washing. Eight or ten under-priests, sitting at a long table, rose and bowed, then sat down again and resumed their eating and drinking. At another table, a half-dozen upper priests nodded to him in casual greeting.

Crossing the room, Ghullam went to the Triple Veil in front of the House of Yat-Zar, where only the highest of the priesthood might go, and parted the curtains, passing through, until he came to the great gilded door. Here he fumbled under his robe and produced a small object like a mechanical pencil, inserting the pointed end in a tiny hole in the door and pressing on the other end. The door opened, then swung shut behind him, and as it locked itself, the lights came on within. Ghullam removed his miter and his false beard, tossing them aside on a table, then undid his sash and peeled out of his robe. His regalia discarded, he stood for a moment in loose trousers and a soft white shirt, with a pistol-like weapon in a shoulder holster under his left arm—no longer Ghullam the high priest of Yat-Zar, but now Stranor Sleth, resident agent on this time-line of the Fourth Level Proto-Aryan Sector for the Transtemporal Mining Corporation. Then he opened a door at the other side of the anteroom and went to the antigrav shaft, stepping over the edge and floating downward.

THERE were temples of Yat-Zar on every time-line of the Proto-Aryan Sector, for the worship of Yat-Zar was ancient among the Hulgun people of that area of paratime, but there were only a few which had such installations as this, and all of them were owned and operated by Transtemporal Mining, which had the fissionable ores franchise for this sector. During the ten elapsed centuries since Transtemporal had begun operations on this sector, the process had become standardized. A few First Level paratimers would transpose to a selected time-line and abduct an upper-priest of Yat-Zar, preferably the high priest of the temple at Yoldav or Zurb. He would be drugged and transposed to the First Level, where he would receive hypnotic indoctrination and, while unconscious, have an operation performed on his ears which would enable him to hear sounds well above the normal audible range. He would be able to hear the shrill sonar-cries of bats, for instance, and, more important, he would be able to hear voices when the speaker used a First Level audio-frequency step-up phone. He would also receive a memory-obliteration from the moment of his abduction, and a set of pseudo-memories of a visit to the Heaven of Yat-Zar, on the other side of the sky. Then he would be returned to his own time-line and left on a mountain top far from his temple, where an unknown peasant, leading a donkey, would always find him, return him to the temple, and then vanish inexplicably.

Then the priest would begin hearing voices, usually while serving at the altar. They would warn of future events, which would always come to pass exactly as foretold. Or they might bring tidings of things happening at a distance, the news of which would not arrive by normal means for days or even weeks. Before long, the holy man, who had been carried alive to the Heaven of Yat-Zar, would acquire a most awesome reputation as a prophet, and would speedily rise to the very top of the priestly hierarchy.

Then he would receive two commandments from Yat-Zar. The first would ordain that all lower priests must travel about from temple to temple, never staying longer than a year at any one place. This would ensure a steady influx of newcomers personally unknown to the local upper-priests, and many of them would be First Level paratimers. Then, there would be a second commandment: A house must be built for Yat-Zar, against the rear wall of each temple. Its dimensions were minutely stipulated; its walls were to be of stone, without windows, and there was to be a single door, opening into the Holy of Holies, and before the walls were finished, the door was to be barred from within. A triple veil of brocaded fabric was to be hung in front of this door. Sometimes such innovations met with opposition from the more conservative members of the hierarchy; when they did, the principal objector would be seized with a sudden and violent illness; he would recover if and when he withdrew his objections.

Very shortly after the House of Yat-Zar would be completed, strange noises would be heard from behind the thick walls. Then, after a while, one of the younger priests would announce that he had been commanded in a vision to go behind the veil and knock upon the door. Going behind the curtains, he would use his door-activator to let himself in, and return by paratime-conveyer to the First Level to enjoy a well-earned vacation. When the high priest would follow him behind the veil, after a few hours, and find that he had vanished, it would be announced as a miracle. A week later, an even greater miracle would be announced. The young priest would return from behind the Triple Veil, clad in such raiment as no man had ever seen, and bearing in his hands a strange box. He would announce that Yat-Zar had commanded him to build a new temple in the mountains, at a place to be made known by the voice of the god speaking out of the box.

This time, there would be no doubts and no objections. A procession would set out, headed by the new revelator bearing the box, and when the clicking voice of the god spoke rapidly out of it, the site would be marked and work would begin. No local labor would ever be employed on such temples; the masons and woodworkers would be strangers, come from afar and speaking a strange tongue, and when the temple was completed, they would never be seen to leave it. Men would say that they had been put to death by the priests and buried under the altar to preserve the secrets of the god. And there would always be an idol to preserve the secrets of the god. And there would always be an idol of Yat-Zar, obviously of heavenly origin, since its workmanship was beyond the powers of any local craftsman. The priests of such a temple would be exempt, by divine decree, from the rule of yearly travel.

Nobody, of course, would have the least idea that there was a uranium mine in operation under it, shipping ore to another time-line. The Hulgun people knew nothing about uranium, and neither did they as much as dream that there were other time-lines. The secret of paratime transposition belonged exclusively to the First Level civilization which had discovered it; and it was a secret that was guarded well.

STRANOR Sleth, dropping to the bottom of the antigrav shaft, cast a hasty and instinctive glance to the right, where the freight conveyers were. One was gone, taking its cargo over hundreds of thousands of parayears to the First Level. Another had just returned empty, and a third was receiving its cargo from the robot mining machines far back under the mountain. Two young men and a girl, in First Level costumes, sat at a bank of instruments and visor-screens, handling the whole operation, and six or seven armed guards, having inspected the newly arrived conveyer and finding that it had picked up nothing inimical en route, were relaxing and lighting cigarettes. Three of them, Stranor Sleth noticed, wore the green uniforms of the Paratime Police.

"When did those fellows get in?" he asked the people at the control desk, nodding toward the green-clad newcomers.

"About ten minutes ago, on the passenger conveyer," the girl told him. "The Big Boy's here. Brannad Klav. And a Paratime Police officer. They're in your office."

"Uh huh; I was expecting that," Stranor Sleth nodded. Then he turned down the corridor to the left.

Two men were waiting for him in his office. One was short and stocky, with an angry, impatient face—Brannad Klav, Transtemporal's vice president in charge of operations. The other was tall and slender with handsome and entirely expressionless features; he wore a Paratime Police officer's uniform, with the blue badge of hereditary nobility on his breast, and carried a sigma-ray needled in a belt holster.

"Were you waiting long, gentlemen?" Stranor Sleth asked. "I was holding Sunset Sacrifice up in the temple."

"No, we just got here," Brannad Klav said. "This is Verkan Vall, Mavrad of Nerros, special assistant to Chief Tortha of the Paratime Police, Stranor Sleth, our resident agent here."

Stranor Sleth touched hands with Verkan Vall.

"I've heard a lot about you, sir," he said. "Everybody working in paratime has, of course. I'm sorry we have a situation here that calls for your presence, but since we have, I'm glad you're here in person. You know what our trouble is, I suppose?"

"In a general way," Verkan Vall replied. "Chief Tortha and Brannad Klav have given me the main outline, but I'd like to have you fill in the details."

"Well, I told you everything," Brannad Klav interrupted impatiently. "It's just that Stranor's let this blasted local king, Kurchuk, get out of control. If I—" He stopped short, catching sight of the shoulder holster under Stranor Sleth's left arm. "Were you wearing that needler up in the temple?" he demanded.

"You're blasted right I was!" Stranor Sleth retorted. "And any time I can't arm myself for my own protection on this time-line, you can have my resignation. I'm not getting into the same jam as those people at Zurb."

"Well, never mind about that," Verkan Vall intervened. "Of course Stranor Sleth has a right to arm himself; I wouldn't think of being caught without a weapon on this time-line, myself. Now, Stranor, suppose you tell me what's been happening, here, from the beginning of this trouble."

"It started, really, about five years ago, when Kurchuk, the King of Zurb, married this Chuldun princess, Darith, from the country over beyond the Black Sea, and made her his queen, over the heads of about a dozen daughters of the local nobility, whom he'd married previously. Then he brought in this Chuldun scribe, Labdurg, and made him Overseer of the Kingdom—roughly, prime minister. There was a lot of dissatisfaction about that, and for a while it looked as though he was going to have a revolution on his hands, but he brought in about five thousand Chuldun mercenaries, all archers—these Hulguns can't shoot a bow worth beans—so the dissatisfaction died down, and so did most of the leaders of the disaffected group. The story I get is that this Labdurg arranged the marriage in the first place. It looks to me as though the Chuldun emperor is intending to take over the Hulgun kingdoms, starting with Zurb.

"Well, these Chulduns all worship a god called Muz-Azin. Muz-Azin is a crocodile with wings like a bat and a lot of knife blades in his tail. He makes this Yat-Zar look downright beautiful. So do his habits. Muz-Azin fancies human sacrifices. The victims are strung up by the ankles on a triangular frame and lashed to death with iron-barbed whips. Nasty sort of a deity, but this is a nasty time-line. The people here get a big kick out of watching these sacrifices. Much better show than our bunny-killing. The victims are usually criminals, or overage or incorrigible slaves, or prisoners of war.

"Of course, when the Chulduns began infiltrating the palace, they brought in their crocodile-god, too, and a flock of priests, and King Kurchuk let them set up a temple in the palace. Naturally, we preached against this heathen idolatry in our temples, but religious bigotry isn't one of the numerous imperfections of this sector. Everybody's deity is as good as anybody else's—indifferentism, I believe, is the theological term. Anyhow, on that basis things went along fairly well, till two years ago, when we had this run of bad luck."

"Bad luck!" Brannad Klav snorted. "That's the standing excuse of every incompetent!"

"Go on, Stranor; what sort of bad luck?" Verkan Vall asked.

"Well, first we had a drought, beginning in early summer, that burned up most of the grain crop. Then, when that broke, we got heavy rains and hailstorms and floods, and that destroyed what got through the dry spell. When they harvested what little was left, it was obvious there'd be a famine, so we brought in a lot of grain by conveyer and distributed it from the temples—miraculous gift of Yat-Zar, of course. Then the main office on First Level got scared about flooding this time-line with a lot of unaccountable grain and were afraid we'd make the people suspicious, and ordered it stopped.

"Then Kurchuk, and I might add that the kingdom of Zurb was the hardest hit by the famine, ordered his army mobilized and started an invasion of the Jumdun country, south of the Carpathians, to get grain. He got his army chopped up, and only about a quarter of them got back, with no grain. You ask me, I'd say that Labdurg framed it to happen that way. He advised Kurchuk to invade in the first place, and I mentioned my suspicion that Chombrog, the Chuldun emperor, is planning to move in on the Hulgun kingdoms. Well, what would be smarter than to get Kurchuk's army smashed in advance?"

"How did the defeat occur?" Verkan Vall asked. "Any suspicion of treachery?"

"Nothing you could put your finger on, except that the Jumduns seemed to have pretty good intelligence about Kurchuk's invasion route and battle plans. It could have been nothing worse than stupid tactics on Kurchuk's part. See, these Hulguns, and particularly the Zurb Hulguns, are spearmen. They fight in a fairly thin line, with heavy-armed infantry in front and light infantry with throwing-spears behind. The nobles fight in light chariots, usually at the center of the line, and that's where they were at this Battle of Jorm. Kurchuk himself was at the center, with his Chuldun archers massed around him.

"The Jumduns use a lot of cavalry, with long swords and lances, and a lot of big chariots with two javelin men and a driver. Well, instead of ramming into Kurchuk's center, where he had his archers, they hit the extreme left and folded it up, and then swung around behind and hit the right from the rear. All the Chuldun archers did was stand fast around the king and shoot anybody who came close to them; they were left pretty much alone. But the Hulgun spearmen were cut to pieces. The battle ended with Kurchuk and his nobles and his archers making a fighting retreat, while the Jumdun cavalry were chasing the spearmen every which way and cutting them down or lancing them as they ran.

"Well, whether it was Labdurg's treachery or Kurchuk's stupidity, in either case, it was natural for the archers to come off easiest and the Hulgun spearmen to pay the butcher's bill. But try and tell these knuckle-heads anything like that! Muz-Azin protected the Chulduns, and Yat-Zar let the Hulguns down, and that was all there was to it. The Zurb temple started losing worshipers, particularly the families of the men who didn't make it back from Jorm.

"If that had been all there'd been to it, though, it still wouldn't have hurt the mining operations, and we could have gotten by. But what really tore it was when the rabbits started to die." Stranor Sleth picked up a cigar from his desk and bit the end, spitting it out disgustedly. "Tularemia, of course," he said, touching his lighter to the tip. "When that hit, they started going over to Muz-Azin in droves, not only at Zurb but all over the Six Kingdoms. You ought to have seen the house we had for Sunset Sacrifice this evening! About two hundred, and we used to get two thousand. It used to be all two men could do to lift the offering box at the door, afterward, and all the money we took in tonight I could put in one pocket!" The high priest used language that would have been considered unclerical even among the Hulguns.

Verkan Vall nodded. Even without the quickie hypno-mech he had taken for this sector, he knew that the rabbit was domesticated among the Proto-Aryan Hulguns and was their chief meat animal. Hulgun rabbits were even a minor import on the First Level, and could be had at all the better restaurants in cities like Dhergabar. He mentioned that.

"That's not the worst of it," Stranor Sleth told him. "See, the rabbit's sacred to Yat-Zar. Not taboo; just sacred. They have to use a specially consecrated knife to kill them—consecrating rabbit knives has always been an item of temple revenue—and they must say a special prayer before eating them. We could have gotten around the rest of it, even the Battle of Jorm—punishment by Yat-Zar for the sin of apostasy—but Yat-Zar just wouldn't make rabbits sick. Yat-Zar thinks too well of rabbits to do that, and it's not been any use claiming he would. So there you are."

"Well, I take the attitude that this situation is the result of your incompetence," Brannad Klav began, in a bullyragging tone. "You're not only the high priest of this temple, you're the acknowledged head of the religion in all the Hulgun kingdoms. You should have had more hold on the people than to allow anything like this to happen."

"Hold on the people!" Stranor Sleth fairly howled, appealing to Verkan Vall. "What does he think a religion is, on this sector, anyhow? You think these savages dreamed up that six-armed monstrosity, up there, to express their yearning for higher things, or to symbolize their moral ethos, or as a philosophical escape-hatch from the dilemma of causation? They never even heard of such matters. On this sector, gods are strictly utilitarian. As long as they take care of their worshipers, they get their sacrifices; when they can't put out, they have to get out. How do you suppose these Chulduns, living in the Caucasus Mountains, got the idea of a god like a crocodile, anyhow? Why, they got it from Homran traders, people from down in the Nile Valley. They had a god, once, something basically like a billy goat, but he let them get licked in a couple of battles, so out he went. Why, all the deities on this sector have hyphenated names, because they're combinations of several deities, worshiped in one person. Do you know anything about the history of this sector?" he asked the Paratime Police officer.

"Well, it develops from an alternate probability of what we call the Nilo-Mesopotamian Basic sector-group," Verkan Vall said. "On most Nilo-Mesopotamian sectors, like the Macedonian Empire Sector, or the Alexandrian-Roman or Alexandrian Punic or Indo-Turanian or Europo-American, there was an Aryan invasion of Eastern Europe and Asia Minor about four thousand elapsed years ago. On this sector, the ancestors of the Aryans came in about fifteen centuries earlier, as neolithic savages, about the time that the Sumerian and Egyptian civilizations were first developing, and overran all southeast Europe, Asia Minor and the Nile Valley. They developed to the Bronze-Age culture of the civilizations they overthrew, and then, more slowly, to an Iron-Age culture. About two thousand years ago, they were using hardened steel and building large stone cities, just as they do now. At that time, they reached cultural stasis. But as for their religious beliefs, you've described them quite accurately. A god is only worshiped as long as the people think him powerful enough to aid and protect them; when they lose that confidence, he is discarded and the god of some neighboring people is adopted instead." He turned to Brannad Klav. "Didn't Stranor report this situation to you when it first developed?" he asked. "I know he did; he speaks of receiving shipments of grain by conveyer for temple distribution. Then why didn't you report it to Paratime Police? That's what we have a Paratime Police Force for."

"Well, yes, of course, but I had enough confidence in Stranor Sleth to think that he could handle the situation himself. I didn't know he'd gone slack—"

"Look, I can't make weather, even if my parishoners think I can," Stranor Sleth defended himself. "And I can't make a great military genius out of a blockhead like Kurchuk. And I can't immunize all the rabbits on this time-line against tularemia, even if I'd had any reason to expect a tularemia epidemic, which I hadn't because the disease is unknown on this sector; this is the only outbreak of it anybody's ever heard of on any Proto-Aryan time-line."

"No, but I'll tell you what you could have done," Verkan Vall told him. "When this Kurchuk started to apostatize, you could have gone to him at the head of a procession of priests, all paratimers and all armed with energy-weapons, and pointed out his spiritual duty to him, and if he gave you any back talk, you could have pulled out that needler and rayed him down and then cried, 'Behold the vengeance of Yat-Zar upon the wicked king!' I'll bet any sum at any odds that his successor would have thought twice about going over to Muz-Azin, and none of these other kings would have even thought once about it."

"Ha, that's what I wanted to do!" Stranor Sleth exclaimed. "And who stopped me? I'll give you just one guess."

"Well, it seems there was slackness here, but it wasn't Stranor Sleth who was slack," Verkan Vall commented.

"Well! I must say; I never thought I'd hear an officer of the Paratime Police criticizing me for trying to operate inside the Paratime Transposition Code!" Brannad Klav exclaimed.

Verkan Vall, sitting on the edge of Stranor Sleth's desk, aimed his cigarette at Brannad Klav like a blaster.

"Now, look," he began. "There is one, and only one, inflexible law regarding outtime activities. The secret of paratime transposition must be kept inviolate, and any activity tending to endanger it is prohibited. That's why we don't allow the transposition of any object of extraterrestrial origin to any time-line on which space travel has not been developed. Such an object may be preserved, and then, after the local population begin exploring the planet from whence it came, there will be dangerous speculations and theories as to how it arrived on Terra at such an early date. I came within inches, literally, of getting myself killed, not long ago, cleaning up the result of a violation of that regulation. For the same reason, we don't allow the export, to outtime natives, of manufactured goods too far in advance of their local culture. That's why, for instance, you people have to hand-finish all those big Yat-Zar idols, to remove traces of machine work. One of those things may be around, a few thousand years from now, when these people develop a mechanical civilization. But as far as raying down this Kurchuk is concerned, these Hulguns are completely nonscientific. They wouldn't have the least idea what happened. They'd believe that Yat-Zar struck him dead, as gods on this plane of culture are supposed to do, and if any of them noticed the needler at all, they'd think it was just a holy amulet of some kind."

"But the law is the law—" Brannad Klav began.

Verkan Vall shook his head. "Brannad, as I understand, you were promoted to your present position on the retirement of Salvan Marth, about ten years ago; up to that time, you were in your company's financial department. You were accustomed to working subject to the First Level Commercial Regulation Code. Now, any law binding upon our people at home, on the First Level, is inflexible. It has to be. We found out, over fifty centuries ago, that laws have to be rigid and without discretionary powers in administration in order that people may be able to predict their effect and plan their activities accordingly. Naturally, you became conditioned to operating in such a climate of legal inflexibility.

"But in paratime, the situation is entirely different. There exist, within the range of the Ghaldron-Hesthor paratemporal-field generator, a number of time-lines of the order of ten to the hundred-thousandth power. In effect, that many different worlds. In the past ten thousand years, we have visited only the tiniest fraction of these, but we have found everything from time-lines inhabited only by subhuman ape-men to Second Level civilizations which are our own equal in every respect but knowledge of paratemporal transposition. We even know of one Second Level civilization which is approaching the discovery of an interstellar hyperspatial drive, something we've never even come close to. And in between are every degree of savagery, barbarism and civilization. Now, it's just not possible to frame any single code of laws applicable to conditions on all of these. The best we can do is prohibit certain flagrantly immoral types of activity, such as slave-trading, introduction of new types of narcotic drugs, or out-and-out piracy and brigandage. If you're in doubt as to the legality of anything you want to do outtime, go to the Judicial Section of the Paratime Commission and get an opinion on it. That's where you made your whole mistake. You didn't find out just how far it was allowable for you to go."

He turned to Stranor Sleth again. "Well, that's the background, then. Now tell me about what happened yesterday at Zurb."

"Well, a week ago, Kurchuk came out with this decree closing our temple at Zurb and ordering his subjects to perform worship and make money offerings to Muz-Azin. The Zurb temple isn't a mask for a mine; Zurb's too far south for the uranium deposits. It's just a center for propaganda and that sort of thing. But they have a House of Yat-Zar, and a conveyer, and most of the upper-priests are paratimers. Well, our man there, Tammand Drav, alias Khoram, defied the king's order, so Kurchuk sent a company of Chuldun archers to close the temple and arrest the priests. Tammand Drav got all his people who were in the temple at the time into the House of Yat-Zar and transposed them back to the First Level. He had orders"—Stranor Sleth looked meaningly at Brannad Klav—"not to resist with energy-weapons or even ultrasonic paralyzers. And while we're on the subject of letting the local yokels see too much, about fifteen of the under-priests he took to the First Level were Hulgun natives."

"Nothing wrong about that; they'll get memory-obliteration and pseudo-memory treatment," Verkan Vall said. "But he should have been allowed to needle about a dozen of those Chulduns. Teach the beggars to respect Yat-Zar in the future. Now, how about the six priests who were outside the temple at the time? All but one were paratimers. We'll have to find out about them, and get them out of Zurb."

"That'll take some doing," Stranor Sleth said. "And it'll have to be done before sunset tomorrow. They are all in the dungeon of the palace citadel, and Kurchuk is going to give them to the priests of Muz-Azin to be sacrificed tomorrow evening."

"How'd you learn that?" Verkan Vall asked.

"Oh, we have a man in Zurb, not connected with the temple," Stranor Sleth said. "Name's Crannar Jurth; calls himself Kranjur, locally. He has a swordmaker's shop, employs about a dozen native journeymen and apprentices who hammer out the common blades he sells in the open market. Then, he imports a few high-class alloy-steel blades from the First Level that'll cut through this local low-carbon armor like cheese. Fits them with locally made hilts and sells them at unbelievable prices to the nobility. He's Swordsmith to the King; picks up all the inside palace dope. Of course, he was among the first to accept the New Gospel and go over to Muz-Azin. He has a secret room under his shop, with his conveyer and a radio.

"What happened was this: These six priests were at a consecration ceremony at a rabbit-ranch outside the city, and they didn't know about the raid on the temple. On their way back, they were surrounded by Chuldun archers and taken prisoner. They had no weapons but their sacrificial knives." He threw another dirty look at Brannad Klav. "So they're due to go up on the triangles at sunset tomorrow."

"We'll have to get them out before then," Verkan Vall stated. "They're our people, and we can't let them down; even the native is under our protection, whether he knows it or not. And in the second place, if those priests are sacrificed to Muz-Azin," he told Brannad Klav, "you can shut down everything on this time-line, pull out or disintegrate your installations, and fill in your mine-tunnels. Yat-Zar will be through on this time-line, and you'll be through along with him. And considering that your fissionables franchise for this sector comes up for renewal next year, your company will be through in this paratime area."

"You believe that would happen?" Brannad Klav asked anxiously.

"I know it will, because I'll put through a recommendation to that effect, if those six men are tortured to death tomorrow," Verkan Vall replied. "And in the fifty years that I've been in the Police Department, I've only heard of five such recommendations being ignored by the commission. You know, Fourth Level Mineral Products Syndicate is after your franchise. Ordinarily, they wouldn't have a chance of getting it, but with this, maybe they will, even without my recommendation. This was all your fault, for ignoring Stranor Sleth's proposal and for denying those men the right to carry energy weapons."

"Well, we were only trying to stay inside the Paratime Code," Brannad Klav pleaded. "If it isn't too late now, you can count on me for every cooperation." He fiddled with some papers on the desk. "What do you want me to do to help?"

"I'll tell you that in a minute." Verkan Vall walked to the wall and looked at the map, then returned to Stranor Sleth's desk. "How about these dungeons?" he asked. "How are they located, and how can we get in to them?"

"I'm afraid we can't," Stranor Sleth told him. "Not without fighting our way in. They're under the palace citadel, a hundred feet below ground. They're spatially co-existent with the heavy water barriers around one of our company's plutonium piles on the First Level, and below surface on any unoccupied time-line I know of, so we can't transpose in to them. This palace is really a walled city inside a city. Here, I'll show you."

Going around the desk, he sat down and, after looking in the index-screen, punched a combination on the keyboard. A picture, projected from the microfilm-bank, appeared on the view-screen. It was an air-view of the city of Zurb—taken, the high priest explained, by infrared light from an airboat over the city at night. It showed a city of an entirely premechanical civilization, with narrow streets, lined on either side by low one- and two-story buildings. Although there would be considerable snow in winter, the roofs were usually flat, probably massive stone slabs supported by pillars within. Even in the poorer sections, this was true except for the very meanest houses and out-buildings, which were thatched. Here and there, some huge pile of masonry would rear itself above its lower neighbors, and where the streets were wider, occasional groups of large buildings would be surrounded by battlemented walls. Stranor Sleth indicated one of the larger of these.

"Here's the palace," he said. "And here's the temple of Yat-Zar, about half a mile away." He touched a large building, occupying an entire block; between it and the palace was a block-wide park, with lawns and trees on either side of a wide roadway connecting the two.

"Now, here's a detailed view of the palace." He punched another combination; the view of the city was replaced by one, taken from directly overhead, of the walled palace area. "Here's the main gate, in front, at the end of the road from the temple," he pointed out. "Over here, on the left, are the slaves' quarters and the stables and workshops and storehouses and so on. Over here, on the other side, are the nobles' quarters. And this,"—he indicated a towering structure at the rear of the walled enclosure—"is the citadel and the royal dwelling. Audience hall on this side; harem over here on this side. A wide stone platform, about fifteen feet high, runs completely across the front of the citadel, from the audience hall to the harem. Since this picture was taken, the new temple of Muz-Azin was built right about here." He indicated that it extended out from the audience hall into the central courtyard. "And out here on the platform, they've put up about a dozen of these triangles, about twelve feet high, on which the sacrificial victims are whipped to death."

"Yes. About the only way we could get down to the dungeons would be to make an airdrop onto the citadel roof and fight our way down with needlers and blasters, and I'm not willing to do that as long as there's any other way," Verkan Vall said. "We'd lose men, even with needlers against bows, and there's a chance that some of our equipment might be lost in the melee and fall into outtime hands. You say this sacrifice comes off tomorrow at sunset?"

"That would be about actual sunset plus or minus an hour; these people aren't astronomers, they don't even have good sundials, and it might be a cloudy day," Stranor Sleth said. "There will be a big idol of Muz-Azin on a cart, set about here." He pointed. "After the sacrifice, it is to be dragged down this road, outside, to the temple of Yat-Zar, and set up there. The temple is now occupied by about twenty Chuldun mercenaries and five or six priests of

Muz-Azin. They haven't, of course, gotten into the House of Yat-Zar; the door's of impervium steel, about six inches thick, with a plating of collapsed nickel under the gilding. It would take a couple of hours to cut through it with our best atomic torch; there isn't a tool on this time-line that could even scratch it. And the insides of the walls are lined with the same thing."

"Do you think our people have been tortured yet?" Verkan Vall asked.

"No." Stranor Sleth was positive. "They'll be fairly well treated until the sacrifice. The idea's to make them last as long as possible on the triangles; Muz-Azin likes to see a slow killing, and so does the mob of spectators."

"That's good. Now, here's my plan. We won't try to rescue them from the dungeons. Instead, we'll transpose back to the Zurb temple from the First Level, in considerable force—say a hundred or so men—and march on the palace, to force their release. You're in constant radio communication with all the other temples on this time-line, I suppose?"

"Yes, certainly."

"All right. Pass this out to everybody, authority Paratime Police, in my name, acting for Tortha Karf. I want all paratimers who can possibly be spared to transpose to First Level immediately and rendezvous at the First Level terminal of the Zurb temple conveyer as soon as possible. Close down all mining operations, and turn over temple routine to the native under-priests. You can tell them that the upper-priests are retiring to their respective Houses of Yat-Zar to pray for the deliverance of the priests in the hands of King Kurchuk. And everybody is to bring back his priestly regalia to the First Level; that will be needed." He turned to Brannad Klav. "I suppose you keep spare regalia in stock on the First Level?"

"Yes, of course; we keep plenty of everything in stock. Robes, miters, false beards of different shades, everything."

"And these big Yat-Zar idols; they're mass-produced on the First Level? You have one available now? Good. I'll want some alterations made on one. For one thing, I'll want it plated heavily, all over, with collapsed nickel. For another, I'll want it fitted with antigrav units and some sort of propulsion-units, and a loud-speaker, and remote control.

"And, Stranor, you get in touch with this swordmaker, Crannar Jurth, and alert him to co-operate with us. Tell him to start calling Zurb temple on his radio about noon tomorrow, and keep it up till he gets an answer. Or, better, tell him to run his conveyer to his First Level terminal, and bring with him an extra suit of clothes appropriate to the role of journeyman-mechanic. I'll want to talk to him, and furnish him with special equipment. Got all that? Well, carry on with it, and bring your own paratimers, priests and mining operators back with you as soon as you've taken care of everything. Brannad, you come with me now. We're returning to First Level immediately. We have a lot of work to do, so let's get started."

"Anything I can do to help, just call on me for it," Brannad Klav promised earnestly. "And, Stranor, I want to apologize. I'll admit, now, that I ought to have followed your recommendations when this situation first developed."

By noon of the next day, Verkan Vall had at least a hundred men gathered in the big room at the First Level fissionables refinery at Jarnabar, spatially co-existent with the Fourth Level temple of Yat-Zar at Zurb. He was having a little trouble distinguishing between them, for every man wore the fringed blue robe and golden miter of an upper-priest, and had his face masked behind a blue false beard. It was, he admitted to himself, a most ludicrous-looking assemblage; one of the most ludicrous things about it was the fact that it would have inspired only pious awe in a Hulgun of the Fourth Level Proto-Aryan Sector. About half of them were priests from the Transtemporal Mining Corporation's temples; the other half were members of the Paratime Police. All of them wore, in addition to their temple knives, holstered sigma-ray needlers. Most of them carried ultrasonic paralyzers, eighteen-inch batonlike things with bulbous ends. Most of the Paratime Police and a few of the priests also carried either heat-ray pistols or neutron-disruption blasters; Verkan Vall wore one of the latter in a left-hand belt holster.

The Paratime Police were lined up separately for inspection, and Stranor Sleth, Tammand Drav of the Zurb temple, and several other high priests were checking the authenticity of their disguises. A little apart from the others, a Paratime Policeman, in high priest's robes and beard, had a square box slung in front of him; he was fiddling with knobs and buttons on it, practicing. A big idol of Yat-Zar, on antigravity, was floating slowly about the room in obedience to its remote controls, rising and lowering, turning about and pirouetting gracefully.

"Hey, Vall!" he called to his superior. "How's this?"

The idol rose about five feet, turned slowly in a half-circle, moved to the right a little, and then settled slowly toward the floor.

"Fine, fine, Horv," Verkan Vall told him, "but don't set it down on anything or turn off the antigravity. There's enough collapsed nickel-plating on that thing to sink it a yard in soft ground."

"I don't know what the idea of that was," Brannad Klav, standing beside him, said. "Understand, I'm not criticizing. I haven't any right to, under the circumstances. But it seems to me that armoring that thing in collapsed nickel was an unnecessary precaution."

"Maybe it was," Verkan Vall agreed. "I sincerely hope so. But we can't take any chances. This operation has to be absolutely right. Ready, Tammand? All right; first detail into the conveyer."

He turned and strode toward a big dome of fine metallic mesh, thirty feet high and sixty in diameter, at the other end of the room. Tammand Drav, and his ten paratimer priests, and Brannad Klav, and ten Paratime Police, followed him in. One of the latter slid shut the door and locked it; Verkan Vall went to the control desk, at the center of the dome, and picked up a two-foot globe of the same fine metallic mesh, opening it and making some adjustments inside, then attaching an electric cord and closing it. He laid the globe on the floor near the desk and picked up the hand battery at the other end of the attached cord.

"Not taking any chances at all, are you?" Brannad Klav asked, watching this operation with interest.

"I never do, unnecessarily. There are too many necessary chances that have to be taken in this work." Verkan Vall pressed the button on the hand battery. The globe on the floor flashed and vanished. "Yesterday, five paratimers were arrested. Any or all of them could have had door-activators with them. Stranor Sleth says they were not tortured, but that is a purely inferential statement. They may have been, and the use of the activator may have been extorted from one of them. So I want a look at the inside of that conveyer-chamber before we transpose into it."

He laid the hand battery, with the loose-dangling wire that had been left behind, on the desk, then lit a cigarette. The others gathered around, smoking and watching, careful to avoid the place from which the globe had vanished. Thirty minutes passed, and then, in a queer iridescence, the globe reappeared. Verkan Vall counted ten seconds and picked it up, taking it to the desk and opening it to remove a small square box. This he slid into a space under the desk and flipped a switch. Instantly, a view-screen lit up and a three-dimensional picture appeared—the interior of a big room a hundred feet square and some seventy in height. There was a big desk and a radio; tables, couches, chairs and an arms-rack full of weapons, and at one end, a remarkably clean sixty-foot circle on the concrete floor, outlined in faintly luminous red.

"How about it?" Verkan Vall asked Tammand Drav. "Anything wrong?"

The Zurb high priest shook his head. "Just as we left it," he said. "Nobody's been inside since we left."

One of the policemen took Verkan Vall's place at the control desk and threw the master switch after checking the instruments. Immediately, the paratemporal-transposition field went on with a humming sound that mounted to a high scream, then settled to a steady drone. The mesh dome flickered with a cold iridescence and vanished, and they were looking into the interior of a great fissionables refinery plant, operated by paratimers on another First Level time-line. The structural details altered, from time-line to time-line, as they watched. Buildings appeared and vanished. Once, for a few seconds, they were inside a cool, insulated bubble in the midst of molten lead. Tammand Drav jerked a thumb at it before it vanished.

"That always bothers me," he said. "Bad place for the field to go weak. I'm fussy as an old hen about inspection of the conveyer, on account of that."

"Don't blame you," Verkan Vall agreed. "Probably the cooling system of a breeder-pile."

They passed more swiftly now, across the Second Level and the Third. Once they were in the midst of a huge land battle, with great tanklike vehicles spouting flame at one another. Another moment was spent in an air bombardment. On any time-line, this section of East Europe was a natural battleground. Once a great procession marched toward them, carrying red banners and huge pictures of a coarse-faced man with a black mustache—Verkan Vall recognized the environment as Fourth Level Europo-American Sector. Finally, as the transposition-rate slowed, they saw a clutter of miserable thatched huts, in the rear of a granite wall of a Fourth Level Hulgun temple of Yat-Zar—a temple not yet infiltrated by Transtemporal Mining Corporation agents. Finally, they were at their destination. The dome around them became visible, and an overhead green light flashed slowly on and off.

Verkan Vall opened the door and stepped outside, his needler drawn. The House of Yat-Zar was just as he had seen it in the picture photographed by the automatic reconnaissance-conveyer. The others crowded outside after him. One of the regular priests pulled off his miter and beard and went to the radio, putting on a headset. Verkan Vall and Tammand Drav snapped on the visi-screen, getting a view of the Holy of Holies outside.

There were six men there, seated at the upper-priests' banquet table, drinking from golden goblets. Five of them wore the black robes with green facings which marked them as priests of Muz-Azin; the sixth was an officer of the Chuldun archers, in gilded mail and helmet.

"Why, those are the sacred vessels of the temple!" Tammand Drav cried, scandalized. Then he laughed in self-ridicule. "I'm beginning to take this stuff seriously, myself; time I put in for a long vacation. I was actually shocked at the sacrilege!"

"Well, let's overtake the infidels in their sins," Verkan Vall said. "Paralyzers will be good enough."

He picked up one of the bulb-headed weapons, and unlocked the door. Tammand Drav and another of the priests of the Zurb temple following and the others crowding behind, they passed out through the veils, and burst into the Holy of Holies. Verkan Vall pointed the bulb of his paralyzer at the six seated men and pressed the button; other paralyzers came into action, and the whole sextet was knocked senseless. The officer rolled from his chair and fell to the floor in a clatter of armor. Two of the priests slumped forward on the table. The others merely sank back in their chairs, dropping their goblets.

"Give each one of them another dose to make sure," Verkan Vall directed a couple of his own men. "Now, Tammand; any other way into the main temple beside that door?"

"Up those steps." Tammand Drav pointed. "There's a gallery along the side; we can cover the whole room from there."

"Take your men and go up there. I'll take a few through the door. There'll be about twenty archers out there, and we don't want any of them loosing any arrows before we can knock them out. Three minutes be time enough?"

"Easily. Make it two," Tammand Drav said.

HE took his priests up the stairway and vanished into the gallery of the temple. Verkan Vall waited until one minute had passed and then, followed by Brannad Klav and a couple of Paratime Policemen, he went under the plinth and peered out into the temple. Five or six archers, in steel caps and sleeveless leather jackets sewn with steel rings, were gathered around the altar, cooking something in a pot on the fire. Most of the others, like veteran soldiers, were sprawled on the floor, trying to catch a short nap, except half a dozen, who crouched in a circle, playing some game with dice—another almost universal military practice.

The two minutes were up. He aimed his paralyzer at the men around the alter and squeezed the button, swinging it from one to another and knocking them down with a bludgeon of inaudible sound. At the same time, Tammand Drav and his detail were stunning the gamblers. Stepping forward and to one side, Verkan Vall, Brannad Klav and the others took care of the sleepers on the floor. In less than thirty seconds, every Chuldun in the temple was incapacitated.

"All right, make sure none of them come out of it prematurely," Verkan Vall directed. "Get their weapons, and be sure nobody has a knife or anything hidden on him. Who has the syringe and the sleep-drug ampoules?"

Somebody had them, it developed, who was still on the First Level, waiting to come up with the second conveyer load. Verkan Vall swore. Something like this always happened on any operation involving more than half a dozen men.

"Well, some of you stay here; patrol around, and use your paralyzers on anybody who even twitches a muscle." Ultrasonics were nice, effective, humane police weapons, but they were unreliable. The same dose that would keep one man out for an hour would paralyze another for no more than ten or fifteen minutes. "And be sure none of them are playing 'possum."

He went back through the door under the plinth, glancing up at the decorated wooden screen and wondering how much work it would take to move the new Yat-Zar in from the conveyers. The five priests and the archer-captain were still unconscious; one of the policemen was searching them.

"Here's the sort of weapons these priests carry," he said, holding up a short iron mace with a spiked head. "Carry them on their belts." He tossed it on the table, and began searching another knocked-out hierophant. "Like this— Hey! Look at this, will you!"

He drew his hand from under the left side of the senseless man's robe and held up a sigma-ray needler. Verkan Vall looked at it and nodded grimly.

"Had it in a regular shoulder holster," the policeman said, handing the weapon across the table. "What do you think?"

"Find anything else funny on him?"

"Wait a minute." The policeman pulled open the robe and began stripping the priest of Muz-Azin; Verkan Vall came around the table to help. There was nothing else of a suspicious nature.

"Could have got it from one of the prisoners, but I don't like the familiar way he's wearing that holster," Verkan Vall said. "Has the conveyer gone back yet?" When the policeman nodded, he continued: "When it returns, take him to the First Level. I hope they bring up the sleep-drug with the next load. When you get him back, take him to Dhergabar by strato-rocket immediately, and make sure he gets back alive. I want him questioned under narco-hypnosis by a regular Paratime Commission psycho-technician, in the presence of Chief Tortha Karf and some responsible Commission official. This is going to be hot stuff."

Within an hour, the whole force was assembled in the temple. The wooden screen had presented no problem—it slid easily to one side—and the big idol floated on antigravity in the middle of the temple. Verkan Vall was looking anxiously at his watch.

"It's about two hours to sunset," he said to Stranor Sleth. "But as you pointed out, these Hulguns aren't astronomers, and it's a bit cloudy. I wish Crannar Jurth would call in with something definite."

Another twenty minutes passed. Then the man at the radio came out into the temple.

"O. K.!" he called. "The man at Crannar Jurth's called in. Crannar Jurth contacted him with a midget radio he has up his sleeve; he's in the palace courtyard now. They haven't brought out the victims yet, but Kurchuk has just been carried out on his throne to that platform in front of the citadel. Big crowd gathering in the inner courtyard; more in the streets outside. Palace gates are wide open."

"That's it!" Verkan Vall cried. "Form up; the parade's starting. Brannad, you and Tammand and Stranor and I in front; about ten men with paralyzers a little behind us. Then Yat-Zar, about ten feet off the ground, and then the others. Forward—*ho-o!*"

They emerged from the temple and started down the broad roadway toward the palace. There was not much of a crowd, at first. Most of Zurb had flocked to the palace earlier, the lucky ones in the courtyard and the latecomers outside. Those whom they did meet stared at them in open-mouthed amazement, and then some, remembering their doubts and blasphemies, began howling for forgiveness. Others—a substantial majority—realizing that it would be upon King Kurchuk that the real weight of Yat-Zar's six hands would fall, took to their heels, trying to put as much distance as possible between them and the palace before the blow fell.

As the procession approached the palace gates, the crowds were thicker, made up of those who had been unable to squeeze themselves inside. The panic was worse here, too. A good many were trampled and hurt in the rush to escape, and it became necessary to use paralyzers to clear a way. That made it worse; everybody was sure that Yat-Zar was striking sinners dead left and right.

Fortunately, the gates were high enough to let the god through without losing altitude appreciably. Inside, the mob surged back, clearing a way across the courtyard. It was only necessary to paralyze a few here, and the levitated idol and its priestly attendants advanced toward the stone platform, where the king sat on his throne, flanked by court functionaries and black-robed priests of Muz-Azin. In front of this, a rank of Chuldun archers had been drawn up.

"Horv; move Yat-Zar forward about a hundred feet and up about fifty," Verkan Vall directed. "Quickly!"

As the six-armed anthropomorphic idol rose and moved closer toward its saurian rival, Verkan Vall drew his needler, scanning the assemblage around the throne anxiously.

"*Where is the wicked King?*" a voice thundered—the voice of Stranor Sleth, speaking into a midget radio tuned to the loud-speaker inside the idol. "*Where is the blasphemer and desecrator, Kurchuk?*"

"There's Labdurg, in the red tunic, beside the throne," Tammand Drav whispered. "And that's Ghromdur, the Muz-Azin high priest, beside him."

Verkan Vall nodded, keeping his eyes on the group on the platform. Ghromdur, the high priest of Muz-Azin, was edging backward and reaching under his robe. At the same time, an officer shouted an order, and the Chuldun archers drew arrows from their quivers and fitted them to their bowstrings. Immediately, the ultrasonic paralyzers of the advancing paratimers went into action, and the mercenaries began dropping.

"*Lay down your weapons, fools!*" the amplified voice boomed at them. "*Lay down your weapons or you shall surely die! Who are you, miserable wretches, to draw bows against Me?*"

At first a few, then all of the Chulduns, lowered or dropped their weapons and began edging away to the sides. At the center, in front of the throne, most of them had been knocked out. Verkan Vall was still watching the Muz-Azin high priest intently; as Ghromdur raised his arm, there was a flash and a puff of smoke from the front of Yat-Zur—the paint over the collapsed nickel was burned off, but otherwise the idol was undamaged. Verkan Vall swung up his needler and rayed Ghromdur dead; as the man in the green-faced black robes fell, a blaster clattered on the stone platform.

"*Is that your puny best, Muz-Azin?*" the booming voice demanded. "*Where is your high priest now!*"

"Horv; face Yat-Zar toward Muz-Azin," Verkan Vall said over his shoulder, drawing his blaster with his left hand. Like all First Level people, he was ambidextrous, although, like all paratimers, he habitually concealed the fact while outtime. As the levitated idol swung slowly to look down upon its enemy on the built-up cart, Verkan Vall aimed the blaster and squeezed.

In a spot less than a millimeter in diameter on the crocodile idol's side, a certain number of neutrons in the atomic structure of the stone from which it was carved broke apart, becoming, in effect, atoms of hydrogen. With a flash and a bang, the idol burst and vanished. Yat-Zar gave a dirty laugh and turned his back on the cart, which was now burning fiercely, facing King Kurchuk again.

"Get your hands up, all of you!" Verkan Vall shouted, in the First Level language, swinging the stubby muzzle of the blaster and the knob-tipped twin tubes of the needler to cover the group around the throne. "Come forward, before I start blasting!"

Labdurg raised his hands and stepped forward. So did two of the priests of Yat-Zar. They were quickly seized by Paratime Policemen, who swarmed up onto the platform and disarmed. All three were carrying sigma-ray needlers, and Labdurg had a blaster as well.

King Kurchuk was clinging to the arms of his throne, a badly frightened monarch trying desperately not to show it. He was a big man, heavy-shouldered, black-bearded; under ordinary circumstances he would probably have cut an imposing figure, in his gold-washed mail and his golden crown. Now his face was a dirty gray, and he was biting nervously at his lower lip. The others on the platform were in an even worse state. The Hulgun nobles were grouped together, trying to disassociate themselves from both the king and the priests of Muz-Azin. The latter were staring in a daze at the blazing cart from which their idol had just been blasted. And the dozen men who were to have done the actual work of the torture-sacrifice had all dropped their whips and were fairly gibbering in fear.

Yat-Zar, manipulated by the robed paratimer, had taken a position directly above the throne and was lowering slowly. Kurchuk stared up at the massive idol descending toward him, his knuckles white as he clung to the arms of his throne. He managed to hold out until he could feel the weight of the idol pressing on his head. Then, with a scream, he hurled himself from the throne and rolled forward almost to the edge of the platform. Yat-Zar moved to one side, swung slightly and knocked the throne toppling, and then settled down on the platform. To Kurchuk, who was rising cautiously on his hands and knees, the big idol seemed to be looking at him in contempt.

"Where are my holy priests, Kurchuk?" Stranor Sleth demanded into his sleeve-hidden radio. *"Let them be brought before me, alive and unharmed, or it shall be better for you had you never been born!"*

The six priests of Yat-Zar, it seemed, were already being brought onto the platform by one of Kurchuk's nobles. This noble, whose name was Yorzuk, knew a miracle when he saw one, and believed in being on the side of the god with the heaviest artillery. As soon as he had seen Yat-Zar coming through the gate without visible means of support, he had hastened to the dungeons with half a dozen of his personal retainers and ordered the release of the six captives. He was now escorting them onto the platform, assuring them that he had always been a faithful servant of Yat-Zar and had been deeply grieved at his sovereign's apostasy.

"Hear my word, Kurchuk," Stranor Sleth continued through the loudspeaker in the idol. *"You have sinned most vilely against me, and were I a cruel god, your fate would be such as no man has ever before suffered. But I am a merciful god; behold, you may gain forgiveness in my sight. For thirty days, you shall neither eat meat nor drink wine, nor shall you wear gold nor fine raiment, and each day shall you go to my temple and beseech me for my forgiveness. And on the thirty-first day, you shall set out, barefoot and clad in the garb of a slave, and journey to my temple that is in the mountains over above Yoldav, and there will I forgive you, after you have made sacrifice to me. I, Yat-Zar, have spoken!"*

The king started to rise, babbling thanks.

"Rise not before me until I have forgiven you!" Yat-Zar thundered. *"Creep out of my sight upon your belly, wretch!"*

THE procession back to the temple was made quietly and sedately along an empty roadway. Yat-Zar seemed to be in a kindly humor; the people of Zurb had no intention of giving him any reason to change his mood. The priests of Muz-Azin and their torturers had been flung into the dungeon. Yorzuk, appointed regent for the duration of Kurchuk's penance, had taken control and was employing Hulgun spearmen and hastily converted Chuldun archers to restore order and, incidentally, purge a few of his personal enemies and political rivals. The priests, with the three prisoners who had been found carrying First Level weapons among them and Yat-Zar floating triumphantly in front, entered the temple. A few of the devout, who sought admission after them, were told that elaborate and secret rites were being held to cleanse the profaned altar, and sent away.

Verkan Vall and Brannad Klav and Stranor Sleth were in the conveyer chamber with the Paratime Policemen and the extra priests; along with them were the three prisoners. Verkan Vall pulled off his false beard and turned to face them. He could see that they all recognized him.

"Now," he began, "you people are in a bad jam. You've violated the Paratime Transposition Code, the Commercial Regulation Code, and the First Level Criminal Code, all together. If you know what's good for you, you'll start talking."

"I'm not saying anything till I have legal advice," the man who had been using the local alias of Labdurg replied. "And if you're through searching me, I'd like to have my cigarettes and lighter back."

"Smoke one of mine, for a change," Verkan Vall told him. "I don't know what's in yours besides tobacco." He offered his case and held a light for the prisoner before lighting his own cigarette. "I'm going to be sure you get back to the First Level alive."

The former Overseer of the Kingdom of Zurb shrugged. "I'm still not talking," he said.

"Well, we can get it all out of you by narco-hypnosis, anyhow," Verkan Vall told him. "Besides, we got that man of yours who was here at the temple when we came in. He's being given a full treatment, as a presumed outtime native found in possession of First Level weapons. If you talk now, it'll go easier with you."

The prisoner dropped the cigarette on the floor and tramped it out.

"Anything you cops get out of me, you'll have to get the hard way," he said. "I have friends on the First Level who'll take care of me."

"I doubt that. They'll have their hands full taking care of themselves, after this gets out." Verkan Vall turned to the two in the black robes. "Either of you want to say anything?" When they shook their heads, he nodded to a group of his policemen; they were hustled into the conveyer. "Take them to the First Level terminal and hold them till I come in. I'll be along with the next conveyer load."

THE conveyer flashed and vanished. Brannad Klav stared for a moment at the circle of concrete floor from whence it had disappeared. Then he turned to Verkan Vall.

"I still can't believe it," he said. "Why, those fellows were First Level paratimers. So was that priest, Ghromdur; the one you rayed."

"Yes, of course. They worked for your rivals, the Fourth Level Mineral Products Syndicate; the outfit that was trying to get your Proto-Aryan Sector fissionables franchise away from you. They operate on this sector already; have the petroleum franchise for the Chuldun country, east of the Caspian

Sea. They export to some of these internal-combustion-engine sectors, like Europo-American. You know, most of the wars they've been fighting, lately, on the Europo-American Sector have been, at least in part, motivated by rivalry for oil fields. But now that the Europo-Americans have begun to release nuclear energy, fissionables have become more important than oil. In less than a century, it's predicted that atomic energy will replace all other forms of power. Mineral Products Syndicate wanted to get a good source of supply for uranium, and your Proto-Aryan Sector franchise was worth grabbing.

"I had considered something like this as a possibility when Stranor, here, mentioned that tularemia was normally unknown in Eurasis on this sector. That epidemic must have been started by imported germs. And I knew that Mineral Products has agents at the court of the Chuldun emperor, Chombrog; they have to, to protect their oil wells on his eastern frontiers. I spent most of last night checking up on some stuff by video-transcription from the Paratime Commission's microfilm library at Dhergabar. I found out, for one thing, that while there is a King Kurchuk of Zurb on every time-line for a hundred parayears on either side of this one, this is the only time-line on which he married a Princess Darith of Chuldu, and it's the only time-line on which there is any trace of a Chuldun scribe named Labdurg.

"That's why I went to all the trouble of having that Yat-Zar plated with collapsed nickel. If there were disguised paratimers among the Muz-Azin party at Kurchuk's court, I expected one of them to try to blast our idol when we brought it into the palace. I was watching Ghromdur and Labdurg in particular; as soon as Ghromdur used his blaster, I needled him. After that, it was easy."

"Was that why you insisted on sending that automatic viewer on ahead?"

"Yes. There was a chance that they might have planted a bomb in the House of Yat-Zar here. I knew they'd either do that or let the place entirely alone. I suppose they were so confident of getting away with this that they didn't want to damage the conveyer or the conveyer chamber. They expected to use them themselves, after they took over your company's franchise."

"Well, what's going to be done about it by the Commission?" Brannad Klav wanted to know.

"Plenty. The syndicate will probably lose their paratime license; any of its officials who had guilty knowledge of this will be dealt with according to law. You know, this was a pretty nasty business."

"You're telling me!" Stranor Sleth exclaimed. "Did you get a look at those whips they were going to use on our people? Pointed iron barbs a quarter-inch long braided into them, all over the lash-ends!"

"Yes. Any punitive action you're thinking about taking on these priests of Muz-Azin—the natives, I mean—will be ignored on the First Level. And that reminds me; you'd better work out a line of policy pretty soon."

"Well, as for the priests and the torturers, I think I'll tell Yorzuk to have them sold to the Bhunguns, to the east. They're always in the market for galley slaves," Stranor Sleth said. He turned to Brannad Klav. "And I'll want six gold crowns made up, as soon as possible. Strictly Hulgun design, with Yat-Zar religious symbolism, very rich and ornate, all slightly different. When I give Kurchuk absolution, I'll crown him at the altar in the name of Yat-Zar. Then I'll invite in the other five Hulgun kings, lecture them on their religious duties, make them confess their secret doubts, forgive them, and crown them, too. From then on, they can all style themselves as ruling by the will of Yat-Zar."

"And from then on, you'll have all of them eating out of your hand," Verkan Vall concluded. "You know, this will probably go down in Hulgun history as the Reformation of Ghullam the Holy. I've always wondered whether the theory of the divine right of kings was invented by the kings, to establish their authority over the people, or by the priests, to establish *their* authority over the kings. It works about as well one way as the other."

"What I can't understand is this," Brannad Klav said. "It was entirely because of my respect for the Paratime Code that I kept Stranor Sleth from using First Level weapons and other techniques to control these people with a show of apparent miraculous powers. But this Fourth Level Mineral Products Syndicate was operating in violation of the Paratime Code by invading our franchise area. Why didn't they fake up a supernatural reign of terror to intimidate these natives?"

"Ha, exactly because they *were* operating illegally," Verkan Vall replied. "Suppose they had started using needlers and blasters and anti-gravity and nuclear-energy around here. The natives would have thought it was the power of Muz-Azin, of course, but what would you have thought? You'd have known, as soon as they tried it, that First Level paratimers were working against you, and you'd have laid the facts before the Commission, and this time-line would have been flooded with Paratime Police. They had to conceal their operations not only from the natives, as you do, but also from us. So they didn't dare make public use of First Level techniques.

"Of course, when we came marching into the palace with that idol on anti-gravity, they knew at once what was happening. I have an idea that they only tried to blast that idol to create a diversion which would permit them to escape—if they could have gotten out of the palace, they'd have made their way, in disguise, to the nearest Mineral Products Syndicate conveyer and transposed out of here. I realized that they could best delay us by blasting our idol, and that's why I had it plated with collapsed nickel. I think that where they made their mistake was in allowing Kurchuk to have those priests arrested, and insisting on sacrificing them to Muz-Azin. If it hadn't been for that, the Paratime Police wouldn't have been brought into this at all.

"Well, Stranor, you'll want to get back to your temple, and Brannad and I want to get back to the First Level. I'm supposed to take my wife to a banquet in Dhergabar tonight, and with the fastest strato-rocket, I'll just barely make it."

LORD KALVAN
OF OTHERWHEN

1

I

TORTHA Karf, Chief of Paratime Police, told himself to stop fretting. He was only three hundred years old, so by the barest life-expectancy of his race he was good for another two centuries. Two hundred more days wouldn't matter. Then it would be Year-End Day, and precisely at midnight, he would rise from this chair and Verkan Vall would sit down in it, and after that he would be free to raise grapes and lemons and wage guerrilla war against the rabbits on the island of Sicily, which he owned outright on one uninhabited Fifth Level time-line. He wondered how long it would take Vall to become as tired of the Chief's seat as he was now.

Actually, Karf knew, Verkan Vall had never wanted to be Chief. Prestige and authority meant little to him, and freedom much. Vall liked to work out-time. But it was a job somebody had to do, and it was the job for which Vall had been trained, so he'd take it, and do it, Karf suspected, better than he'd done it himself. The job of policing a near-infinity of worlds, each of which was this same planet Earth, would be safe with Verkan Vall.

Twelve thousand years ago, facing extinction on an exhausted planet, the First Level race had discovered the existence of a second, lateral, time-dimension and a means of physical transposition to and from a near-infinity of worlds of alternate probability parallel to their own. So the conveyers had gone out by stealth, bringing back wealth to Home Time-Line—a little from this one, a little from that, never enough to be missed anywhen.

It all had to be policed. Some paratimers were less than scrupulous in dealing with outtime races—he'd have retired ten years ago except for the discovery of a huge paratemporal slave-trade, only recently smashed. More often, somebody's bad luck or indiscretion would endanger the Paratime Secret, or some incident—nobody's fault, something that just happened—would have to be explained away. But, at all costs, the Paratime Secret must be preserved. Not merely the actual technique of transposition—that went without saying—but the very existence of a race possessing it. If for no other reason (and there *were* many others), it would be utterly immoral to make any outtime race live with the knowledge that there were among them aliens indistinguishable from themselves, watching and exploiting. It was a big police-beat.

Second Level: that had been civilized almost as long as the First, but there had been dark-age interludes. Except for paratemporal transposition, most of its sectors equaled First Level, and from many, Home Time Line had learned much. The Third Level civilizations were more recent, but still of respectable antiquity and advancement. Fourth Level had started late and progressed slowly; some Fourth Level genius was first domesticating animals long after the steam engine was obsolescent all over the Third. And Fifth Level: on a few sectors, subhuman brutes, speechless and fireless, were cracking nuts and each other's heads with stones, and on most of it nothing even vaguely humanoid had appeared.

Fourth Level was the big one. The others had devolved from low-probability genetic accidents; it was the maximum probability. It was divided into many sectors and subsectors, on most of which human civilization had first appeared in the valleys of the Nile and Tigris-Euphrates, and on the Indus and Yangtze. Europo-American Sector: they might have to pull out of that entirely, but that would be for Chief Verkan to decide. Too many thermonuclear weapons and too many competing national sovereignties. That had happened all over Third Level at one time or another within Home Time Line experience. Alexandrian-Roman: off to a fine start with the pooling of Greek theory and Roman engineering talent, and then, a thousand years ago, two half-forgotten religions had been rummaged out of the dustbin and fanatics had begun massacring one another. They were still at it, with pikes and matchlocks, having lost the ability to make anything better. Europo-American could come to that if its rival political and economic sectarians kept on. Sino-

Hindic: that wasn't a civilization; it was a bad case of cultural paralysis. And so was Indo-Turanian—about where Europo-American had been ten centuries ago.

And Aryan-Oriental: the Aryan migration of three thousand years ago, instead of moving west and south, as on most sectors, had rolled east into China. And Aryan-Transpacific, an offshoot: on one sector, some of them had built ships and sailed north and east along the Kuriles and the Aleutians and settled in North America, bringing with them horses and cattle and iron-working skills, exterminating the Amerinds, warring with one another, splitting into diverse peoples and cultures. There was a civilization, now decadent, on the Pacific coast, and nomads on the central plains herding bison and crossbreeding them with Asian cattle, and a civilization around the Great Lakes and one in the Mississippi Valley, and a new one, five or six centuries old, along the Atlantic and in the Appalachians. Technological level pre-mechanical, water-and-animal power; a few subsectors had gotten as far as gunpowder.

But Aryan-Transpacific was a sector to watch. They were going forward; things were ripe to start happening soon.

Let Chief Verkan watch it, for the next couple of centuries. After Year-End Day, ex-Chief Tortha would have his vineyards and lemon-groves to watch.

II

RYLLA tried to close her mind to the voices around her in the tapestried room, and stared at the map spread in front of her and her father. There was Tarr-Hostigos overlooking the gap, only a tiny fleck of gold on the parchment, but she could see it in her mind's eye—the walled outer bailey with the sheds and stables and workshops inside, the inner bailey and the citadel and keep, the watchtower pointing a blunt finger skyward. Below, the little Darro flowed north to join the Listra and, with it, the broad Athan to the east. Hostigos Town, white walls and slate roofs and busy streets; the checkerboard of fields to the west and south; the forest, broken by farms, to the west.

A voice, louder and harsher than the others, brought her back to reality. Her cousin, Sthentros.

"He'll do nothing at all? Well, what in Dralm's holy name is a Great King for, but to keep the peace?"

She looked along the table, from one to another. Phosg, the speaker for the peasants, at the foot, uncomfortable in his feast-day clothes and ill at ease seated among his betters. The speakers for the artisans' guilds, and for the merchants and the townsfolk; the lesser family members and marriagekin; the barons and landholders. Old Chartiphon, the chief-captain, his golden beard streaked with gray like the lead splotches on his gilded breastplate, his long sword on the table in front of him. Xentos, the cowl of his priestly robe thrown back from his snowy head, his blue eyes troubled. And beside her, at the table's head, her father, Prince Ptosphes, his mouth tight between pointed gray mustache and pointed gray beard. How long it had been since she had seen her father smile!

Xentos passed a hand negatively across his face.

"King Kaiphranos said that it was every Prince's duty to guard his own realm; that it was for Prince Ptosphes, not for him, to keep bandits out of Hostigos."

"Bandits? They're Nostori soldiers!" Sthentros shouted. "Gormoth of Nostor means to take all Hostigos, as his grandfather took Sevenhills Valley after the traitor we don't name sold him Tarr-Dombra."

That was a part of the map her eyes had shunned: the bowl valley to the east, where Dombra Gap split the Mountains of Hostigos. It was from thence that Gormoth's mercenary cavalry raided into Hostigos.

"And what hope have we from Styphon's House?" her father asked. He knew the answer; he wanted the others to hear it at first hand.

"The Archpriest wouldn't talk to me; the priests of Styphon hold no speech with priests of other gods," Xentos said.

"The Archpriest wouldn't talk to me, either," Chartiphon said. "Only one of the upper-priests of the temple. He took our offerings and said he would pray to Styphon for us. When I asked for fireseed, he would give me none."

"None at all?" somebody down the table cried. "Then we are indeed under the ban."

Her father rapped with the pommel of his poignard. "You've heard the worst, now. What's in your minds that we should do? You first, Phosg."

The peasant representative rose and cleared his throat.

"Lord Prince, this castle is no more dear to you than my cottage is to me. I'll fight for mine as you would for yours."

There was a quick mutter of approval along the table. "Well said, Phosg!" "An example for all of us!" The others spoke in turn; a few tried to make speeches. Chartiphon said: "Fight. What else."

"I am a priest of Dralm," Xentos said, "and Dralm is a god of peace, but I say, fight with Dralm's blessing. Submission to evil men is the worst of all sins."

"Rylla," her father said.

"Better die in armor than live in chains," she replied. "When the time comes, I will be in armor with the rest of you."

Her father nodded. "I expected no less from any of you." He rose, and all with him. "I thank you. At sunset we will dine together; until then servants will attend you. Now, if you please, leave me with my daughter. Chartiphon, you and Xentos stay."

Chairs scraped and feet scuffed as they went out. The closing door cut off the murmur of voices. Chartiphon had begun to fill his stubby pipe.

"I know there's no use looking to Balthar of Beshta," Rylla said, "but wouldn't Sarrask of Sask aid us? We're better neighbors to him than Gormoth would be."

"Sarrask of Sask's a fool," Chartiphon said shortly. "He doesn't know that once Gormoth has Hostigos, his turn will come next."

"He knows that," Xentos differed. "He'll try to strike before Gormoth does, or catch Gormoth battered from having fought us. But even if he wanted to help us, he dares not. Even King Kaiphranos dares not aid those whom Styphon's House would destroy."

"They want that land in Wolf Valley, for a temple-farm," she considered. "I know that would be bad, but . . ."

"Too late," Xentos told her. "They have made a compact with Gormoth, to furnish him fireseed and money to hire mercenaries, and when he has conquered Hostigos he will give them the land." He paused and added: "And it was on my advice, Prince, that you refused them."

"I'd have refused against your advice, Xentos," her father said. "Long ago I vowed that Styphon's House should never come into Hostigos while I lived, and by Dralm and by Galzar neither shall they! They come into a princedom, they build a temple, they make temple-farms and slaves of everybody on them. They tax the Prince, and make him tax the people, till nobody has anything left. Look at that temple-farm in Sevenhills Valley!"

"Yes, you'd hardly believe it," Chartiphon said. "Why, they even make the peasants for miles around cart their manure in, till they have none left for their own fields. Dralm only knows what they do with it." He puffed at his pipe. "I wonder why they want Sevenhills Valley."

"There's something in the ground there that makes the water of those springs taste and smell badly," her father said.

"Sulfur," said Xentos, "But why do they want sulfur?"

III

CORPORAL Calvin Morrison, Pennsylvania State Police, squatted in the brush at the edge of the old field and looked across the small brook at the farmhouse two hundred yards away. It was scabrous with peeling yellow paint, and festooned with a sagging porch-roof. A few white chickens pecked uninterestedly in the littered barnyard; there was no other sign of life, but he knew that there was a man inside. A man with a rifle, who would use it; a man who had murdered once, broken jail, would murder again.

He looked at his watch; the minute-hand was squarely on the nine. Jack French and Steve Kovac would be starting down from the road above, where they had left the car. He rose, unsnapping the retaining-strap of his holster.

"Watch that middle upstairs window," he said. "I'm starting now."

"I'm watching it." Behind him, a rifle-action clattered softly as a cartridge went into the chamber. "Luck."

He started forward across the seedling-dotted field. He was scared, as scared as he had been the first time, back in '51, in Korea, but there was nothing he could do about that. He just told his legs to keep moving, knowing that in a few moments he wouldn't have time to be scared.

He was within a few feet of the little brook, his hand close to the butt of the Colt, when it happened.

There was a blinding flash, followed by a moment's darkness. He thought he'd been shot; by pure reflex, the .38-special was in his hand. Then, all around him, a flickering iridescence of many colors glowed, a perfect hemisphere fifteen feet high and thirty across, and in front of him was an oval desk with an instrument-panel over it, and a swivel-chair from which a man was rising. Young, well-built; a white man but, he was sure, not an American. He wore loose green trousers and black ankle-boots and a pale green shirt. There was a shoulder holster under his left arm, and a weapon in his right hand.

He was sure it was a weapon, though it looked more like an electric soldering-iron, with two slender rods instead of a barrel, joined, at what should be the muzzle, by a blue ceramic or plastic knob. It was probably something that made his own Colt Official Police look like a kid's cap-pistol, and it was coming up fast to line on him.

He fired, held the trigger back to keep the hammer down on the fired chamber, and flung himself to one side, coming down, on his left hand and left hip, on a smooth, polished floor. Something, probably the chair, fell with a crash. He rolled, and kept on rolling until he was out of the nacreous dome of light and bumped hard against something. For a moment he lay still, then rose to his feet, letting out the trigger of the Colt.

What he'd bumped into was a tree. For a moment he accepted that, then realized that there should be no trees here, nothing but low brush. And this tree, and the ones all around, were huge; great rough columns rising to support a green roof through which only a few stray gleams of sunlight leaked. Hemlocks; must have been growing here while Columbus was still conning Isabella into hocking her jewelry. He looked at the little stream he had been about to cross when this had happened. It was the one thing about this that wasn't completely crazy. Or maybe it was the craziest thing of all.

He began wondering how he was going to explain this.

"While approaching the house," he began, aloud and in a formal tone, "I was intercepted by a flying saucer landing in front of me, the operator of which threatened me with a ray-pistol. I defended myself with my revolver, firing one round . . ."

No. That wouldn't do at all.

He looked at the brook again, and began to suspect that there might be nobody to explain to. Swinging out the cylinder of his Colt, he replaced the fired round. Then he decided to junk the regulation about carrying the hammer on an empty chamber, and put in another one.

IV

VERKAN Vall watched the landscape outside the almost invisible shimmer of the transposition-field; now he was in the forests of the Fifth Level. The mountains, of course, were always the same, but the woods around flickered and shifted. There was a great deal of randomness about which tree grew where, from time-line to time-line. Now and then he would catch fleeting glimpses of open country, and the buildings and airport installations of his own people. The red light overhead went off and on, a buzzer sounding each time. The conveyer dome became a solid iridescence, and then a mesh of cold inert metal. The red light turned green. He picked up a sigma-ray needler from the desk in front of him and holstered it. As he did, the door slid open and two men in Paratime Police green, a lieutenant and a patrolman, entered. When they saw him, they relaxed, holstering their own weapons.

"Hello, Chief's Assistant," the lieutenant said. "Didn't pick anything up, did you?"

In theory, the Ghaldron-Hesthor transposition-field was impenetrable; in practice, especially when two paratemporal vehicles going in opposite "directions" interpenetrated, the field would weaken briefly, and external objects, sometimes alive and hostile, would intrude. That was why paratimers kept weapons ready at hand, and why conveyers were checked immediately upon materializing. It was also why some paratimers didn't make it home.

"Not this trip. Is my rocket ready?"

"Yes, sir. Be a little delay about an aircar for the rocket-port." The patrolman had begun to take the transposition record-tapes out of the cabinet. "They'll call you when it's ready."

He and the lieutenant strolled out into the noise and colorful confusion of the conveyor-head rotunda. He got out his cigarette case and offered it; the lieutenant flicked his lighter. They had only taken a few puffs when another conveyer quietly materialized in a vacant circle a little to their left.

A couple of Paracops strolled over as the door opened, drawing their needlers, and peeped inside. Immediately, one backed away, snatching the hand-phone of his belt radio and speaking quickly into it. The other went inside. Throwing away their cigarettes, he and the lieutenant hastened to the conveyer.

Inside, the chair at the desk was overturned. A Paracop lay on the floor, his needler a few inches from his outflung hand. His tunic was off and his shirt, pale green, was darkened by blood. The lieutenant, without touching him, bent over him.

"Still alive," he said. "Bullet or sword-thrust?"

"Bullet. I smell nitro powder." Then he saw the hat lying on the floor, and stepped around the fallen man. Two men were entering with an antigrav stretcher; they got the wounded man onto it and floated him out. "Look at this, Lieutenant."

The lieutenant looked at the hat—gray felt, wide-brimmed, the crown peaked by four indentations.

"Fourth Level," he said. "Europo-American, Hispano-Columbian Subsector."

He picked up the hat and glanced inside. The lieutenant was right. The sweat-band was stamped in golden Roman-alphabet letters, JOHN B. STETSON COMPANY. PHILADELPHIA, PA., and, hand-inked, *Cpl. Calvin Morrison, Penna'a State Police,* and a number.

"I know that crowd," the lieutenant said. "Good men, every bit as good as ours."

"One was a split second better than one of ours." He got out his cigarette case. "Lieutenant, this is going to be a real baddie. This pickup's going to be missed, and the people who'll miss him will be one of the ten best constabulary organizations in the world, on their time-line. We won't satisfy them with the kind of lame-brained explanations that usually get by in that sector. And we'll have to find out where he emerged, and what he's doing. A man who can beat a Paracop to the draw after being sucked into a conveyer won't just sink into obscurity on any time-line. By the time we get to him, he'll be kicking up a small fuss."

"I hope he got dragged out of his own subsector. Suppose he comes out on a next-door time-line, and reports to his police post, where a duplicate of himself, with duplicate fingerprints, is on duty."

"Yes. Wouldn't that be dandy, now?" He lit a cigarette. "When the aircar comes, send it back. I'm going over the photo-records myself. Have the rocket held; I'll need it in a few hours. I'm making this case my own personal baby."

2

CALVIN Morrison dangled his black-booted legs over the edge of the low cliff and wished, again, that he hadn't lost his hat. He knew exactly where he was: he was right at the same place he had been, sitting on the little cliff above the road where he and Larry Stacey and Jack French and Steve Kovac had left the car, only there was no road there now, and never had been one. There was a hemlock, four feet thick at the butt, growing where the farmhouse should have been, and no trace of the stonework of the foundations of house or barn. But the really permanent features, like the Bald Eagles to the north and Nittany Mountain to the south, were exactly as they should be.

That flash and momentary darkness could have been subjective; put that in the unproven column. He was sure the strangely beautiful dome of shimmering light had been real, and so had the desk and the instrument-panel, and the man with the odd weapon. And there was nothing at all subjective about all this virgin timber where farmlands should have been. So he puffed slowly on his pipe and tried to remember and to analyze what had happened to him.

He hadn't been shot and taken to a hospital where he was now lying delirious, he was sure of that. This wasn't delirium. Nor did he consider for an instant questioning either his sanity or his senses, nor did he indulge in dirty language like "incredible" or "impossible." Extraordinary—now there was a good word. He was quite sure that something extraordinary had happened to him. It seemed to break into two parts: one, blundering into that dome of pearly light, what had happened inside of it, and rolling out of it; and two, this same-but-different place in which he now found himself.

What was wrong with both was anachronism, and the anachronisms were mutually contradictory. None of the first part belonged in 1964 or, he suspected, for many centuries to come; portable energy-weapons, for instance. None of the second part belonged in 1964, either, or for at least a century in the past.

His pipe had gone out. For awhile he forgot to relight it, while he tossed those two facts back and forth in his mind. He still didn't use those dirty words. He used one small boys like to scribble on privy walls.

In spite—no, because—of his clergyman father's insistence that he study for and enter the Presbyterian ministry, he was an agnostic. Agnosticism, for him, was refusal to accept or to deny without proof. A good philosophy for a cop, by the way. Well, he wasn't going to reject the possibility of time-machines; not after having been shanghaied aboard one and having to shoot his way out of it. That thing had been a time-machine, and whenever he was now, it wasn't the twentieth century, and he was never going to get back to it. He settled that point in his mind and accepted it once and for all.

His pipe was out; he started to knock out the heel, then stirred it with a twig and relit it. He couldn't afford to waste anything now. Sixteen rounds of ammunition; he couldn't do a hell of a lot of Indian-fighting on that. The blackjack might be some good at close quarters. The value of the handcuffs and the whistle was problematical. When he had smoked the contents of his pipe down to ash, he emptied and pocketed it and climbed down from the little cliff, going to the brook and following it down to where it joined a larger stream.

A bluejay made a fuss at his approach. Two deer ran in front of him. A small black bear regarded him suspiciously and hastened away. Now, if he could only find some Indians who wouldn't throw tomahawks first and ask questions afterward. . . .

A road dipped in front of him to cross the stream. For an instant he accepted that calmly, then caught his breath. A real, wheel-rutted road. And brown horse-droppings in it—they were the most beautiful things he had ever seen. They meant he hadn't beaten Columbus here, after all. Maybe he might have trouble giving a plausible account of himself, but at least he could do it in English. He waded through the little ford and started down the road, toward where he thought Bellefonte ought to be. Maybe he was in time to get into the Civil War. That would be more fun than Korea had been.

The sun went down in front of him. By now he was out of the big hem-locks; they'd been lumbered off on both sides of the road, and there was a re-spectable second growth, mostly hardwoods. Finally, in the dusk, he smelled freshly turned earth. It was full dark when he saw a light ahead.

The house was only a dim shape; the light came from one window on the end and two in front, horizontal slits under the roof overhang. Behind, he thought, were stables. And a pigpen—his nose told him that. Two dogs, out-side, began whauff-whauffing in the road in front of him.

"Hello, in there!" he called.

Through the open windows, too high to see into, he heard voices: a man's, a woman's, another man's. He called again, and came closer. A bar scraped, and the door swung open. For a moment a heavy-bodied woman in a sleeve-less dark dress stood in it. Then she spoke to him and stepped inside. He en-tered.

It was a big room, lighted by two candles, one on a table spread with a meal and the other on the mantel, and by the fire on the hearth. Double-deck bunks along one wall, fireplace with things stacked against it. There were three men and another, younger, woman, besides the one who had admitted him. Out of the corner of his eye he could see children peering around a door that seemed to open into a shed-annex. One of the men, big and blonde-bearded, stood with his back to the fireplace, holding what looked like a short gun.

No, it wasn't, either. It was a crossbow, bent, with a quarrel in the groove.

The other two men were younger—probably his sons. Both were bearded, though one's beard was only a blonde fuzz. He held an axe; his older brother had a halberd. All three wore sleeveless leather jerkins, short-sleeved shirts, and cross-gartered hose. The older woman spoke in a whisper to the younger woman, who went through the door at the side, hustling the children ahead of her.

He had raised his hands pacifically as he entered. "I'm a friend," he said. "I'm going to Bellefonte; how far is it?"

The man with the crossbow said something. The woman replied. The youth with the axe said something, and they all laughed.

"My name's Morrison. Corporal, Pennsylvania State Police." Hell, they wouldn't know the State Police from the Swiss Marines. "Am I on the road to Bellefonte?" They ought to know where that was, it'd been settled in 1770, and this couldn't be any earlier than that.

More back-and-forth. They weren't talking Pennsylvania Dutch—he knew a little of it. Maybe Polish . . . no, he'd heard enough of that in the hard-coal country to recognize it, at least. He looked around while they argued, and noticed, on a shelf in the far corner, three images. He meant to get a closer look at them. Roman Catholics used images, so did Greek Catholics, and he knew the difference.

The man with the crossbow laid the weapon down, but kept it bent with the quarrel in place, and spoke slowly and distinctly. It was no language he had ever heard before. He replied, just as distinctly, in English. They looked at one another, and passed their hands back and forth across their faces. On a thousand-to-one chance, he tried Japanese. It didn't pay off. By signs, they invited him to sit and eat with them, and the children, six of them, trooped in.

The meal was ham, potatoes and succotash. The eating tools were knives and a few horn spoons; the plates were slabs of corn-bread. The men used their belt-knives. He took out his jackknife, a big switchblade he'd taken off a j.d. arrest, and caused a sensation with it. He had to demonstrate several times. There was also elderberry wine, strong but not particularly good. When they left the table for the women to clear, the men filled pipes from a tobacco-jar on the mantel, offering it to him. He filled his own, lighting it, as they had, with a twig from the hearth. Stepping back, he got a look at the images.

The central figure was an elderly man in a white robe with a blue eight-pointed star on his breast. Flanking him, on the left, was a seated female figure, nude and exaggeratedly pregnant, crowned with wheat and holding a cornstalk; and on the right a masculine figure in a mail shirt, holding a spiked mace. The only really odd thing about him was that he had the head of a wolf. Father god, fertility goddess, war god. No, this crowd weren't Catholics— Greek, Roman or any other kind.

He bowed to the central figure, touching his forehead, and repeated the gesture to the other two. There was a gratified murmur behind him; anybody could see he wasn't any heathen. Then he sat down on a chest with his back to the wall.

They hadn't re-barred the door. The children had been herded back into the annex by the younger woman. Now that he recalled, there'd been a vacant place, which he had taken, at the table. Somebody had gone off somewhere with a message. As soon as he finished his pipe, he pocketed it, managing, unobtrusively, to unsnap the strap of his holster.

Some half an hour later, he caught the galloping thud of hooves down the road—at least six horses. He pretended not to hear it; so did the others. The father moved to where he had put down the crossbow; the older son got hold of the halberd, and the fuzz-chinned youth moved to the door. The horses stopped outside; the dogs began barking frantically. There was a clatter of accoutrements as men dismounted. He slipped the .38 out and cocked it.

The youth went to the door, but before he could open it, it flew back in his face, knocking him backward, and a man—bearded face under a high-combed helmet, steel long sword in front of him—entered. There was another helmeted head behind, and the muzzle of a musket. Everybody in the room shouted in alarm; this wasn't what they'd been expecting, at all. Outside, a pistol banged, and a dog howled briefly.

Rising from the chest, he shot the man with the sword. Half-cocking with the double-action and thumbing the hammer back the rest of the way, he shot the man with the musket, which went off into the ceiling. A man behind him caught a crossbow quarrel in the forehead and pitched forward, dropping a long pistol unfired.

Shifting the Colt to his left hand, he caught up the sword the first man had dropped. Double-edged, with a swept guard, it was lighter than it looked, and beautifully balanced. He stepped over the body of the first man he had shot, to be confronted by a swordsman from outside, trying to get over the other two. For a few moments they cut and parried, and then he drove the point into his opponent's unarmored face, then tugged his blade free as the man went down. The boy, who had gotten hold of the dropped pistol, fired past him and hit a man holding a clump of horses in the road. Then he was outside, and the man with the halberd along with him, chopping down another of the party. The father followed; he'd gotten the musket and powder-flask, and was reloading it.

Driving the point of the sword into the ground, he holstered his Colt and as one of the loose horses passed, caught the reins, throwing himself into the saddle. Then, when his feet had found the stirrups, he stooped and retrieved the sword, thankful that even in a motorized age the state police taught their men to ride.

The fight was over, at least here. Six attackers were down, presumably dead; two more were galloping away. Five loose horses milled about, and the two young men were trying to catch them. Their father had charged the short musket, and was priming the pan.

This had only been a sideshow fight, though. The main event was a half mile down the road; he could hear shots, yells and screams, and a sudden orange glare mounted into the night. While he was quieting the horse and trying to accustom him to the change of ownership, a couple more fires blazed up. He was wondering just what he had cut himself in on when the fugitives began streaming up the road. He had no trouble identifying them as such; he'd seen enough of that in Korea.

There were more than fifty of them—men, women and children. Some of the men had weapons: spears, axes, a few bows, one musket almost six feet long. His bearded host shouted at them, and they paused.

"What's going on down there?" he demanded.

Babble answered him. One or two tried to push past; he cursed them luridly and slapped at them with his flat. The words meant nothing, but the tone did. That had worked for him in Korea, too. They all stopped in a clump, while the bearded man spoke to them. A few cheered. He looked them over; call it twenty effectives. The bodies in the road were stripped of weapons; out of the corner of his eye he saw the two women passing things out the cottage door. Four of the riderless horses had been caught and mounted. More fugitives came up, saw what was going on, and joined.

"All right, you guys! You want to live forever?" He swung his sword to include all of them, then pointed down the road to where a whole village must now be burning. "Come on, let's go get them!"

A general cheer went up as he started his horse forward, and the whole mob poured after him, shouting. They met more and more fugitives, who saw that a counter-attack had been organized, if that was the word for it. The shooting ahead had stopped. Nothing left in the village to shoot at, he supposed.

Then, when they were within four or five hundred yards of the burning houses, there was a blast of forty or fifty shots in less than ten seconds, and loud yells, some in alarm. More shots, and then mounted men came pelting toward them. This wasn't an attack; it was a rout. Whoever had raided that village had been hit from behind. Everybody with guns or bows let fly at once. A horse went down, and a saddle was emptied. Remembering how many shots it had taken for one casualty in Korea, that wasn't bad. He stood up in his stirrups, which were an inch or so too short for him to begin with, waved his sword, and shouted, *"Chaaarge!"* Then he and the others who were mounted kicked their horses into a gallop, and the infantry—axes, scythes, pitchforks and all—ran after them.

A horseman coming in the opposite direction aimed a sword-cut at his bare head. He parried and thrust, the point glancing from a breastplate. Before either could recover, the other man's horse had carried him on past and among the spears and pitchforks behind. Then he was trading thrusts for cuts with another rider, wondering if none of these imbeciles had ever heard that a sword had a point. By this time the road for a hundred yards in front, and the fields on either side, were full of horsemen, chopping and shooting at one another in the firelight.

He got his point in under his opponent's arm, the memory-voice of a history professor of long ago reminded him of the gap in a cuirass there, and almost had the sword wrenched from his hand before he cleared it. Then another rider was coming at him, unarmored, wearing a cloak and a broad hat, aiming a pistol almost as long as the arm that held it. He swung back for a cut, urging his horse forward, and knew he'd never make it. *All right, Cal; your luck's run out!*

There was an upflash from the pan, a belch of flame from the muzzle, and something hammered him in the chest. He hung onto consciousness long enough to kick his feet free of the stirrups. In that last moment, he realized that the rider who had shot him had been a girl.

3

I

RYLLA sat with her father at the table in the small study. Chartiphon was at one end and Xentos at the other, and Harmakros, the cavalry captain, in a chair by the hearth, his helmet on the floor beside him. Vurth, the peasant, stood facing them, a short horseman's musketoon slung from his shoulder and a horn flask and bullet-bag on his belt.

"You did well, Vurth," her father commended. "By sending the message, and in the fighting, and by telling Princess Rylla that the stranger was a friend. I'll see you're rewarded."

Vurth smiled. "But, Prince, I have this gun, and fireseed for it," he replied. "And my son caught a horse, with all its gear, even pistols in the holsters, and the Princess says we may keep it all."

"Fair battle-spoil, yours by right. But I'll see that something's sent to your farm tomorrow. Just don't waste that fireseed on deer. You'll need it to kill more Nostori before long."

He nodded in dismissal, and Vurth grinned and bowed, and backed out, stammering thanks. Chartiphon looked after him, remarking that there went a man Gormoth of Nostor would find costly to kill.

"He didn't pay cheaply for anything tonight," Harmakros said. "Eight houses burned, a dozen peasants butchered, four of our troopers killed and six wounded, and we counted better than thirty of his dead in the village on the road, and six more at Vurth's farm. And the horses we caught, and the weapons." He thought briefly. "I'd question if a dozen of them got away alive and hale."

Her father gave a mirthless chuckle. "I'm glad some did. They'll have a fine tale to carry back. I'd like to see Gormoth's face at the telling."

"We owe the stranger for most of it," she said. "If he hadn't rallied those people at Vurth's farm and led them back, most of the Nostori would have gotten away. And then I had to shoot him myself!"

"You couldn't know, kitten," Chartiphon told her. "I've been near killed by friends myself, in fights like that." He turned to Xentos. "How is he?"

"He'll live to hear our thanks," the old priest said. "The ornament on his breast broke the force of the bullet. He has a broken rib, and a nasty hole in him—our Rylla doesn't load her pistols lightly. He's lost more blood than I'd want to, but he's young and strong, and Brother Mytron has much skill. We'll have him on his feet again in a half-moon."

She smiled happily. It would be terrible for him to die, and at her hand, a stranger who had fought so well for them. And such a handsome and valiant stranger, too. She wondered who he was. Some noble, or some great captain, of course.

"We owe much to Princess Rylla," Harmakros insisted. "When this man from the village overtook us, I was for riding back with three or four to see about this stranger of Vurth's, but the Princess said, 'We've only Vurth's word there's but one; there may be a hundred Vurth hasn't seen.' So back we all went, and you know the rest."

"We owe most of all to Dralm." Old Xentos's face lit with a calm joy. "And Galzar Wolfhead, of course," he added. "It is a sign that the gods will not turn their backs upon Hostigos. This stranger, whoever he may be, was sent by the gods to be our aid."

II

VERKAN Vall put the lighter back on the desk and took the cigarette from his mouth, blowing a streamer of smoke.

"Chief, it's what I've been saying all along. We'll have to do something." After Year-End Day, he added mentally, I'll do something. "We know what causes this: conveyers interpenetrating in transposition. It'll have to be stopped."

Tortha Karf laughed. "The reason I'm laughing," he explained, "is that I said just that, about a hundred and fifty years ago, to old Zarvan Tharg, when I was taking over from him, and he laughed at me just as I'm laughing at you, because he'd said the same thing to the retiring Chief when he was taking over. Have you ever seen an all-time-line conveyer-head map?"

No. He couldn't recall. He blanked his mind to everything else and concentrated with all his mental power.

"No, I haven't."

"I should guess not. With the finest dots, on the biggest map, all the inhabited areas would be indistinguishable blotches. There must be a couple of conveyers interpenetrating every second of every minute of every day. You know," he added gently, "we're rather extensively spread out."

"We can cut it down." There had to be *something* that could be done. "Better scheduling, maybe."

"Maybe. How about this case you're taking an interest in?"

"Well, we had one piece of luck. The pickup time-line is one we're on already. One of our people, in a newspaper office in Philadelphia, messaged us that same evening. He says the press associations have the story, and there's nothing we can do about that."

"Well, just what did happen?"

"This man Morrison and three other state police officers were closing in on a house in which a wanted criminal was hiding. He must have been a dangerous man—they don't go out in force like that for chicken-thieves. Morrison and another man were in front; the other two were coming in from behind. Morrison started forward, with his companion covering for him with a rifle. This other man is the nearest thing to a witness there is, but he was watching the front of the house and only marginally aware of Morrison. He says he heard the other two officers pounding on the back door and demanding admittance, and then the man they were after burst out the front door with a rifle in his hands. This officer—Stacey's his name—shouted to him to drop the rifle and put up his hands. Instead, the criminal tried to raise it to his shoulder; Stacey fired, killing him instantly. Then, he says, he realized that Morrison was nowhere in sight.

"He called, needless to say without response, and then he and the other two hunted about for some time. They found nothing, of course. They took this body in to the county seat and had to go through a lot of formalities; it was evening before they were back at the substation, and it happened that a reporter was there, got the story, and phoned it to his paper. The press associations then got hold of it. Now the state police refuse to discuss the disappearance, and they're even trying to deny it."

"They think their man's nerve snapped, he ran away in a panic, and is ashamed to come back. They wouldn't want a story like that getting around; they'll try to cover up."

"Yes. This hat he lost in the conveyer, with his name in it—we'll plant it about a mile from the scene, and then get hold of some local, preferably a boy of twelve or so, give him narco-hyp instructions to find the hat and take it to the state police substation, and then inform the reporter responsible for the original news-break by an anonymous phone call. After that, there will be the usual spate of rumors of Morrison being seen in widely separated localities."

"How about his family?"

"We're in luck there, too. Unmarried, parents both dead, no near relatives."

The Chief nodded. "That's good. Usually there are a lot of relatives yelling their heads off. Particularly on sectors where they have inheritance laws. Have you located the exit time-line?"

"Approximated it; somewhere on Aryan-Transpacific. We can't determine the exact moment at which he broke free of the field. We have one positive indication to look for at the scene."

The Chief grinned. "Let me guess. The empty revolver cartridge."

"That's right. The things the state police use don't eject automatically; he'd have to open it and take the empty out by hand. And as soon as he was outside the conveyer and no longer immediately threatened, that's precisely what he'd do: open his revolver, eject the empty, and replace it with a live round. I'm as sure of that as though I watched him do it. We may not be able to find it, but if we do it'll be positive proof."

4

MORRISON woke, stiff and aching, under soft covers, and for a moment lay with his eyes closed. Near him, something clicked with soft and monotonous regularity; from somewhere an anvil rang, and there was shouting. Then he opened his eyes. It was daylight, and he was on a bed in a fairly large room with paneled walls and a white plaster ceiling. There were two windows at one side, both open, and under one of them a woman, stout and gray-haired, in a green dress, sat knitting. It had been her needles that he had heard. Nothing but blue sky was visible through the windows. There was a table, with things on it, and chairs, and, across the room, a chest on the top of which his clothes were neatly piled, his belt and revolver on top. His boots, neatly cleaned, stood by the chest, and a long unsheathed sword with a swept guard and a copper pommel leaned against the wall.

The woman looked up quickly as he stirred, then put her knitting on the floor and rose. She looked at him, and went to the table, pouring a cup of water and bringing it to him. He thanked her, drank, and gave it back. The cup and pitcher were of heavy silver, elaborately chased. This wasn't any peasant cottage. Replacing the cup on the table, she went out.

He ran a hand over his chin. About three days' stubble. The growth of his fingernails checked with that. The whole upper part of his torso was tightly bandaged. Broken rib, or ribs, and probably a nasty hole in him. He was still alive after three days. Estimating the here-and-now medical art from the general technological level as he'd seen it so far, that probably meant that he had a fair chance of continuing so. At least he was among friends and not a prisoner. The presence of the sword and the revolver proved that.

The woman returned, accompanied by a man in a blue robe with an eight-pointed white star on the breast, the colors of the central image on the peasants' god-shelf reversed. A priest, doubling as doctor. He was short and chubby, with a pleasant round face; advancing, he laid a hand on Morrison's brow, took his pulse, and spoke in a cheerfully optimistic tone. The bedside manner seemed to be a universal constant. With the woman's help, he got the bandages, yards of them, off. He did have a nasty wound, uncomfortably close to his heart, and his whole left side was black and blue. The woman brought a pot from the table; the doctor-priest smeared the wound with some dirty-looking unguent, they put on fresh bandages, and the woman took out the old ones. The doctor-priest tried to talk to him; he tried to talk to the doctor-priest. The woman came back with a bowl of turkey-broth, full of finely minced meat, and a spoon. While he was finishing it, two more visitors arrived.

One was a man, robed like the doctor, his cowl thrown back from his head, revealing snow-white hair. He had a gentle, kindly face, and was smiling. For a moment Morrison wondered if this place might be a monastery of some sort, and then saw the old priest's definitely un-monastic companion.

She was a girl, twenty, give or take a year or so, with blonde hair cut in what he knew as a page-boy bob. She had blue eyes and red lips and an impudent tilty little nose dusted with golden freckles. She wore a jerkin of something like brown suede, sewn with gold thread, and a yellow under-tunic with a high neck and long sleeves, and brown knit hose and thigh-length jackboots. There was a gold chain around her neck, and a gold-hilted dagger on a belt of gold links. No, this wasn't any monastery, and it wasn't any peasant hovel, either.

As soon as he saw her, he began to laugh. He'd met that young lady before.

"You shot me!" he accused, aiming an imaginary pistol and saying "Bang!" and then touching his chest.

She said something to the older priest, he replied, and she said something to Morrison, pantomiming sorrow and shame, covering her face with one hand, and winking at him over it. Then they both laughed. Perfectly natural mistake—how could she have known which side he'd been on?

The two priests held a colloquy, and then the younger brought him about four ounces of something dark brown in a glass tumbler. It tasted alcoholic and medicinally bitter. They told him, by signs, to go back to sleep, and left him, the girl looking back over her shoulder as she went out.

He squirmed a little, decided that he was going to like it, here-and-now, and dozed off.

LATE in the afternoon he woke again. A different woman, thin, with mouse-brown hair, sat in the chair under the window, stitching on something that looked like a shirt. Outside, a dark was barking, and farther off somebody was drilling troops—a couple of hundred, from the amount of noise they were making. A voice was counting cadence: *Heep, heep, heep, heep!* Another universal constant.

He smiled contentedly. Once he got on his feet again, he didn't think he was going to be on unemployment very long. A soldier was all he'd ever been, since he'd stopped being a theological student at Princeton between sophomore and junior years. He'd owed a lot of thanks to the North Korean Communists for starting that war; without it, he might never have found the moral courage to free himself from the career into which his father had been forcing him. His enlisting in the Army had probably killed his father; the Rev. Alexander Morrison simply couldn't endure not having his own way. At least, he died while his son was in Korea.

Then there had been the year and a half, after he came home, when he'd worked as a bank guard, until his mother died. That had been soldiering of a sort; he'd worked armed and in uniform, at least. And then, when he no longer had his mother to support, he'd gone into the state police. That had really been soldiering, the nearest anybody could come to it in peacetime.

And then he'd blundered into that dome of pearly light, that time-machine, and come out of it into—into here-and-now, that was all he could call it.

When *here* was was fairly easy. It had to be somewhere within, say, ten or fifteen miles of where he had been time-shifted, which was just over the Clinton County line, in Nittany Valley. They didn't use helicopters to evacuate the wounded here-and-now, that was sure.

When *now* was was something else. He lay on his back, looking up at the white ceiling, not wanting to attract the attention of the woman sewing by the window. It wasn't the past. Even if he hadn't studied history—it was about the only thing at college he had studied—he'd have known that Penn's Colony had never been anything like this. It was more like sixteenth century Europe, though any sixteenth-century French or German cavalryman who was as incompetent a swordsman as that gang he'd been fighting wouldn't have lived to wear out his first pair of issue boots. And enough Comparative Religion had rubbed off on him to know that those three images on that peasant's shelf didn't belong in any mythology back to Egypt and Sumeria.

So it had to be the future. A far future, long after the world had been devastated by atomic war, and man, self-blasted back to the Stone Age, had bootstrap-lifted himself back this far. A thousand years, ten thousand years; ten dollars if you guess how many beans in the jar. The important thing was that here-and-now was when-where he would stay, and he'd have to make a place for himself. He thought he was going to like it.

That lovely, lovely blonde! He fell asleep thinking about her.

BREAKFAST the next morning was cornmeal mush cooked with meat-broth and tasting rather like scrapple, and a mug of sassafras tea. Coffee, it seemed, didn't exist here-and-now, and *that* he was going to miss. He sign-talked for his tunic to be brought, and got his pipe, tobacco and lighter out of it. The woman brought a stool and set it beside the bed to put things on. The lighter opened her eyes a trifle, and she said something, and he said something in a polite voice, and she went back to her knitting. He looked at the tunic; it was torn and blood-soaked on the left side, and the badge was lead-splashed and twisted. That was why he was still alive.

The old priest and the girl were in about an hour later. This time she was wearing a red and gray knit frock that could have gone into Bergdorf-Goodman's window with a $200 price-tag any day, though the dagger on her belt wasn't exactly Fifth Avenue. They had slates and soapstone sticks with them; paper evidently hadn't been rediscovered yet. They greeted him, then pulled up chairs and got down to business.

First, they taught him the words for *you* and *me* and *he* and *she,* and, when he had that, names. The girl was Rylla. The old priest was Xentos. The younger priest, who dropped in for a look at the patient, was Mytron. The names, he thought, sounded Greek; it was the only point of resemblance in the language.

Calvin Morrison puzzled them. Evidently they didn't have surnames, here-and-now. They settled on calling him Kalvan. There was a lot of picture-drawing on the slates, and play-acting for verbs, which was fun. Both Rylla and Xentos smoked; Rylla's pipe, which she carried on her belt with her dagger, had a silver-inlaid redstone bowl and a cane stem. She was intrigued by his Zippo, and showed him her own lighter. It was a tinderbox, with a flint held down by a spring against a quarter-circular striker pushed by hand and returned by another spring for another push. With a spring to drive instead of return the striker it would have done for a gunlock. By noon, they were able to tell him that he was their friend because he had killed their enemies, which seemed to be the definitive test of friendship, here-and-now, and he was able to assure Rylla that he didn't blame her for shooting him in the skirmish on the road.

They were back in the afternoon, accompanied by a gentleman with a gray imperial, wearing a garment like a fur-collared bathrobe and a sword-belt over it. He had a most impressive gold chain around his neck. His name was Ptosphes, and after much sign-talk and picture-making, it emerged that he was Rylla's father, and also Prince of this place. This place, it seemed, was Hostigos. The raiders with whom he had fought had come from a place called Nostor, to the north and east. Their Prince was named Gormoth, and Gormoth was not well thought of in Hostigos.

The next day, he was up in a chair, and they began giving him solid food, and wine to drink. The wine was excellent; so was the local tobacco. Maybe he'd get used to sassafras tea instead of coffee. The food was good, though sometimes odd. Bacon and eggs, for instance; the eggs were turkey eggs. Evidently they didn't have chickens, here-and-now. They had plenty of game, though. The game must have come back nicely after the atomic wars.

Rylla was in to see him twice a day, sometimes alone and sometimes with Xentos, or with a big man with a graying beard, Chartiphon, who seemed to be Ptosphes' top soldier. He always wore a sword, long and heavy, with a two-hand grip; not a real two-hander, but what he'd known as a hand-and-a-half, or bastard, sword. Often he wore a gilded back-and-breast, ornately wrought but nicked and battered. Sometimes, too, he visited alone, or with a young cavalry officer, Harmakros.

Harmakros wore a beard, too, obviously copied after Prince Ptosphes's. He decided to stop worrying about getting a shave; you could wear a beard, here-and-now, and nobody'd think you were either an Amishman or a beatnik. Harmakros had been on the patrol that had hit the Nostori raiders from behind at the village, but, it appeared, Rylla had been in command.

"The gods," Chartiphon explained, "did not give our Prince a son. A Prince should have a son, to rule after him, so our little Rylla must be as a son to her father."

The gods, he thought, ought to provide Prince Ptosphes with a son-in-law, name of Calvin Morrison . . . or just Kalvan. He made up his mind to give the gods some help on that.

There was another priest in to see him occasionally: a red-nosed, gray-bearded character named Tharses, who had a slight limp and a scarred face. One look was enough to tell which god he served; he wore a light shirt of finely linked mail and a dagger and a spiked mace on his belt, and a wolfskin hood topped with a jewel-eyed wolf head. As soon as he came in, he would toss that aside, and as soon as he sat down somebody would provide him with a drink. He almost always had a cat or a dog trailing him. Everybody called him Uncle Wolf.

Chartiphon showed him a map, elaborately illuminated on parchment. Hostigos was all Centre County, the southern corner of Clinton, and all Lycoming south of the Bald Eagles. Hostigos Town was exactly on the site of otherwhen Bellefonte; they were at Tarr-Hostigos, or Hostigos Castle, overlooking it from the end of the mountain east of the gap. To the south, the valley of the Juniata, the Besh, was the Princedom of Beshta, ruled by a Prince Balthar. Nostor was Lycoming County north of the Bald Eagles, Tioga County to the north, and parts of Northumberland and Montour Counties, to the forks of the Susquehanna. Nostor Town would be about Hughesville. Potter and McKean Counties were Nyklos, ruled by a Prince Armanes. Blair and parts of Clearfield, Huntington and Bedford Counties made up Sask, whose prince was called Sarrask.

Prince Gormoth of Nostor was a deadly enemy. Armanes was a friendly neutral. Sarrask of Sask was no friend of Hostigos; Balthar of Beshta was no friend of anybody's.

On a bigger map, he saw that all this was part of the Great Kingdom of Hos-Harphax—all of Pennsylvania, Maryland, Delaware and southern New Jersey—ruled by a King Kaiphranos at Harphax City, at the mouth of the Susquehanna, the Harph. No, he substituted—just reigned over lightly. To judge from what he'd seen on the night of his arrival, King Kaiphranos's authority would be enforced for about a day's infantry march around his capital and ignored elsewhere.

He had a suspicion that Hostigos was in a bad squeeze between Nostor and Sask. He could hear the sounds of drilling soldiers every day, and something was worrying these people. Too often, while Rylla was laughing with him—she was teaching him to read, now, and that was fun—she would remember something she wanted to forget, and then her laughter would be strained. Chartiphon seemed always preoccupied; at times he'd forget, for a moment, what he'd been talking about. And he never saw Ptosphes smile.

Xentos showed him a map of the world. The world, it seemed, was round, but flat like a pancake. Hudson's Bay was in the exact center, North America was shaped rather like India, Florida ran almost due east, and Cuba north and south. Asia was attached to North America, but it was all blankly unknown. An illimitable ocean surrounded everything. Europe, Africa and South America simply weren't.

Xentos wanted him to show the country from whence he had come. He'd been expecting that to come up, sooner or later, and it had worried him. He couldn't risk lying, since he didn't know on what point he might be tripped up, so he had decided to tell the truth, tailored to local beliefs and preconceptions. Fortunately, he and the old priest were alone at the time.

He put his finger down on central Pennsylvania. Xentos thought he misunderstood.

"No, Kalvan. This is your home now, and we want you to stay with us always. But from what place did you come?"

"Here," he insisted. "But from another time, a thousand years in the future. I had an enemy, an evil sorcerer, of great power. Another sorcerer, who was not my friend but was my enemy's enemy, put a protection about me, so that I might not be sorcerously slain. So my enemy twisted time for me, and hurled me far back into the past, before my first known ancestor had been born, and now here I am and here I must stay."

Xentos's hand described a quick circle around the white star on his breast, and he muttered rapidly. Another universal constant.

"How terrible! Why, you have been banished as no man ever was!"

"Yes. I do not like to speak, or even think, of it, but it is right that you should know. Tell Prince Ptosphes, and Princess Rylla, and Chartiphon, pledging them to secrecy, and beg them not to speak of it to me. I must forget my old life, and make a new one here and now. For all others, it may be said that I am from a far country. From here." He indicated what ought to be the location of Korea on the blankness of Asia. "I was there, once, fighting in a great war."

"Ah! I knew you had been a warrior." Xentos hesitated, then asked: "Do you also know sorcery?"

"No. My father was a priest, as you are, and our priests hated sorcery." Xentos nodded in agreement with that. "He wished me also to become a priest, but I knew that I would not be a good one, so when this war came, I left my studies and joined the army of my Great King, Truman, and went away to fight. After the war, I was a warrior to keep the peace in my own country."

Xentos nodded again. "If one cannot be a good priest, one should not be a priest at all, and to be a good warrior is the next best thing. What gods did your people worship?"

"Oh, my people had many gods. There was Conformity, and Authority, and Expense Account, and Opinion. And there was Status, whose symbols were many, and who rode in the great chariot Cadillac, which was almost a god itself. And there was Atom-bomb, the dread destroyer, who would some day come to end the world. None were very good gods, and I worshiped none of them. Tell me about your gods, Xentos."

Then he filled his pipe and lit it with the tinderbox that replaced his now fuelless Zippo. He didn't need to talk any more; Xentos was telling him about his gods. There was Dralm, to whom all men and all other gods bowed; he was a priest of Dralm himself. Yirtta Allmother, the source of all life. Galzar the war god, all of whose priests were called Uncle Wolf; lame Tranth, the craftman god; fickle Lytris, the weather goddess; all the others.

"And Styphon," he added grudgingly. "Styphon is an evil god, and evil men serve him, but to them he gives wealth and great power."

5

AFTER that, he began noticing a subtle change in manner toward him. Occasionally he caught Rylla regarding him in awe tinged with compassion. Chartiphon merely clasped his hand and said, "You'll like it here, Lord Kalvan." It amused him that he had accepted the title as though born to it. Prince Ptosphes said casually, "Xentos tells me there are things you don't want to talk about. Nobody will speak of them to you. We're all happy that you're with us; we'd like you to make this your home always."

The others treated him with profound respect; the story for public consumption was that he was a Prince from a distant country, beyond the Western Ocean and around the Cold Lands, driven from his throne by treason. That was the ancient and forgotten land of wonder; that was the Home of the Gods. And Xentos had told Mytron, and Mytron told everybody else, that the Lord Kalvan had been sent to Hostigos by Dralm.

As soon as he was on his feet again, they moved him to a suite of larger rooms, and gave him personal servants. There were clothes for him, more than he had ever owned at one time in his life, and fine weapons. Rylla contributed a pair of her own pistols, all of two feet long but no heavier than his Colt .38-special, the barrels tapering to almost paper thinness at the muzzles. The locks worked with the tinderboxes, flint held tightly against moving striker, like wheel-locks but with a simpler and more efficient mechanism.

"I shot you with one of them," she said.

"If you hadn't," he said, "I'd have ridden on, after the fight, and never come to Tarr-Hostigos."

"Maybe it would have been better for you if you had."

"No, Rylla. This is the most wonderful thing that ever happened to me."

As soon as he could walk unaided, he went down and outside to watch the soldiers drilling. They had nothing like uniforms, except blue and red scarves or sashes, Prince Ptosphes' colors. The flag of Hostigos was a blue halberd-head on a red field. The infantry wore canvas jacks sewn with metal plates, or brigandines, and a few had mail shirts; their helmets weren't unlike the one he had worn in Korea. A few looked like regulars; most of them were peasant levies. Some had long pikes; more had halberds or hunting-spears or scythe-blades with the tangs straightened and fitted to eight-foot staves, or woodcut-ters' axes with four-foot helves.

There was about one firearm to three polearms. Some were huge muskets, five to six feet long, 8- to 6-bore, aimed and fired from rests. There were ar-quebuses, about the size and weight of an M-1 Garrand, 16- to 20-bore, and calivers about the size of the Brown Bess musket of the Revolution and the Napoleonic Wars. All were fitted with the odd back-acting flintlocks; he won-dered which had been adapted from which, the gunlock or the tinderbox. There were also quite a few crossbowmen.

The cavalry wore high-combed helmets and cuirasses; they were armed with swords and pistols, a pair in saddle-holsters and, frequently, a second pair down the boot-tops. Most of them also carried short musketoons or lances. They all seemed to be regulars. One thing puzzled him: while the crossbow-man practiced constantly, he never saw a firearm discharged at a target. Maybe a powder-shortage was one of the things that was worrying the people here.

The artillery was laughable; it would have been long out of date in the six-teenth century of his own time. The guns were all wrought-iron, built up by welding bars together and strengthened with shrunk-on iron rings. They didn't have trunnions; evidently nobody here-and-now had ever thought of that. What passed for field-pieces were mounted on great timbers, like oversized gunstocks, and hauled on four-wheel carts. They ran from four to twelve pound bore. The fixed guns on the castle walls were bigger, some huge bom-bards firing fifty, one hundred, and even two-hundred pound stone balls.

Fifteenth century stuff; Henry V had taken Harfleur with just as good, and John of Bedford had probably bombarded Orleans with better. He decided to speak to Chartiphon about this.

He took the broadsword he had captured on the night of his advent here-

and-now to the castle bladesmith, to have it ground down into a rapier. The bladesmith thought he was crazy. He found a pair of wooden practice swords and went outside with a cavalry lieutenant to demonstrate. Immediately, the lieutenant wanted a rapier, too. The bladesmith promised to make real ones, to his specifications, for both of them. His was finished the next evening, and by that time the bladesmith was swamped with orders for rapiers.

Almost everything these people used could be made in the workshops inside the walls of Tarr-Hostigos, or in Hostigos Town, and he seemed to have an unlimited expense-account with them. He began to wonder what, besides being the guest from the Land of the Gods, he was supposed to do to earn it. Nobody mentioned that; maybe they were waiting for him to mention it.

He brought the subject up, one evening, in Prince Ptosphes's study, where he and the Prince and Rylla and Xentos and Chartiphon were smoking over a flagon of after-dinner wine.

"You have enemies on both sides—Gormoth of Nostor and Sarrask of Sask—and that's not good. You have taken me in and made me one of you. What can I do to help against them?"

"Well, Kalvan," Ptosphes said, "perhaps you could better tell us that. We don't want to talk of what distresses you, but you must come of a very wise people. You've already taught us new things, like the thrusting-sword"—he looked admiringly at the new rapier he had laid aside—"and what you've told Chartiphon about mounting cannon. What else can you teach us?"

Quite a lot, he thought. There had been one professor at Princeton whose favorite pupil he had been, and who had been his favorite teacher. A history prof, and an unusual one. Most academic people at the middle of the twentieth century took the same attitude toward war that their Victorian opposite numbers had toward sex: one of those deplorable facts nice people don't talk about, and maybe if you don't look at the horrid thing it'll go away. This man had been different. What happened in the cloisters and the guild-halls and the parliaments and council-chambers was important, but none of them went into effect until ratified on the battlefield. So he had emphasized the military aspect of history in a freshman from Pennsylvania named Morrison, a divinity student, of all unlikely things. So, while he should have been studying homiletics and scriptural exegesis and youth-organization methods, that freshman, and a year later that sophomore, had been reading Sir Charles Oman's *Art of War.*

"Well, I can't tell you how to make weapons like that six-shooter of mine, or ammunition for it," he began, and then tried, as simply as possible, to explain about mass production and machine industry. They only stared in incomprehension and wonder. "I can show you a few things you can do with the things you have. For instance, we cut spiral grooves inside the bores of our guns, to make the bullet spin. Such guns shoot harder, straighter and farther than smoothbores. I can show you how to build cannon that can be moved rapidly and loaded and fired much more rapidly than what you have. And another thing." He mentioned never having seen any practice firing. "You have very little powder—fireseed, you call it. Is that it?"

"There isn't enough fireseed in all Hostigos to load all the cannon of this castle for one shot," Chartiphon told him. "And we can get no more. The priests of Styphon have put us under the ban and will let us have none, and they send cartload after cartload to Nostor."

"You mean you get your fireseed from the priests of Styphon? Can't you make your own?"

They all looked at him as though he was a cretin.

"Nobody can make fireseed but the priests of Styphon," Xentos told him. "That was what I meant when I told you that Styphon's House has great power. With Styphon's aid, they alone can make it, and so they have great power, even over the Great Kings."

"Well I'll be Dralm-damned!"

He gave Styphon's House that grudging respect any good cop gives a really smart crook. Brother, what a racket! No wonder this country, here-and-now, was divided into five Great Kingdoms, and each split into a snakepit of warring Princes and petty barons. Styphon's House wanted it that way; it was good for business. A lot of things became clear. For instance, if Styphon's House did the weaponeering as well as the powder-making, it would explain why small-arms were so good; they'd see to it that nobody without fireseed stood an outside chance against anybody with it. But they'd keep the brakes on artillery development. Styphon House wouldn't want bloody or destructive wars—they'd be bad for business. Just wars that burned lots of fireseed; that would be why there were all these great powder-hogs of bombards around.

And no wonder everybody in Hostigos had monkeys on their backs. They knew they were facing the short end of a war of extermination. He set down his goblet and laughed.

"You think nobody but those priests of Styphon can make fireseed?" There was nobody here that wasn't security-cleared for the inside version of his cover-story. "Why, in my time, everybody, even the children, could do that." (Well, children who'd gotten as far as high school chemistry; he'd almost been expelled, once) "I can make fireseed right here on this table." He refilled his goblet.

"But it is a miracle; only by the power of Styphon . . ." Xentos began.

"Styphon's a big fake!" he declared. "A false god; his priests are lying swindlers." That shocked Xentos; good or bad, a god was a god and shouldn't be talked about like that. "You want to see me do it? Mytron has everything in his dispensary I'll need. I'll want sulfur, and saltpeter." Mytron prescribed sulfur and honey (they had no molasses here-and-now), and saltpeter was supposed to cool the blood. "And charcoal, and a brass mortar and pestle, and a flour-sieve and something to sift into, and a pair of balance-scales." He picked up an unused goblet. "This'll do to mix it in."

Now they were all staring at him as though he had three heads, and a golden crown on each one.

"Go on, man! Hurry!" Ptosphes told Xentos. "Have everything brought here at once."

Then the Prince threw back his head and laughed—maybe a trifle hysterically, but it was the first time Morrison had heard Ptosphes laugh at all. Chartiphon banged his fist on the table.

"Ha, Gormoth!" he cried. "Now see whose head goes up over whose gate!"

Xentos went out. Morrison asked for a pistol, and Ptosphes brought him one from a cabinet behind him. It was loaded; opening the pan, he spilled out the priming on a sheet of parchment and touched a lighted splinter to it. It scorched the parchment, which it shouldn't have done, and left too much black residue. Styphon wasn't a very honest powder maker; he cheapened his product with too much charcoal and not enough saltpeter. Morrison sipped from his goblet. Saltpeter was seventy-five percent, charcoal fifteen, sulfur ten.

After a while Xentos returned, accompanied by Mytron, bringing a bucket of charcoal, a couple of earthen jars, and the other things. Xentos seemed slightly dazed; Mytron was frightened and making a good game try at not showing it. He put Mytron to work grinding saltpeter in the mortar. The sulfur was already pulverized. Finally, he had about a half pint of it mixed.

"But it's just dust," Chartiphon objected.

"Yes. It has to be moistened, worked into dough, pressed into cakes, dried, and ground. We can't do all that here. But this will flash."

Up to about 1500, all gunpowder had been like that—meal powder, they had called it. It had been used in cannon for a long time after grain powder was being used in small arms. Why, in 1588, the Duke of Medina-Sidonia had been very happy that all the powder for the Armada was corned arquebus powder, and not meal powder. He primed the pistol with a pinch from the mixing goblet, aimed at a half-burned log in the fireplace, and squeezed. Outside somebody shouted, feet pounded up the hall, and a guard with a halberd burst into the room.

"The Lord Kalvan is showing us something about a pistol," Ptosphes told him. "There may be more shots; nobody is to be alarmed."

"All right," he said, when the guard had gone out and closed the door. "Now let's see how it'll fire." He loaded with a blank charge, wadding it with a bit of rag, and handed it to Rylla. "You fire the first shot. This is a great moment in the history of Hostigos. I hope."

She pushed down the striker, set the flint down, aimed at the fireplace, and squeezed. The report wasn't quite as loud, but it did fire. Then they tried it with a ball, which went a half inch into the log. Everybody thought that was very good. The room was full of smoke, and they were all coughing, but nobody cared. Chartiphon went to the door and shouted into the hall for more wine.

Rylla had her arms around him. "Kalvan! You really did it!" she was saying.

"But you said no prayers," Mytron faltered. "You just made fireseed."

"That's right. And before long, everybody'll be just making fireseed. Easy as cooking soup." And when that day comes, he thought, the priests of Styphon will be out on the sidewalk, beating a drum for pennies.

Chartiphon wanted to know how soon they could march against Nostor. "It will take more fireseed than Kalvan can make on this table," Ptosphes told him. "We will need saltpeter, and sulfur, and charcoal. We will have to teach people how to get the sulfur and the saltpeter for us, and how to grind and mix them. We will need many things we don't have now, and tools to make them. And nobody knows all about this but Kalvan, and there is only one of him."

Well, glory be! Somebody had gotten something from his lecture on production, anyhow.

"Mytron knows a few things, I think." He pointed to the jars of sulfur and saltpeter. "Where did you get these?" he asked.

Mytron had gulped his first goblet of wine without taking it from his lips. He had taken three gulps to the second. Now he was working on his third, and coming out of shock nicely. It was about as he thought. The saltpeter was found in crude lumps under manure-piles, then refined; the sulfur was evaporated out of water from the sulfur springs in Wolf Valley. When that was mentioned, Ptosphes began cursing Styphon's House bitterly. Mytron knew both processes, on a quart-jar scale. He explained how much of both they would need.

"But that'll take time," Chartiphon objected. "And as soon as Gormoth hears that we're making our own fireseed, he'll attack at once."

"Don't let him hear about it. Clamp down the security." He had to explain about that. Counter-intelligence seemed to be unheard of, here-and-now. "Have cavalry patrols on all the roads out of Hostigos. Let anybody in, but let nobody out. Not just to Nostor; to Sask and Beshta, too." He thought for a moment. "And another thing. I'll have to give orders people aren't going to like. Will I be obeyed?"

"By anybody who wants to keep his head on his shoulders," Ptosphes said. "You speak with my voice."

"And mine, too!" Chartiphon cried, reaching his sword across the table for him to touch the hilt. "Command me and I will obey, Lord Kalvan."

He established himself, the next morning, in a room inside the main gateway to the citadel, across from the guardroom, a big flagstone-floored place with the indefinable but unmistakable flavor of a police-court. The walls were white plaster; he could write and draw diagrams on them with charcoal. Nobody, here-and-now, knew anything about paper. He made a mental note to do something about that, but no time for it now. Rylla appointed herself his adjutant and general Girl Friday. He collected Mytron, the priest of Tranth, all the master-craftsmen in Tarr-Hostigos, some of the craftsmen's guild people from Hostigos Town, a couple of Chartiphon's officers, and a half dozen cavalrymen to carry messages.

Charcoal would be no problem—there was plenty of that, burned exclusively in the iron-works in the Listra Valley and extensively elsewhere. There was coal, from surface out-croppings to the north and west, and it was used for a number of purposes, but the sulfur content made it unsuitable for iron-furnaces. He'd have to do something about coke some time. Charcoal for gunpowder, he knew, ought to be willow or alder or something like that. He'd do something about that, too, but at present he'd have to use what he had available.

For quantity evaporation of sulfur he'd need big iron pans, and sheet-metal larger than skillets and breastplates didn't seem to exist. The iron-works were forges, not rolling mills. So they'd have to beat the sheet-iron in two-foot squares and weld them together like patch quilts. He and Mytron got to work on planning the evaporation works. Unfortunately, Mytron was not pictorial-minded, and made little or no sense of the diagrams he drew.

Saltpeter could be accumulated all over. Manure-piles would be the best source, and cellars and stables and underground drains. He set up a saltpeter commission, headed by one of Chartiphon's officers, with authority to go anywhere and enter any place, and orders to behead any subordinate who misused his powders and to deal just as summarily with anybody who tried to obstruct or resist. Mobile units, wagons and oxcarts loaded with caldrons, tubs, tools and the like, to go from farm to farm. Peasant women to be collected and taught to leech nitrated soil and purify nitrates. Equipment, manufacture of.

Grinding mills: there was plenty of water-power, and by good fortune he didn't have to invent the waterwheel. That was already in use, and the master-millwright understood what was needed in the way of converting a gristmill to a fireseed mill almost at once. Special grinding equipment, invention of. Sifting screens, cloth. Mixing machines; these would be big wine-casks, with counter-revolving paddlewheels inside. Presses to squeeze dough into cakes. Mills to grind caked powder; he spent considerable thought on regulations to prevent anything from striking a spark around them, with bloodthirsty enforcement threats.

During the morning he managed to grind up the cake he'd made the evening before from what was left of the first experimental batch, running it through a sieve to about FFFg fineness. A hundred grains of that drove a ball from an 8-bore musket an inch deeper into a hemlock log than an equal charge of Styphon's best.

By noon he was almost sure that almost all of his War Production Board understood most of what he'd told them. In the afternoon there was a meeting, in the outer bailey, of as many people who would be working on fireseed production as could be gathered. There was an invocation of Dralm by Xentos, and an invocation of Galzar by Uncle Wolf, and an invocation of Tranth by his priest. Ptosphes spoke, emphasizing that the Lord Kalvan had full authority to do anything, and would be backed to the limit, by the headsman if necessary. Chartiphon made a speech, picturing the howling wilderness they would shortly make of Nostor. (Prolonged cheering.) He made a speech, himself, emphasizing that there was nothing of a supernatural nature whatever about fireseed, detailing the steps of manufacture, and trying to give some explanation of what made it explode. The meeting then broke up into small groups, everybody having his own job explained to him. He was kept running back and forth, explaining to the explainers.

In the evening they had a feast. By that time he and Rylla had gotten a rough table of organization charcoaled onto the wall of his headquarters.

Of the next four days, he spent eighteen hours each in that room, talking to six or eight hundred people. Some of them he suffered patiently if not gladly; they were trying to do their best at something they'd never been expected to do before. Some he had trouble with. The artisans' guilds bickered with one another about jurisdiction, and they all complained about peasants invading their crafts. The masters complained that the journeymen and apprentices were becoming intractable, meaning that they'd started thinking for themselves. The peasants objected to having their byres invaded and their dunghills forked down, and to being put to unfamiliar work. The landlords objected to having their peasants taken out of the fields, predicting that the year's crop would be lost.

"Don't worry about that," he told them. "If we win, we'll eat Gormoth's crops. If we lose, we'll all be too dead to eat."

And the Iron Curtain went down. Within a few days, indignant packtraders and wagoners were being collected in Hostigos Town, trapped for the duration, protesting vehemently but unavailingly. Sooner or later, Gormoth and Sarrask would begin to wonder why nobody was coming out of Hostigos, and would send spies slipping through the woods to find out. *Counterespionage; organize soonest.* And a few of his own spies in Sask and Nostor. And an anti-Styphon fifth column in both princedoms. *Discuss with Xentos.*

By the fifth day, the Wolf Valley sulfur-evaporation plant was ready to go into operation, and saltpeter production was up to some ten pounds a day. He put Mytron in charge at Tarr-Hostigos, hoping for something better than the worst, and got into his new armor. He and Rylla and a half dozen of Harmakros's cavalrymen trotted out the gate and down the road from the castle into Hostigos Gap. It was the first time he'd been outside the castle since he had been brought there unconscious, tied onto a horse-litter.

It was not until they were out of the gap and riding toward the town, spread around the low hill above the big spring, that he turned in his saddle to look back at the castle. For a moment he couldn't be certain what was wrong, but he knew something was. Then it struck him.

There was no trace whatever of the great stone-quarries.

There should have been. No matter how many thousands of years had passed since he had been in and out of that dome of shifting light that had carried him out of his normal time, there would have been some evidence of quarrying there. Normal erosion would have taken not thousands but hundreds of thousands' of years to obliterate those stark man-made cliffs, and enough erosion to have done that would have reduced the whole mountain by half. He remembered how unchanged the little cliff, under which he and Larry and Jack and Steve had parked the car, had been when he had . . . emerged. No. That mountain had never been quarried, at any time in the past.

288 · H. BEAM PIPER

So he wasn't in the future; that was sure. And he wasn't in the past, unless every scrap of history everybody had ever written or taught was an organized lie, and that he couldn't swallow.

Then when the hell was he?

Rylla had reined in her horse and stopped beside him. The six troopers came to an unquestioning halt.

"What is it, Kalvan?"

"I was just . . . just thinking of the last time I saw this place."

"You mustn't think about that, any more." Then, after a moment: "Was there somebody . . . somebody you didn't want to leave?"

He laughed. "No, Rylla. The only somebody like that is right beside me now."

They shook their reins and started off again, the six troopers clattering behind them.

6

I

VERKAN Vall watched Tortha Karf spin the empty revolver cartridge on his desk. It was a very valuable empty cartridge; it had taken over forty days and cost ten thousand man-hours of crawling on hands and knees and pawing among dead hemlock needles to find it.

"That was a small miracle, Vall," the Chief said. "Aryan-Transpacific?"

"Oh, yes; we were sure of that from the beginning. Styphon's House Sub-sector." He gave the exact numerical designation of the time-line. "They're all basically alike; the language, culture, taboo and situation-response tapes we have will do."

The Chief was fiddling with the selector for the map screen; when he had gotten geographical area and run through level and sector, he lit it with a map of eastern North America, divided into five Great Kingdoms. First, Hos-Zygros—he chose to identify it in the terms the man he was hunting would use—its use—its capital equivalent with Quebec, taking in New England and southeastern Canada to Lake Ontario. Second, Hos-Agrys: New York, western Quebec Province and northern New Jersey. Third, Hos-Harphax, where the pickup incident had occurred. Fourth, Hos-Ktemnos: Virginia and North Carolina. Finally, Hos-Bletha, south from there to the tip of Florida and west along the Gulf to Mobile Bay. And also Trygath, which was not Hos-, or *great,* in the Ohio Valley. Glancing at a note in front of him, Tortha Karf made a dot of light in the middle of Hos-Harphax.

"That's it. Of course, that was over forty days ago. A man can go a long way, even on foot, in that time."

The Chief knew that. "Styphon's House," he said. "That's that gunpowder theocracy, isn't it?"

It was. He'd seen theocracies all over paratime, and liked none of them; priests in political power usually made themselves insufferable, worse than any secular despotism. Styphon's House was a particularly nasty case in point. About five centuries ago, Styphon had been a minor healer-god; still was on most of Aryan-Transpacific. Some deified ancient physician, he supposed. Then, on one time-line, some priest experimenting with remedies had mixed a batch of saltpeter, sulfur and charcoal—a small batch, or he wouldn't have survived it.

For a century or so, it had merely been a temple miracle, and then the propellant properties had been discovered, and Styphon had gone out of medical practice and into the munitions business. Priestly researchers had improved the powder and designed and perfected weapons to use it. Nobody had discovered fulminating powder and invented the percussion-cap, but they had everything short of that. Now, through their monopoly on this essential tool for maintaining or altering the political status quo, Styphon's House ruled the whole Atlantic seaboard, while the secular sovereigns merely reined.

He wondered if Calvin Morrison knew how to make gunpowder, and while he was wondering silently, the Chief did so aloud, adding:

"If he does, we won't have any trouble locating him. We may afterward, though."

That was how pickup jobs usually were, on the exit end; the pickup either made things easy or impossibly difficult. Many of these paratemporal DP's, suddenly hurled into an unfamiliar world, went hopelessly insane, their minds refusing to cope with what common sense told them was impossible. Others were quickly killed through ignorance. Others would be caught by the locals, and committed to mental hospitals, imprisoned, sold as slaves, executed as spies, burned as sorcerers, or merely lynched, depending on local mores. Many accepted and blended into their new environment and sank into traceless obscurity. A few created commotions and had to be dealt with.

"Well, we'll find out. I'm going outtime myself to look into it."

"You don't need to, Vall. You have plenty of detectives who can do that."

He shook his head obstinately. "On Year-End Day, that'll be a hundred and seventy-four days, I'm going to be handcuffed to that chair you're sitting in. Until then, I'm going to do as much outtime work as I possibly can." He leaned over and turned a dial on the map-selector, got a large-scale map of Hos-Harphax and increased the magnification and limited the field. He pointed. "I'm going in about there. In the mountains in Sask, next door. I'll be a pack-trader—they go everywhere and don't have to account for themselves to anybody. I'll have a saddle-horse and three pack-horses loaded with wares. It'll take about five or six days to collect and verify what I'll take with me. I'll travel slowly, to let word seep ahead of me. It may be that I'll hear something about this Morrison before I enter Hostigos."

"What'll you do about him when you find him?"

That would depend. Sometimes a pickup could be taken alive, moved to Police Terminal on the Fifth Level, given a complete memory obliteration, and then returned to his own time-line. An amnesia case; that was always a credible explanation. Or he would be killed with a sigma-ray needler, which left no traceable effects. Heart failure or "He just died." Amnesia and heart failure were wonderful things, from the Paratime Police viewpoint. Anybody with any common sense would accept either. Common sense was a wonderful thing, too.

"Well, I don't want to kill the fellow; after all, he's a police officer, too. But with the explanation we're cobbling up for his disappearance, returning him to his own time-line wouldn't be any favor to him." He paused, thinking. "We'll have to kill him, I'm afraid. He knows too much."

"What does he know, Vall?"

"One, he's seen the inside of a conveyer, something completely alien to his own culture's science. Two, he knows he's been shifted in time, and time-travel is a common science-fiction concept in his own world. If he can disregard verbalisms about fantasies and impossibilities, he will deduce a race of time-travelers.

"Only a moron, which no Pennsylvania State Police officer is, would be so ignorant of his own world's history as to think for a moment that he'd been shifted into the past. And he'll know he hasn't been shifted into the future, because that area, on all of Europo-American, is covered with truly permanent engineering works of which he'll find no trace. So what does that leave?"

"A lateral shift in time, and a race of lateral time travelers," the Chief said. "Why, that's the Paratime Secret itself!"

II

THEY were feasting at Tarr-Hostigos that evening. All morning, pigs and cattle had been driven in, lowing and squealing, to be slaughtered in the outer bailey. Axes thudded for firewood; the roasting-pits were being cleaned out from the last feast; casks of wine were coming up from the cellars. Morrison wished the fireseed mills were as busy as the castle bakery and kitchen.

A whole day's production shot to hell. He said as much to Rylla.

"But, Kalvan, they're all so happy." She was pretty happy, herself. "And they've worked so hard."

He had to grant that, and maybe the morale gain would offset the production loss. And they did have something to celebrate: a full hundredweight of fireseed, fifty percent better than Styphon's Best, and half of it made in the last two days.

"It's been so long since any of us had anything to be really happy about," she was saying. "When we'd have a feast, everybody'd try to get drunk as soon as they could, to keep from thinking about what was coming. And now maybe it won't come at all."

And now, they were all drunk on a hundred pounds of black powder. Five thousand caliver or arquebus rounds at most. They'd have to do better than twenty-five pounds a day—get it up above a hundred at least. Saltpeter production was satisfactory, and Mytron had figured a couple of angles at the evaporation plant that practically gave them sulfur running out their ears. The bottleneck was mixing and caking, and grinding the cakes. That meant more machinery, and there weren't enough men competent to build it. It would mean stopping work on the other things.

The carriages for the new light four-pounders. The iron-works had turned out four of them, so far—welded wrought-iron, of course, since nobody knew how to cast iron, here-and-now, and neither did he, but made with trunnions. They only weighed four hundred pounds, the same as Gustavus Adolphus's, and with four horses the one prototype already completed could keep up with cavalry on any kind of decent ground. He was happier about that little gun than anything else—except Rylla, of course.

And they were putting trunnions on some old stuff, big things, close to a ton metal-weight but only six and eight pounders, and he hoped to get field-carriages under them, too. They'd take eight horses apiece, and they would never keep up with cavalry.

And rifling-benches—long wooden frames in which the barrel would be clamped, with grooved wooden cylinders to slide in guides to rotate the cutting-heads. One turn in four feet—that, he remembered, had been the usual pitch for the Kentucky rifles. So far, he had one in the Tarr-Hostigos gunshop.

And drilling troops—he had to do most of that himself, too, till he could train some officers. Nobody knew anything about foot-drill by squads; here-and-now troops maneuvered in columns of droves.

It would take a year to build the sort of an army he wanted. And Gormoth of Nostor would give him a month, at most.

He brought that up at the General Staff meeting that afternoon. Like rifled firearms and trunnions on cannon, General Staffs hadn't been invented here-and-now, either. You just hauled a lot of peasants together and armed them; that was Mobilization. You picked a reasonably passable march-route; that was Strategy. You lined up your men and shot or hit anything in front of you; that was Tactics. And Intelligence was what mounted scouts, if any, brought in at the last minute from a mile ahead. It cheered him to recall that that would probably be Prince Gormoth's notion of the Art of War. Why, with twenty thousand men, Gustavus Adolphus, or the Duke of Parma, or Gonzalo de Córdoba could have gone through all five of these Great Kingdoms like a dose of croton oil. And what Turenne could have done!

Ptosphes and Rylla were present as Prince and Heiress-Apparent. The Lord Kalvan was Commander-in-Chief of the Armed Forces of Hostigos. Chartiphon, gratifyingly unresentful at seeing an outlander promoted over his head, was Field Marshal and Chief of Operations. An elderly "captain"—actual functioning rank about brigadier-general—was quartermaster, paymaster, drillmaster, inspector-general and head of the draft board. A civilian merchant, who wasn't losing any money at it, had charge of procurement and supply. Mytron was surgeon-general, and the priest of Tranth had charge of production. Uncle Wolf Tharses was Chief of Chaplains. Harmakros was G2, mainly because his cavalry were patrolling the borders and keeping the Iron Curtain tight, but he'd have to be moved out of that. He was too good a combat man to be stuck with a Pentagon Job, and Xentos was now doing most of the Intelligence work. Besides his ecclesiastical role as highpriest of Dralm, and his political function as Ptosphes' Chancellor, he was in contact with his co-religionists in Nostor, all of whom hated Styphon's House inexpressibly and were organizing an active Fifth Column. Like Iron Curtain, Fifth Column was now part of the local lexicon.

The first blaze of optimism, he was pleased to observe, had died down on the upper echelon.

"Dralm-damn fools!" Chartiphon was growling. "One keg of fireseed—they'll want to shoot that all away tonight celebrating—and they think we're saved. Making our own fireseed's given us a chance, and that's all." He swore again, this time an oath that made Xentos frown. "We have three thousand under arms; if we take all the boys with bows and arrows and all the old peasants with pitchforks, we might get that up to five thousand, but not another child or dotard more. And Gormoth'll have ten thousand: four thousand of his own people and those six thousand mercenaries he has."

"I'd call it eight thousand," Harmakros said. "He won't take the peasants out of the fields; he needs them there."

"Then he won't wait till the harvest's in; he'll invade sooner," Ptosphes said.

He looked at the relief-map on the long table. The idea that maps were important weapons of war was something else he'd had to introduce. This one was only partly finished; he and Rylla had done most of the work on it, in time snatched from everything else that ought to have been done last week at the latest. It was based on what he remembered from the U.S. Geological Survey quadrangle sheets he'd used on the State Police, on interviews with hundreds of soldiers, woodsmen, peasants and landlords, and on a good bit of personal horseback reconnaissance.

Gormoth could invade up the Listra Valley, crossing the river at the equivalent of Lock Haven, but that wouldn't give him a third of Hostigos. The whole line of the Bald Eagles was strongly defended everywhere but at Dombra Gap. Tarr-Dombra guarding it, had been betrayed seventy-five years ago to Prince Gormoth's grandfather, and Sevenhills Valley with it.

"Then we'll have to do something to delay him. This Tarr-Dombra . . . say we take that, and occupy Sevenhills Valley. That'll cut off his best invasion route."

They all stared at him, just as he'd been stared at when he'd first spoken of making fireseed. It was Chartiphon who first found his voice:

"Man! You never saw Tarr-Dombra or you wouldn't talk like that! Nobody can take Tarr-Dombra unless they buy it, like Prince Galtrath did, and we haven't enough money for that."

"That's right," said the retread "captain" who was G1 and part of G4. "It's smaller than Tarr-Hostigos, of course, but it's twice as strong."

"Do the Nostori think it can't be taken, too? Then it can be. Prince, are there any plans of that castle here?"

"Well, yes. On a big scroll, in one of my coffers. It was my grandfather's, and we've always hoped that some time . . ."

"I'll want to see that. Later will do. Do you know if any changes have been made since the Nostori got it?"

None on the outside, at least. He asked about the garrison; five hundred, Harmakros thought. A hundred of Gormoth's regulars, and four hundred mercenary cavalry to patrol Sevenhills Valley and raid into Hostigos.

"Then we stop killing raiders who can be taken alive. Prisoners can be made to talk." He turned to Xentos. "Is there a priest of Dralm in Sevenhills Valley? Can you get in touch with him, and will he help us? Explain to him that this is not a war against Prince Gormoth, but against Styphon's House."

"He knows that, and he will help as much as he can, but he can't get into Tarr-Dombra. There is a priest of Galzar there for the mercenaries, and a priest of Styphon for the lord of the castle and his gentlemen, but among the Nostori, Dralm is but a god for the peasants."

Yes, and that rankled, too. The priests of Dralm would help, all right.

"Good enough. He can talk to people who can get inside, can't he? And he can send messages, and organize an espionage apparatus. I want to know everything that can be found out about Tarr-Dombra, no matter how trivial. Particularly, I want to know the guard-routine, and I want to know how the castle is supplied. And I want it observed at all times. Harmakros, you find men to do that. I take it we can't storm the place. Then we'll have to get in by trickery."

III

VERKAN the pack-trader went up the road, his horse plodding unhurriedly and the three pack-horses on the lead-line trailing behind. He was hot and sticky under his steel back-and-breast, and sweat ran down his cheeks from under his helmet into his new beard, but nobody ever saw an unarmed pack-trader, so he had to endure it. A paratimer had to be adaptable, if nothing else. The armor was from an adjoining, nearly identical time-line, and so were his clothes, the short carbine in the saddle-sheath, his sword and dagger, the horse-gear, and the loads of merchandise—all except the bronze coffer on one pack-load.

Reaching the brow of the hill, he started slowly down the other side, and saw a stir in front of a whitewashed and thatch-roofed roadside cottage. Men

mounting horses, sun-glints on armor, and the red and blue colors of Hostigos. Another cavalry post, the third since he'd crossed the border from Sask.
The other two had ignored him, but this crowd meant to stop him. Two had
lances, and a third a musketoon, and a fourth, who seemed to be in command,
had his holsters open and his right hand on his horse's neck. Two more, at the
cottage, were getting into the road on foot with musketoons.

He pulled up; the pack-horses, behind, came to a well-trained stop.

"Good cheer, soldiers," he greeted.

"Good cheer, trader," the man with his hand close to his pistol-butt
replied. "From Sask?"

"Sask latest. From Ulthor, this trip; Grefftscharr by birth." Ulthor was the
lake port in the north; Grefftscharr was the kingdom around the Great Lakes.
"I'm for Agrys City."

One of the troopers chuckled. The sergeant asked: "Have you fireseed?"

He touched the flask on his belt. "About twenty charges. I was going to
buy some in Sask Town, but when the priests heard I was passing through
Hostigos they'd sell me none. Doesn't Styphon's House like you Hostigi?"

"We're under the ban." The sergeant didn't seem greatly distressed about
it. "But I'm afraid you'll not get out of here soon. We're on the edge of war
with Nostor, and Lord Kalvan wants no tales carried to him, so he's ordered
that none may leave Hostigos."

He cursed; that was expected of him. The Lord Kalvan, now?

"I'd feel ill-used, too, in your place, but you know how it is," the sergeant
sympathized. "When lords command, commonfolk obey, if they want to keep
their heads on. You'll make out all right, though. You'll find ready sale for all
your wares at good price, and then if you're skilled at any craft, work for good
pay. Or you might take the colors. You're well horsed and armed, and Lord
Kalvan welcomes all such."

"Lord Kalvan? I thought Ptosphes was Prince of Hostigos. Or have there
been changes?"

"No; Dralm bless him, Ptosphes is still our Prince. But the Lord Kalvan,
Dralm bless him, too, is our new war leader. It's said he's a Prince himself,
from a far land, which he well could be. It's also said he's a sorcerer, but that
I doubt."

"Yes. Sorcerers are more heard of than seen," Vall commented. "Are there
many more traders caught here as I am?"

"Oh, the Styphon's own lot of them; the town's full of them. You'd best go
to the Sign of the Red Halberd; the better sort of them all stay there. Give the

landlord my name"—he repeated it several times to make sure it would be remembered—"and you'll fare well."

He chatted pleasantly with the sergeant and his troopers, about the quality of local wine and the availability of girls and the prices things fetched at sale, and then bade them good luck and rode on.

The Lord Kalvan, indeed! Deliberately, he willed himself no longer to think of the man in any other way. And a Prince from a far country, no less. He passed other farmhouses; around them some work was going on. Men were forking down dunghills and digging under them, and caldrons steamed over fires. He added that to the cheerfulness with which the cavalrymen had accepted the ban of Styphon's House.

Styphon, it appeared, had acquired a competitor.

Hostigos Town, he saw, was busier and more crowded than Sask Town had been. There were no mercenaries around, but many local troops. The streets were full of carts and wagons, and the artisans' quarter was noisy with the work of smiths and joiners. He found the inn to which the sergeant had directed him, mentioning his name to make sure he got his rake-off, put up his horses, safe-stowed his packs and had his saddlebags, valise and carbine carried to his room. He followed the inn-servant with the bronze coffer on his shoulder. He didn't want anybody else handling that and finding out how light it was.

When he was alone, he went to the coffer, an almost featureless rectangular block without visible lock or hinges, and pressed his thumbs on two bright steel ovals on the top. The photoelectric lock inside responded to his thumbprint patterns with a click, and the lid rose slowly. Inside were four globes of gleaming coppery mesh, a few instruments with dials and knobs, and a little sigma-ray needler, a ladies' model, small enough to be covered by his hand but as deadly as the big one he usually carried.

There was also an antigrav unit attached to the bottom of the coffer; it was on, with a tiny red light glowing. When he switched it off, the floorboards under the coffer creaked. Lined with collapsed metal, it now weighed over half a ton. He pushed down the lid which only his thumbprints could open, and heard the lock click.

The command-room downstairs was crowded and noisy. He found a vacant place at one of the long tables, across from a man with a bald head and a straggling red beard, who grinned at him.

"New fish in the net?" he asked. "Welcome, brother. Where from?"

"Ulthor, with three horse-loads of Grefftscharr wares. My name's Verkan."

"Mine's Skranga." The bald man was from Agrys City, on the island at the mouth of the Hudson. He had been trading for horses in the Trygath country.

"These people here took the lot, fifty of them. Paid me less than I asked, but more than I expected, so I guess I got a fair price. I had four Trygathi herders—they all took the colors in the cavalry. I'm working in the fireseed mill, till they let me leave here."

"The what?" He made his voice sound incredulous. "You mean they're making their own fireseed? But only the priests of Styphon can do that."

Skranga laughed. "That's what I used to think, too, but anybody can do it. It's easy as boiling maple-sugar. See, they get saltpeter from under dung-hills . . ."

He detailed the process step by step. The man next to him joined the conversation; he even understood, roughly, the theory: the charcoal was what burned, the sulfur was the kindling, and the saltpeter made the air to blow up the fire and blow the bullet out of the gun. And there was no secrecy about it, Vall mused as he listened. If a man who had been a constabulary corporal, and a combat soldier before that, wasn't keeping any better security it was because he didn't care. Lord Kalvan just didn't want word getting into Nostor till he had enough fireseed to fight a war with.

"I bless Dralm for bringing me here," Skranga was saying. "When I can leave here, I'm going somewhere and set up making fireseed myself. Hos-Ktemnos—no, I don't want too close to Styphon's House Upon Earth. Maybe Hos-Bletha, or Hos-Zygros. But I'll make myself rich at it. So can you, if you keep your eyes and ears open."

The Agrysi finished his meal, said he had to go back to work, and left. A cavalry officer, a few places down, promptly picked up his goblet and flagon and moved into the vacated seat.

"You just got in?" he asked. "From Nostor?"

"No, from Sask." The answer seemed to disappoint the cavalryman; he went into the Ulthor-Grefftscharr routine again. "How long will I have to stay here?"

The officer shrugged. "Dralm and Galzar only know. Till we fight the Nostori and beat them. What do the Saski think we're doing here?"

"Waiting for Gormoth to cut your throats. They don't know you're making your own fireseed."

The officer laughed. "Ha! Some of those buggers'll get theirs cut, if Prince Sarrask doesn't mind his step. You say you have three pack-loads of Grefftscharr wares. Any sword-blades?"

"About a dozen; I sold a few in Sask Town. Some daggers, a dozen gun-locks, four good shirts of rivet-link mail, a lot of bullet-moulds. And jewelry, and tools, and brassware."

"Well, take your stuff up to Tarr-Hostigos. They have a little fair in the outer bailey each evening; you can get better prices from the castle-folk than here in town. Go early. Use my name." He gave it, and his cavalry unit. "See Captain Harmakros; he'll be glad of any news you can give him."

Late in the afternoon, he re-packed his horses and went up the road to the castle on the mountain above the gap. The workshops along the wall of the outer bailey were all busy. Among other things, he saw a new carriage for a field-piece being put together—not a four-wheel cart, but two big wheels and a trail, to be hauled with a limber, which was also being built. The gun was a welded iron four-pounder, which was normal for Styphon's House Subsector, but it had trunnions, which was not. Lord Kalvan, again.

Like all the local gentry, Harmakros had a small neat beard. His armor was rich but commendably well battered; his sword, instead of the customary cut-and-thrust (mostly cut) broadsword, was a long rapier, quite new. Kalvan had evidently introduced the revolutionary concept that swords had points, which should be used. He asked a few exploratory questions, then listened to a detailed account of what the Grefftscharr trader had seen in Sask, including mercenary companies Prince Sarrask had lately hired, with the names of the captains.

"You've kept your eyes and ears open," he commended, "and you know what's worth telling about. I wish you'd come through Nostor instead. Were you ever a soldier?"

"All free-traders are soldiers, in their own service."

"Yes; that's so. Well, when you've sold your loads, you'll be welcome in ours. Not as a common trooper—I know you traders too well for that. As a scout. You want to sell your pack-horses, too? We'll give you a good price for them."

"If I can sell my loads, yes."

"You'll have no trouble doing that. We'll buy the mail, the gunlocks, the sword-blades and that sort of thing ourselves. Stay about; have your meals with the officers here. We'll find something for you."

He had some tools, both for wood and metal work. He peddled them among the artisans in the shops along the outer wall, for a good price in silver and a better one in information. Besides rapiers and cannon with trunnions, Lord Kalvan had introduced rifling in firearms. Nobody knew whence he had come, except that it was far beyond the Western Ocean. The more pious were positive that he had been guided to Hostigos by the very hand of Dralm.

The officers with whom he ate listened avidly to what he had picked up in Sask Town. Nostor first and then Sask seemed to be the schedule. When they talked about Lord Kalvan, the coldest expressions were of deep respect, shading from there up to hero-worship. But they knew nothing about him before the night he had appeared to rally some fleeing peasants for a counter-attack on Nostori raiders and had been shot, by mistake, by Princess Rylla herself.

Vall sold the mail and sword-blades and gunlocks as a lot, and spread his other wares for sale in the bailey. There was a crowd, and the stuff sold well. He saw Lord Kalvan, strolling about from display to display, in full armor— probably wearing it all the time to accustom himself to the weight, Vall decided. Kalvan was carrying a .38 Colt on his belt along with his rapier and dagger, and clinging to his arm was a beautiful blonde girl in male riding-dress. That would be Prince Ptosphes's daughter, Rylla. The happy possessiveness with which she clung to him, and the tenderness with which he looked at her, made him smile. Then the thought of his mission froze the smile on his lips. He didn't want to kill that man, and break that girl's heart, but . . .

They came over to his display, and Lord Kalvan picked up a brass mortar and pestle.

"Where did you get this?" he asked. "Where did it come from?"

"It was made in Grefftscharr, Lord; shipped down the lakes by boat to Ulthor."

"It's cast. Are there no brass foundries nearer than Grefftscharr?"

"Oh, yes, Lord. In Zygros City there are many." Lord Kalvan put down the mortar. "I see. Thank you. Captain Harmakros tells me he's been talking to you. I'd like to talk to you, myself. I think I'll be around the castle all morning, tomorrow; ask for me, if you're here."

Returning to the Red Halberd, Vall spent some time and a little money in the common-room. Everybody, as far as he could learn, seemed satisfied that the mysterious Lord Kalvan had come to Hostigos in a perfectly normal manner, with or without divine guidance. Finally, he went up to his room.

Opening the coffer, he got out one of the copper-mesh globes, and from it drew a mouthpiece on a small wire, into which he spoke for a long time.

"So far," he concluded, "there seems to be no suspicion of anything paranormal about the man in anybody's mind. I have been offered an opportunity to take service with his army as a scout. I intend doing this; assistance can be given me in performing this work. I will find a location for an antigrav conveyer to land, somewhere in the woods near Hostigos Town; when I do, I will send a message-ball through from there."

Then he replaced the mouthpiece, set the timer for the transposition-field generator, and switched on the antigrav. Carrying the ball to an open window, he tossed it outside, and then looked up as it vanished in the night. After a few seconds, high above, there was an instant's flash among the many visible stars. It looked like a meteor; a Hostigi, seeing it, would have made a wish.

7

KALVAN sat on a rock under a tree, wishing he could smoke, and knowing that he was getting scared again. He cursed mentally. It didn't mean anything—as soon as things started happening he'd forget about it but it always happened, and he hated it. That sort of thing was all right for a buck private, or a platoon-sergeant, or a cop going to arrest some hillbilly killer, but, for Dralm's sake, a five-star general, now!

And that made him think of what Churchill had called Hitler: the lance-corporal who had promoted himself to commander-in-chief at one jump. Corporal Morrison had done that, cut Hitler's time by quite a few years, and gotten into the peerage, which Hitler hadn't.

It was quiet on the mountain top, even though there were two hundred men squatting or lying around him, and another five hundred, under Chartiphon and Prince Ptosphes, five hundred yards behind. And, in front, at the edge of the woods, a skirmish line of thirty riflemen, commanded by Verkan, the Grefftscharr trader.

There had been some objections to giving so important a command to an outlander; he had informed the objectors rather stiffly that until recently he had been an outlander and a stranger himself. Verkan was the best man for it. Since joining Harmakros's scouts, he had managed to get closer to Tarr-Dombra than anybody else, and knew the ground ahead better than any. He wished he could talk the Grefftscharrer into staying in Hostigos. He'd fought bandits all over, as any trader must, and Trygathi, and nomads on the western plains, and he was a natural rifle-shot and a born guerrilla. Officer type, too. But free-traders didn't stay anywhere; they all had advanced cases of foot-itch and horizon-fever.

And out in front of Verkan and his twenty rifled calivers at the edge of the woods, the first on any battlefield in here-and-now history, were a dozen men with rifled 8-bore muskets, fitted with peep-sights and carefully zeroed in, in what was supposed to be cleared ground in front of the castle gate. The condition of that approach ground was the most promising thing about the whole operation.

It had been cleared, all right—at least, the trees had been felled and the stumps rooted out. But the Nostori thought Tarr-Dombra couldn't be taken and they'd gone slack: the ground hadn't been brushed for a couple of years. There were bushes all over it as high as a man's waist, and not a few that a man could hide behind standing up. And his men would have been hard enough to see even if it had been kept like a golf-course.

The helmets and body-armor had all been carefully rusted; there'd been anguished howls about that. So had every gun-barrel and spearhead. Nobody wore anything but green or brown, and most of them had bits of greenery fastened to helmets and clothing. The whole operation had been rehearsed four times back of Tarr-Hostigos, starting with twelve hundred men and eliminating down to the eight hundred best.

There was a noise, about what a wild-turkey would make feeding, and a soft voice called, "Lord Kalvan!" It was Verkan; he carried a rifle and wore a dirty gray-green smock with a hood; his sword and belt were covered with green and brown rags.

"I never saw you till you spoke," Morrison commended him.

"The wagons are coming up. They're at the top switchback now."

He nodded. "We start, then." His mouth was dry. What was that thing in *For Whom the Bell Tolls* about spitting to show you weren't afraid? He couldn't have done that now. He nodded to the boy squatting beside him; the boy picked up his arquebus and started back to where Ptosphes and Chartiphon were waiting.

And Rylla. He cursed vilely—in English, since he still couldn't get much satisfaction out of taking the names of these local gods in vain. She'd announced that she was coming along. He'd told her she'd do nothing of the sort; so had her father and Chartiphon. She'd thrown a tantrum, and thrown other things as well. She had come along. He was going to have his hands full with that girl, after they were married.

"All right," he said softly to the men around him. "Let's start earning our pay."

The men around and behind him rose quietly, two spears or halberds or long-handled scythe-blades to every caliver or arquebus, though some of the spearmen had pistols in their belts. He and Verkan advanced to the edge of the woods, where riflemen crouched in pairs behind trees. Across four hundred yards of clearing rose the limestone walls of Tarr-Dombra, the castle that couldn't be taken, above the chasm that had been quarried straight across the mountain top. The drawbridge was down and the portcullis up, and a few soldiers with black and orange scarves and sashes—his old college colors; he ought to be ashamed to shoot them—loitered in the gateway or kept perfunctory watch from the battlements.

Ptosphes and Chartiphon—and Rylla, damn it!—came up with the rest of the force, with a frightful clatter and brush-crashing which nobody at the castle seemed to hear. There was one pike or spear or halberd or something—too often something—to every two arquebuses or calivers. Chartiphon wore a long brown sack with arm and neck holes over his armor. Ptosphes wore brown, and browned armor; so did Rylla. They nodded greetings, and peered through the bushes to where the road from Sevenhills Valley came up to the summit of the mountain.

Finally, four cavalrymen, with black and orange pennons and scarves, came into view. They were only fake Princeton men; he hoped they'd get rid of that stuff before some other Hostigi shot them by mistake. A long ox-wagon, piled high with hay which covered eight Hostigi infantrymen, followed. Then a few false-color cavalry, another big haywagon, more cavalry, two more wagons, and a dozen cavalry behind.

The first four clattered over the drawbridge, spoke to the guards, and rode through the gate. Two wagons followed vanishing through the gate. Great Galzar, if anybody noticed anything now! The third rumbled onto the drawbridge and stopped directly below the portcullis; that was the one with the log framework under the hay, and the log slung underneath; the driver must have cut the strap to let it drop, jamming the wagon. The fourth, the one loaded with rocks to the top of the bed, stopped on the end of the drawbridge, weighting it down.

Then a pistol banged inside, and another; there were shouts of "Hostigos!" and "Ptosphes!" He blew his State Police whistle, and six of the big elephant-size muskets went off in front, from places where he'd have sworn there'd been nobody at all. The rest of Verkan's rifle-platoon began firing, sharp whipcrack reports entirely different from the smoothbores. He hoped they'd remember to patch their bullets when they reloaded; that was something new for them. He blew his whistle twice and started running forward.

The men who had been showing themselves on the walls were gone now, but a musket-shot or so showed that the snipers in front hadn't gotten all of them. He ran past a man with fishnet over his helmet stuck full of twigs, ramming a ball into his musket; another, near him, who had been waiting till he was half through, fired. Gray powder smoke hung in the gateway; all the Hostigi were inside now, and there was an uproar of shouting—"Hostigos!" "Nostor!"—and shots and blade-clashing. He broke step to look behind him; his two hundred were pouring in after him and Ptosphes's spearmen; the arquebusiers and calivermen had advanced to two hundred yards and were plastering the battlements as fast as they could load and fire, without bothering to aim. Aimed smoothbore fire at that range was useless; they were just trying to throw as much lead as they could.

A cannon went off above him when he was almost to the end of the drawbridge, and then, belatedly, the portcullis slammed down and stopped eight feet from the ground on the log framework hidden under the hay of the third wagon. They'd tested that a couple of times with the portcullis at Tarr-Hostigos, first. All six of the oxen on the last wagon were dead; the drivers and the infantrymen inside had been furnished short broadaxes to make sure of that. The oxen of the portcullis wagon had been cut loose and driven inside. There were a lot of ripped-off black and orange scarves on the ground, and more on corpses. The gate, and the two gate-towers, had been secured.

But shots were coming from the citadel, across the bailey, and a mob of Nostori was pouring out the gate from it. This, he thought, was the time to expend some .38-specials. Standing with his feet apart and his left hand on his hip, he drew the Colt and began shooting, timed-fire rate. He killed six men with six shots (he'd done that well on silhouette targets often enough), and they were the front six men. The rest stopped, just long enough for the men behind him to come up and sweep forward, arquebuses banging. Then he holstered the empty Colt—he had only eight rounds left for it—and drew his rapier and poignard. Another cannon thundered from the outside wall; he hoped Rylla and Chartiphon hadn't been in front of it. Then he was fighting his way through the citadel gate, shoulder to shoulder with Prince Ptosphes.

Behind, in the bailey, something else besides "Ptosphes!" and "Gormoth!" and "Hostigos!" was being shouted. It was:

"Mercy, comrade! Mercy; I yield! Oath to Galzar!"

There was much more of that as the morning passed; before noon, all the garrison had either cried for mercy or hadn't needed it. There had only been those two cannon-shots, though between them they had killed or wounded fifty men. Nobody would be crazy enough to attack Tarr-Dombra, so the cannon had been left empty, and they'd only had time to load and fire two.

The hardest fighting was inside the citadel. He ran into Rylla there, with Chartiphon hurrying to keep up with her. There was a bright sword-nick on her brown helmet, and blood on her light rapier; she was laughing happily. Then the melee swept them apart. He had expected that taking the keep would be even grimmer work, but as soon as they had the citadel, it surrendered. By that time, he had used the last of his irreplaceable cartridges. Muzzle-loaders for him, from now on.

They hauled down Gormoth's black flag with the orange lily and ran up the halberd-head of Hostigos. They found four huge bombards, throwing hundred-pound stone balls, loaded them, hand-spiked them around, and sent the huge gunstones crashing into the roofs of the town of Dyssa, at the mouth of Gorge River, to announce that Tarr-Dombra was under new management. They set the castle cooks to work skinning and cutting up the dead wagon-oxen for a barbecue. Then they turned their attention to the prisoners, herded into the inner bailey.

First, there were the mercenaries. They all agreed to enter Prince Ptosphes's service. They couldn't be used against Gormoth until the term of their contract with him expired; they would be sent to patrol the Sask border. Then there were Gormoth's own subject troops. They couldn't be made to bear arms at all, but they could be put to work, as long as they were given soldiers' pay and soldierly treatment. Then there was the governor of the castle, a Count Pheblon, cousin to Gormoth, and his officers. They would be released on oath to send their ransoms to Hostigos. The castle priest of Galzar, after administering the oaths, elected to go to Hostigos with his parishioners.

As for the priest of Styphon, Chartiphon wanted to question him under torture, and Ptosphes thought he should be beheaded out of hand.

"Send him to Nostor with Pheblon," Morrison said. "No, send him to Balph, in Hos-Ktemnos, with a letter to the Supreme Priest, Styphon's Voice, telling him that we make our own fireseed, that we will teach everybody else to make it, and that we are the enemies of Styphon's House until Styphon's House is destroyed."

Everybody, including those who had been suggesting novel and interesting ways of putting the priest to death, shouted approval.

"And a letter to Gormoth," he continued, "offering him peace and friendship. Tell him we'll put his soldiers to work in the fireseed mill and teach them the whole art, and when we release them, they can teach it in Nostor."

Ptosphes was horrified. "Kalvan! What god has addled your wits, man? Gormoth's our enemy by birth, and he'll be our enemy as long as he lives."

"Well, if he tries to make his own fireseed without joining us, that won't be long. Styphon's House will see to that."

8

I

VERKAN the Grefftscharrer led the party that galloped back to Hostigos Town in the late afternoon with the good news—Tarr-Dombra taken, with over two hundred prisoners, a hundred and fifty horses, four tons of fireseed, twenty cannon, and rich booty of small arms, armor and treasure. And Sevenhills Valley was part of Hostigos again. Harmakros had defeated a large company of mercenary cavalry, killing over twenty of them and capturing the rest. And he had taken the Styphon temple-farm, a nitriary, freeing the slaves and putting the priests to death. And the long-despised priest of Dralm had gathered his peasant flock and was preaching to them that the Hostigi had come not as conquerors but as liberators.

That sounded familiar to Verkan Vall; he'd heard the like on quite a few time-lines, including Morrison/Kalvan's own. Come to think of it, in the war in which Morrison had fought, both sides had made that claim.

He also brought copies of the letters Prince Ptosphes had written—more likely, that Kalvan had written and Ptosphes had signed—to Gormoth and to Sesklos, Styphon's Voice. The man was clever; those letters would do a lot of harm, where harm would do the most good.

Dropping a couple of troopers to spread the news in the town, he rode up to the castle; as he approached the gate, the great bell of the town hall began pealing. It took some time to tell the whole story to Xentos, counting interruptions while the old priest-chancellor told Dralm about it. When he got away from Xentos, he was dragged bodily into the officers' mess, where a barrel of wine had already been broached. Fortunately, he had some First Level alcodote-vitamin pills with him. By the time he got down to Hostigos Town it was dark, everybody was roaring drunk, the bell was still ringing, and somebody was wasting fireseed in the square with a little two-pounder.

He was mobbed there, too; the troopers who had come in with him betrayed him as one of the heroes of Tarr-Dombra. Finally he managed to get into the inn and up to his room. Getting another message-ball and a small radioactive beacon from his coffer, he hid them under his cloak, got his horse, and managed to get out of town, riding to a little clearing two miles away.

Pulling out the mouthpiece, he recorded a message, concluding:

"I wish especially to thank Skordran Kirv and the people with him for the reconnaissance work at Tarr-Dombra, on this and adjoining time-lines. The information so secured, and the success this morning resulting from it, places me in an excellent position to carry out my mission.

"I will need the assistants, and the equipment, at once. The people should come in immediately; there is a big victory celebration in the town, everybody's drunk, and they could easily slip in unnoticed. There will be a formal thanksgiving ceremony in the temple of Dralm, followed by a great feast, three days from now. At this time the betrothal of Lord Kalvan to the Princess Rylla will be announced."

Then he set the transposition timer, put the ball on antigrav, and tossed it up with a gesture like a falconer releasing his hawk. There was a slight overcast, and it flashed just below the ceiling, but that didn't matter. On this night, nobody would be surprised at portents in the sky over Hostigos. Then, after stripping the shielding from the beacon and planting it to guide the conveyer in, he sat down with his back to a tree and lit his pipe. Half an hour transposition time to Police Terminal, maybe an hour to get the men and equipment together, and another half hour to transpose in.

He wouldn't be bored waiting. First Level people never were. He had too many interesting things in his memory, all of which were available to total recall.

II

INVITED to sit, the Agrysi horse-trader took the chair facing the desk in the room that had been fitted up as Lord Kalvan's private office. He was partly bald, with a sparse red beard; about fifty, five-eight, a hundred and forty-five. The sort of character Corporal Calvin Morrison would have taken a professional interest in: he'd have a record, was probably wanted somewhere, for horse-theft at a guess. Shave off that beard and he'd double for a stolen-car fence he had arrested a year ago. A year before he'd gone elsewhen, anyhow. The horse-trader, Skranga, sat silently, wondering why he'd been brought in, and trying to think of something they might have on him. Another universal constant, he thought.

"Those were excellent horses we got from you," he began. "The officers snapped most of them up before they could get to the remount corrals."

"I'm glad to hear you say so, Lord Kalvan," Skranga said cautiously. "I try to deal only in the best."

"You've been working in the fireseed mill since. I'm told you've learned all about making fireseed."

"Well, Lord, I try to learn what I'm doing, when I'm supposed to do something."

"Most commendable. Now, we're going to open the frontiers. There's no point in keeping them closed since we took Tarr-Dombra. Where had you thought of going?"

Skranga shrugged. "Back to the Trygath country for more horses, I suppose."

"If I were you, I'd go to Nostor, before Gormoth closes his frontiers. Speak to Prince Gormoth privately, and be sure the priests of Styphon don't find out about it. Tell him you can make fireseed, and offer to make it for him. You'll be making your fortune if you do."

That was the last thing Skranga had expected. He was almost successful in concealing his surprise.

"But, Lord Kalvan! Prince Gormoth is your enemy." Then he stopped, scenting some kind of top-level double-crossing. "At least, he's Prince Ptosphes's enemy."

"And Prince Ptosphes's enemies are mine. But I like my enemies to have all the other enemies possible, and if Styphon's House find out that Gormoth is making his own fireseed, they'll be his. You worship Dralm? Then, before you speak to Prince Gormoth, go to the Nostor temple of Dralm, speak secretly to the high priest there, tell him I sent you, and ask his advice. You mustn't let Gormoth know about that. Dralm, or somebody, will reward you well."

Skranga's eyes widened for a moment, then narrowed craftily.

"Ah. I understand, Lord Kalvan. And if I get into Gormoth's palace, I'll find means of sending word to the priests of Dralm, now and then. Is that it, Lord Kalvan?"

"You understand perfectly, Skranga. I suppose you'd like to stay for the great feast, but if I were you, I'd not. Go the first thing in the morning, tomorrow. And before you go, speak to High Priest Xentos; ask the blessing of Dralm before you depart."

He'd have to get somebody into Sask and start Prince Sarrask up in fireseed production, too, he thought. That might be a little harder. And after the feast, all these traders and wagoners who'd been caught in the Iron Curtain would be leaving, fanning out all over the five Great Kingdoms. He watched Skranga go out, and then filled and lit a pipe—not the otherwhen Dunhill, but a local corncob, regular Douglas MacArthur model—and lit it at the candle on his desk.

Styphon's House was the real enemy. Beat Gormoth properly, on his own territory, and he'd stay beaten. Sarrask of Sask was only a Mussolini to Gormoth's Hitler; a decisive defeat of Nostor would overawe him. But Styphon's House wouldn't stop till Hostigos was destroyed; their prestige, which was their biggest asset, demanded it. And Styphon's House was big; it spread over all the Great Kingdoms, from the St. Lawrence to the Gulf.

Big but vulnerable, and he knew, by now, the vulnerable point. Styphon wasn't a popular god, like Dralm or Galzar or Yirtta Allmother. The priests of Styphon never tried for a following among the people, or even the minor nobility and landed gentry who were the backbone of here-and-now society. They ruled by pressure on the Great Kings and the Princes, and as soon as the pressure was relieved, as soon as the fireseed monopoly was broken, those rulers and their people with them would turn on Styphon's House. The war against Styphon's House was going to be won in little independent powder mills all over the Five Kingdoms.

But beating Gormoth was the immediate job. He didn't know how much good Skranga would be able to do, or Xentos's Dralm-temple Fifth Column. You couldn't trust that kind of thing. Gormoth would have to be beaten on the battlefield. Taking Tarr-Dombra had been a good start. The next morning, two thousand Nostori troops, mostly mercenaries, had tried to force a crossing at Dyssa Ford, at the mouth of Pine Creek; they'd been stopped by artillery fire. That night, Harmakros had taken five hundred cavalry across the West Branch at Vryllos Gap, and raided western Nostor, firing thatches, running off cattle, and committing all the usual atrocities.

He frowned slightly. Harmakros was a fine cavalry leader, and a nice guy to sit down and drink with, but Harmakros was just a trifle atrocity-prone. That massacre at the Sevenhills temple-farm, for instance. Well, if that was the way they made war, here-and-now, that would be the way to make it.

Then he sat for a while longer, thinking about the Art of War, here-and-now. He hoped taking Tarr-Dombra would hold Gormoth off for the rest of this year, and give him a chance to organize a real army, trained in the tactics he could remember from the history of the sixteenth and seventeenth centuries of his own time.

Light cannon, the sort Gustavus Adolphus had smashed Tilly's unwieldy tercios at Breitenfeld with. And plenty of rifles, and men trained to use them. There was a lot of forest country, here-and-now, and oddly, no game laws to speak of; everybody was a hunter. And bore-standardization, so that bullets could be issued, instead of every soldier having to carry his own bullet-mould and make his own bullets. He wondered how soon he could get socket bayonets, unknown here-and-now, produced. Not by the end of this year, not along with everything else. But if he could get rid of all these bear spears, and these scythe-blade things, whatever they were called, and get the spearmen armed with eighteen-foot Swiss pikes, then they'd keep the cavalry off his arquebusiers and calivermen.

He dug the heel out of his pipe and put it down, rising and looking at his watch (the only one in the world, and what would he do if he broke it?). It was 1700; dinner in an hour and a half. He went out, returning the salute of the halberdier at the door, and up the stairway.

His servant had the things piled on a table in his parlor, on a white sheet. The tunic with the battered badge that had saved his life; the gray shirt, torn and blood-stained. The breeches; he left the billfold in the hip pocket. He couldn't spend the paper currency of a nonexistent United States, and the identification cards belonged to a man similarly nonexistent here-and-now. He didn't want the boots, either; the castle cordwainer did better work, now that he had learned to make right and left feet. The Sam Browne belt, with the empty cartridge-loops and the holster and the handcuff-pouch. Anybody you needed handcuffs for, here-and-now, you knocked on the head or shot. He tossed the blackjack down contemptuously; blackjacks didn't belong here-and-now. Rapiers and poignards did.

He picked up the .38 Colt Official Police, swung out the cylinder and checked it by habit-reflex, and dry-practiced a few rounds at a knot-hole in the paneling. He didn't want to part with that, even if there were no more cartridges for it, but the rest of this stuff would be rather meaningless without it. He slipped it into the holster and buttoned down the retaining-strap.

"That's the lot," he told the servant. "Take them to High Priest Xentos."

The servant put them compactly together, one boot on either side, and wrapped them in the sheet. Tomorrow, at the thanksgiving ceremony, they would be deposited as votive offerings in the temple of Dralm. He didn't believe in Dralm, or any other god, but now, besides being a general and an ordnance engineer and an industrialist, he had to be a politician and no politician can afford to slight his constituents' religion. If nothing else, a parsonage childhood had given him a talent for hypocritical lip-service.

He watched the servant carry the bundle out. There goes Corporal Calvin Morrison, he thought. Long live Lord Kalvan of Hostigos.

III

VERKAN Vall, his story finished, relaxed in his chair and sipped his tall drink. There was no direct light on the terrace, only a sky-reflection of the city lights below, dim enough that the tip of Tortha Karf's cigarette glowed visibly. There were four of them around the low table: the Chief of Paratime Police; the Director of the Paratime Commission, who acted only on the Chief's suggestion; the Chairman of the Paratemporal Trade Board, who did as the Commission Director told him; and himself, who, in a hundred and twenty-odd days, would have all Tortha Karf's power and authority—and all his headaches.

"You took no action?" the Paratime Commission Director was asking.

"None whatever. None was needed. The man knows he was in some kind of a time-machine, which shifted him not into the past or future of his own world but laterally, in another time-dimension, and from that he can deduce the existence, somewhen, of a race of lateral time-travelers. That, in essence, is the Paratime Secret, but this Calvin Morrison—Lord Kalvan, now—is no threat to it. He's doing a better job of protecting it in his own case than we could. He has good reason to.

"Look what he has, on his new time-line, that his old one could never have given him. He's a great nobleman; they've gone out of fashion on Europo-America, where the Common Man is the ideal. He's going to marry a beautiful princess, and they've even gone out of fashion for children's fairy-tales. He's a sword-swinging soldier of fortune, and they've vanished from a nuclear-weapons world. He's commanding a good little army, and making a better one of it, the work he loves. And he has a cause worth fighting for, and an enemy worth beating. He's not going to jeopardize his position with those people.

"You know what he did? He told Xentos, under pledge of secrecy, that he had been banished by sorcery from his own time, a thousand years in the future. Sorcery, on that time-line, is a perfectly valid explanation for anything. With his permission, Xentos gave that story to Rylla, Ptosphes and Chartiphon; they handed it out that he is an exiled Prince from a country completely outside local geographical knowledge. See what he has? Regular defense in depth; we couldn't have done nearly as well ourselves."

"Well, how'd it leak to you?" the Board Chairman wanted to know.

"From Xentos, at the big victory feast. I got him off to one side, got him into a theological discussion, and spiked his drink with some hypno truth-drug. He doesn't even remember, now, that he told me."

"Nobody on that time-line'll get it that way," the Board Chairman agreed. "But didn't you take a chance on getting that stuff of his out of the temple?"

He shook his head. "We ran a conveyer in the night of the feast, when it was empty. The next morning, when the priests discovered that the uniform and the revolver and the other things had vanished, they cried, 'Lo! Dralm has accepted the offering! A miracle!' I was there, and saw it. Kalvan doesn't believe in any miracles; he thinks some of these transients that left Hostigos that day when the borders were opened stole the stuff. I know Harmakros's cavalry were stopping people at all the exit roads and searching wagons and packs. Publicly, of course, Kalvan had to give thanks to Dralm for accepting the offering."

"Well, was it necessary?"

"Not on that time-line. On the pickup line, yes. The stuff will be found . . . first the clothing and the badge with his number on it. Not too far from where he vanished; I think at Altoona. We have a man planted on the city police force there. Later, maybe in a year, the revolver will turn up, in connection with a homicide we will arrange. The Sector Regional Subchief can take care of that. There are always plenty of prominent people on any time-line who wouldn't be any great loss."

"But that won't explain anything," the Commission Director objected.

"No; it'll be an unsolved mystery. Unsolved mysteries are just as good as explanations, as long as they're mysterious within a normal framework."

"Well, gentlemen, all this is very interesting, but how does it concern me officially?" the Paratemporal Trade Board Chairman asked.

The Commission Director laughed. "You disappoint me! This Styphon's House racket is perfect for penetration of that subsector, and in a couple of centuries, long before either of us retire, it'll be a good area to have penetrated. We'll just move in on Styphon's House and take over the same way we did the Yat-Zar temples on the Hulgun Sector, and build that up to general political and economic control."

"You'll have to stay off Morrison's—Kalvan's—time-line," Tortha Karf said.

"I should say they will! You know what's going to be done with that? We're going to turn that over to the University of Dhergabar as a study-area, and five adjoining time-lines for controls. You know what we have here?" He was becoming excited about it. "We have the start of an entirely new subsector, identified from the exact point of divarication, something we've never been able to do before, except from history. I'm already established on that time-line as Verkan the Grefftscharr trader; Kalvan thinks that I'm traveling on horseback to Zygros City to recruit brass-founders for him, to teach his people how to cast brass cannon. In about forty or so days, I can return with them. They will, of course, be the University study-team. And I will be back, every so often, as often as horse-travel rates would plausibly permit. I'll put in a trade depot, which can mask the conveyer-head . . ."

Tortha Karf began laughing. "I knew you'd figure yourself some way! And, of course, it's such a scientifically important project that the Chief of Paratime Police would have to give it his personal attention, so you'll be getting outtime even after I retire and you take over."

"Well, all right. We all have our hobbies; you've been going to that farm of yours on Fifth Level Sicily for as long as I've been on the Paracops. Well, my hobby farm's going to be Kalvan Subsector, Fourth Level Aryan Transpacific. I'm only a hundred and thirty; by the time I'm ready to retire . . ."

9

IN the quiet of the Innermost Circle, in Styphon's House Upon Earth, at Balph, the great image looked down, and Sesklos, Supreme Priest and Styphon's Voice, returned the carven stare almost as stonily. Sesklos did not believe in Styphon or in any other god; if he had, he would not be sitting here. The policies of Styphon's House were too important to entrust to believers, and such could never hope to rise above the white robed outer circle, or at most don the black robes of under-priests. None might wear the yellow robe, let alone the flame-colored robe of primacy. The image, he knew, was of a man—the old high priest who had, by discovering the application of a minor temple secret, taken the cult of a minor healer-god out of its mean back-street shrines and made it the power that ruled the rulers of all the Five Kingdoms. If it had been in Sesklos to worship anything, he would have worshiped the memory of that man.

And now, the first Supreme Priest looked down upon the last one. Sesklos lowered his eyes to the sheets of parchment in front of him, flattening one with his hands to read again:

PTOSPHES, Prince of Hostigos, to SESKLOS, calling himself Styphon's Voice, these: False priest of a false god, impudent swindler, liar and cheat!

Know that we in Hostigos, by simple mechanic arts, now make for ourselves that fireseed which you pretend to be the miracle of your fraudulent god, and that we propose teaching these arts to all, that hereafter Kings and Princes minded to make war may do so for their own defense and advancement, and not to the enrichment of Styphon's House of Iniquities.

In proof thereof, we send fireseed of our own make, enough for twenty musket charges, and set forth how it is made, thus:

To three parts of refined saltpeter and three fifths of one part of charcoal and two fifths of one part of sulfur, all ground to the fineness of bolted wheat flour. Mix thoroughly, moisten the mixture, and work it to a heavy dough, then press into cakes and dry them, and when they are fully dry, grind and sieve them.

And know that we hold you and all in Styphon's House of Iniquities our deadly enemies, and the enemies general of all men, to be dealt with as wolves are, and that we will not rest content until Styphon's House of Iniquities is utterly cast down and destroyed.

PTOSPHES,

Prince of and for the nobles and people of Hostigos.

That had been the secret of the power of Styphon's House. No ruler, Great King or petty lord, could withstand his enemies if they had fireseed and he had none; no ruler sat secure upon his throne except by the favor of Styphon's House. Given here, armies marched to victory; withheld there, terms of peace were accepted. In every council of state, Styphon's House spoke the deciding word. Wealth poured in to be loaned out again at usury and return more wealth.

And now, the contemptible Prince of a realm a man could ride across without tiring his horse was bringing it down, and Styphon's House had provoked him to it. There had been sulfur springs in Hostigos, and of Styphon's Trinity, sulfur was hardest to get. Well, they'd demanded the land of him, and he'd refused, and none could be allowed to defy Styphon's House, so his enemy, Prince Gormoth, had been given gifts of money and fireseed. Things like that were done all the time.

Three moons ago, Ptosphes and his people had been desperate; now he was writing thus, to Styphon's Voice Himself. The impiety of it shocked Sesklos. Then he pushed aside Ptosphes's letter and looked again at the one from Vyblos, the high priest at Nostor Town. Three moons ago, a stranger, calling himself Kalvan and claiming to be an exiled Prince from a far country, had appeared in Hostigos. A moon later, Ptosphes had made this Kalvan commander of all his soldiers, and had set guards on his borders, that none might leave. He had been informed of that, but had thought nothing of it.

Then, six days ago, the Hostigi had taken Tarr-Dombra, the castle securing Gormoth's best route of invasion into Hostigos, and a black-robe priest who had been there had been released to bear this letter to him. Vyblos had sent the letter on by swift couriers; the priest was following more slowly to tell his tale in person.

It had, of course, been this Kalvan who had given Ptosphes the fireseed secret. He wondered briefly if this Kalvan might be some renegade from Styphon's House, then shook his head. No; the full secret, as Ptosphes had set it down, was known only to yellow-robe priests of the Inner Circle, upper priests, high priests and archpriests. If one of these had absconded, the news would have reached him as fast as relays of galloping horses could bring it. Some Inner Circle priest might have written it down, a thing utterly forbidden, and the writing might have fallen into unconsecrated hands, but he doubted that. The proportions were different: more saltpeter and less charcoal. He would have Ptosphes's sample tried; he suspected that it might be better than their own.

A man, then, who had rediscovered the secret for himself? That could be, though it had taken many years and the work of many priests to perfect the process, especially the caking and grinding. He shrugged. That was not important. The important thing was that the secret was out. Soon everybody would be making fireseed, and then Styphon's House would be only a name, and a name of mockery at that.

He might, however, postpone that day for as long as mattered to him. He was near his ninetieth year; he would not live to see many more, and for each man the world ends when he dies.

Letters of urgency to the archpriests of the five Great Temples, plainly telling them all, each to tell those under him as much as he saw fit. A story to be circulated among the secular rulers that fireseed stolen by bandits was being smuggled and sold. Prompt investigation of reports of anyone gathering sulfur or saltpeter, or building or altering grinding-mills. Death by assassination of anyone suspected of knowing the secret.

That would only do for the moment; he knew that. Something better must be devised, and quickly. And care must be taken not to spread, while trying to suppress, the news that someone outside Styphon's House was making fireseed. A Great Council of all the archpriests, but that later.

And, of course, immediate destruction of Hostigos, and all in it, not one to be spared even for slavery. Gormoth had been waiting until his own people could harvest their crops; he must be made to move at once. An archpriest of Styphon's House Upon Earth to be sent to Nostor, since this was entirely beyond poor Vyblos's capacities. Krastokles, he thought. Lavish gifts of fire-seed and silver and arms for Gormoth.

He glanced again at Vyblos's letter. A copy of Ptosphes's letter to himself had gone to Gormoth, by the hand of the castellan of Tarr-Dombra, released on ransom-oath. Why, Ptosphes had given his enemy the fireseed secret! He rebuked himself for not having noticed that before. That had been a daring, and a fiendishly clever, thing to do.

So, with Krastokles would go fifty mounted Guardsmen of the Temple, their captain to be an upper priest without robe. And more silver, to corrupt Gormoth's courtiers and mercenary captains.

And a special letter to the high priest of the Sask Town temple. It had been planned to use Prince Sarrask as a counterpoise to Gormoth, when the latter had grown too great by the conquest of Hostigos. Well, the time for that was now. Gormoth was needed to destroy Hostigos; as soon as that was accomplished, he, too, must be destroyed.

Sesklos struck the gong thrice, and as he did, he thought again of this mysterious Kalvan. That was nothing to shrug off. It was important to learn who he was, and whence he had come, and with whom he had been in contact before he had appeared—he was intrigued by Vyblos's choice of the word—in Hostigos. He could have come from some far country where the making of fireseed was commonly known. He knew of none such, but the world might well be larger than he thought.

Or could there be other worlds? The idea had occurred to him, now and then, as an idle speculation.

II

THE man called Lord Kalvan—except in retrospect, he never thought of himself as anything else now—sipped from the goblet and set it on the stand beside his chair. It was what they called winter-wine: set out in tubs to freeze, and the ice thrown off until it was sixty to seventy proof, the nearest they had to spirits, here-and-now. *Distillation,* he added to the long list of mental memos; *invent and introduce.* Bourbon, he thought; they grew plenty of corn.

It was past midnight; a cool breeze fluttered the curtains at the open windows, and flickered the candles. He was tired, and he knew that he would have to rise at dawn tomorrow, but he knew that he would lie awake a long while if he went to bed now. There was too much to think about.

Troop strengths: better than two to one against Hostigos. If Gormoth waited till his harvests were in and used all his peasant levies, more than that. Of course, if he waited, they'd be a little better prepared in training and matériel, but not much. Three thousand regular infantry, meaning they had been organized into companies and given a modicum of drill. Two thousand were pikemen and halberdiers, and too many of the pikes were short hunting-spears, and too many of the halberds were those scythe-blade things (he still didn't know what else to call them), and a thousand calivermen, arquebusiers and musketeers. And fifty riflemen, though in another thirty days there would be a hundred more. And eight hundred cavalry, all of whom could be called regulars—nobles and gentlemen-farmers, and their attendants.

Artillery—there was the real bright spot. Four of the light four-pounders were finished and in service, gun-crews training with them, and two more would be finished in another eight or ten days. And the old guns had been re-mounted; they were at least three hundred percent better than anything Gor-moth would have.

All right, they couldn't do anything about numbers; then cut the odds by concentrating on mobility and firepower. It didn't really matter who had the mostest; just git th'ar fustest and fire the most shots and score the most hits with them. But he didn't want to think about that right now.

He emptied the goblet and debated pouring himself more, lighting his pipe. Instead, he turned to something he hadn't had time to think about lately: the question of just when now was.

He wasn't at any time in the past or the future of May 19, 1964, when he'd walked into that dome of light. He'd settled that in his mind definitely. So what did that leave? Another time-dimension.

Say time was a plane, like a sheet of paper. *Paper; experiment with man-ufacture of;* that mental memo popped up automatically, and was promptly shoved down again. He wished he'd read more science fiction; time-dimensions were a regular science-fiction theme, and a lot of it carefully thought out. Well, say he was an insect, capable of moving only in one direc-tion, crawling along a line on the paper, and say somebody picked him up and set him down on another line.

That figured. And say, long ago, one of these lines of time had forked, maybe before the beginning of recorded history. Or say these lines had always existed, an infinite number of them, and on each one, things happened differ-ently. That could be it. He was beginning to be excited; Dralm-dammit, now he'd be awake half the night, thinking about this. He got up and filled the gob-let with almost-brandy.

He'd found out a little about these people's history. Their ancestors had been living on the Atlantic coast for over five hundred years; they all spoke the same language, and were of the same stock: Zarthani. They hadn't come from across the Atlantic, but from the west, across the continent. Some of that was recorded history he had read, and some was legend; all of it was supported by the maps, which showed all the important seacoast cities at the mouths of rivers. There were no cities on the sites of such excellent harbors as Boston, Baltimore or Charleston. There was the Grefftscharr Kingdom, at the west end of the Great Lakes, and Dorg at the confluence of the Mississippi and Missouri, and Xiphlon at the site of New Orleans. But there was nothing but a trading town at the mouth of the Ohio, and the Ohio valley was full of semi-savages. Rivers flowing east and south had been the pathway.

So these people had come from across the Pacific. But they weren't Asiatics, as he used the word; they were blond Caucasians. Aryans! Of course; the Aryans had come out of Central Asia, thousands of years ago, sweeping west and south into India and the Mediterranean basin, and west and north to Scandinavia. On this line of events, they'd gone the other way.

The names sounded Greek—all those -*os* and -*es* and -*on* endings—but the language wasn't even the most corrupt Greek. It wasn't even grammatically the same. He'd had a little Greek in college, dodging it as fast as it was thrown at him, but he knew that.

Wait a minute. The words for "father" and "mother." German, *vater;* Spanish, *padre;* Latin, *pater;* Greek, as near that as didn't matter; Sanskrit, *pitr.* German, *mutter;* Spanish, *madre;* Latin, *mater;* Greek, *meter;* Sanskrit, *matr.* In Zarthani, they were *phadros* and *mavra.*

III

I<small>T</small> was one of those small late-afternoon gatherings, nobody seeming to have a care in the world, lounging indolently, sipping tall drinks, nibbling canapes, talking and laughing. Verkan Vall held his lighter for his wife, Hadron Dalla, then applied it to his own cigarette. Across the low table, Tortha Karf was mixing himself a drink, with the concentrated care of an alchemist compounding the Elixir of Life. The Dhergabar University people—the elderly professor of Paratemporal Theory, the lady professor of Outtime History (IV), and the young man who was director of outtime study operations—were all smiling like three pussy-cats at a puddle of spilled cream.

"You'll have it all to yourselves," Vall told them. "The Paratime Commission has declared that time-line a study-area, and it's absolutely quarantined to everybody but University personnel and accredited students. I'm making it my personal business to see that the quarantine is enforced."

Tortha Karf looked up. "After I retire, I'm taking a seat on the Paratime Commission," he said. "I'll see to it that the quarantine isn't revoked or modified."

"I wish we could account for those four hours from the time he got out of that transposition field until he stopped at that peasant's cottage," the paratemporal theorist said. "We have no idea what he was doing."

"Wandering in the woods, trying to orient himself," Dalla said. "Sitting and thinking, most of the time, I'd say. Getting caught in a conveyer field must be a pretty shattering experience if you don't know what it is, and he seems to have adjusted very nicely by the time he had those Nostori to fight. I don't believe he was changing history all by himself."

"You can't say that," the old professor chided. "He could have shot a rattlesnake which would otherwise have bitten and killed a child who would otherwise have grown up to be an important personage. That sounds far-fetched and trivial, but paratemporal alternate probability is built on different trivialities. Who knows what started the Aryan migration eastward on that sector instead of westward, as on all the others? Some tribal chief's hangover; some wizard's nightmare."

"Well, that's why you're getting those five adjoining time-lines for controls," the outtime study operations director said. "And I'd keep out of Hostigos on all of them. We don't want our people massacred along with the resident population by Gormoth's gang, or forced to defend themselves with Home Time-Line weapons."

"What bothers me," the lady professor of history said, "is Vall's beard."

"It bothers me, too," Dalla said, "but I'm getting used to it."

"He hasn't shaved it off since he came back from Kalvan's time-line, and it begins to look like a permanent fixture. And I notice that Dalla's a blonde, now. Blondes are less conspicuous on Aryan-Transpacific. They're both going to be on and off that time-line all the time."

"Well, nobody's exclusive rights to anything outtime excludes the Paratime Police. I told you I was going to give that time-line my personal attention. And Dalla is officially Special Chief's Assistant's Special Assistant, now; she'll be promoted automatically along with me."

"Well, you won't introduce a lot of probability contamination, will you?"

the elderly theorist asked anxiously. "We want to observe the effect of this man's appearance on that time-line . . ."

"You know any kind of observation that doesn't contaminate the thing observed, professor?" Tortha Karf, who had gotten the drink mixed, asked.

"If anything, I'll be able to minimize the amount of contamination his study-teams introduce. I'm already well established with these people as Verkan the Grefftscharr trader. Why, Lord Kalvan offered me a commission in his army, commanding a rifle regiment he's raising, and right now I'm supposed to be recruiting brass-founders for him in Zygros." Vall turned to the operations director. "I can't plausibly get back to Hostigos for another thirty days. Can you have your first team ready by then? They'll have to know their trade; if they cast cannon that blow up on the first shot, I know where their heads will go, and I won't try to intervene for them."

"Oh, yes. They have everything now but local foundry techniques and correct Zygrosi accent. Thirty days will be plenty."

"But that's contamination!" the professor of Paratemporal Theory objected. "You're teaching his people to make cannon, and . . ."

"Just to make better cannon, and if I didn't bring in fake Zygrosi founders, Kalvan would send somebody else to bring in real ones. I will help him in any other way a wandering pack-trader could; information and things like that. I may even go into battle with him again—with one of those back-acting flint-locks. But I want *him* to win. I admire the man too much to want to hand him an unearned victory on a platter."

"He sounds like a lot of man to me," the lady historian said. "I'd like to meet him, myself."

"Better not, Eldra," Dalla warned. "That princess of his is handy with a pistol, and I don't think she cares much who she shoots."

10

I

THE general staff had a big room of their own to meet in, just inside the door of the keep, and the relief map was finished and set up. The General Staff were all new at it. So was he, but he had some vague idea of what a General Staff was supposed to do, which put him several up on any of the rest of them. Xentos was reporting what he had gotten from the Nostori Fifth Column.

"The bakeries work night and day," he said. "And milk cannot be bought at any price—it is all being made into cheese. And most of the meat is being made into smoked sausages."

Stuff a soldier could carry in a haversack and eat uncooked: field-rations. That stuff, even the bread, could be stored, Kalvan thought, but Xentos was also reporting that wagons and oxen were being commandeered, and peasants impressed as drivers. They wouldn't do that too long in advance.

"Then Gormoth isn't waiting to get his harvests in," Ptosphes said. "He'll strike soon, and taking Tarr-Dombra didn't stop him at all."

"It delayed him, Prince," Chartiphon said. "He'd be pouring mercenaries into Nostor now through Sevenhills Valley if we hadn't."

"I grant that." There was a smile on Ptosphes's lips. He'd been learning to smile again, since the powder mills had gone into operation, and especially since Tarr-Dombra had fallen. "We'll have to be ready for him a little sooner than I'd expected, that's all."

"We'll have to be ready for him yesterday at the latest," Rylla said. She'd picked that expression up from him. "What do you think he'll hit us with?"

"Well, he's been shifting troops around," Harmakros said. "He seems to be moving all his mercenaries east, and all his own soldiers west."

"Marax Ford," Ptosphes guessed. "He'll throw the mercenaries at us first."

"Oh, no, Prince!" Chartiphon dissented. "Go all the way around the mountains and all the way up through East Hostigos? He wouldn't do that. Here's how he'll come in."

He drew his big hand-and-a-half sword—none of these newfangled pokers for him—and gave it a little toss in his hand to get the right grip on it, then pointed on the map to where the Listra flowed into the Athan.

"There—Listra-Mouth. He can move his whole army up the river in his own country, force a crossing here—if we let him—and take all Listra Valley to the Saski border. That's where all our iron-works are."

Now that was something. Not so long ago, to Chartiphon, weapons had been just something you fought with; he'd taken them for granted. Now he was realizing that they had to be produced.

That started an argument. Somebody thought Gormoth would try to force one of the gaps. Not Dombra; that was too strong. Maybe Vryllos Gap.

"He'll attack where we don't expect him, that's where," Rylla declared.

"Well, that means we have to expect him everywhere."

"Great Galzar!" Ptosphes exploded, drawing his rapier. "That means we have to expect him everywhere from here"—he touched the point to the map to the mouth of the Listra—"to here," which was about where Lewisburg had been in Calvin Morrison's world. "That means that with half Gormoth's strength, we'll have to be stronger than he is at every point."

"Then we'll have to move what men we have around faster," his daughter told him.

Well, good girl! She'd seen what none of the others had, what he'd been thinking about last night, that mobility could make up for lack of numbers.

"Yes," he said. "Harmakros, how many infantrymen could you put horses under? They don't have to be good horses, just good enough to take them where they'll fight on foot."

Harmakros was scandalized. Mounted soldiers were *cavalry;* everybody knew it took years to train a cavalryman; he had to be practically born at it.

Chartiphon was scandalized, too. Infantrymen were *foot* soldiers; they had no business on horses.

"It'll mean," he continued, "that in action about one out of four will have to hold horses for the others, but they'll get into action before the battle's over, and they can wear heavier armor. Now, how many infantry can you find mounts for?"

Harmakros looked at him, decided that he was serious, thought for a moment, then grinned. It always took Harmakros a moment or so to recover from the shock of a new idea, but he always came up punching before the count was over.

"Just a minute; I'll see."

He pulled the remount officer aside; Rylla joined them with a slate and soapstone. Among other things, Rylla was the mathematician. She'd learned Arabic numerals, even the reason for having a symbol for nothing at all. Very high on the *I love Rylla, reasons why* list was the fact that the girl had a brain and wasn't afraid to use it.

He turned to Chartiphon and began talking about the defense of Listra-Mouth. They were still discussing it when Rylla and Harmakros came over and joined them.

"Two thousand," Rylla said. "They all have four legs, and we think they were all alive last evening."

"Eighteen hundred," Harmakros cut it. "We'll need some for pack-train and replacements."

"Sixteen hundred," Kalvan decided. "Eight hundred pikemen, with pikes and not hunting-spears or those scythe-blade things, and eight hundred arque-busiers, with arquebuses and not rabbit-guns. Can you do that, Chartiphon?"

Chartiphon could. All men who wouldn't fall off their horses, too.

"It'll make a Styphon's own hole in the army, though," he added.

Aside from the Mobile Force, that would leave twelve hundred pikemen and two hundred with firearms. Of course, there was the militia: two thousand peasant levies, anybody who could do an hour's foot-drill without dropping dead, armed with anything at all. They would fight bravely if unskillfully. A lot of them were going to get killed.

And, according to best intelligence estimates, Gormoth had six thousand mercenaries, of whom four thousand were cavalry, and four thousand of his own subjects, including neither the senile nor the adolescent and none of them armed with agricultural implements or crossbows. He looked at the map again. Gormoth would attack where he could use his cavalry superiority to best advantage. Either Listra-Mouth or Marax Ford.

"Good. And all the riflemen." All fifty of them. "Put them on the best horses, they'll have to be everywhere at once. And five hundred regular cavalry."

Everybody howled at that. There weren't that many, not uncommitted. Swords flashed over the map, indicating places where they only had half enough now. Contradictions were shouted. One of these days somebody was going to use a sword for something besides map-pointing in one of these arguments. Finally, by robbing Peter and Paul both, they scraped up five hundred for the Mobile Force.

"And I want all those musketoons and lances turned in," he said. "The lances are better pikes than half our pikemen have, and the musketoons are almost as good as arquebuses. We won't have cavalrymen burdened with infantry weapons when the infantry need them as desperately as they do."

Harmakros wanted to know what the cavalry would fight with.

"Swords and pistols. The purpose of cavalry is to scout and collect information, neutralize enemy cavalry, harass enemy movement and communications, and pursue fugitives. It is not to fight on foot—that's why we're organizing mounted infantry—and it is not to commit suicide by making attacks on massed pikemen—that's why we're building these light four-pounders. The lances and musketoons will go to the infantry, and the fowling-pieces and scythe-blade things they replace can go to the militia.

"Now, you'll command this Mobile Force, Harmakros. Turn all your intelligence work over to Xentos; Prince Ptosphes and I will help him. You'll have all four of the four-pounders, and the two being built as soon as they're finished, and pick out the lightest four of the old eight-pounders. You'll be based in Sevenhills Valley; be prepared to move either east or west as soon as you have orders.

"And another thing: battle-cries." They had to be shouted constantly, to keep friend from killing friend. "Besides 'Ptosphes!' and 'Hostigos!' we will shout 'Down Styphon!'"

That met with general approval. They all knew who the real enemy was.

II

GORMOTH, Prince of Nostor, set down the goblet, wiping his bearded lips on the back of his hand. The candles in front of him and down the long tables at the sides flickered. Tableware clattered, and voices were loud.

"Lost everything!" The speaker was a baron driven from Sevenhills Valley when Tarr-Dombra had fallen almost a moon ago. "My house, a score of farms, a village . . ."

"You think we've lost nothing?" another noble demanded. "They crossed the river the night after they chased you out, and burned everything on my land. It was Styphon's own miracle I got out with my own blood unspilled."

"For shame!" cried Vyblos, the high priest of the temple of Styphon, sitting with him at the high table. "You speak of cow-byres and peasant-huts; what of the temple-farm of Sevenhills, a holy place pillaged and desecrated? What of fifteen consecrated priests and novices, and a score of lay guards, all cruelly murdered? 'Dealt with as wolves are,'" he quoted.

"That's Styphon's business; let him look to his own," the lord from western Nostor said. "I want to know why our Prince isn't looking to the protection of Nostor."

"It can be stopped, Prince." That was the mayor, and wealthiest merchant, of Nostor Town. "Prince Ptosphes has offered peace, now that Hostigos has Tarr-Dombra again. He's a man of his word."

"Peace tossed like a bone to a cur?" yelled Netzigon, the chief captain of Nostor. "Friendship shot at us out of cannon?"

"Peace with a desecrator of holy places, and a butcher of Styphon's priests?" Vyblos fairly screamed. "Peace with a blasphemer who pretends, with his mortal hands, to work Styphon's own miracle, and make fireseed without Styphon's aid?"

"More than pretends!" That was Gormoth's cousin, Count Pheblon. He still hadn't taken Pheblon back into his favor after losing Tarr-Dombra, but for those words he was close to it. "By Dralm, the Hostigi burned more fireseed taking Tarr-Dombra than we thought they had in all Hostigos. I was there, which you weren't. And when they opened the magazines, they only sneered and said, 'That filthy trash; don't get it mixed with ours.'"

"That's all aside," the baron from Listra-Mouth said. "I want to know what's being done to keep their raiders out of Nostor. Why, they've harried all the strip between the mountains and the river; there isn't a house standing there now."

Weapons clattered at the door. Somebody else sneered: "That's Ptosphes, now! Under the tables, everybody!" A man in mail and black leather strode in, advancing and saluting; the captain of the dungeons.

"Lord Prince, the special prisoner has been made to talk. He will tell all."

"Ha!" Gormoth knew what that meant. Then he laughed at the looks of concern on faces down the side tables. Not a few at his court had cause to dread somebody telling all about something. He drew his poignard and cut a line across the candle in front of him, a thumb's breadth from the top.

"You bring good news. I'll go to hear him in that time."

As he nodded dismissal, the captain bowed and backed away. He rapped loudly on the table with the pommel of the dagger.

"Be silent, all of you; I've little time, so give heed. Klestreus," he addressed the elected captain-general of the mercenary free-companies, "you have four thousand horse, two thousand foot, and ten cannon. Add to them a thousand of my infantry and such guns of mine as you think fit. You'll cross the Athan at Marax Ford. Be on the road before the dew's off the grass tomorrow; before dawn of the next day, take and hold the ford, put the best of your cavalry across at once, and let the others follow as speedily as they can.

"Netzigon," he told his own chief-captain, "you'll gather every man you can, down to the very peasant rabble, and such cannon as Klestreus leaves you. Post companies to confront every pass in the mountains from across the river; use the peasants for that. With the rest of your force, march to Listra-Mouth and Vryllos Gap. As Klestreus moves west through East Hostigos, he will attack each gap from behind; when he does, your people will cross over and give aid. Tarr-Dombra we'll have to starve out; the rest must be taken by storm. When Klestreus is as far as Vryllos Gap, you will cross the Athan and move up Listra Valley. After that, we'll have Tarr-Hostigos to take. Galzar only knows how long we'll be at that, but by the end of the moon-half all else in Hostigos should be ours."

There were gratified murmurs all along the table; this made good hearing, and they had waited long to hear it. Only the high priest, Vyblos, was ill-pleased.

"But why so soon, Prince?"

"Soon? By the Mace of Galzar, you've been bawling for it like a branded calf since greenleaf-time. Well, now you have your invasion—yet you object. Why?"

"A few more days would cost nothing, Prince," Vyblos said. "Today I had word from Styphon's House Upon Earth, from the pen of His Divinity, Styphon's Voice Himself. An archpriest, His Sanctity Krastokles, is traveling hither with rich gifts and the blessing of Styphon. It were poor reverence not to await His Sanctity's coming."

Another cursed temple-rat, bigger and fatter and more insolent than this one. Well, let him come after the victory, and content himself with what bones were tossed to him.

"You heard me," he told the two captains. "I rule here, not this priest. Be about it; send out your orders now, and move in the morning."

Then he rose, pushing back the chair before the servant behind him could touch it. The line was still visible at the top of the candle.

Guards with torches attended him down the winding stairs into the dungeons. The air stank. His breath congealed; the heat of summer never penetrated here. From the torture chamber shrieks told of some wretch being questioned; idly he wondered who. Stopping at an iron-bound door, he unlocked it with a key from his belt and entered alone, closing it behind him.

The room within was large, warmed by a fire on a hearth in the corner and lighted by a great lantern from above. Under it, a man bent over a littered table, working with a mortar and pestle. As the door closed, he straightened and turned. He had a bald head and a red beard, and wore a most unprisoner-like dagger on his belt. A key for the door lay on the table, and by them a pair of heavy horseman's pistols. He smiled.

"Greetings, Prince; it's done. I tried some, and it's as good as they make in Hostigos, and better than the dirt the priests sell."

"And no prayers to Styphon, Skranga?"

Skranga was chewing tobacco. He spat brownly on the floor.

"That in the face of Styphon! You want to try it, Prince? The pistols are empty."

There was a bowl half full of fireseed on the table. He measured a charge and poured it into one, loaded and wadded a ball on top of it, primed the pan, readied the flint and striker. Aiming at a billet of wood by the hearth, he fired, then laid the pistol down and went to probe the hole with a straw. The bullet had gone in almost a little finger's length; Styphon's powder wouldn't do that much.

"Well, Skranga!" he laughed. "We'll have to keep you hidden for awhile yet, but from this hour you're first nobleman of Nostor after myself. Style yourself Duke. There'll be rich lands for you in Hostigos, when Hostigos is mine."

"And in Nostor the Styphon temple-farms?" Skranga asked. "If I'm to make fireseed for you, there's all there that I'll need."

"Yes, by Galzar, that too! After I've dealt with Ptosphes, I'll have a reckoning with Vyblos, and before I let him die, he'll be envying Ptosphes."

Snatching up a pewter cup without looking to see if it were clean, he went to the wine-barrel and drew it full. He tasted the wine, then spat it out.

"Is this the swill they've given you to drink?" he demanded. "Whoever's at fault won't see tomorrow's sun set!" He flung open the door and bellowed into the hall: "Wine! Wine for Prince Gormoth and Duke Skranga! And silver cups!" He hurled the pewter, still half full of wine, at a guard. "Move your feet, you bastard! And see it's fit for nobles to drink!"

11

I

MOBILE force HQ had been the mansion of a Nostori noble driven from Sevenhills Valley on D-for-Dombra Day. Kalvan's name had been shouted ahead as he rode to it through the torchlit, troop-crowded village, and Harmakros and some of his officers met him at the door.

"Great Dralm, Kalvan!" Harmakros laughed. "Don't tell me you're growing wings on horses, now. Our messengers only got off an hour ago."

"Yes, I met them at Vryllos Gap." They crossed the outer hall and entered the big room beyond. "We got the news at Tarr-Hostigos just after dark. What have you heard since?"

At least fifty candles burned in the central chandelier. Evidently the cavalry had gotten here before the peasants, on D-Day, and hadn't looted too destructively themselves. Harmakros led him to an inlaid table on which a map, scorched with hot needles on white deerskin, was spread.

"We have reports from all the watchtowers along the mountains. They're too far back from the river for anything but dust to be seen, but the column's over three miles long. First cavalry, then infantry, then guns and wagons, and then more infantry and some cavalry. They halted at Nirfë at dusk and built hundreds of campfires. Whether they left them burning and moved on after dark, and how far ahead the cavalry are now, we don't know. We expect them at Marax Ford by dawn."

"We got a little more than that. The Nostor priest of Dralm got a messenger off a little after noon, but he didn't get across the river till twilight. Your column's commanded by Klestreus, the mercenary captain-general. All Gormoth's mercenaries, four thousand cavalry and two thousand infantry, a thousand of his own infantry, and fifteen guns, he didn't say what kind, and a train of wagons that must be simply creaking with loot. At the same time, Netzigon's moving west on Listra-Mouth with an all-Nostori army; dodging them was what delayed this messenger. Chartiphon's at Listra-Mouth with what he can scrape up; Ptosphes is at Vryllos Gap with a small force."

"That's it," Harmakros said. "Double attack, but the one from the east will be the heavy one. We can't do anything to help Chartiphon, can we?"

"Beat Klestreus as badly as we can; that's all I can think of." He had gotten out his pipe; as soon as he had it filled, one of the staff officers was offering a light. That was another universal constant. "Thank you. What's been done here, so far?"

"I started my wagons and the eight-pounders east on the main road; they'll halt just west of Fitra, here." He pointed on the map to a little farming village. "As soon as I'm all collected, here, I'll start down the back road, which joins the main road at Fitra. After I'm past, the heavy stuff will follow on. I have two-hundred militia—the usual odd-and-sods, about half with crossbows—marching with the wagons."

"That was all smart."

He looked again at the map. The back road, adequate for cavalry and four-pounders but not for wagons or the heavy guns, followed the mountain and then bent south to join the main valley road. Harmakros had gotten the slow stuff off first, and wouldn't be impeded by it on his own march, and he was waiting to have all his force together, instead of feeding it in to be chopped up by detail.

"Where had you thought of fighting?"

"Why, on the Athan, of course." Harmakros was surprised that he should ask. "Klestreus will have some of his cavalry across before we get there, but that can't be helped. We'll kill them or run them back, and then defend the line of the river."

"No." Kalvan touched the stem of his corncob on the Fitra road-junction. "We fight here."

"But, Lord Kalvan! That's miles inside Hostigos!" one of the officers expostulated. Maybe he owned an estate down there. "We can't let them get that far!"

"Lord Kalvan," Harmakros began stiffly. He was going to be insubordinate; he never bothered with titles otherwise. "We cannot give up a foot of Hostigi ground. The honor of Hostigos forbids it."

Here we are, back in the Middle Ages! He seemed to hear the voice of the history professor, inside his head, calling a roll of battles lost on points of honor. Mostly by the French, though they weren't the only ones. He decided to fly into a rage.

"To Styphon with that!" he yelled, banging his fists on the table. "We're not fighting this war for honor, and we're not fighting this war for real-estate. We're fighting this Dralm-damned war for survival, and the only way we can win it is to kill all the damned Nostori we can, and get as few of our men killed doing it as we can.

"Now, here," he continued quietly, the rage having served its purpose. "Here's the best place to do it. You know what the ground's like there. Klestreus will cross here at Marax. He'll rush his best cavalry ahead, and after he's secured the ford, he'll push on up the valley. His cavalry'll want to get in on the best looting before the infantry come up. By the time the infantry are over, they'll be strung out all up East Hostigos.

"And they'll be tired, and, more important, their horses will be tired. We'll all have gotten to Fitra by daylight, and by the time they begin coming up, we'll have our position prepared, our horses will be fresh again, all the men will have at least an hour or so sleep, and a hot meal. You think that won't make a difference? Now, what troops have we east of here?"

A hundred-odd cavalry along the river; a hundred and fifty regular infantry, and about twice as many militia. Some five hundred, militia and some regulars, at posts in the gaps.

"All right . . . get riders off at once, somebody who won't be argued with. Have that force along the river move back, the infantry as rapidly as possible, and the cavalry a little ahead of the Nostori, skirmishing. They will not attempt to delay them; if the ones in front are slowed down, the ones behind will catch up with them, and we don't want that."

Harmakros had been looking at the map, and also looking over the idea. He nodded.

"East Hostigos," he declared, "will be the graveyard of the Nostori."

That took care of the honor of Hostigos.

"Well, mercenaries from Hos-Agrys and Hos-Ktemnos. Who hired those mercenaries, anyhow—Gormoth or Styphon's House?"

"Why, Gormoth. Styphon's House furnished the money, but the mercenary captains contracted with Gormoth."

"Stupid of Styphon. The reason I asked, the Rev. What's-his-name, in Nostor, included an interesting bit of gossip in his report. It seems that this morning Gormoth had one of his under-stewards put to death. Forced a funnel into his mouth, and had close to half a keg of wine poured into him. The wine was of inferior quality, and had been furnished to a prisoner, or supposed prisoner, for whom Gormoth had commanded good treatment."

One of the officers made a face. "Sounds like Gormoth." Another laughed and named a couple of innkeepers in Hostigos Town who deserved the same. Harmakros wanted to know who this pampered prisoner was.

"You know him. That Agrysi horse-trader, Skranga."

"Yes, we got some good horses from him. I'm riding one, myself," Harmakros said. "Hey! He was working in the fireseed mill. Do you think he's making fireseed for Gormoth now?"

"If he's doing what I told him to he is." There was an outcry; even Harmakros stared at him in surprise. "If Gormoth starts making his own fireseed, Styphon's House will find it out, and you know what'll happen then. That's why I was wondering who'd be able to use those mercenaries against whom. That's another thing. We can't be bothered with Nostori prisoners, but take all the mercenaries who'll surrender. We'll need them when Sarrask's turn comes up."

II

DAWN was only a pallor in the east, and the whitewashed walls were dim blurs under dark thatches, but the village of Fitra was awake, and the shouting began as he approached: "Lord Kalvan! Dralm bless Lord Kalvan!" He was used to it now; it didn't give him the thrill it had at first. Light streamed from open doors and windows, and a fire blazed on the little common, and there was a crowd of villagers and cavalrymen who had ridden on ahead. Behind him, hooves thudded on the road, and far back he could hear the four-pounders clattering over the pole bridge at the mill. He had to make a speech from the saddle, while orders were shouted and reshouted to the rear and men and horses crowded off the road to make way for the guns.

Then he and Harmakros and four or five other officers rode forward, reining in where the main road began to dip into the little hollow. The eastern pallor had become a bar of yellow light. The Mountains of Hostigos were blackly plain on the left, and the jumble of low ridges on the right were beginning to take shape. He pointed to a ravine between two of them.

"Send two hundred cavalry around that ridge and into that little valley, where those three farms are clumped together," he said. "They're not to make fires or let themselves be seen. They're to wait till we're engaged here, and the second batch of Nostori come up. Then they'll come out and hit them from behind."

An officer galloped away to attend to it. The yellow light spread; only a few of the larger and brighter stars were still visible. In front, the ground fell away to the small brook that ran through the hollow, to join a larger stream that flowed east along the foot of the mountain. The mountain rose steeply to a bench, then sloped up to the summit. On the right was broken ground, mostly wooded. In front, across the hollow, was mostly open farmland. There were a few trees around them, in the hollow and on the other side. This couldn't have been better if he'd had Dralm create it to special order.

The yellow light had reached the zenith, and the eastern horizon was a dazzle. Harmakros squinted at it and said something about fighting with the sun in their eyes.

"No such thing; it'll be overhead before they get here. Now, you go take a nap. I'll wake you in time to give me some sack-time. As soon as the wagons get here, we'll give everybody a hot meal."

An ox-cart appeared on the brow of the hill across the hollow, piled high, a woman and a boy trudging beside the team and another woman and some children riding. Before they were down to the brook, a wagon had come into sight. This was only the start; there'd be a perfect stream of them soon. They couldn't be allowed on the main road west of Fitra until the wagons and the eight-pounders were through.

"Have them turned aside," he ordered. "And use the wagons and carts for barricades, and the oxen to drag trees."

The village peasants were coming out now, with four- and six-ox teams dragging chains. Axes began thudding. More refugees were coming in; there were loud protests at being diverted and at having wagons and oxen commandeered. The axe-men were across the hollow now, and men shouted at straining oxen as felled trees were dragged in to build an abatis.

He strained his eyes against the sunrise; he couldn't see any smoke. Too far away, but he was sure it was there. The enemy cavalry had certainly crossed the Athan by now, and pyromania was as fixed in the mercenary character as kleptomania. The abatis began to take shape, trees dragged into line with the tops to the front and the butts to the rear, with spaces for three of the six four-pounders on either side of the road and a barricade of wagons and farm carts a little in advance at either end. He rode forward now and then to get an enemy's-eye view of it. He didn't want it to look too formidable from in front, or too professional—for one thing, he wanted to make sure that the guns were completely camouflaged. Finally he began to notice smears of smoke against the horizon, maybe six or eight miles away. Klestreus's mercenaries weren't going to disappoint him after all.

A company of infantry came up. They were regulars, a hundred and fifty of them, with two pikes (and one of them a real pike) to every caliver, marching in good order. They'd come all the way from the Athan, reported fighting behind them, and were disgusted at marching away from it. He told them they'd get all they wanted before noon, and to fall out and rest. A couple of hundred militia, some with crossbows, dribbled in. There were more smokes on the eastern horizon, but he still couldn't hear firing. At seven-thirty, the supply wagons, the four eight-pounders, and the two hundred militia arrived. That was good. The refugees, now a steady stream, could be sent on up the road. He saw to it that fires were lit and a hot meal started, and then went into the village.

He found Harmakros asleep in one of the cottages, wakened him, and gave him the situation to date.

"Send somebody to wake me," he finished, "as soon as you see smoke within three miles, as soon as our cavalry skirmishers start coming in, and in any case in two and a half hours."

Then he pulled off his helmet and boots, unbuckled his sword-belt, and lay down in the rest of his armor on the cornshuck tick Harmakros had vacated, hoping that it had no small inhabitants or, if so, that none of them would find lodgement under his arming-doublet. It was cool in here behind the stone walls and under the thick thatch. The wet heat of his body became a clammy chill. He shifted positions a few times, decided that fewer things gouged into him when lying on his back, and closed his eyes.

So far, everything had gone nicely; all he was worried about was who was going to let him down, and how badly. He hoped some valiant fool wouldn't get a rush of honor to the head and charge when he ought to stand fast, like the Saxons at Hastings.

If he could bring this off just half as well as he'd planned it, which would be about par for any battle, he could go to Valhalla when he died and drink at the same table with Richard Coeur-de-Lion, the Black Prince and Henry of Navarre. A complete success would entitle him to take a salute from Stonewall Jackson. He fell asleep receiving the commendation of George S. Patton.

III

An infantry captain wakened him at a little before ten.

"They're burning Systros now," he said. That was a town of some two thousand, two and a half miles away. "A couple of the cavalry who've been keeping contact with them just came in. The first batch, about fifteen hundred, are coming up fast, and there's another lot, about a thousand, a mile and a half behind them. And we've been hearing those big bombards at Narza Gap."

Between Montoursville and Muncy; that would be Klestreus's infantry on this side, and probably some of Netzigon's ragtag and bobtail on the other. He pulled on his boots and buckled on his belt, and somebody brought him a bowl of beef stew with plenty of onion in it, and a mug of sour red wine. When his horse was brought, he rode forward to the line, noticing in passing that the Mobile Force Uncle Wolf and the village priest of Dralm and priestess of Yirtta had set up a field hospital in the common, and that pole-and-blanket stretchers were being made. He hoped he wouldn't be wounded. No anesthetics, here-and-now, though the priests of Galzar used sandbags.

A big cloud of smoke dirtied the sky over Systros. Silly buggers—first crowd in had fired it. Here-and-now mercenaries were just the same as Tilly's or Wallenstein's. Now the ones behind would have to bypass it, which would bring them to Fitra in even worse order.

The abatis was finished, and he cantered forward for a final look at it. He couldn't see a trace of any of the guns, and it looked, as he had wanted it to, like the sort of thing a lot of peasant home-guards would throw up. At each end, between the abatis itself and the short barricades of carts, was an opening big enough for cavalry to sortie out. The mounted infantry horse-lines were back of the side road, with the more poorly armed militia holding horses.

Away off, one of the Narza Gap bombards boomed; they were still holding out. Then he began to hear the distant, and then not-so-distant, pop of small arms. Cavalry drifted up the road, some reloading pistols as they came. The shots grew louder; more cavalry, in more of a hurry, arrived. Finally, four of them topped the rise and came down the slope; the last one over the top turned in his saddle and fired a pistol behind him. A dozen Nostori cavalry appeared as they were splashing through the brook.

Immediately, a big 8-bore rifled musket bellowed from behind the abatis, and then another and another. His horse dance-stepped daintily. Across the hollow, a horse was down, kicking, another reared, riderless, and a third, also empty saddled, trotted down to the brook and stopped to drink. The mercenaries turned and galloped away out of sight into the dead ground beyond the rise. He was wondering where Harmakros had put the rest of the riflemen when a row of smoke-puffs blossomed along the edge of the bench above the stream on the left, and shots cracked like a string of firecrackers. There were yells from out of sight across the hollow, and musketoons thumped in reply. Wasting Styphon's good fireseed—at four hundred yards, they couldn't have hit Grant's Tomb with smoothbores.

He wished he had five hundred rifles up there. Hell, why not wish for twenty medium tanks and half a dozen Sabre-Jets, while he was at it?!

Then Klestreus's mercenary cavalry came up in a solid front on the brow of the hill—black and orange pennons and helmet-plumes and scarves, polished breastplates. Lancers all in front, musketoon-men behind. A shiver ran along the front as the lances came down.

As though that had been the signal, and it probably had been, six four-pounders and four eight-pounders went off together. It wasn't a noise, but a palpable blow on the ears. His horse started to buck; by the time he had him under control the smoke was billowing out over the hollow, and several perfect rings were floating up against the blue, and everybody behind the abatis was yelling, "Down Styphon!"

Roundshot; he could see where it had torn furrows back into the group of black and orange cavalry. Men were yelling, horses rearing, or down and screaming horribly, as only wounded horses can. The charge had stopped before it had started. On either side of him, gun-captains were shouting, "Grapeshot! Grapeshot!" and cannoneers were jumping to their pieces before they had stopped recoiling with double-headed swabs, one end wet to quench lingering powder-bag sparks and one end dry.

The cavalry charge slid forward in broken chunks, down the slope and into the hollow. When they were twenty yards short of the brook, four hundred arquebuses crashed. The whole front went down, horses behind falling over dropped horses in front. The arquebusiers who had fired stepped back, drawing the stoppers of their powder-flasks with their teeth. *Spring powder-flasks, self-measuring; get made and issued soonest.* He also added cartridge-paper to the paper memo.

When they were half reloaded, the other four hundred arquebuses crashed. The way those cavalry were jammed down there, it would take an individual miracle for any bullet to miss something. The smoke was clogging the hollow like spilled cotton now, but through it he could see another wave of cavalry coming up on the brow of the opposite hill. A four-pounder spewed grapeshot into them, then another and another, till the whole six had fired.

Gustavus Adolphus's four-pounder crews could load and fire faster than musketeers, the dry lecture-room voice was telling him. Of course, the muskets they'd been timed against had been matchlocks; that had made a big difference. Lord Kalvan's were doing almost as well: the first four-pounder had fired on the heels of the third arquebus volley. Then one of the eight-pounders fired, and that was a small miracle.

A surprising number of Klestreus's cavalry had survived the fall of their horses. Well, not so surprising; horses were bigger targets, and they didn't wear breastplates. Having nowhere else to go, the men were charging on foot, using their lances as pikes. A few among them had musketoons; they'd been in the rear. Quite a few were shot coming up, and more were piked trying to get through the abatis. A few did get through. As he galloped to help deal with one of these parties, he heard a trumpet sound on the left, and another on the right, and there was a clamor of "Down Styphon!" at both ends. That would be the cavalry going out; he hoped the artillery wouldn't get excited.

Then he was in front of a dozen unhorsed Nostori cavalrymen, pulling up his horse and aiming a pistol at them.

"Yield, comrades! We spare mercenaries!"

An undecided second and a half, then one of them lifted a reversed musketoon.

"We yield; oath to Galzar."

That, he thought, they would keep. Galzar didn't like oath-breaking soldiers; he let them get killed at the next opportunity. *Cult of Galzar; encourage.*

Some peasants ran up, brandishing axes and pitchforks. He waved them back with his pistol, letting them have a look at the muzzle.

"Keep your weapons," he told the mercenaries. "I'll find somebody to guard you."

He detailed a couple of Mobile Force arquebusiers; they impressed some militia. Then he had to save a wounded mercenary from having his throat cut. Dralm-damned civilians! He'd have to detail prisoner-guards. Disarm these mercenaries and the peasants'd cut their throats; leave them armed, and the temptation might overcome the fear of Galzar.

Along the abatis, the firing had stopped, but the hollow below was a perfect hell's bedlam—pistol shots, clashing steel, "Down Styphon!" and, occasionally, "Gormoth!" Over his shoulder he could see villagers, even women and children, replacing militiamen on the horse-lines. Captains were shouting,

"Pikes forward!" and pikemen were dodging among the branches to get through the abatis. Dimly, through the smoke, he could see red and blue on horsemen at the brow of the opposite hill. *Uniforms; do something about. Brown, or dark green.*

The road had been left unobstructed, and he trotted through and down toward the brook. What he saw in the hollow made his stomach heave, and it didn't heave easily. It was the horses that bothered him more than anything else, and he wasn't the only one. The infantry, going forward, were stopping to cut wounded horses' throats, or brain them, or shoot them with pistols from saddle-holsters. They shouldn't do that, they ought to keep on, but he couldn't stand seeing horses suffer.

Stretcher-bearers were coming forward to, and villagers to loot. Corpse-robbing was the only way the here-and-now civil population had of getting a little of their own back after a battle. Most of them had clubs or hatchets, to make sure that what they were robbing really were corpses.

There were a lot of good weapons lying around. They ought to be collected before they rusted into uselessness, but there was no time for that now. Stopping to do that, once, had been one of Stonewall Jackson's few mistakes. Something was being done toward that, though: he saw crossbows lying around, and each one meant a militiaman who had armed himself with an enemy cavalry musketoon.

The battle had passed on eastward; unopposed infantry were forming up, blocks of pikemen with blocks of arquebusiers between, and men were running back to bring up horses. Away ahead, there was an uproar of battle; that would be the two hundred cavalry he had posted on the far right hitting another batch of Gormoth's mercenaries, who, by now, would be disordered by fugitives streaming back from the light at the hollow. The riflemen on the bench were drifting eastward, too, firing as they went.

And enemy cavalry were coming in in groups, holding their helmets up on their sword-points, calling out, "We yield, oath to Galzar." One of the officers of the flanking party, with four troopers, was coming in with close to a hundred of them, regretting that so many had gotten away. And all the infantry who had marched in from the Athan, and many of the local militia, had mounted themselves on captured horses.

There was a clatter behind him, and he got his horse off the road to let the four-pounders pass in column. Their captain waved to him and told him, laughing, that the eights would be along in a day or so.

"Where do we get some more shooting?" he asked.

"Down the road a piece; just follow along and we'll show you plenty to shoot at."

He slipped back the knit cuff under his mail sleeve and looked at his watch. It was still ten minutes to noon, Hostigos Standard Sundial Time.

12

By 1730, they were down the road a really far piece, and there had been considerable shooting on the way. Now they were two miles west of the Athan, on the road to Marax Ford, and the Nostori wagons and cannon were strung out for half a mile each way. He was sitting, with his helmet off, on an upended wine keg at a table made by laying a shed-door across some boxes, with Harmakros's pyrographed deerskin map spread in front of him, and a mug where he could reach it. Beside the road, some burned out farm buildings were still smoking, and the big oaks which shaded him were yellowed on one side from heat. Several hundred prisoners squatted in the field beyond, eating rations from their own wagons.

Harmakros, and the commander of mounted infantry, Phrames—he'd be about two-star rank—and the brigadier-general commanding cavalry, and the Mobile Force Uncle Wolf—somewhat younger than the Tarr-Hostigos priest of Galzar and about chaplain-major equivalent—sat or squatted around him. The messenger from Sevenhills Valley, who had just caught up with him, paced back and forth, trying to walk the stiffness out of his legs. He drank from a mug as he talked. He was about U.S. first lieutenant equivalent.

Titles of rank; regularize. This business of calling everybody from company commander up to commander-in-chief a captain just wouldn't do. He'd made a start with that, on the upper echelons; he'd have to carry it down to field and company level. *Rank, insignia of; establish.* He thought he'd adopt the Confederate Army system—it was simpler, with no oak and maple leaves and no gold and silver distinctions. Then he pulled his attention back to what the messenger was saying.

"That's all we know. All morning, starting before mess call, there was firing up the river. Cannon-fire, and then small arms, and, when the wind was right, we could hear shouting. About first morning drill break, some of our cavalry, who'd been working up the river along the mountains, came back and reported that Netzigon had crossed the river in front of Vryllos Gap, and they couldn't get through to Ptosphes and Princess Rylla."

He cursed, first in Zarthani and then in English. "Is she at Vryllos Gap, too?"

Harmakros laughed. "You ought to know that girl by now, Kalvan; you're going to marry her. Just try and keep her out of battles."

That he would, by Dralm! With how much success, though, was something else.

The messenger, having taken time out for a deep drink, continued:

"Finally, a rider came in from this side of the mountain. He said that the Nostori were across and pushing Prince Ptosphes back into the gap. He wanted to know if the captain of Tarr-Dombra could send him help."

"Well?"

The messenger shrugged. "We only had two hundred regulars and two hundred and fifty militia, and it's ten miles to Vryllos along the river, and an even longer way around the mountains on the south side. So the captain left a few cripples and kitchen-women to hold the castle, and crossed the river at Dyssa. They were just starting when I left; I could hear cannon-fire as I was leaving Sevenhills Valley."

"That was about the best thing he could do."

Gormoth would have a couple of hundred men at Dyssa. Just a holding-force; they'd given up the idea of any offensive operations against Dombra Gap. If they could be run out and the town burned, it would start a scare that might take a lot of pressure off Ptosphes and Chartiphon both.

"Well, I hope nobody expects any help from us," Harmakros said. "Our horses are ridden into the ground; half our men are mounted on captured horses, and they're in worse shape than what we have left of our own."

"Some of my infantrymen are riding two to a horse," Phrames said. "You can figure what kind of a march they'd make. They'd do almost as well on foot."

"And it would be midnight before any of us could get to Vryllos Gap, and that would be less than a thousand."

"Five hundred, I'd make it," the cavalry brigadier said. "We've been losing by attrition all the way east."

"But I'd heard that your losses had been very light."

"You heard? From whom?"

"Why, the men guarding prisoners. Great Galzar, Lord Kalvan, I never saw so many prisoners . . ."

"That's been our losses: prisoner-guard details. Every one of them is as much out of it as though he'd been shot through the head."

But the army Klestreus had brought across the Athan had ceased to exist. Not improbably as many as five hundred had re-crossed at Marax Ford. Six hundred had broken out of Hostigos at Narza Gap. There would be several hundred more, singly and in small bands, dodging through the woods to the south; they'd have to be mopped up. The rest had all either been killed or captured.

First, there had been the helter-skelter chase east from Fitra. For instance, twenty riflemen, firing from behind rocks and trees, had turned back two hundred trying to get through at the next gap down. Mostly, anybody who was overtaken had simply pulled off his helmet or held up a reversed weapon and cried for quarter.

He'd only had to fight once, himself; he and two Mobile Force cavalrymen had caught up to ten fleeing mercenaries and shouted to them to yield. Maybe this crowd were tired of running, maybe they were insulted at the demand from so few, or maybe they'd just been bullheaded. Instead, they had turned and charged. He had half-dodged and half parried a lance and spitted the lancer in the throat, and then had been fighting two swordsmen, and good ones, when a dozen mounted had come up.

Then, they'd had a small battle a half-mile west of Systros. Fifteen hundred infantry and five hundred cavalry, all mercenaries, had just gotten onto the main road again after passing on both sides of the burning town when the Fitra fugitives came dashing into them. Their own cavalry were swept away, and the infantry were trying to pike off the fugitives, when mounted Hostigi infantry arrived, dismounted, gave them an arquebus volley, and then made a pike charge, and then a couple of four-pounders came up and began throwing case-shot, leather tubes full of pistol balls. The Fitra fugitives had never been exposed to case-shot before, and after about two hundred were casualties they began hoisting their helmets and invoking Galzar.

Galzar was being a big help today. Have to do something nice for him.

That had been where the mercenary general, Klestreus, had been captured. Phrames had taken his surrender; Kalvan and Harmakros had been too busy chasing fugitives. A lot of these had turned toward Narza Gap.

Hestophes, the Hostigi CO there, had been a real cool cat. He'd had two hundred and fifty men, two old bombards, and a few lighter pieces. Klestreus's infantry had attacked Nirfë Gap, the last one down, and, with the help of Netzigon's people from the other side, swamped it. A few survivors had managed to get away along the mountain top and brought him warning. An hour later, he was under attack from both sides, too.

He had beaten off three attacks, by a probable total of two thousand, and was bracing for a fourth when his lookouts on the mountain reported seeing the fugitives from Fitra and Systros streaming east. Immediately he had spiked his guns and pulled his men up the mountain. The besieging infantry on the south were swept through by fleeing cavalry, and they threw the Nostori on the other side into confusion. Hestophes spattered them generously with small-arms fire to discourage loitering and let them go to spread panic on the other side. By now, they would be spreading it in Nostor Town.

Then, just west of the river, they had run into the wagon train and artillery, inching along under ox-power, accompanied by a thousand of Gormoth's subject troops and another five hundred mercenary cavalry. This had been Systros over again, except it had been a massacre. The fugitive cavalry had tried to force a way past, the infantry had resisted them, the four-pounders—only five of them, now; one was off the road just below Systros with a broken axle—arrived and began firing case-shot, and then two eight-pounders showed up. Some of the mercenaries attempted to fight—when they later found the paychests in one of the wagons, they understood why—but the Nostori simply emptied their arquebuses and calivers and ran. Along with "Down Styphon!" the pursuers were shouting "Dralm and no Quarter!" He wondered what Xentos would think of that; Dralm wasn't supposed to be that kind of a god, at all.

"You know," he said, getting out his pipe and tobacco, "we didn't have a very big army to start with. What do we have now?"

"Five hundred, and four hundred along the river," Phrames said. "We lost about five hundred, killed and wounded. The rest are guarding prisoners all the way back to Fitra." He looked up at the sun. "Back almost to Hostigos Town, by now."

"Well, we can help Ptosphes and Chartiphon from here," he said. "That gang Hestophes let through Narza Gap will be in Nostor Town by now, panting their story out, and the way they'll tell it, it will be five times worse than it really was." He looked at his watch. "By this time, Gormoth should be getting ready to fight the Battle of Nostor." He turned to Phrames. "You're in charge of this stuff here. How many men do you really need to guard it? Two hundred?"

Phrames looked up and down the road, and then at the prisoners, and then, out of the corner of his eye, at the boxes under the improvised table. They hadn't gotten around to weighing that silver yet, but there was too much of it to be careless with.

"I ought to have twice that many."

"The prisoners are mercenaries, and have agreed to take Prince Ptosphes's colors," the priest of Galzar said. "Of course, they may not bear arms against Prince Gormoth or any in his service until released from their oaths to him. In the sight of the war god, helping guard these wagons would be the same, for it would release men of yours to fight. But I will speak to them, and I will answer that they will not break their surrender. You will need some to keep the peasants from stealing, though."

"Two hundred," Phrames agreed. "We have some walking wounded who can help."

"All right. Take two hundred; men with the worst beat up horses and those men who are riding double, and mind the store. Harmakros, you take three hundred and two of the four-pounders, and cross at the next ford down. I'll take the other four hundred and three guns and work north and east. You might split into two columns, a hundred men and one gun, but no smaller. There'll be companies and parts of companies over there, trying to re-form. Break them up. And burn the whole country out—everything that'll catch fire and make a smoke by daylight or a blaze at night. Any refugees, head them up the river, give them a good scare and let them go. We want Gormoth to think we're across the river with three or four thousand men. By Dralm, that'll take some pressure off Ptosphes and Chartiphon!"

He rose, and Phrames took his seat. Horses were brought, and he and Harmakros mounted. The messenger from Sevenhills Valley sat down, stretching his legs in front of him. He rode slowly along the line of wagons, full of food the Nostori wouldn't eat this winter, and would curse Gormoth for it, and fireseed the Styphon temple-farm slaves would have to toil to replace. Then he came to the guns, and saw one that caught his eye. It was a long brass eighteen-pounder, on a two-wheel cart, with the long tail of the heavy timber stock supported by a four-wheel cart. There were two more behind it, and an officer with a ginger-brown beard sat morosely smoking a pipe on the limber-cart of the middle one. He pulled up.

"Your guns, Captain?"

"They were. They're Prince Ptosphes's guns now, I suppose."

"They're still yours, if you take our colors, and good pay for the use of them. We have other enemies besides Gormoth, you know."

The captain grinned. "So I've heard. Well, I'll take Ptosphes's colors. You're the Lord Kalvan? Is it true that you people make your own fireseed?"

"What do you think we were shooting at you, sawdust? You know what the Styphon stuff's like. Try ours and see the difference."

"Well, Down Styphon, then!"

They chatted for a little. The mercenary artilleryman's name was Alkides; his home, to the extent that any free-captain had one, was in Agrys City, on Manhattan Island. His guns, of which he was inordinately proud, and almost tearfully happy at being able to keep, had been cast in Zygros City. They were very good; if Verkan could collect a few men capable of casting guns like that, with trunnions . . .

"Well, go back there by that burned house, by those big trees. You'll find one of my officers, Count Phrames, and our Uncle Wolf there. You'll find a keg of something, too. Where are your men?"

"Well, some were killed before we cried quits. The rest are back with the other prisoners."

"Gather them up. Tell Count Phrames you're to have oxen—we have no horses to spare—and get your company and guns on the road for Hostigos Town as soon as you can. I'll talk to you later. Good luck, Captain Alkides."

Or *Colonel* Alkides; if he was as good as he seemed to be, maybe Brigadier-General Alkides.

There were dead infantry all along the road, mostly killed from behind. Another case of cowardice carrying its own penalty; infantry who stood against cavalry had a chance, often a good one, but infantry who turned tail and ran had none. He didn't pity them a bit.

It grew progressively worse as he neared the river, where the crews of the four-pounders and the two eight-pounders were swabbing and polishing their pieces, and dark birds rose cawing and croaking and squawking when disturbed. Must be every crow and raven and buzzard in Hos-Harphax; he even saw eagles.

The river, horse-knee deep at the ford, was tricky; his mount continually stumbled on armor-weighted corpses. That had been case-shot, mostly, he thought.

13

I

So your boy did it, all by himself," the lady history professor was saying.

Verkan Vall grinned. They were in a seminar room at the University, their chairs facing a big map of Fourth Level Aryan-Transpacific Hostigos, Nostor, northeastern Sask and northern Beshta. The pin-points of light he had been shifting back and forth on it were out, now.

"Didn't I tell you he was a genius?"

"Just how much genius did it take to lick a bunch of klunks like that?" said Talgan Dreth, the outtime studies director. "The way I heard it, they licked themselves."

"Well, considerable, to predict their errors accurately and plan to exploit them," argued old Professor Shalgro, the paratemporal probability theorist. To him, it was a brilliant theoretical achievement, and the battle was merely the experiment which had vindicated it. "I agree with Chief's Assistant Verkan; the man is a genius, and the fact that he was only able to become a minor police officer on his own time-line shows how these low-order cultures allow genius to go to waste."

"He knew the military history of his own time-line, and he knew how to apply it on Aryan-Transpacific." The historian wasn't letting her own subject be slighted. "Actually, I think Gormoth planned an excellent campaign—

against people like Ptosphes and Chartiphon. If it hadn't been for Kalvan, he'd have won."

"Well, Chartiphon and Ptosphes fought a battle of their own and won it, didn't they?"

"More or less." He began punching buttons on the arm of his chair and throwing on red and blue lights. "Netzigon was supposed to wait here, at Listra-Mouth, till Klestreus got up to here. Chartiphon began cannonading him—ordnance engineering by Lord Kalvan—and Netzigon couldn't take it. He attacked prematurely."

"Why didn't he just pull back? He had that river in front of him. Chartiphon couldn't have gotten his guns across that, could he?" Talgan Dreth asked.

"Oh, that wouldn't have been honorable. Besides, he didn't want the mercenaries to win the war; he wanted the glory of winning it himself."

The historian laughed. "How often I've heard *that!*" she said. "But don't these Hostigi go in for all this honor and glory jazz too?"

"Sure—till Kalvan talked them out of it. As soon as he started making fireseed, he established a moral ascendancy. And then, the new tactics, the new swordplay, the artillery improvements; now it's 'Trust Lord Kalvan. Lord Kalvan is always right.'"

"He'll have to work at that now," Dreth said. "He won't dare make any mistakes. What happened to Netzigon?"

"He made three attempts to cross the river, which is a hundred yards wide, in the face of artillery superiority. That was how he lost most of his cavalry. Then he threw his infantry across here at Vryllos, pushed Ptosphes back into the gap, and started a flank attack up the south bank on Chartiphon. Ptosphes wouldn't stay pushed; he waited till Netzigon was between the river and the mountain, and then counter-attacked. Then Rylla took what cavalry they had across the river, burned Netzigon's camp, butchered some camp-followers, and started a panic in his rear. That was when everything came apart and the pieces began breaking up, and then the commander at Tarr-Dombra, there, took some of his men across, burned Dyssa, and started another panic."

"It was too bad about Rylla," the lady historian said.

"Yes." He shrugged. "Things like that happen, in battles." That was why Dalla was always worried when she heard he'd been in one. "We had a couple of antigrav conveyers in, after dark. They had to stay up to twenty thousand feet, since we didn't want any heavenly portents on top of everything else, but they got some good infrared telephoto views. Big fires all over western Nostor, and around Dyssa, and more of them, the whole countryside, in the southwest—that was Kalvan and Harmakros. And a lot of hasty fortifying and entrenching around Nostor Town; Gormoth seems to think he's going to have to fight the next battle there."

"Oh, that's ridiculous," Talgan Dreth said. "It'll be a couple of weeks before Kalvan has his army in shape for an offensive, after those battles. And how much powder do you think he has left?"

"Six or seven tons. That came in just before I came here, from our people in Hostigos Town. After he crossed the river last evening, Harmakros captured a big wagon train. A Styphon's House archpriest, on his way to Nostor Town, with four tons of fireseed and seven thousand ounces of gold. Subsidies for Gormoth."

"Now that's what's called making war support war," the history professor commented.

"And another ton or so in Klestreus's supply train, and the pay-chests for his army," he added. "Hostigos came out of this all right."

"Wait till I get this all worked up," old Professor Shalgro was gloating. "Absolute proof of the decisive effect of one superior individual on the course of history. Kalthar Morth and his Historical Inevitability, and his vast, impersonal social forces, indeed!"

"Well, what are we going to do now?" Talgan Dreth asked. "We have the study-team organized, the five men who'll be the brass-founders, and the three girls who'll be the pattern-makers."

"Well, we have horseback travel-time between Zygros City and Hostigos Town to allow for. They've been familiarizing on adjoining near-identical time-lines? Send them all to Zygros City on the Kalvan time-line. I have a couple of Paracops planted there already. Let them make local contacts and call attention to themselves. Dalla and I will do the same. Then we won't have to worry about some traveler from Zygros showing up in Hostigos Town and punching holes in our stories."

"How about conveyer-heads?"

He shook his head. "You'll have to have your team established in Hostigos Town before they can put one in there. You have a time-line for operations on Fifth Level, of course; work from there. You'll have to get onto Kalvan time-line by an antigrav conveyer drop."

"Horses and all?"

"Horses and all. That will be mounts for myself and Dalla, for two Paracops who will pose as hired guards, and for your team. Seventeen saddle-horses. And twelve pack horses, with loads of Zygrosi and Grefftscharr wares. Lord Kalvan's friend Verkan is a trader; traders have to have merchandise."

Talgan Dreth whistled softly. "That'll mean at least two hundred-foot conveyers. Where had you thought of landing them?"

"Up here." He twisted the dial; the map slid down until he had the southern corner of the Princedom of Nyklos, north and west of Hostigos. "About here," he said, making a spot of light.

II

GORMOTH of Nostor stood inside the doorway of his presence-chamber, his arm over the shoulder of the newly ennobled Duke Skranga, and together they surveyed the crowd within. Netzigon, who had come stumbling in after midnight with all his guns and half his army lost and the rest a frightened rabble. His cousin, Count Pheblon, his ransom still unpaid; he'd hoped Ptosphes wouldn't be alive to be paid by the moon's end. The nobles of the Elite Guard, who had attended him here at Tarr-Hostigos, waiting for news of victory until news of defeat had come in. Three of Klestreus's officers, who had broken through at Narza Gap to bring it, and a few more who had gotten over Marax Ford and back to Nostor alive. And Vyblos, the high priest, and with him the Archpriest Krastokles from Styphon's House Upon Earth, and his blackarmored guard-captain, who had arrived at dawn with half a dozen troopers on broken-down horses.

He hated the sight of all of them, and the two priests most of all. He cut short their greetings.

"This is Duke Skranga," he told them. "Next to me, he is first nobleman of Nostor. He takes precedence over all here." The faces in front of his went slack with amazement, then stiffened angrily. A mutter of protest was hushed almost as soon as it began. "Do any object? Then it had better be one who's served me at least half as well as this man, and I see none such here." He turned to Vyblos. "What do you want, and who's this with you?"

"His Sanctity, the Archpriest Krastokles, sent by His Divinity, Styphon's Voice," Krastokles began furiously. "And how has he fared since entering your realm? Set upon by Hostigi heathens, hounded like a deer through the hills, his people murdered, his wagons pillaged . . ."

"His wagons, you say? Well, great Galzar, what of my gold and my fireseed, sent me by Styphon's Voice in his care, and look how he's cared for them, he and Styphon between them."

"You blaspheme!" Archpriest Krastokles cried. "And it was not your gold and fireseed, but the god's, to be given you in the god's service at my discretion."

"And lost at your indiscretion. You witless fool in a yellow bedgown, didn't you know a battle when you were riding into one?"

"Sacrilege!"

A dozen voices said it at once: Vyblos's and Krastokles's, and, among others, Netzigon's. By the Mace of Galzar, now didn't he have a fine right to open his mouth here? Anger almost sickened him; in a moment he was afraid that he would vomit pure bile. He strode to Netzigon, snatching the golden chief-captain's chain from over his shoulder.

"All the gods curse you, and all the devils take you! I told you to wait at Listra-Mouth for Klestreus, not to throw your army away along with his. By Galzar, I ought to have you flayed alive!" He struck Netzigon across the face with the chain. "Out of my sight, while you're still alive!" Then he turned to Vyblos. "You, too—out of here, and take the Archpimp Krastokles with you. Go to your temple and stay there; return here either at my bidding or at your peril."

He watched them leave: Netzigon shaken, the black-armored captain stolidly, Vyblos and Krastokles stiff with rage. A few of Netzigon's officers and gentlemen attended him; the rest drew back from them as though from contamination. He went to Pheblon and threw the golden chain over his head.

"I still don't thank you for losing me Tarr-Dombra, but that's a handful of dried peas to what that son of a horse-leech's daughter cost me. Now, Galzar help you, you'll have to make an army out of what he left you."

"My ransom still needs paying," Pheblon reminded him. "Till that's done, I'm oath-bound to Prince Ptosphes and Lord Kalvan."

"So you are; twenty thousand ounces of silver for you and those taken with you. You know where to find it? I don't."

"I do, Prince," Duke Skranga said. "There's ten times that in the treasure-vault of the temple of Styphon."

III

COUNT Netzigon waited until he was outside to touch a handkerchief to his cheek. It was bleeding freely, and had dripped onto his doublet. Now, by Styphon, the cleaning of that would cost Gormoth dear!

It wasn't his fault, anyhow. Great Styphon, was he to sit still while Chartiphon cannonaded him from across the river? And how had he known what sort of cannon Chartiphon had? The Hostigi really must be making fireseed; he hadn't believed that until yesterday. Three times he had sent his cavalry splashing into the river, and three times the guns had murdered them. He'd never seen guns throw small-shot so far. So then he'd sent his infantry over at Vryllos, and driven those with Prince Ptosphes back into the gap, and then, while he was driving against Chartiphon's right and the day had seemed won, Ptosphes had brought his beaten soldiers back, fighting like panthers, and that she-devil daughter of his—he'd heard, later, that she'd been killed. Styphon bless whoever did it!

Then everything had gone down in bloody ruin. Driven back across the river again, the Hostigi pouring after them, and then riders from Nostor Town with word that Klestreus's army was beaten in East Hostigos and orders to fall back, and they had retreated, with the whole country burning around them, fire and smoke at Dyssa and fugitives screaming that a thousand Hostigi were pouring out of Dombra Gap, and his worthless peasant levies throwing away their weapons and taking to their heels. . . .

Sorcery, that's what it was! That cursed foreign wizard, Kalvan!

Someone touched his arm. His hand flew to his poignard, and then he saw that it was the archpriest's guard-captain. He relaxed.

"You were ill-used, Count Netzigon," the man in black armor said. "By Styphon, it ired me to see a brave soldier used like a thievish serf!"

"His Sanctity wasn't reverently treated, nor His Holiness Vyblos. It shocked me to hear such words to the consecrated of Styphon," he replied. "What good can come to a realm whose Prince so insults the anointed of the god?"

"Ah!" The captain smiled. "It's a pleasure, in such a court, to hear such piety. Now, Count Netzigon, if you could have a few words with His Sanctity—this evening, say, at the temple. Come after dark, cloaked and in commoner's dress."

14

I

KALVAN'S horse stumbled, jerking him awake. Behind him, fifty-odd riders clattered, many of them more or less wounded, none seriously. There had been a score on horse litters, or barely able to cling to their mounts, but they had been left at the base hospital in Sevenhills Valley. He couldn't remember how long it had been since he had had his clothes, or even all his armor, off; except for quarter-hour pauses, now and then, he had been in the saddle since daylight, when he had recrossed the Athan with the smoke of southern Nostor behind him.

That had been as bad as Phil Sheridan in the Shenandoah, but every time some peasant's thatching blazed up, he knew it was burning another hole in Prince Gormoth's morale. He'd felt better about it today, after following the mile-wide swath of devastation west from Marax Ford and seeing it stop, with dramatic suddenness, at Fitra.

And the story Harmakros's stragglers had told him: fifteen eight-horse wagons, four tons of fireseed, seven thousand ounces of gold—that would come to about $150,000—two wagon-loads of armor, three hundred new calivers, six hundred pistols, and all of a Styphon's House archpriest's personal baggage and vestments. He was sorry the archpriest had gotten away; his execution would have been an interesting feature of the victory celebration.

He had passed prisoners marching east, all mercenaries, under arms and in good spirits, at least one pike or lance in each detachment sporting a red and blue pennon. Most of them shouted, "Down Styphon!" as he rode by. The back road from Fitra to Sevenhills Valley hadn't been so bad, but now, in what he had formerly known as Nittany Valley, traffic had become heavy again. Militia from Listra-Mouth and Vryllos, marching like regulars, which was what they were, now. Trains of carts and farm-wagons, piled with sacks and barrels or loaded with cabbages and potatoes, or with furniture that must have come from manor-houses. Droves of cattle, and droves of prisoners, not armed, not in good spirits, and under heavy guard: Nostori subjects headed for labor-camps and intensive Styphon-is-a-fake indoctrination. And guns, on four-wheel carts, that he couldn't remember from any Hostigi ordnance inventory.

Hostigos Town was in an all-time record traffic-jam. He ran into Alkides, the mercenary artilleryman, with a strip of blue cloth that seemed to have come from a bedspread and a strip of red from the bottom of a petticoat. He was magnificently drunk.

"Lord Kalvan!" he shouted. "I saw your guns; they're wonderful! What god taught you that? Can you mount mine that way?"

"I think so. I'll have a talk with you about it tomorrow, if I'm awake then."

Harmakros was on his horse in the middle of the square, his rapier drawn, trying to untangle the chaos of wagons and carts and riders. Kalvan shouted to him, above the din:

"What the Styphon—when did we start using three-star generals for traffic-cops?"

Military Police; organize soonest. Mercenaries, tough ones.

"Just till I get a detail here. I sent all my own crowd up with the wagons." He started to say something else, then stopped short and asked, "Did you hear about Rylla?"

"No, for Dralm's sake." He went cold under his scalding armor. "What about her?"

"Well, she was hurt—late yesterday, across the river. Her horse threw her; I only know what I got from one of Chartiphon's aides. She's at the castle."

"Thanks; I'll see you there later."

He swung his horse about and plowed into the crowd, drawing his sword and yelling for way. People crowded aside, and yelled his name to others beyond. Outside town, the road was choked with troops, and with things too big and slow to get out of the way; he rode mostly in the ditch. The wagons Harmakros had captured, great canvas-covered things like Conestogas, were going up to Tarr-Hostigos. He thought he'd never get past them: there always seemed to be more ahead. Finally he got through the outer gate and galloped across the bailey.

Throwing his reins to somebody at the foot of the keep steps, he stumbled up them and through the door. From the Staff Room, he heard laughing voices, Ptosphes's among them. For an instant he was horrified, then reassured; if Ptosphes could laugh, it couldn't be too bad.

He was mobbed as soon as he entered, everybody shouting his name and thumping him on the back; he was glad for his armor. Chartiphon, Ptosphes, Xentos, Uncle Wolf, most of the General Staff crowd. And a dozen officers he had never seen before, all wearing new red and blue scarves. Ptosphes was presenting a big man with a florid face and gray hair and beard.

"Kalvan, this is General Klestreus, late of Prince Gormoth's service, now of ours."

"And most happy at the change, Lord Kalvan," the mercenary said. "An honor to have been conquered by such a soldier."

"Our honor, General. You fought most brilliantly and valiantly." He'd fought like a damned imbecile, and gotten his army chopped to hamburger, but let's be polite. "I'm sorry I hadn't time to meet you earlier, but things were a trifle pressing." He turned to Ptosphes. "Rylla? What happened to her?"

"Why, she broke a leg," Ptosphes began.

That frightened him. People had died from broken legs in his own world when the medical art was at least equal to its here-and-now level. They used to amputate. . . .

"She's in no danger, Kalvan," Xentos assured him. "None of us would be here if she were. Brother Mytron is with her. If she's awake, she'll want to see you."

"I'll go to her at once." He clinked goblets with the mercenary and drank. It was winter-wine, aged quite a few winters, and evidently frozen down in a very cold one. It warmed and relaxed him. "To your good fortune in Hostigos, General. Your capture," he lied, "was Gormoth's heaviest loss, yesterday, and our greatest gain." He set down the goblet, took off his helmet and helmet-coif and detached his sword from his belt; then picked up the wine again and finished it. "If you'll excuse me now, gentlemen. I'll see you all later."

Rylla, whom he had expected to find gasping her last, sat propped against a pile of pillows in bed, smoking one of her silver-inlaid redstone pipes. She was wrapped in a loose gown, and her left leg, extended, was buckled into a bulky encasement of leather—no plaster casts, here-and-now. Mytron, the chubby and cherubic physician-priest, was with her, and so were several of the women who functioned as midwives, hexes, herb-boilers and general nurses. Rylla saw him first, and her face lighted like a sunrise.

"Hi, Kalvan! Are you all right? When did you get in? How was the battle?"

"Rylla, darling!" The women sprayed away from in front of him like grasshoppers. She flung her arms around his neck as he bent over her; he thought Mytron stepped in to relieve her of her pipe. "What happened to you?"

"You stopped in the Staff Room," she told him, between kisses. "I smell it on you."

"How is she, Mytron?" he asked over his shoulder.

"Oh, a beautiful fracture, Lord Kalvan!" the doctor enthused. "One of the priests of Galzar set it; he did an excellent job . . ."

"Gave me a fine lump on the head, too," Rylla added. "Why, my horse fell on me. We were burning a Nostori village, and he stepped on a hot ember. He almost threw me, and then fell over something, and down we both went, the horse on top of me. I was carrying an extra pair of pistols in my boots and I fell on one of them. The horse broke a leg, too. They shot him. I guess they thought I was worth making an effort about. . . . Kalvan! Never hug a girl so tight when you're wearing mail sleeves!"

"It's nothing to worry about, Lord Kalvan," Mytron was saying. "Not the first time for this young lady, either. She broke an ankle when she was eight, trying to climb a cliff to rob a hawk's nest, and a shoulder when she was twelve, firing a musket-charge out of a carbine."

"And now," Rylla was saying, "it'll be a moon, at least, till we can have the wedding."

"We could have it right now, sweetheart . . ."

"I will not be married in my bedroom," she declared. "People make jokes about girls who have to do that. And I will not limp to the temple of Dralm on crutches."

"All right, Princess; it's your wedding." He hoped the war with Sask that everybody expected would be out of the way before she was able to ride again. He'd have a word with Mytron about that. "Somebody," he said, "go and have a hot bath brought to my rooms, and tell me when it's ready. I must stink to the very throne of Dralm."

"I was wondering when you were going to mention that, darling," Rylla said.

II

He did speak to Mytron the next day, catching him between a visit to Rylla and his work at the main army hospital in Hostigos Town. Mytron thought, at first, that he was impatient for Rylla's full recovery and the wedding.

"Oh, Lord Kalvan, quite soon. You know, of course, that broken bones take time to knit, but our Rylla is young and young bones knit fast. Inside a moon, I'd say."

"Well, Mytron; you know we're going to have to fight Sarrask of Sask now. When war with Sask comes, I'd be most happy if she were still in bed, with that thing on her leg. So would Prince Ptosphes."

"Yes. Our Rylla, shall we say, is a trifle heedless of her own safety." That was a generous five hundred percent understatement. Mytron put on his professional portentous frown. "You must understand, of course, that it is not good for any patient to be kept too long in bed. She should be able to get up and walk about as soon as possible. And wearing the splints is not pleasant."

He knew that. It wasn't any light plaster cast; it was a frame of heavily padded steel splints, forged from old sword-blades, buckled on with a case of saddle leather. It weighed about ten pounds, and it would be even more confining and hotter than his armor. But the next thing she broke might be her neck, or she might stop a two-ounce musket ball, and then his luck would run out along with hers. His mind shied like a frightened horse from the thought of no more happy, lovely Rylla.

"I'll do my best, Lord Kalvan, but I can't keep her in bed forever."

War with Sask wouldn't wait that long, either. Xentos was in contact with the priests of Dralm in Sask Town; they reported that the news of Fitra and Listra-Mouth had stunned Sarrask's court briefly, then thrown Sarrask into a furor of activity. More mercenaries were being hired, and some sort of negotiations, the exact nature undetermined, were going on between Sarrask and Balthar of Beshta. A Styphon archpriest, one Zothnes, had arrived in Sask Town, with a train of wagons as big as the one taken by Harmakros in southern Nostor.

A priest of Galzar arrived at Tarr-Hostigos from Nostor Town with an escort and a thousand ounces of gold—gold and silver seemed to be on a twenty-to-one ratio, here-and-now—to pay the ransoms of Count Pheblon and the other gentlemen taken at Tarr-Dombra. The news was that Pheblon was now Gormoth's chief-captain and was trying to reorganize what was left of the Nostori army. Gormoth would be back in the ring for another bout in the spring; that meant that Sarrask must be dealt with this fall.

He was having his own reorganization problems. They'd taken heavier losses than he'd liked, mostly the poorly armed and partly trained militia who'd fought at Listra-Mouth. On the other hand, they'd acquired over a thousand mercenary infantry and better than two thousand cavalry. They were a headache; they'd have to be integrated into the army of Hostigos. He didn't want any mercenary troops at all. Mercenary soldiers, as individual soldiers, were as good as any; in fact, any regular army man was simply a mercenary in the service of his own country. But mercenary troops, as troops, weren't good at all. They didn't fight for the Prince who hired them; they fought for their own captains, who paid them from what the Prince had paid him. *Mercenary captains,* he could hear his history professor quoting Machiavelli, *are either very capable men or not. If they are, you cannot rely upon them, for they will always aspire to their own greatness, either by oppressing you, their master, or by oppressing others against your intentions; but if the captain is not an able man, he will generally ruin you.* Most of the captains captured in East Hostigos seemed to be quite able.

Klestreus was one exception. As a battle commander, he was an incompetent—Fitra had proven that. He wasn't a soldier at all; he was a military businessman. He could handle sales, promotion and public relations, but not management and operations. That was how he'd gotten elected captain-general in Nostor. But he did have a wide knowledge of political situations, knew most of the Princes of Hos-Harphax, and knew the composition and command of all the mercenary outfits in the Five Kingdoms. So Kalvan appointed him Chief of Intelligence, where he could really be of use, and wouldn't be able to lead troops in combat. He was quite honored and flattered.

Nothing could be done about breaking up the mercenary cavalry companies, numbering over two thousand men. The mercenary infantry, however, were broken up and put into militia companies, one mercenary to three militiamen. This almost started a mutiny, until he convinced them that they were being given posts of responsibility and the rank of private first class, with badges. The sergeants were all collected into a quickie OCS company, to emerge second lieutenants.

Alkides, the artilleryman, was made captain of Tarr-Esdreth-of-Hostigos, and sent there with his three long brass eighteens, now fitted with trunnions on welded-on iron bands and mounted on proper field-carriages. Tarr-Esdreth-of-Hostigos was a sensitive spot. The Sask-Hostigos border followed the east branch of the Juniata, the Besh, and ran through Esdreth Gap. Two castles dominated the gap, one on either side; until one or the other could be taken, the gap would be closed both to Hostigos and Sask.

TEN days after Fitra and Listra-Mouth, an unattached mercenary, wearing the white and black colors of unemployment, put in an appearance at Tarr-Hostigos. There were many such; they were equivalent to the bravos of Renaissance Italy. This one produced letters of credence, which Xentos found authentic, from Prince Armanes of Nyklos. His client, he said, wanted to buy fireseed, but wished to do so secretly; he was not ready for an open break with Styphon's House. When asked if he would trade cavalry and artillery horses, the unofficial emissary instantly agreed.

Well, that was a beginning.

15

I

SESKLOS rested his elbows on the table and palmed his smarting eyes. Around him, pens scratched on parchment and tablets clattered. He longed for the cool quiet and privacy of the Innermost Circle, but there was so much to do, and he must order the doing of all of it himself.

There were frantic letters from everywhere; the one before him was from the Archpriest of the Great Temple of Hos-Agrys. News of Gormoth's defeat was spreading rapidly, and with it rumors that Prince Ptosphes, who had defeated him, was making his own fireseed. Agents-inquisitory were reporting that the ingredients, and even the proportions, were being bandied about in taverns; it would take an army of assassins to deal with everybody who seemed to know them. Even a pestilence couldn't wipe out everybody who knew at least some of the secret. Oddly, it was even better known in far northern Zygros City than elsewhere. And they all wanted him to tell them how to check the spread of such knowledge.

Curse and blast them! Did they have to ask him about anything? Couldn't any of them think for themselves?

He opened his eyes. Why, admit it; better that than try to deny what would soon be proven everywhere. Let everyone in Styphon's House, even the lay Guardsmen, know the full secret, but for those outside, and for the few believers within, insist that special rites and prayers, known only to the yellow-robes of the Inner Circle, were essential.

But why? Soon it would be known that fireseed made by unconsecrated hands would fire just as well, and, to judge from Prince Ptosphes's sample, with more force and less fouling.

Well, there were devils, malignant spirits of the netherworld; everybody knew that. He smiled, imagining them thronging about—scrawny bodies, bat-wings, bristling beards, clawed and fanged. In fireseed, there were many—they made it explode—and only the prayers of anointed priests of Styphon could slay them. If fireseed were made without the aid of Styphon, the devils would be set free as soon as the fireseed burned, to work manifold evils and frights in the world of men. And, of course, the curse of Styphon was upon any who presumed profanely to make fireseed.

But Ptosphes had made fireseed, and he had pillaged a temple-farm, and put consecrated priests cruelly to death, and then he had defeated the army of Gormoth, which had marched under Styphon's blessing. How about that?

But wait! Gormoth himself was no better than Ptosphes. He too had made fireseed—both Krastokles and Vyblos were positive of that. And Gormoth had blasphemed Styphon and despitefully used a holy archpriest, and forced a hundred thousand ounces of silver out of the Nostor temple, at as close to pistol-point as made no difference. To be sure, most of that had happened after the day of battle, but outside Nostor who knew that? Gormoth, he decided, had suffered defeat for his sins.

He was smiling happily now, wondering why he hadn't thought of that before. And what was known in Nostor would matter little more than what was known in Hostigos before long. Both would have to be destroyed utterly.

He wondered how many more Princedoms he would have to doom to fire and sword. Not too many—a few sharp examples at the start ought to be enough. Maybe just Hostigos and Nostor, and Sarrask of Sask and Balthar of Beshta could attend to both. An idea began to seep up in his mind, and he smiled.

Balthar's brother, Balthames, wanted to be a Prince, himself; it would take only a poisoned cup or a hired dagger to make him Prince of Beshta, and Balthar knew it. He should have had Balthames killed long ago. Well, suppose Sarrask gave up a little corner of Sask, and Balthar gave up a similar piece of Beshta, adjoining and both bordering on western Hostigos, to form a new Princedom; call it Sashta. Then, to that could be added all western Hostigos south of the mountains; why, that would be a nice little Princedom for any young couple. He smiled benevolently. And the father of the bride and the brother of the groom could compensate themselves for their generosity, respectively, with the Listra Valley, rich in iron, and East Hostigos, manured with the blood of Gormoth's mercenaries.

This must be done immediately, before winter put an end to campaigning. Then, in the spring, Sarrask, Balthar and Balthames could hurl their combined strength against Nostor.

And something would have to be done about fireseed making in the meantime. The revelation about the devils would have to be made public everywhere. And call a Great Council of Archpriests, here at Balph—no, at Harphax City: let Great King Kaiphranos bear the costs—to consider how they might best meet the threat of profane fireseed making, and to plan for the future. It could be, he thought hopefully, that Styphon's House might yet survive.

II

VERKAN Vall watched Dalla pack tobacco into a little cane-stemmed pipe. Dalla preferred cigarettes, but on Aryan-Transpacific they didn't exist. No paper; it was a wonder Kalvan wasn't trying to do something about that. Behind them, something thumped heavily; voices echoed in the barnlike pre-fab shed. Everything here was temporary—until a conveyor-head could be established at Hostigos Town, nobody knew where anything should go at Fifth Level Hostigos Equivalent.

Talgan Dreth, sitting on the edge of a packing case with a clipboard on his knee, looked up, then saw what Dalla was doing and watched as she got out her tinderbox, struck sparks, blew the tinder aflame, lit a pine splinter, and was puffing smoke, all in fifteen seconds.

"Been doing that all your life," he grinned.

"Why, of course," Dalla deadpanned. "Only savages have to rub sticks together, and only sorcerers can make fire without flint and steel."

"You checked the pack-loads, Vall?" he asked.

"Yes. Everything perfectly in order, all Kalvan time-line stuff. I liked that touch of the deer and bear skins. We'd have to shoot for the pot, on the way south, and no trader would throw away saleable skins."

Talgan Dreth almost managed not to show how pleased he was. No matter how many outtime operations he'd run, a back-pat from the Paratime Police still felt good.

"Well, then we make the drop tonight," he said. "I had a reconnaissance-crew checking it on some adjoining time-lines, and we gave it a looking over on the target time-line last night. You'll go in about fifteen miles east of the Hostigos-Nyklos road."

"That's all right. They're hauling powder to Nyklos and bringing back horses. That road's being patrolled by Harmakros's cavalry. We make camp fifteen miles off the road and start around sunrise tomorrow; we ought to run into a Hostigi patrol before noon."

"Well, you're not going to get into any more battles, are you?" Dalla asked.

"There won't be any more battles," Talgan Dreth told her. "Kalvan won the war while Vall was away."

"He won *a* war. How long it'll stay won I don't know, and neither does he. But *the* war won't be over till he's destroyed Styphon's House. That is going to take a little doing."

"He's destroyed it already," Talgan Dreth said. "He destroyed it by proving that anybody can make fireseed. Why, it was doomed from the start. It was founded on a secret, and no secret can be kept forever."

"Not even the Paratime Secret?" Dalla asked innocently.

"Oh, Dalla!" the University man cried. "You know that's different. You can't compare that with a trick like mixing saltpeter and charcoal and sulfur."

III

THE late morning sun baked the open horsemarket; heat and dust and dazzle, and flies at which the horses switched constantly. It was hot for so late in the year; as nearly as Kalvan could estimate it from the way the leaves were coloring, it would be mid-October. They had two calendars here-and-now—lunar, for daily reckoning, and solar, to keep track of the seasons—and they never matched. *Calendar reform; do something about.* He seemed to recall having made that mental memo before.

And he was sweat-sticky under his armor, forty pounds of it—quilted arming-doublet with mail sleeves and skirt, quilted helmet-coif with mail throat-guard, plate cuirass, plate tassets down his thighs into his jackboots, high combed helmet, rapier and poignard. It wasn't the weight—he'd carried more, and less well distributed, as a combat infantryman in Korea—but he questioned if anyone ever became inured to the heat and lack of body ventilation. *Like a rich armor worn in heat of day, That scalds with safety*—if

Shakespeare had never worn it himself except on the stage, he'd known plenty of men who had, like that little Welsh pepperpot Williams, who was the original of Fluellen.

"Not a bad one in the lot!" Harmakros, riding beside him, was enthusing. "And a dozen big ones that'll do for gun-horses."

And fifty-odd cavalry horses; that meant, at second or third hand, that many more infantrymen could get into line when and where needed, in heavier armor. And another lot coming in tonight; he wondered where Prince Armanes was getting all the horses he was trading for bootleg fireseed. He turned in his saddle to say something about it to Harmakros.

As he did, something hit him a clanging blow on the breastplate, knocking him almost breathless and nearly unhorsing him. He thought he heard the shot; he did hear the second, while he was clinging to his seat and clawing a pistol from his saddlebow. Across the alley, he could see two puffs of smoke drifting from back upstairs windows of one of a row of lodginghouse-wineshop-brothels. Harmakros was yelling; so was everybody else. There was a kicking, neighing confusion among the horses. His chest aching, he lifted the pistol and fired into one of the windows. Harmakros was firing, too, and behind him an arquebus roared. Hoping he didn't have another broken rib, he holstered the pistol and drew its mate.

"Come on!" he yelled. "And Dralm-dammit, take them alive! We want them for questioning."

Torture. He hated that, had hated even the relatively mild third-degree methods of his own world, but when you need the truth about something, you get it, no matter how. Men were throwing poles out of the corral gate; he sailed past them, put his horse over the fence across the alley, and landed in the littered backyard beyond. Harmakros took the fence behind him, with a Mobile Force arquebusier and a couple of horse-wranglers with clubs following on foot.

He decided to stay in the saddle; till he saw how much damage the bullet had done, he wasn't sure how much good he'd be on foot. Harmakros flung himself from his horse, shoved a half-clad slattern out of the way, drew his sword, and went through the back door into the house, the others behind him. Men were yelling, women screaming; there was commotion everywhere except behind the two windows from which the shots had come. A girl was bleating that Lord Kalvan had been murdered. Looking right at him, too.

He squeezed his horse between houses to the street, where a mob was forming. Most of them were pushing through the front door and into the house; from within came yells, screams, and sounds of breakage. Hostigos Town would be the better for one dive less if they kept at that.

Up the street, another mob was coagulating; he heard savage shouts of "Kill! Kill!" Cursing, he holstered the pistol and drew his rapier, knocking a man down as he spurred forward, shouting his own name and demanding way. The horse was brave and willing, but untrained for riot work; he wished he had a State Police horse under him, and a yard of locust riot-stick instead of this sword. Then the combination provost-marshal and police chief of Hostigos Town arrived, with a dozen of his men laying about them with arquebus-butts. Together they rescued two men, bloodied, half-conscious and almost ripped naked. The mob fell back, still yelling for blood.

He had time, now, to check on himself. There was a glancing dent on the right side of his breastplate, and a lead-splash, but the plate was unbroken. *That scalds with safety*—Shakespeare could say that again. Good thing it hadn't been one of those great armor-smashing brutes of 8-bore muskets. He drew the empty pistol and started to reload it, and then he saw Harmakros approaching on foot, his rapier drawn and accompanied by a couple of soldiers, herding a pot-bellied, stubble-chinned man in a dirty shirt, a blowsy woman with "madam" stamped all over her, and two girls in sleazy finery.

"That's them! That's them!" the man began, as they came up, and the woman was saying, "Dralm smite me dead, I don't know nothing about it!"

"Take these two to Tarr-Hostigos," Kalvan directed the provost-marshal. "They are to be questioned rigorously." Euphemistic police-ese; another universal constant. "This lot, too. Get their statements, but don't harm them unless you catch them trying to lie to you."

"You'd better go to Tarr-Hostigos yourself, and let Mytron look at that," Harmakros told him.

"I think it's only a bruise; plate isn't broken. If it's another broken rib, my back-and-breast'll hold it for awhile. First we go to the temple of Dralm and give thanks for my escape. Temple of Galzar, too." He'd been building a reputation for piety since the night of his appearance, when he'd bowed down to those three graven images in the peasant's cottage; not doing that would be out of character, now. "And we go slowly, and roundabout. Let as many people see me as possible. We don't want it all over Hostigos that I've been killed."

16

I

As a child, he had heard his righteous Ulster Scots father speak scornfully of smoke-filled-room politics and boudoir diplomacy. The Rev. Alexander Morrison should have seen this—it was both, and for good measure, two real idolatrous heathen priests were sitting in on it. They were in Rylla's bedroom because it was easier for the rest of Prince Ptosphes's Privy Council to gather there than to carry her elsewhere, they were all smoking, and because the October nights were as chilly as the days were hot, the windows were all closed.

Rylla's usually laughing eyes were clouded with anxiety. "They could have killed you, Kalvan." She'd said that before. She was quite right, too. He shrugged.

"A splash on my breastplate, and a big black-and-blue place on me. The other shot killed a horse; I'm really provoked about that."

"Well, what's being done with them?" she demanded.

"They were questioned," her father said distastefully. He didn't like using torture, either. "They confessed. Guardsmen of the Temple—that's to say, kept cutthroats of Styphon's House—sent from Sask Town by Archpriest Zothnes, with Prince Sarrask's knowledge. They told us there's a price of five hundred ounces gold on Kalvan's head, and as much on mine. Tomorrow," he added, "they will be beheaded in the town square."

"Then it's war with Sask." She looked down at the saddler's masterpiece on her leg. "I hope I'm out of this before it starts."

Not between him and Mytron she wouldn't; Kalvan set his mind at rest on that.

"War with Sask means war with Beshta," Chartiphon said sourly. "And together they outnumber us five to two."

"Then don't fight them together," Harmakros said. "We can smash either of them alone. Let's do that, Sask first."

"Must we always fight?" Xentos implored. "Can we never have peace?"

Xentos was a priest of Dralm, and Dralm was a god of peace, and in his secular capacity as Chancellor Xentos regarded war as an evidence of bad statesmanship. Maybe so, but statesmanship was operating on credit, and sooner or later your credit ran out and you had to pay off in hard money or get sold out.

Ptosphes saw it that way, too. "Not with neighbors like Sarrask of Sask and Balthar of Beshta we can't," he told Xentos. "And we'll have Gormoth of Nostor to fight again in the Spring, you know that. If we haven't knocked Sask and Beshta out by then, it'll be the end of us."

The other heathen priest, alias Uncle Wolf, concurred. As usual, he had put his wolfskin vestments aside; and as usual, he was nursing a goblet, and playing with one of the kittens who made Rylla's room their headquarters.

"You have three enemies," he said. *You,* not *we*; priests of Galzar advised, but they never took sides. "Alone, you can destroy each of them; together, they will destroy you."

And after they had beaten all three, what then? Hostigos was too small to stand alone. Hostigos, dominating Sask and Beshta, with Nostor beaten and Nyklos allied, could, but then there would be Great King Kaiphranos, and back of him, back of everything, Styphon's House.

So it would have to be an empire. He'd reached that conclusion long ago.

Klestreus cleared his throat. "If we fight Balthar first, Sarrask of Sask will hold to his alliance and deem it an attack on him," he pronounced. "He wants war with Hostigos anyhow. But if we attack Sask, Balthar will vacillate, and take counsel of his doubts and fears, and consult his soothsayers, whom we are bribing, and do nothing until it is too late. I know them both." He drained his goblet, refilled it, and continued:

"Balthar of Beshta is the most cowardly, and the most miserly, and the most suspicious, and the most treacherous Prince in the world. I served him, once, and Galzar keep me from another like service. He goes about in an old black gown that wouldn't make a good dust-clout, all hung over with wizards' amulets. His palace looks like a pawnshop, and you can't go three lance-lengths anywhere in it without having to shove some impudent charlatan of a soothsayer out of your way. He sees murderers in every shadow, and a plot against him whenever three gentlemen stop to give each other good day."

He drank some more, as though to wash the taste out of his mouth.

"And Sarrask of Sask's a vanity-swollen fool who thinks with his fists and his belly. By Galzar, I've known Great Kings who hadn't half his arrogance. He's in debt to Styphon's House beyond belief, and the money all gone for pageants and feasts and silvered armor for his guards and jewels for his light-o'-loves, and the only way he can get quittance is by conquering Hostigos for them."

"And his daughter's marrying Balthar's brother," Rylla added. "They're both getting what they deserve. The Princess Amnita likes cavalry troopers, and Duke Balthames likes boys."

And he, and all of them, knew what was back of that marriage—this new Princedom of Sashta that there was talk of, to be the springboard for conquest and partition of Hostigos, and when that was out of the way, a concerted attack on Nostor. Since Gormoth had started making his own fireseed, Styphon's House wanted him destroyed, too.

It all came back to Styphon's House.

"If we smash Sask now, and take over some of these mercenaries Sarrask's been hiring on Styphon's expense-account, we might frighten Balthar into good behavior without having to fight him." He didn't really believe that, but Xentos brightened a little.

Ptosphes puffed thoughtfully at his pipe. "If we could get our hands on young Balthames," he said, "we could depose Balthar and put Balthames on the throne. I think we could control him."

Xentos was delighted. He realized that they'd have to fight Sask, but this looked like a bloodless—well, almost—way of conquering Beshta.

"Balthames would be willing," he said eagerly. "We could make a secret compact with him, and loan him, say, two thousand mercenaries, and all the Beshtan army and all the better nobles would join him."

"No, Xentos. We do not want to help Balthames take his brother's throne," Kalvan said. "We want to depose Balthar ourselves, and then make Balthames do homage to Ptosphes for it. And if we beat Sarrask badly enough, we might depose him and make him do homage for Sask."

That was something Xentos seemed not to have thought of. Before he could speak, Ptosphes was saying, decisively:

"Whatever we do, we fight Sarrask now; beat him before that old throttlepurse of a Balthar can send him aid."

Ptosphes, too, wanted war now, before Rylla could mount a horse again. Kalvan wondered how many decisions of state, back through the history he had studied, had been made for reasons like that.

"I'll make sure of that," Chartiphon promised. "He won't send any troops up the Besh."

That was why Hostigos now had two armies: the Army of the Listra, which would make the main attack on Sask, and the Army of the Besh, commanded by Chartiphon in person, to drive through southern Sask and hold the Beshtan border.

"How about Tarr-Esdreth?" Harmakros asked.

"You mean Tarr-Esdreth-of-Sask? Alkides can probably shoot rings around anybody they have there. Chartiphon can send a small force to hold the lower end of the gap, and you can do the same from the Listra side."

"Well, how soon can we get started?" Chartiphon wanted to know. "How much sending back and forth will there have to be first?"

Uncle Wolf put down his goblet, and then lifted the kitten from his lap and set her on the floor. She mewed softly, looked around, and then ran over to the bed and jumped up with her mother and brothers and sisters who were keeping Rylla company.

"Well, strictly speaking," he said, "you're at peace with Prince Sarrask, now. You can't attack him until you've sent him letters of defiance, setting forth your causes of emnity."

Galzar didn't approve of undeclared wars, it seemed. Harmakros laughed.

"Now, what would they be, I wonder?" he asked. "Send them Kalvan's breastplate."

"That's a just reason," Uncle Wolf nodded. "You have many others. I will carry the letter myself." Among other things, priests of Galzar acted as heralds. "Put it in the form of a set of demands, to be met on pain of instant war—that would be the quickest way."

"Insulting demands," Klestreus specified.

"Well, give me a slate and a soapstone, somebody," Rylla said. "Let's see how we're going to insult him."

"A letter to Balthar, too," Xentos said thoughtfully. "Not of defiance, but of friendly warning against the plots and treacheries of Sarrask and Balthames. They're scheming to involve him in war with Hostigos, let him bear the brunt of it, and then fall on him and divide his Princedom between them. He'll believe that—it's what he'd do in their place."

"Your job, Klestreus," Kalvan said. A diplomatic assignment would be just right for him, and would keep him from combat command without hurting his feelings. "Leave with it for Beshta Town tomorrow. You know what Balthar will believe and what he won't; use your own judgment."

"We'll get the letters written tonight," Ptosphes said. "In the morning, we'll hold a meeting of the Full Council of Hostigos. The nobles and people should have a voice in the decision for war."

As though the decision hadn't been made already, here in Princess Rylla's smoke-filled boudoir. Real democracy, this was. Just like Pennsylvania.

II

THE Full Council of Hostigos met in a long room, with tapestries on one wall and windows opening onto the inner citadel garden on the other. The speaker for the peasants, a work-gnarled graybeard named Phosg, sat at the foot of the table, flanked by the speaker for the shepherds and herdsmen on one side, and for the woodcutters and charcoal burners on the other. They graded up from there, through the artisans, the master-craftsmen, the merchants, the yeomen farmers, the professions, the priests, the landholding gentry and nobility, to Prince Ptosphes, at the head of the table, in a magnificent fur robe, with a heavy gold chain on his shoulders. He was flanked, on the left, by the Lord Kalvan, in a no less magnificent robe and an only slightly less impressive gold chain. The place on his right was vacant, and everybody was looking at it.

It had been talked about—Kalvan and Xentos and Chartiphon and Harmakros had seen to that—that the Princess Rylla would, because of her injury, be unable to attend. So, when the double doors were swung open at the last moment and six soldiers entered carrying Rylla propped up on a couch, there were exclamations of happiness and a general ovation. Rylla was really loved in Hostigos.

She waved her hand in greeting and replied to them, and the couch was set down at Ptosphes' right. Ptosphes waited until the clamor had subsided, then drew his poignard and rapped on the table with the pommel.

"You all know why we're here," he began without preamble. "The last time we met, it was to decide whether to have our throats cut like sheep or die fighting like men. Well, we didn't have to do either. Now, the question is, shall we fight Sarrask of Sask now, at our advantage, or wait and fight Sarrask and Balthar together at theirs? Let me hear what is in your minds about it."

It was like a council of war; junior rank first. Phosg was low man on the totem-pole. He got to his feet.

"Well, Lord Prince, it's like I said the last time. If we have to fight, let's fight."

"Different pack of wolves, that's all," the shepherds' and herdsmen's speaker added. "We'll have another wolf-hunt like Fitra and Listra-Mouth."

It went up the table like that. The speaker for the lawyers, naturally, wanted to know if they were really sure Prince Sarrask was going to attack. Somebody asked him why not wait and have his throat cut, his house burned and his daughters raped, so that he could really be sure. The priestess of Yirtta abstained; a servant of the Allmother could not vote for the shedding of the blood of mothers' sons. Uncle Wolf just laughed. Then it got up among the nobility.

"Well, who wants this war with Sask?" one of them demanded. "That is, besides this outlander who has grown so great in so short a time among us, this Lord Kalvan."

He leaned right a little to look. Yes, Sthentros. He was some kind of an in-law of Ptosphes . . . had a barony over about where Boalsburg ought to be. He'd made trouble when the fireseed mills were being started—refused to let his peasants be put to work collecting saltpeter. Kalvan had threatened to have his head off, and Sthentros had run spluttering to Ptosphes. The interview had been private, nobody knew exactly what Ptosphes had told him, but he had emerged from it visibly shaken. The peasants had gone to work collecting saltpeter.

"Just who is this Kalvan?" Sthentros persisted. "Why, until five moons ago, nobody in Hostigos had even heard of him!"

A couple of other nobles, including one who had just sworn to wade to his boot-tops in Saski blood, muttered agreement. Another, who had fought at Fitra, said:

"Well, nobody'd ever heard of *you* in Hostigos, either, till your uncle's wife's sister married our Prince."

Uncle Wolf laughed again. "They've heard of Kalvan since, and in Nostor, too, by the war god's mace!"

"Yes," another noble said, "I grant that. But you'll have to grant that the man's an outlander, and it's a fine thing indeed to see him rise so swiftly over the heads of nobles of old Hostigi family. Why, when he came among us, he couldn't speak a word that anybody could understand."

"By Dralm, we understand him well enough now!" That was another new-comer to the Full Council—the speaker for the fireseed makers. There were murmurs of agreement; quite a few got the point.

Sthentros refused to be silenced. "How do we know that he isn't some runaway priest of Styphon himself?"

Mytron, present as speaker for the physicians, surgeons and apothecaries, rose.

"When Kalvan came among us, I tended his wounds. He is not circum-cised, as all priests of Styphon are."

Then he sat down. That knocked that on the head. It was a good thing the Rev. Morrison had refused to let the doctor load the bill with what he'd con-sidered non-essentials when his son had been born. He'd never say another word against Scotch-Irish frugality. Sthentros, however, was staying with it.

"Well, maybe that's worse," he argued. "It's flatly against nature for any-thing to act like fireseed. I think there are devils in it that make it explode, and maybe the priests of Styphon do something to keep the devils from getting out when it explodes . . . something that we don't know anything about."

The speaker for the fireseed makers was on his feet.

"I make the stuff; I know what goes in it. Saltpeter and sulfur and char-coal, and there aren't any devils in any of them." He didn't know anything about oxidization, but he knew that the saltpeter made the rest of it burn fast. "Next thing, he'll be telling us there are devils in wine, or in dough to make the bread rise, or in . . ."

"Has anybody heard of any devils around Fitra?" somebody else asked. "We burned plenty of fireseed there."

"What in Galzar's name does Sthentros know about Fitra?—he wasn't there!"

"I'm going to have a little talk with that fellow, after this is over," Ptosphes said quietly to Kalvan. "All he is in Hostigos, he is by my favor, and my favor to him is getting frayed now."

"Well, devils or not, the question is Lord Kalvan's place among us," the noble who had sided with Sthentros said. "He is no Hostigi—what right has he to sit at the Council table?"

"Fitra!" somebody cried, from a place or two above Sthentros; "Tarr-Dombra!" added another voice, from across the table.

"He sits here," Rylla said icily, "as my betrothed husband, by my choice. Do you question that, Euklestes?"

"He sits here as heir-matrimonial to the throne of Hostigos, and as my son-adoptive," Ptosphes added. "I hope none of you presume to question that."

"He sits here as commander of our army," Chartiphon roared, "and as a soldier I am proud to obey. If you want to question that, do it with your sword against mine!"

"He sits here as one sent by Dralm. Do you question the Great God?" Xentos asked.

Euklestes gave Sthentros a look-what-you-got-me-into look.

"Great Dralm, no!"

"Well, then. We still have the question of war with Sask to be voted," Ptosphes said. "How vote you, Lord Sthentros?"

"Oh, war, of course; I'm as loyal a Hostigi as any here."

There was no more argument. The vote was unanimous. As soon as Ptosphes had thanked them, Harmakros was on his feet.

"Then, to show that we are all in loyal support of our Prince, let us all vote that whatever decision he may make in the matter of our dealings with Sask, with Beshta, or with Nostor, either in making war or in making peace afterward, shall stand approved in advance by the Full Council of Hostigos."

"What?" Ptosphes asked in a whisper. "Is this some idea of yours, Kalvan?"

"Yes. We don't know what we're going to have to do, but whatever it is, we may have to do it in a hurry, and afterward we won't want anybody like Sthentros or Euklestes whining that they weren't consulted."

"That's probably wise. We'd do it anyhow, but this way there'll be no argument."

Harmakros's motion was also carried unanimously. The organization steamroller ran up the table without a bump.

III

VERKAN, the free-trader from Grefftscharr, waited till the others—Prince Ptosphes, old Xentos, and the man of whom he must never under any circumstances think as Calvin Morrison—were seated, and then dropped into a chair at the table in Ptosphes's study.

"Have a good trip?" Lord Kalvan was asking him.

He nodded, and ran quickly over the fictitious details of the journey to Zygros City, his stay there, and his return to Hostigos, checking them with the actual facts. Then he visualized the panel, and his hand reaching out and pressing the black button. Other Paratimers used different imagery, but the result was the same. The pseudo-memories fed to him under hypnosis took over, the real memories of visits on this time-line to Zygros City were suppressed, and a complete blockage imposed on anything he knew about Fourth Level Europo-American, Hispano-Columbian Subsector.

"Not bad," he said. "I had a little trouble at Glarth Town, in Hos-Agrys. I'd sold those two kegs of Tarr-Dombra fireseed to a merchant, and right away they were after me, the Prince of Glarth's soldiers and Styphon's House agents. It seems Styphon's House had put out a story about one of their wagon-trains being robbed by bandits, and everybody's on the lookout for unaccountable fireseed. They'd arrested and tortured the merchant; he put them onto me. I killed one and wounded another, and got away."

"When was that?" Xentos asked sharply.

"Three days after I left here."

"Eight days after we took Tarr-Dombra and sent that letter to Sesklos," Ptosphes said. "That story'll be all over the Five Kingdoms by now."

"Oh, they've dropped that. They have a new story, now. They admit that some Prince in Hos-Harphax is making his own fireseed, but it isn't good fireseed."

Kalvan laughed. "It only shoots half again as hard as theirs, with half as much fouling."

"Ah, but there are devils in your fireseed. Of course, there are devils in all fireseed—that's what makes it explode—but the priests of Styphon have secret rites that cause the devils to die as soon as they've done their work. When yours explodes, the devils escape alive. I'll bet East Hostigos is full of devils, now."

He laughed, then stopped when he saw that none of the others were. Kalvan cursed; Ptosphes mentioned a name.

"That story has appeared here," Xentos said. "I hope none of our people believe it. It comes from Sask Town."

"This Sthentros, a kinsman by marriage of mine," Ptosphes said. "He's jealous of Kalvan's greatness among us. I spoke to him, gave him a good fright. He claimed he thought of it himself, but I know he's lying. Somebody from Sask's been at him. Trouble is, if we tortured him, all the other nobles would be around my ears like a swarm of hornets. We're having him watched."

"They move swiftly," Xentos said, "and they act as one. Their temples are everywhere, and each temple has its post station, with relays of fast horses.

Styphon's Voice can speak today at Balph, in Hos-Ktemnos, and in a moon-quarter his words are heard in every temple in the Five Kingdoms. Their lies can travel so fast and far that the truth can never overtake them."

"Yes, and see what'll happen," Kalvan said. "From now on, everything—plague, famine, drought, floods, hailstorms, forest-fires, hurricanes—will be the work of devils out of our fireseed. Well, you got out of Glarth; what then?"

"After that, I thought it better to travel by night. It took me eight days to reach Zygros City. My wife, Dalla, met me there, as we'd arranged when I started south from Ulthor. In Zygros City, we recruited five brass-founders—two are cannon-founders, one's a bell-founder, one's an image-maker and knows the wax-runoff method, and one's a general foundry foreman. And three girls, wood-carvers and pattern makers, and two mercenary sergeants I hired as guards.

"I gave the fireseed secret to the gunmakers' guild in Zygros City, in exchange for making up twelve long rifled fowling-pieces and rifling some pistols. They'll ship you rifled caliver barrels at the cost of smoothbore barrels. They'd heard the devil story; none of them believe it. And I gave the secret to merchants from my own country; they will spread it there."

"And by this time next year, Grefftscharr fireseed will be traded down the Great River to Xiphlon," Kalvan said. "Good. Now, how soon can this gang of yours start pouring cannon?"

"Two moons; a special miracle for each day less."

He started to explain about the furnaces and moulding sand; Kalvan understood.

"Then we'll have to fight this war with what we have. We'll be fighting in a moon-quarter, I think. We sent our Uncle Wolf off to Sask Town today with demands on Prince Sarrask. As soon as he hears them, they'll have to chain Sarrask up to keep him from biting people."

"Among other things, we're demanding that Archpriest Zothnes and the Sask Town high priest be sent here in chains, to be tried for plotting Kalvan's death and mine," Ptosphes said. "If Zothnes has the influence over Sarrask I think he has, that alone will do it."

"You'll command the Mounted Rifles again, won't you?" Kalvan asked. "It's carried on the Army List as a regiment, so you'll be a colonel. We have a hundred and twenty rifles, now."

Dalla wouldn't approve. Well, that was too bad, but people who didn't help their friends fight weren't well thought of around here. Dalla would just have to adjust to it, the way she had to his beard.

Ptosphes finished his wine. "Shall we go up to Rylla's room?" he asked. "I'm glad you brought your wife with you, Verkan. Charming girl, and Rylla likes her. They made friends at once. She'll be company for Rylla while we're away."

"Rylla's sore at us," Kalvan said. "She thinks we're keeping that bundle of splints on her leg to keep her from going to war with us." He grinned. "She's right; we are. Maybe Dalla'll help keep her amused."

Vall didn't doubt that. Rylla and Dalla would get along together, all right; what he was worried about was what they'd get *into* together. Those two girls were just two cute little sticks of the same brand of dynamite; what one wouldn't think of, the other would.

17

I

THE common-room of the village inn was hot and stuffy in spite of the open door; it smelled of woolens drying, of oil and sheep-tallow smeared on armor against the rain, of wood smoke and tobacco and wine, unwashed humanity and ancient cooking-odors. The village outside was jammed with the Army of the Listra; the inn with officers, steaming and stinking and smoking, drinking mugs of mulled wine or strong sassafras tea, crowding around the fire at the long table where the map was unrolled, spooning stew from bowls or gnawing meat impaled on dagger-points. Harmakros was saying, again and again, "Dralm damn you, hold that dagger back; don't drip grease on this!" And the priest of Galzar, who had carried the ultimatum to Sask Town and gotten this far on his return, and who had lately been out among the troops, sat in his shirt with his back to the fire, his wolfskin hood and cape spread to dry and a couple of village children wiping and oiling his mail. He had a mug in one hand, and with the other stroked the head of a dog that squatted beside him. He was laughing jovially.

"So I read them your demands, and you should have heard them! When I came to the part about dismissing the newly hired mercenaries, the captain-general of free companies bawled like a branded calf: I took it on myself to tell him you'd hire all of them with no loss of pay. Did I do right, Prince?"

"You did just right, Uncle Wolf," Ptosphes told him. "When we come to battle, along with 'Down Styphon' we'll shout, 'Quarter for mercenaries.' How about the demands touching on Styphon's House?"

"Ha! The Archpriest Zothnes was there, sitting next to Sarrask, with the Chancellor of Sask shoved down one place to make room for him, which shows you who rules in Sask now. He didn't bawl like a calf; he screamed like a panther. Wanted Sarrask to have me seized and my head off right in the throne-room. Sarrask told him his own soldiers would shoot him dead on the throne if he ordered it, which they would have. The mercenary captain-general wanted Zothnes's head off, and half drew his sword for it. There's one with small stomach to fight for Styphon's House. And this Zothnes was screaming that there was no god at all but Styphon; now what do you think of that?"

Gasps of horror, and exclamations of shocked piety. One officer was charitable enough to say that the fellow must be mad.

"No. He's just a—" A monotheist, Kalvan wanted to say, but there was no word in the language for it. "One who respects no gods but his own. We had that in my own country." He caught himself just before saying, "in my own time"; of those present, only Ptosphes was security-cleared for that version of his story. "They are people who believe in only one god, and then they believe that the god they worship is the only true one, and all others are false, and finally they believe that the only true god must be worshiped in only one way, and that those who worship otherwise are vile monsters who should be killed." The Inquisition; the wicked and bloody Albigensian Crusade; Saint Bartholomew's; Haarlem; Magdeburg. "We want none of that here."

"Lord Prince," the priest of Galzar said, "you know how we who serve the war god stand. The war god is the Judge of Princes, his courtroom the battle-field. We take no sides. We minister to the wounded without looking at their colors; our temples are havens for the war-maimed. We preach only Galzar's Way: be brave, be loyal, be comradely; obey your officers; respect yourselves and your weapons and all other good soldiers; be true to your company and to him who pays you.

"But Lord Prince, this is no common war, of Hostigos against Sask and Ptosphes against Sarrask. This is a war for all the true gods against false Styphon and Styphon's foul brood. Maybe there is some devil called Styphon, I don't know, but if there is, may the true gods trample him under their holy feet as we must those who serve him."

A shout of "Down Styphon!" rose. So this was what he had said they must have none of, and an old man in a dirty shirt, a mug of wine in his hand and a black and brown mongrel thumping his tail on the floor beside him, had spelled it out. A religious war, the vilest form an essentially vile business can take. Priests of Dralm and Galzar preaching fire and sword against Styphon's House. Priests of Styphon rousing mobs against the infidel devil-makers. *Styphon wills it!* Atrocities. Massacres. *Holy Dralm and no quarter!*

And that was what he'd brought to here-and-now. Well, maybe for the best; give Styphon's House another century or so in power and there'd be no gods, here-and-now, but Styphon.

"And then?"

"Well, Sarrask was in a fine rage, of course. By Styphon, he'd meet Prince Ptosphes's demands where they should be met, on the battlefield, and the war'd start as soon as I took my back out of sight across the border. That was just before noon. I almost killed a horse, and myself, getting here. I haven't done much hard riding, lately," he parenthesized. "As soon as I got here, Harmakros sent riders out."

They'd reached Tarr-Hostigos at cocktail time, another alien rite introduced by Lord Kalvan, and found him and Ptosphes and Xentos and Rylla and Dalla in Rylla's room. Hasty arming and saddling, hastier good-bys, and then a hard mud-splashing ride up Listra Valley, reaching this village after dark. The war had already started; from Esdreth Gap they could hear the distant dull thump of cannon.

Outside, the Army of the Listra was still moving forward; an infantry company marched past with a song:

Roll another barrel out, the party's just begun.
We beat Prince Gormoth's soldiers; you oughta seen them run!
And then we crossed the Athan, and didn't we have fun,
While we were marching through Nostor!

Galloping hoofs; cries of "Way! Way! Courier!" The song ended in shouted imprecations from mud-splashed infantrymen. The galloping horse stopped outside. The march, and the song, was resumed:

Hurrah! Hurrah! We burned the bastards out!
Hurrah! Hurrah! We put them all to rout!
We stole their pigs and cattle and we dumped their sauerkraut,
While we were marching through Nostor!

A muddy cavalryman stumbled through the door, looked around blinking, and then made for the long table, saluting as he came.

"From Colonel Verkan, Mounted Rifles. He and his men have Fyk; they beat off a counter-attack, and now the whole Saski army's coming at him. I found some Mobiles and a four-pounder on the way back; they've gone to help him.

"By Dralm, the whole Army of the Listra's going to help him. Where is this Fyk place?"

Harmakros pointed on the map—beyond Esdreth Gap, on the main road to Sask Town. There was a larger town, Gour, a little beyond. Kalvan pulled on his quilted coif and fastened the throat-guard; while he was settling his helmet on his head, somebody had gone to the door and was bawling into the dripping night for horses.

II

THE rain had stopped, an hour later, when they reached Fyk. It was a small place, full of soldiers and lighted by bonfires. The civil population had completely vanished; all fled when the shooting had started. A four-pounder pointed up the road to the south, with the dim shape of an improvised barricade stretching away in the darkness on either side. Off ahead, an occasional shot banged, and he could distinguish the sharper reports of Hostigos-made powder from the slower-burning stuff put out by Styphon's House. Maybe Uncle Wolf was right that this was a war between the true gods and false Styphon; it was also a war between two makes of gunpowder.

He found Verkan and a Mobile Force major in one of the village cottages; Verkan wore a hooded smock of brown canvas, and a short chopping-sword on his belt and a powder-horn and bullet-pouch slung from his shoulder. The major's cavalry armor was browned and smeared with tallow. They had one of the pyrographed deerskin field-maps spread on the table in front of them. *Paper, invention of;* he'd made that mental memo a thousand times already.

"There were about fifty cavalry here when we arrived," Verkan was saying. "We killed them or ran them out. In half an hour there were a couple of hundred back. We beat them off, and that was when I sent the riders back. Then Major Leukestros came up with his men and a gun, just in time to help beat off another attack. We have some cavalry and mounted arquebusiers out in front and on the flanks; that's the shooting you're hearing. There are some thousand cavalry at Gour, and probably all Sarrask's army following."

"I'm afraid we're going to have to make a wet night of it," Kalvan said. "We'll have to get our battle-line formed now; we can't take chances on what they may do."

He shoved the map aside and began scribbling and diagraming an order of battle on the white-scrubbed table top. Guns to the rear, in column along a side road north of the village, four-pounders in front; horses to be unhitched, but fed and rested in harness, ready to move out at once. Infantry in a line to both sides of the road a thousand yards ahead of the village, Mobile Force infantry in the middle. Cavalry on the flank; mounted infantry horses to the rear. A battle-order that could be converted instantly into a march-order if they had to move on in the morning.

The army came stumbling in for the next hour or so, in bits and scraps, got themselves sorted out, and took their positions astride of the road on the slope south of the village. The air had grown noticeably warmer. He didn't like that; it presaged fog, and he wanted good visibility for the battle tomorrow. Cavalry skirmishers began drifting back, reporting pressure of large enemy forces in front.

An hour after he had his line formed, the men lying in the wet grass on blankets, or whatever bedding they could snatch from the village, the Saski began coming up. There was a brief explosion of small-arms fire as they ran into his skirmishers, then they pulled back and began forming their own battle-line.

Hell of a situation, he thought disgustedly, lying on a cornshuck tick he and Ptosphes and Harmakros had stolen from some peasant's abandoned bed. Two blind armies, not a thousand yards apart, waiting for daylight, and when daylight came . . .

A cannon went off in front and on his left, with a loud, dull *whump*! A couple of heartbeats later, something whacked behind the line. He rose on his hands and knees, counting seconds as he peered into the darkness. Two minutes later, he glimpsed an orange glow on his left, and two seconds after that heard the report. Call it eight hundred yards, give or take a hundred. He hissed to a quartet of officers on a blanket next to him.

"They're overshooting us a little. Pass the word along the line, both ways, to move forward three hundred paces. And not a sound; dagger anybody who speaks above a whisper. Harmakros, get the cavalry and the mounted infantry horses back on the other side of the village. Make a lot of noise about five hundred yards behind us."

The officers moved off, two to a side. He and Ptosphes picked up the mattress and carried it forward, counting three hundred paces before dropping it. Men were moving up on both sides, with a gratifying minimum of noise.

The Saski guns kept on firing. At first there were yells of simulated fright; Harmakros and his crowd. Finally, a gun fired almost in front of him; the cannonball passed overhead and landed behind with a swish and whack like a headsman's sword coming down. The next shot was far on his left. Eight guns, at two minute intervals—call it fifteen minutes to load. That wasn't bad, in the dark and with what the Saski had. He relaxed, lying prone with his chin rested on his elbows. After awhile Harmakros returned and joined him and Ptosphes on the shuck tick. The cannonade went on in slow procession from left to right and left to right again. Once there was a bright flash instead of a dim glow, and a much sharper crack. Fine! One of the guns had burst! After that, there were only seven rounds to the salvo. Once there was a rending crash behind, as though a roundshot had hit a tree. Every shot was a safe over.

Finally, the firing stopped. The distant intermittent dueling between the two Castles Esdreth had ceased, too. He let go of wakefulness and dropped into sleep.

PTOSPHES, stirring beside him, wakened him. His body ached and his mouth tasted foul, as every body and mouth on both battle-lines must. It was still dark, but the sky above was something less than black, and he made out his companions as dim shapes. Fog.

By Dralm that was all they needed! Fog, and the whole Saski army not five hundred yards away, and all their advantages of mobility and artillery superiority lost. Nowhere to move, no room to maneuver, visibility down to less than pistol-shot, even the advantage of their hundred-odd rifled calivers nullified.

This looked like the start of a bad day for Hostigos.

They munched the hard bread and cold pork and cheese they had brought with them and drank some surprisingly good wine from a canteen and talked in whispers, other officers creeping in until a dozen and a half were huddled around the headquarters mattress.

"Couldn't we draw back a little?" That was Mnestros, the mercenary "captain"—approximately major-general—in command of the militia. "This is a horrible position. We're halfway down their throats."

"They'd hear us," Ptosphes said, "and start with their guns again, and this time they'd know where to shoot."

"Bring up our own guns and start shooting first," somebody suggested.

"Same objection; they'd hear us and open fire before we could. And for Dralm's sake keep your voices down," Kalvan snapped. "No, Mnestros said it. We're halfway down their throats. Let's jump the rest of the way and kick their guts out from the inside."

The mercenary was a book-soldier. He was briefly dubious, then admitted:

"We are in line to attack, and we know where they are and they don't know where we are. They must think we're back at the village, from the way they were firing last night. Cavalry on the flanks?" He deprecated that. According to the here-and-now book, cavalry should be posted all along the line, between blocks of infantry.

"Yes, half the mercenaries in each end, and a solid line of infantry, two ranks of pikes, and arquebuses and calivers to fire over the pikemen's shoulders," Kalvan said. "Verkan, have your men pass the word along the line. Everybody stay put and keep quiet till we can all go forward together. I want every pan reprimed and every flint tight; we'll all move off together, and no shouting till the enemy sees us. I'll take the extreme right. Prince Ptosphes, you'd better take center; Mnestros, command the left. Harmakros, you take the regular and Mobile Force cavalry and five hundred Mobile Force infantry, and move back about five hundred yards. If they flank us or break through, attend to it."

By now, the men around him were individually recognizable, but everything beyond twenty yards was fog-swollowed. Their saddle-horses were brought up. He reprimed the pistols in the holsters, got a second pair from a saddlebag, renewed the priming, and slipped one down the top of each jack-boot. The line was stirring with a noise that stood his hair on end under his helmet-coif, until he realized that the Saski were making too much noise to hear it. He slipped back the cuff under his mail sleeve and looked at his watch. Five forty-five; sunrise in half an hour. They all shook hands with one another, and he started right along the line.

Soldiers were rising, rolling and slinging cloaks and blankets. There were quilts and ticks and things from the village lying on the ground; mustn't be a piece of bedding left in Fyk. A few were praying, to Dralm or Galzar. Most of them seemed to take the attitude that the gods would do what they wanted to without impertinent human suggestions.

He stopped at the extreme end of the line, on the right of five hundred regular infantry, like all the rest lined four deep, two ranks of pikes and two of calivers. Behind and on the right, the mercenary cavalry were coming up in a block of twenty ranks, fifty to the rank. The first few ranks were heavy-armed, plate rerebraces and vambraces on their arms instead of mail sleeves, heavy pauldrons protecting their shoulders, visored helmets, mounted on huge chargers, real old style brewery-wagon horses. They came to a halt just behind him. He passed the word of readiness left, then sat stroking his horse's neck and talking softly to him.

After awhile the word came back with a moving stir along the line through the fog. He lifted a long pistol from his right-hand holster, readied it to fire, and shook his reins. The line slid forward beside him, front rank pikes waist high, second rank pike-points a yard behind and breast high, calivers behind at high port. The cavalry followed him with a slow fluviatile *clop-clatter-clop*. Things emerged from the fog in front—seedling pines, clumps of tall weeds, a rotting cartwheel, a whitened cow's skull—but the gray nothingness marched just twenty yards in front.

This, he recalled, was how Gustavus Adolphus had gotten killed, riding forward into a fog like this at Lützen.

An arquebus banged on his left; that was a charge of Styphon's Best. Half a dozen shots rattled in reply, most of them Kalvan's Unconsecrated, and he heard yells of "Down Styphon!" and "Sarrask of Sask!" The pikemen stiffened; some of them lost step and had to hop to make it up. They all seemed to crouch over their weapons, and the caliver muzzles poked forward. By this time, the firing was like a slate roof endlessly sliding off a house, and then, much farther to the left, there was a sudden ringing crash like sheet-steel falling into a scrap-car.

The Fyk corpse-factory was in full production.

But in front, there was only silence and the slowly receding curtain of fog, and pine-dotted pastureland broken by small gullies in which last night's rainwater ran yellowly. Ran straight ahead of them—that wasn't right. The Saski position was up a slope from where they had lain under the midrange trajectory of the guns, and now the noise of battle was not only to the left but behind them. He flung up the hand holding the gold-mounted pistol.

"Halt!" he called out. "Pass the word left to stand fast!"

He knew what had happened. Both battle-lines, formed in the dark, had overlapped the other's left. So he had flanked them, and Mnestros, on the Hostigi left, was also flanked.

"You two," he told a pair of cavalry lieutenants. "Ride left till you come to the fighting. Find a good pivot-point, and one of you stay with it. The other will come back along the line, passing the word to swing left. We'll start swinging from this end. And find somebody to tell Harmakros what's happened, if he doesn't know it already. He probably does. No orders; just use his own judgment."

Everybody would have to use his own judgment, from here out. He wondered what was happening to Mnestros. He hadn't the liveliest confidence in Mnestros's judgment when he ran into something the book didn't cover. Then he sat, waiting for centuries, until one of the lieutenants came thudding back behind the infantry line, and he gave the order to start the leftward swing.

The level pikes and slanting calivers kept line on his left; the cavalry clop-clattered behind him. The downward slope swung in front of them, until they were going steeply uphill, and then the ground was level under their feet, and he could feel a freshening breeze on his cheek.

He was shouting a warning when the fog tore apart for a hundred yards in front and two or three on either side, and out of it came a mob of infantry, badged with Sarrask's green and gold. He pulled his horse back, fired his pistol into them, holstered it, and drew the other from his left holster. The major commanding the regular infantry blew his whistle and screamed above the din:

"Action front! Fire by ranks, odd numbers only!"

The front rank pikemen squatted as though simultaneously stricken with diarrhea. The second rank dropped to one knee, their pikes advanced. Over their shoulders, half the third rank blasted with calivers, then dodged for the fourth rank to fire over them. As soon as the second volley crashed, the pike-men were on their feet and running at the disintegrating front of the Saski infantry, all shouting, "Down Styphon!"

He saw that much, then raked his horse with his spurs and drove him forward, shouting, "Charge!" The heavily armed mercenaries thundered after him, swinging long swords, firing pistols almost as big as small carbines, smashing into the Saski infantry from the flank before they could form a new front. He pistoled a pikeman who was thrusting at his horse, then drew his sword.

Then the fog closed down again, and dim shapes were dodging among the horses. A Saski cavalryman bulked in front of him, firing almost in his face. The bullet missed him, but hot grains of powder stung his cheek. Get a coal-miner's tattoo out of that, he thought, and then his wrist hurt as he drove the point into the fellow's throat-guard, spreading the links. *Plate gorgets; issue to mounted troops as soon as can be produced.* He wrenched the point free, and the Saski slid gently out of his saddle.

"Keep moving!" he screamed at the cavalry with him. "Don't let them slow you down!"

In a mess like this, stalled cavalry were all but helpless. Their best weapon was the momentum of a galloping horse, and once lost, that took at least thirty yards to regain. Cavalry horses ought to be crossed with jackrabbits; but that was something he couldn't do anything about at all. One mass of cavalry, the lancers and musketoon-men who had ridden behind the heavily armed men, had gotten hopelessly jammed in front of a bristle of pikes. He backed his horse quickly out of that, then found himself at the end of a line of Mobile Force infantry, with short arquebuses and cavalry lances for pikes. He directed them to the aid of the stalled cavalry, and then realized that he was riding across the road at right angles. That meant that he—and the whole battle, since all the noise was either to his right or left along the road—was now facing east instead of south. Of the heavily armed mercenary cavalry who had been with him at the beginning, he could see nothing.

A horseman came crashing at him out of the fog, shouting "Down Styphon!" and thrusting at him with a sword. He had barely time to beat it aside with his own and cry, "Ptosphes!" and a moment later:

"Ptosphes, by Dralm! How did you get here?"

"Kalvan! I'm glad you parried that one. Where are we?"

He told the Prince, briefly. "The whole Dralm-damned battle's turned at right angles; you know that?"

"Well, no wonder. Our whole left wing's gone. Mnestros is dead—I heard that from an officer who saw his body. The regular infantry on our extreme left are all but wiped out; what few are left, and what's left of the militia next to them, reformed on Harmakros, in what used to be our rear. That's our left wing, now."

"Well, their left wing's in no better shape; I swung in on that and smashed it up. What's happened to the cavalry we had on the left?"

"Dralm knows; I don't. Took to their heels out of this, I suppose." Ptosphes drew one of his pistols and took a powder-flask from his belt. "Watch over my shoulder, will you, Kalvan."

He drew one of his own holster-pair and poured a charge into it. The battle seemed to have moved out of their immediate vicinity, though off in the fog in both directions there was a bedlam of shooting, yelling and steel-clashing. Then suddenly a cannon, the first of the morning, went off in what Kalvan took to be the direction of the village. An eight-pounder, he thought, and certainly loaded with Made-in-Hostigos. On its heels came another, and another.

"That," Ptosphes said, "will be Harmakros."

"I hope he knows what he's shooting at." He primed the pistol, holstered it, and started on its mate. "Where do you think we could do the most good?"

Ptosphes had his saddle pair loaded, and was starting on one from a boot-top.

"Let's see if we can find some of our own cavalry, and go looking for Sarrask," he said. "I'd like to kill or capture him, myself. If I did, it might give me some kind of a claim on the throne of Sask. If this cursed fog would only clear."

From off to the right, south up the road, came noises like a boiler-shop starting up. There wasn't much shooting—everybody's gun was empty and no one had time to reload—just steel, and an indistinguishable *waw-waw-waw*-ing of voices. The fog was blowing in wet rags, now, but as fast as it blew away, more closed down. There was a limit to that, though; overhead the sky was showing a faint sunlit yellow.

"Come on, Lytris, come on!" he invoked the weather goddess. "Get this stuff out of here! Whose side are you fighting on, anyhow?"

Ptosphes finished the second of his spare pair, he had the last one of his own four to prime. Ptosphes said, "Watch behind you!" and he almost spilled the priming, then closed the pan and readied the pistol to fire. It was some twenty of the heavy-armed cavalry who had gone in with him. Their sergeant wanted to know where they were.

He hadn't any better idea than they had. Shoving the flint away from the striker, he pushed the pistol into his boot and drew his sword; they all started off toward the noise of fighting. He thought he was still going east until he saw that he was riding, at right angles, onto a line of mud-trampled quilts and bedspreads and mattresses, the things that had been appropriated in the village the night before. He glanced left and right. Ptosphes knew what they were, too, and swore.

Now the battle had made a full 180-degree turn. Both armies were facing in the direction from whence they had come; the route of either would be in the direction of the enemy's country.

Galzar, he thought irreverently, must have overslept this morning.

But at least the fog was definitely clearing, gilded above by sunlight, and the gray tatters around them were fewer and more threadbare, visibility now better than a hundred yards. They found a line of battle extending, apparently, due east of Fyk, and came up behind a hodgepodge of militia, regulars and Mobiles, any semblance of unit organization completely lost. Mobile Force cavalry were trotting back and forth behind them, looking for soft spots where breakthroughs, in either direction, might happen. He yelled to a Mobile Force captain who was fighting on foot:

"Who's in front of you?"

"How should I know? Same mess of odds-and-sods we are. This Dralm-damned battle . . ."

Officially, he supposed, it would be the Battle of Fyk, but nobody who'd been in it would ever call it anything but the Dralm-damned Battle.

Before he could say anything, there was a crash on his left like all the boiler-shops in creation together. He and Ptosphes looked at one another.

"Something new has been added," he commented. "Well, let's go see."

They started to the left with their picked up heavy cavalry, not too rapidly, and with pistols drawn. There was a lot of shouting—"Down Styphon!" of course, and "Ptosphes!" and "Sarrask of Sask!" There were also shouts of "Balthames!" That would be the retinue Balthar's brother, the prospective Prince of Sashta, had brought to Sask Town—some two hundred and fifty, he'd heard. Then, there were cries of "Treason! Treason!"

Now there was a hell of a thing to yell on any battlefield, let alone in a fog. He was wondering who was supposed to be betraying whom when he found the way blocked by the backs of Hostigi infantry at right angles to the battle-line; not retreating, just being pushed out of the way of something. Beyond them, through the thinning fog, he could see a rush of cavalry, some wearing black and pale yellow surcoats over their armor. They'd be Balthames's Beshtans; they were firing and chopping indiscriminately at anything in front of them, and, mixed with them, were green-and-gold Saski, fighting with them and the Hostigi both. All he and Ptosphes and the mercenary men-at-arms could do was sit on their horses and fire pistols at them over the heads of their own infantry.

Finally, the breakthrough, if that was what it had been, was over. The Hostigi infantry closed in behind them, piking and shooting, and there were cries of "Comrade, we yield!" and "Oath to Galzar!" and "Comrade, spare mercenaries!"

"Should we give them a chase?" Ptosphes asked, looking after the Saski-Beshtan whatever-it-had-been.

"I shouldn't think so. They're charging in the right direction. What the Styphon do you think happened?"

Ptosphes laughed. "How should I know? I wonder if it really was treason."

"Well, let's get through here." He raised his voice. "Come on—forward! Somebody's punched a hole for us; let's get through it!"

SUDDENLY, the fog was gone. The sun shone from a cloudless sky; the mountainside, nearer than he thought, was gaudy with Autumn colors; all the drifting puffs and hanging bands of white on the ground were powder-smoke. The village of Fyk, on his left, was ringed with army wagons like a Boer laager, guns pointing out between them. That was the strong point on which Harmakros had rallied the wreckage of the left wing.

In front of him, the Hostigi were moving forward, infantry running beside the cavalry, and in front of them the Saski line was raveling away, men singly and in little groups and by whole companies turning and taking to their heels, trying to join two or three thousand of their comrades who had made a porcupine. He knew it from otherwhen history as a Swiss hedgehog: a hollow circle bristling pikes in all directions. Hostigi cavalry were already riding around it, firing into it, and Verkan's riflemen were sniping at it. There seemed to be no Saski cavalry whatever; they must all have joined the rush to the south at the time of the breakthrough.

Then three four-pounders came out from the village at a gallop, unlimbered at three hundred yards, and began firing case-shot. When two eight-pounders followed more sedately, helmets began going up on pike-points and caliver muzzles.

Behind him, the fighting had ceased entirely. Hostigi soldiers had scattered through the brush and trampled cornstalks, tending to their wounded, securing prisoners, robbing corpses, collecting weapons, all the routine after-battle chores, and the battle wasn't over yet. He was worrying about where all the Saski cavalry had gotten, and the possibility that they might rally and counterattack, when he saw a large mounted column approaching from the south. This is it, he thought, and we're all scattered to Styphon's House and gone—He was shouting at the men nearest him to drop what they were doing and start earning their pay when he saw blue and red colors on lances, saddle-pads, scarves. He trotted forward to meet them.

Some were mercenaries, some were Hostigi regulars; with them were a number of green-and-gold prisoners, their helmets hung on saddlebows. A captain in front shouted a greeting as he came up.

"Well, thank Galzar you're still alive, Lord Kalvan! Where's the Prince?"

"Back at the village, trying to get things sorted out. How far did you go?"

"Almost to Gour. Better than a thousand of them got away; they won't stop short of Sask Town. The ones we have are the ones with the slow horses. Sarrask may have gotten away; we know Balthames did."

"Dralm and Galzar and all the true gods curse that Beshtan bastard!" one of the prisoners cried. "Devils eat his soul forever! The Dralm-damned lackwit cost us the battle, and only Galzar's counted how many dead and maimed."

"What happened? I heard cries of treason."

"Yes, that dumped the whole bagful of devils on us," the Saski said. "You want to know what happened? Well, in the darkness we formed with our right wing far beyond your left; yours beyond ours, I suppose, from the looks of things. On our right, we carried all before us, drove your cavalry from the field and smashed your infantry. Then this boy-lover from Beshta—we can fight our enemies, but Galzar guard us from our allies—took his own men and near a thousand of our mercenary horse off on a rabbit-hunt after your fleeing cavalry, almost to Esdreth.

"Well, you know what happened in the meantime. Our right drove in your left, and yours ours, and the whole battle turned like a wheel, and we were all facing in the way we'd come, and then back comes this Balthames of Beshta, smashing into our rear, thinking that he was saving the day.

"And to make it worse, the silly fool doesn't shout 'Sarrask of Sask,' as he should have; no, he shouts 'Balthames!'—he and all his, and the mercenaries with him took it up to curry favor with him. Well, great Dralm, you know how much anybody can trust anybody from Beshta; we thought the bugger'd turned his coat, and somebody cried treason. I'll not deny crying it myself, after I was near spitted on a Beshtan lance, and me crying 'Sarrask!' at the top of my lungs. So we were carried away in the rout, and I fell in with mercenaries from Hos-Ktemnos. We got almost to Gour and tried to make a stand, and were ridden over and taken."

"Did Sarrask get away? Galzar knows I want to spill his blood badly enough, but I want to do it honestly."

The Saski didn't know; none of Sarrask's silver-armored personal guard had been near him in the fighting.

"Well, don't blame Duke Balthames too much." Looking around, he saw over a score of Saski and mercenary prisoners within hearing. If we're going to have a religious war, let's start it now. "It was," he declared, "the work of the true gods! Who do you think raised the fog, but Lytris the Weather Goddess? Who confounded your captains in arraying your line, and caused your gunners to overshoot, harming not one of us, but Galzar Wolfhead, the Judge of Princes? And who but Great Dralm himself addled poor Balthames's wits, leading him on a fool's chase and bringing him back to strike you from behind? At long last," he cried, "the true gods have raised their mighty hands against false Styphon and the blasphemers of Styphon's House!"

There were muttered amens, some from the Saski prisoners. Styphon's stock had dropped quite a few points. He decided to let it go at that, and put them in with the other prisoners and let them talk.

18

PTOSPHES was shocked by the casualties. Well, they *were* rather shocking—only forty-two hundred effectives left out of fifty-eight hundred infantry, and eighteen hundred of a trifle over three thousand cavalry. The body count didn't meet the latter figure, however, and he remembered what the Saski officer had said about Balthames's chase almost to Esdreth Gap. Most of the mercenaries on the left wing had simply bugged out; by now, they'd be fleeing into Listra Valley, spreading tales of a crushing Hostigi defeat. He cursed; there wasn't anything else he could do about it.

Some cavalry arrived from Esdreth Gap: Chartiphon's Army of the Besh men. During the night, they reported, infantry from both the army of the Besh and the Army of the Listra had gotten onto the mountain back of Tarr-Esdreth-of-Sask, and taken it by storm just before daylight. Alkides had moved his three treasured brass eighteen-pounders and some lighter pieces down into the gap, and was holding it at both ends with a mixed force. As the fog had started to blow away, a large body of Saski cavalry had tried to force a way through; they had been driven off by gunfire. Perturbed by the presence of enemy troops so far north, he had sent to find out what was going on. Riders were sent to reassure him, and order him to come up in person and bring his eighteens with him.

There was no telling what they might have to break into before the day was over. The long eighteen-pounders were excellent burglar-tools.

Harmakros got off at ten, with the Mobile Force and all the four-pounders, up the main road for Sask Town. All the captured mercenaries agreed to take Prince Ptosphes's colors and were released under oath and under arms. The Saski subjects were disarmed and put to work digging trenches for mass graves and collecting salvageable equipment. Mytron and his staff preempted the better cottages and several of the larger and more sanitary barns for hospitals. Taking five hundred of the remaining cavalry, Kalvan started out a little before noon, leaving Ptosphes to await the arrival of Alkides and the eighteen-pounders.

Gour was a market town of some five thousand. He found bodies, already stripped of armor, in the square, and a mob of townsfolk and disarmed Saski prisoners working to put out several fires, guarded by some lightly wounded mounted arquebusiers. He dropped two squads to help them and rode on.

He thought he knew this section; he'd been stationed in Blair County five otherwhen years ago. He hadn't realized how much the Pennsylvania Railroad Company had altered the face of Logan Valley. At about what ought to be Allegheny Furnace, he was stopped by a picket-post of Mobile Force cavalry and warned to swing right and come in on Sask Town from behind. Tarr-Sask was being held, either by or for Prince Sarrask, and was cannonading the town. While he talked with them, he could hear the occasional distant boom of a heavy bombard.

Tarr-Sask stood on the south end of Brush Mountain, Sarrask's golden-rayed sun on green flying from the watchtower. The arrival of his cavalry at the other side of the town must have been observed; four bombards let go with strain-everything charges of Styphon's Best, hurling hundred and fifty pound stone cannonballs among the houses. This, he thought, wouldn't do much to improve relations between Sarrask and his subjects. Harmakros, who had nothing but four-pounders, which was to say nothing, was not replying. Wait, he thought, till Alkides gets here.

Battering-pieces, thirty-two-pounders, about six; get cast as soon as Verkan's gang gets a foundry going. And cast shells; do something about.

There had been no fighting inside the town; Harmakros's blitzkrieg had hit it too fast, before resistance could be organized. There had been some looting—that was to be expected—but no fires. Arson for arson's sake, without a valid strategic reason as in Nostor, was discountenanced in the Hostigos army. Most of the civil population had either refugeed out or were down in the cellar.

The temple of Styphon had been taken first of all. It stood on almost the exact site of the Hollidaysburg courthouse, a circular building under a golden dome, with rectangular wings on either side. If, as he suspected, that dome was really gold, it might go a long way toward paying the cost of the war. A Mobile Force infantryman was up a ladder with a tarpot and a brush, painting DOWN STYPHON over the door. Entering, the first thing he saw was a twenty-foot image, its face newly spalled and pitted and lead-splashed. The Puritans had been addicted to that sort of small-arms practice, he recalled, and so had the Huguenots. There was a lot of gold ornamentation around; guards had been posted.

He found Harmakros in the Innermost Circle, his spurred heels resting on the high priest's desk. He sprang to his feet.

"Kalvan! Did you bring any guns?"

"No, only cavalry. Ptosphes is bringing Alkides's three eighteens. He'll be here in about three hours. What happened here?"

"Well, as you see, Balthames got here a little ahead of us and shut himself up in Tarr-Sask. We sent the local Uncle Wolf up to parley with him. He says he's holding the castle in Sarrask's name, and won't surrender without Sarrask's orders as long as he has fireseed."

"Then he doesn't know where Sarrask is, either."

Sarrask could be dead and his body stripped on the field by common soldiers—it'd be worth stripping—and tumbled anonymously into one of those mass graves. If so, they might never be sure, and then, every year for the next thirty years, some fake Sarrask would be turning up somewhere in the Five Kingdoms, conning suckers into financing a war to recover his throne. That had happened occasionally in otherwhen history.

"Did you get the priests along with this temple?"

"Oh, yes, Zothnes and all. They were packing to leave when we got here, and argued about what to take along. We have them in chains in the town jail, now. Do you want to see them?"

"Not particularly. We'll have their heads off tomorrow or the next day, when we find time for it. How about the fireseed mill?"

Harmakros laughed. "Verkan's surrounding it with his riflemen. As soon as we get a dozen or so men dressed in priestly robes, about a hundred more will chase them in, with a lot of yelling and shooting. If that gets the gate open, we may be able to take the place before some fanatic blows it up. You know, some of these under-priests and novices really believe in Styphon."

"Well, what did you get here?"

Harmakros waved a hand about him. "All this gold and fancywork. Then there's gold and silver, specie and bullion, in the vaults, to about fifty thousand gold ounces, I'd say."

That was a lot of money. Around a million U.S. dollars. He could believe it, though; besides making fireseed, Styphon's House was in the loan-shark business, at something like ten percent per lunar month, compound interest. *Anti-usury laws; do something about.* Except for a few small-time pawnbrokers, they were the only money-lenders in Sask.

"Then," Harmakros continued, "there's a magazine and armory. We haven't taken inventory yet, but I'd say ten tons of fireseed, three or four hundred stand of arquebuses and calivers, and a lot of armor. And one wing's packed full of general merchandise, probably taken in as offerings. We haven't even looked at that, yet; just put it under guard. A lot of barrels that could be wine; we don't want the troops getting at that yet."

The guns of Tarr-Sask kept on firing slowly, smashing a house now and then. None of the roundshot came near the temple; Balthames was evidently still in awe of Styphon's House. The main army arrived about 1630; Alkides got his brass eighteen-pounders and three twelves in position and began shooting back. They didn't throw the huge granite globes Balthames's bombards did, but they fired every five minutes instead of every half hour, and with something approaching accuracy. A little later, Verkan rode in to report the fireseed mill taken intact. He didn't think much of the equipment—the mills were all slave-powered—but there had been twenty tons of finished fireseed, and over a hundred of sulfur and saltpeter. He had had some trouble preventing a massacre of the priests when the slaves had been unshackled.

At 1815, in the gathering dusk, riders came in from Esdreth, reporting that Sarrask had been captured, in Listra Valley, while trying to reach the Nostori border to place himself under the questionable protection of Prince Gormoth.

"He was captured," the sergeant in command finished, "by the Princess Rylla and Colonel Verkan's wife, Dalla."

He and Ptosphes and Harmakros and Verkan all shouted at once. A moment later, the roar of one of Alkides's eighteens was almost an anticlimax. Verkan was saying, "*That's* the girl who wanted *me* to stay out of battles!"

"But Rylla can't get out of bed," Ptosphes argued.

"I wouldn't know about that, Prince," the sergeant said. "Maybe the Princess calls a saddle a bed, because that's what she was in when I saw her."

"Well, did she have that cast—that leather thing—on her leg?" Kalvan asked.

"No, sir—just regular riding boots, with pistols in them."

He and Ptosphes cursed antiphonally. Well, at least they'd kept her out of that blindfold slaughterhouse at Fyk.

"Sound Cease Fire, and then Parley," he ordered. "Send Uncle Wolf up the hill again; tell Balthames we have his pa-in-law."

They got a truce arranged; Balthames sent out a group of neutrals, merchants and envoys from other princedoms, to observe and report. Bonfires were lit along the road up to the castle. It was full dark when Rylla and Dalla arrived, with a mixed company of mounted Tarr-Hostigos garrison troops, fugitive mercenaries rallied along the road south, and overage peasants on overage horses. With them were nearly a hundred of Sarrask's elite guard, in silvered harness that looked more like table-service than armor, and Sarrask himself in gilded armor.

"Where's that lying quack of a Mytron?" Rylla demanded, as soon as she was within hearing. "I'll doctor him when I catch him—a double orchidectomy! You know what? Yes, of course you do; you put him up to it! Well, Dalla had a look at my leg this morning, she's forgotten more about doctoring than Mytron ever learned, and she said that thing ought to have been off half a moon ago."

"Well, what's the story?" Kalvan asked. "How did you pick all this up?" He indicated Sarrask, glowering at them from his saddle, with his silver-plated guardsmen behind him.

"Oh, this band of heroes you took to a battle you tried to keep me out of," Rylla said bitterly. "About noon, they came clattering into Tarr-Hostigos— that's the ones with the fastest horses and the sharpest spurs—screaming that all was lost, the army destroyed, you killed, father killed, Harmakros killed, Verkan killed, Mnestros killed; why, they even had Chartiphon, down on the Beshtan border, killed!"

"Well, I'm sorry to say that Mnestros *was* killed," her father told her.

"Well, I didn't believe a tenth of it, but even at that something bad could have happened, so I gathered up what men I could mount at the castle, appointed Dalla my lieutenant—she was the best man around—and we started south, gathering up what we could along the way. Just this side of Darax, we ran into this crowd. We thought they were the cavalry screen for a Saski invasion, and we gave them an argument. That was when Dalla captured Prince Sarrask."

"I did not," Verkan's wife denied. "I just shot his horse. Some farmers captured him, and you owe them a lot of money, or somebody does. We rode into this gang on the road, and there was a lot of shooting, and this big man in gilded armor came at me swinging a sword as long as I am. I fired at him, and as I did his horse reared and caught it in the chest and fell over backward, and while he was trying to get clear some peasants with knives and hatchets and things jumped on him, and he began screaming, 'I am Prince Sarrask of Sask; my ransom is a hundred thousand ounces of silver!' Well, right away, they lost interest in killing him."

"Who are they, do you know?" Ptosphes asked. "I'll have to make that good to them."

"Styphon will pay," Kalvan said.

"Styphon ought to; he got Sarrask into this mess in the first place," Ptosphes commented. He turned back to Rylla. "What then?"

"Well, when Sarrask surrendered, the rest of them began pulling off helmets and holding swords up by the blades and crying, 'Oath to Galzar!' They all admitted they'd taken an awful beating at Fyk, and were trying to get into Nostor. Now wouldn't that have been nice?"

"Our gold-plated friend here didn't want to come along with us," Dalla said. "Rylla told him he didn't need to; we could take his head along easier than all of him. You know, Prince, your daughter doesn't fool. At least, Sarrask didn't think so."

She hadn't been fooling, and Sarrask had known it.

"So," Rylla picked it up, "we put him on a horse one of his guards didn't need any more, and brought him along. We thought you might find a use for him. We stopped at Esdreth Gap—I saw our flag on the Sask castle; that looked pretty, but Sarrask didn't think so . . ."

"Prince Ptosphes!" Sarrask burst out. "I am a Prince, as you are. You have no right to let these—these girls—make sport of me!"

"They're as good soldiers as you are," Ptosphes snapped. "They captured you, didn't they?"

"It was the true gods who made sport of you, Prince Sarrask!" Kalvan went into the same harangue he had given the captured officers at Fyk, in his late father's best denunciatory pulpit style. "I pray all the true gods," he finished, "that now that they have humbled you, they will forgive you."

Sarrask was no longer defiant; he was a badly scared Prince, as badly scared as any sinner at whom the Rev. Alexander Morrison had thundered hellfire and damnation. Now and then he looked uneasily upward, as though wondering what the gods were going to hit him with next.

It was almost midnight before Kalvan and Ptosphes could sit down privately in a small room behind Sarrask's gaudy presence chamber. There had been the takeover of Tarr-Sask, and the quartering of troops, and the surrendered mercenaries to swear into Ptosphes's service, and the Saski troops to disarm and confine to barracks. Riders had been coming and going with messages. Chartiphon, on the Beshtan border, was patching up a field truce with Balthar's officers on the spot, and had sent cavalry to seize the lead mines in Sinking Valley. As soon as things stabilized, he was turning the Army of the Besh over to his second in command and coming to Sask Town.

Ptosphes had let his pipe go out. Biting back a yawn, he leaned forward to relight it from a candle.

"We have a panther by the tail here, Kalvan; you know that?" he asked. "What are we going to do now?"

"Well, we clean Styphon's House out of Sask, first of all. We'll have the heads off all those priests, from Zothnes down." Counting the lot that had been brought in from the different temple-farms, that would be about fifty. They'd have to gather up some headsmen. "That will have to be policy, from now on. We don't leave any of that gang alive."

"Oh, of course," Ptosphes agreed. "'To be dealt with as wolves are.' But how about Sarrask and Balthames? If we behead them, the other Princes would criticize us."

"No, we want both of them alive, as your vassals. Balthames is going to marry that wench of Sarrask's if I have to stand behind him with a shotgun, and then we'll make him Prince of Sashta, and occupy all that territory Balthar agreed to cede him. In return, he'll guarantee us the entire output of those lead mines. Lead, I'm afraid, is going to be our chief foreign-exchange monetary metal for a long time to come.

"To make it a little tighter," he continued, "we'll add a little of Hostigos, east of the mountains, say to the edge of the Barrens—"

"Are you crazy, Kalvan? Give up Hostigi land? Not as long as I'm Prince of Hostigos!"

"Oh, I'm sorry. I must have forgotten to tell you. You're not Prince of Hostigos any more. I am." Ptosphes's face went blank, for an instant, with shocked incredulity. Then he was on his feet with an oath, his poignard half drawn. "No," Kalvan continued, before his father-in-law-to-be could say anything else. "You are now His Majesty, Ptosphes the First, Great King of Hos-Hostigos. As Prince by betrothal of your Majesty's domain of Old Hostigos, let me be the first to do homage to your Majesty."

Ptosphes resumed his chair, solely by force of gravity. He stared for a moment, then picked up his goblet and drained it.

This was a Hos- of another color.

"If the people in that section don't want to live under the rule of Balthames, for which I shouldn't blame them, we'll buy them out and settle them elsewhere. We'll fill that country with mercenaries we've had to take over and don't want to carry on the payroll. The officers can be barons, and the privates will all get forty acres and a mule, and we'll make sure they all have something to shoot with. That'll keep them out of worse mischief, and keep Prince Balthames's hands full. If we need them, we can always call them up again. Styphon, as usual, will pay.

"I don't know how long it'll take us to get Beshta—a moon or so. We'll let Balthar find out how much gold and silver we're getting out of this temple here. Balthar is fond of money. Then, after he's broken with Styphon's House, he'll find that he'll have to join us."

"Armanes, too," Ptosphes considered, toying with his golden chain. "He owes Styphon's House a lot of money. What do you think Kaiphranos will do about this?"

"Well, he won't be happy about it, but who cares? He only has some five thousand troops of his own; if he wants to fight us, he'll either have to raise a mercenary army—and there's a limit to how many mercenaries anybody, even financed by Styphon's House, can hire—or he'll have to levy on his subject Princes. Half of them won't send troops to help coerce a fellow Prince— it might be their turn next—and the rest will all be too jealous of their own dignities to take orders from him. And in any case, he won't move till spring."

Ptosphes had started to lift the chain from around his neck. He replaced it.

"No, Kalvan," he said firmly. "I will remain Prince of Old Hostigos. You must be Great King."

NOW, look here, Ptosphes; Dralm-dammit, you *have* to be Great King!" For a moment, he was ten years old again, arguing who'd be cops and who'd be robbers. "You have some standing; you're a Prince. Nobody in Hos-Harphax knows me from a hole in the ground."

Ptosphes slapped the table till the goblets jiggled.

"That's just it, Kalvan! They know me all too well. I'm just a Prince, no better than they are; every one of these other Princes would say he had as much right to be Great King as I do. But they don't know who you are; all they know is what you've done. That and the story we told at the beginning, that you come from far across the Western Ocean, around the Cold Lands.

Why, that's the Home of the Gods! We can't claim that you're a god, yourself; the real gods wouldn't like that. But anybody can plainly see that you've been taught by the gods, and sent by them. It would be nothing but plain blasphemy to deny it!"

Ptosphes was right; none of these haughty Princes would kneel to one of their own ilk. But Kalvan, Galzar-taught and Dralm-sent; that was a Hos- of another color, too. Rylla's father had risen to kneel to him.

"Oh, sit down; sit down! Save that nonsense for Sarrask and Balthames to do. We'll have to talk to some of our people tonight; best do that in the presence chamber."

Harmakros was still up and more or less awake. He took the announcement quite calmly; by this time he was beyond surprise at anything. They had to waken Rylla; she'd had a little too much, for her first day up. She merely nodded drowsily. Then her eyes widened. "Hey, doesn't this make me Great Queen, or something?" Then she went back to sleep.

Chartiphon, arriving from the Beshtan border, was informed. He asked, "Why not Ptosphes?" then nodded agreement when the reasons were explained. About the necessity for establishing a Great Kingdom he had no doubt. "What else are we now? We'll have Beshta next."

A score of others, Hostigi nobles and top army brass, were gathered in the presence chamber. Among them was Sthentros; maybe he hadn't been at Fitra, but nobody could say he hadn't been at Fyk. He might have envied Lord Kalvan, but Great King Kalvan was completely beyond envy. They were all half out on their feet—they'd only marched all day yesterday, tried to sleep in a wet cowpasture with cannon firing over them, fought a "great murthering battle" in the morning, marched fifteen more miles, and taken Sask Town and Tarr-Sask—but they wanted to throw a party to celebrate. They were persuaded to have one drink to their new sovereign and then go to bed.

The rank-and-file weren't in any better shape; half a den of Cub Scouts could have taken Tarr-Sask and run the lot of them out.

19

I

THE next morning Kalvan's orderly, who didn't seem to have gotten much sleep, wakened him at nine-thirty. Should have done it earlier, but he'd probably just gotten awake himself. He bathed, put on clothes he'd never seen before—*have things brought from Tarr-Hostigos, soonest*—and breakfasted with Ptosphes, who had also been outfitted from some Saski nobleman's wardrobe. There were more messages: from Klestreus, in Beshta Town, who had bullied Balthar into agreeing to a truce and pulling his troops back to the line agreed on the treaty with Sarrask; and from Xentos, at Tarr-Hostigos. Xentos was disturbed about reports of troop mobilization in Nostor; Gormoth, he knew, had recently hired five hundred mercenary cavalry. Immediately, Ptosphes became equally disturbed. He wanted to march at once down the Listra Valley.

"No, for Dralm's sake!" Kalvan protested. "We have a panther by the tail, here. In a day or so, when we're in control, we can march a lot of these new mercenaries to Listra-Mouth, but right now we mustn't let anybody know we're frightened or they'll all jump us."

"But if Gormoth's invading Hostigos—"

"I don't think he is. Just to make sure, we'll send Phrames off with half the

Mobile Force and four four-pounders; they can hold anything Gormoth's moving against us for a few days."

He gave the necessary orders, saw to it that the troops left Sask Town quietly, and tried to ignore the subject. He was glad, though, that Rylla had gotten out of her splints and come to Sask Town; she might be safer here.

So they had Sarrask and Balthames brought in.

Both seemed to be expecting to be handed over to the headsman, and were trying to be nonchalant about it. Ptosphes informed them abruptly that they were now subjects of the Great King of Hos-Hostigos.

"Who's he?" Sarrask demanded, with a truculence the circumstances didn't quite justify. "You?"

"Oh, no. I am Prince of Old Hostigos. His Majesty, Kalvan the First, is Great King."

They were both relieved. Ptosphes had been right; the sovereignty of the mysterious and possibly supernatural Kalvan would be acceptable; that of a self-elevated equal would not. When the conditions under which they would reign as Princes, respectively, of Sashta and Sask were explained, Balthames was delighted. He'd come out of this as well as if Sask had won the war. Sarrask was somewhat less so, until informed that he was now free of all his debts to Styphon's House and would share in the loot of the temple and be given the fireseed mill.

"Well, Dralm save your Majesty!" he cried, and then loosed a torrent of invective against Styphon's House and all in it. "You'll let me put these thieving priests to death, won't you, your Majesty?"

"They are offenders against the Great King; his justice will deal with them," Ptosphes informed him.

Then they had in the foreign envoys, representatives of Prince Kestophes of Ulthor, on Lake Erie, and Armanes of Nyklos, and Tythanes of Kyblos, and Balthar of Beshta, and other neighboring Princes. There had been no such diplomatic corps at Tarr-Hostigos, because of the ban of Styphon's House. The Ulthori minister immediately wanted to know what the new Great Kingdom included.

"Well, at the moment, the Princedom of Old Hostigos, the Princedom of Sask, and the new Princedom of Sashta. Any other Princes who may elect to join us will be made welcome under our rule and protection; those which do not will be respected in their sovereignty as long as they respect us in ours. Or what they may conceive to be their sovereignty as subjects of this Great King of Hos-Harphax, Kaiphranos."

He shrugged Kaiphranos off as too trivial for consideration. Several of them laughed. The Beshtan minister began to bristle:

"This Princedom of Sashta, now; does that include territory ruled by my master, Prince Balthar of Beshta?"

"It includes territory your master ceded to our subject, Prince Balthames, in a treaty with our subject Prince Sarrask, which we recognized and confirm, and which we are prepared to enforce. As to how we are prepared to enforce it, I trust I don't have to remind you of what happened at Fyk yesterday morning."

He turned to the others. "Now, if your respective Princes don't wish to acknowledge our sovereignty, we hope they will accept our friendship and extend their own," he said. "We also hope that mutually satisfactory arrangements for trade can be made. For example, before long we expect to be producing fireseed in sufficient quantities for export, of better quality and at lower price than Styphon's House."

"We know that," the Nyklosi envoy said. "I can't, of course, commit my Prince to accepting the sovereignty of Hos-Hostigos, though I will strongly advise it. We've been paying tribute to King Kaiphranos and getting absolutely nothing in return for it. But in any case, we'll be glad to get all the fireseed you can send us."

"Well, look here," the Beshtan began. "What's all this about devils? The priests of Styphon make the devils in fireseed die when it burns, and yours lets them loose."

The Ulthori nodded. "We've heard about that, too," he said. "We have no use for King Kaiphranos; for all he does, we might as well not have a Great King. But we don't want Ulthor being filled with evil spirits."

"We've been using Hostigos fireseed in Nyklos, and we haven't had any trouble with devils," the Nyklosi said.

"There are no devils in fireseed," Kalvan declared. "It's nothing but saltpeter and charcoal and sulfur, mixed without any prayers or rites or magic whatever. You know how much of it we burned at Fitra and Listra-Mouth. Nobody's seen any devils there, since."

"Well, but you can't see the devils," the envoy from Kyblos said. "They fill the air, and make bad weather, and make the seed rot in the ground. You wait till spring, and see what kind of crops you have around Fitra. And around Fyk."

The Beshtan was frankly hostile, the Ulthori unconvinced. That devil story was going to have to be answered, and how could you prove the nonexistence of something, especially an invisible something, that didn't exist? That was why he was an agnostic instead of an atheist.

They got rid of the diplomatic corps, and had in the priests and priestesses of all the regular, non-Styphon, pantheon. The one good thing about monotheism, he thought, was that it reduced the priesthood problem. Hadn't the Romans handled that through a government-appointed pontifex maximus? *Think over, seriously.* The good thing about polytheism was that the gods operated in non-competitive fields, and their priests had a common basis of belief, and mutual respect for each other's deities. The high priest of Dralm seemed to be the acknowledged dean of the sacred college. Assisted by all his colleagues, he would make the invocation and proclaim Kalvan Great King in the name of all the gods. Then they had in a lot of Sarrask's court functionaries, who bickered endlessly about protocol and precedence. And they made sure that each of the mercenary captains swore a new oath of service to the Great King.

After noon-meal, they assembled everybody in Prince Sarrask's throne-room.

In Korea, another sergeant in Calvin Morrison's company had seen the throne-room of Napoleon at Fontainebleau.

"You know," his comrade had said, "I never really understood Napoleon till I saw that place. If Al Capone had ever seen it, he'd have gone straight back to Chicago and ordered one for himself, twice as big, because he couldn't possibly have gotten one twice as flashy or in twice as bad taste."

That described Sarrask's throne-room exactly.

The high priest of Dralm proclaimed him Great King, chosen by all the true gods; the other priests and priestesses ratified that on behalf of their deities. Divine right of kings was another innovation, here-and-now. He then seated Rylla on the throne beside him, and then invested her father with the throne of Old Hostigos, emphasizing that he was First Prince of the Great Kingdom. Then he accepted the homage of Sarrask and Balthames, and invested them with their Princedoms. The rest of the afternoon was consumed in oaths of fealty from the more prominent nobles.

When he left the throne, he was handed messages from Klestreus, in Beshta Town, and Xentos. Klestreus reported that Prince Balthar had surrounded the temple of Styphon with troops, to protect it from mobs incited by priests of Dralm and Galzar. Xentos reported confused stories of internal fighting in Nostor, and no incidents on the border, where Phrames was on watch.

That evening, they had a feast.

THE next morning, after assembling the court, the priests and priestesses of all the regular deities, and all the merchants, itinerant traders and other travelers in Sask Town, the priests of Styphon, from Zothnes down, were hustled in. They were a sorry-looking lot, dungeon-soiled, captivity-scuffed, and loaded with chains. Prodded with pike-butts, they were formed into a line facing the throne, and booed enthusiastically by all.

"Look at them!" Balthames jeered. "See how Styphon cares for his priests!"

"Throw their heads in Styphon's face!" Sarrask shouted.

Other suggestions were forthcoming, most of which would have horrified the Mau-Mau. A few, black-robe priests and white-robe under-priests, were defiant. He remembered what Harmakros had said about some on the lower echelons really believing in Styphon. Most of them didn't, and were in no mood for martyrdom. Zothnes, who should have been setting an example, was in a pitiable funk.

Finally, he commanded silence. "These people," he said, "are criminals against all men and against all the true gods. They must be put to death in a special manner, reserved for them and those like them. Let them be blown from the muzzles of cannon!"

Well, the British had done that during the Sepoy Mutiny, in the reign of her enlightened Majesty, Victoria, and could you get any more respectable than that? He was making a bad pun about cannon-ized martyrs. There was a general shout of approval—original, effective, uncomplicated, and highly appropriate. A yellow-robe upper priest fainted.

Kalvan addressed his mercenary Chief of Artillery: "Alkides, say we use the three eighteens and three twelve; how long would it take your men to finish off this lot?"

"Six at a time." Alkides looked the job-lot over. "Why, if we started right after noon-meal, we could be through in time for dinner." He thought for a moment. "Look, Lord Kal—pardon, your Majesty. Suppose we use the big bombards, here. We could load the skinny ones all the way in, and the fat ones up to the hips." He pointed at Zothnes. "I think that one would go all the way in a fifty-pounder, almost."

Kalvan frowned. "But I'd wanted to do it in the town square. The people ought to watch it."

"But it would make an awful mess in the square," Rylla objected.

"The people could come out from town to watch," Sarrask suggested helpfully. "More than could see it in the square. And vendors could come out and sell honey-cakes and meat-pies."

Another priest fainted. Kalvan didn't want too many of them doing that, and nodded unobtrusively to Ptosphes.

"Your Majesty," the First Prince of the Great Kingdom said, "I understand this is a fate reserved only for the priests of the false god Styphon. Now, suppose, before they can be executed, some of these criminals abjure their false god, recant their errors, and profess faith in the true gods. What then?"

"Oh, in that case we'd have no right to put them to death at all. If they make public abjuration of Styphon, renounce their priesthood, profess faith in Dralm and Galzar and Yirtta Allmother and the other true gods, and recant all their false teachings, we would have to set them free. To those willing to enter our service, honorable employment, appropriate to their condition, would be given. If Zothnes, say, were to do so, I'd think something around five hundred ounces of gold a year—"

A white-robe under-priest shouted that he would never deny his god. A yellow-robe upper priest said, "Shut your fool's mouth!" and hit him across the face with the slack of his fetter-chain. Zothnes was giggling in half-hysterical relief.

"Dralm bless your Majesty; of course we will, all of us!" he babbled. "Why, I spit in the face of Styphon! You think any true god would suffer his priests to be treated as we've been?"

XENTOS reached Sask Town that evening. The news from Nostor was a little more definite: according to his sources there, Gormoth had started mobilizing for a blitz attack on Hostigos on hearing the first, false, news of a Hostigi disaster at Fyk. As soon as he had learned better, he had used his troops to seize the Nostor Town temple of Styphon and the temple-farm up Lycoming Creek. Now there was savage fighting all over Nostor, between Gormoth's new mercenaries and supporters of Styphon's House, and the Nostori regular army was split by mutiny and counter-mutiny. There had been an unsuccessful attack on Tarr-Nostor. Gormoth still seemed to be in control.

The Sask Town priestcraft all deferred to Xentos; it was evident that he was Primate of the Great Kingdom, Archbishop of Canterbury or something of the sort. *Established Church of Hos-Hostigos; think over carefully.* He immediately called an ecclesiastical council and began working out a program for the auto-da-fé.

Held the next day, it was a great success. Procession of the penitents from Tarr-Sask to the Sask Town temple of Dralm, in sackcloth and ashes, guarded by enough pikemen to keep the mob from pelting them with anything more lethal than rotten cabbage and dead cats. Token flagellation. Recantation of all heresies, special emphasis on fireseed, supernatural nature and devil content of. He was pleased to observe the reactions of the diplomatic corps to this. Sermon of the Faith, preached by the Hostigos Uncle Wolf; as a professional performance, at least, the Rev. Alexander Morrison would have approved. And, finally, after profession of faith in the true gods and absolution, a triumphant march through the streets, the new converts robed in white and crowned with garlands. And free wine for everybody. This was even more fun than shooting them out of cannons would have been. The public was delighted.

They had another feast that evening.

The next day, Klestreus reported that Balthar had seized the temple of Styphon and massacred the priests; the mob was parading their heads on pike-points. He refused, however, to renounce his sovereignty and accept the rule of Great King Kalvan. Evidently he never considered his vassalage to Great King Kaiphranos, which wasn't surprising. Late in the afternoon, a troop of cavalry from Nyklos Town arrived, escorting one of Prince Armanes's chief nobles with a petition that Nyklos be annexed to the Great Kingdom of Hos-Hostigos, and also a pack-horse loaded with severed heads. Prince Armanes was more interested in liquidating his debts by liquidating the creditors than he was in winning converts for the true gods. Prince Kestophes of Ulthor blew his priests of Styphon off the guns of his lakeside fort; along with his allegiance he gave Hos-Hostigos a port on the Great Lakes. By that time the demolition of the Sask Town temple of Styphon had begun, starting with the gold dome. It was real gold, twelve thousand ounces, of which Sarrask, after his ransom was paid, received three thousand.

When he returned to Tarr-Hostigos, Klestreus was there, seeking instructions. Prince Balthar was now ready to accept the sovereignty of King Kalvan. It seemed that, after seizing the temple, massacring the priests, and incurring the ban of Styphon's House, he discovered that there was no fireseed mill at all in Beshta; all the fireseed the priests had furnished him had been made in Sask. He was, in spite of the Sask Town auto-da-fé, still worried about the possible devil content of Kalvan's Unconsecrated. The ex-Archpriest Zothnes, now with the Ministry of State at six thousand ounces, gold, a year, was sent to reassure him.

It took more reassurance to induce him to come to Tarr-Hostigos to do homage; outside Tarr-Beshta, Balthar was violently agoraphobic. He came, however, in a mail-curtained wagon, guarded by two hundred of Harmakros's cavalry.

The news from Nostor was still confused. A civil war was raging, that was definite, but exactly who against whom was less clear. It sounded a little like France at the time of the War of the Three Henries. Netzigon, the former chief-captain, and Krastokles, who had escaped the massacre when Gormoth had taken the temple, were in open revolt, though relations between them were said to be strained. Fighting continued in the streets of Nostor Town after the abortive attack on the castle. Count Pheblon, Gormoth's cousin and Netzigon's successor, commanded about half the army; the other half adhered to their former commander. The nobles, each with a formidable following, were split about evenly. Then there were minor factions: anti-Gormoth-and-anti-Styphon, pro-Styphon-and-pro-Gormoth, anti-Gormoth-and-pro-Pheblon. In addition, several large mercenary companies had invaded Nostor on their own and were pillaging indiscriminately, committing all the usual atrocities, while trying to auction their services.

Not liking all this anarchy next door, Kalvan wanted to intervene. Chartiphon and Harmakros were in favor of that; so was Armanes of Nyklos, who hoped to pick up a few bits of real estate on his southeast border. Xentos, of course, wanted to wait and see, and, rather surprisingly, he was supported by Ptosphes, Sarrask and Klestreus. Klestreus probably knew more about the situation in Nostor than any of them. That persuaded Kalvan to wait and see.

Tythanes of Kyblos arrived to do homage, attended by a large retinue, and bringing with him twenty-odd priests of Styphon, yoked neck-and-neck like a Guinea Coast slave-kaffle. Baron Zothnes talked to them; there was an auto-da-fé and public recantation. Some went to work in the fireseed mill and some became novices in the temple of Dralm, all under close surveillance. Kestophes of Ulthor came in a few days later. Balthar of Beshta was still at Tarr-Hostigos, which, by then, was crowded like a convention hotel. *Royal palace; get built.* Something that could accommodate a mob of subject Princes and their attendants, but not one of these castles. Castles, once he began making cast-iron roundshot and hollow explosive shells and heavy brass guns, would become scenic features, just as these big hooped iron bombards would become war memorials. Something simple and homelike, he thought. On the order of Versailles.

When the Princes were all at Tarr-Hostigos, he and Rylla were married, and there was a two-day feast, with an extra day for hangovers. He'd never been married before. He liked it. It couldn't possibly have happened with anybody nicer than Rylla.

Some time during the festivities, Prince Balthames and Sarrask's daughter Amnita were married. There was also a minor and carefully hushed scandal about Balthames and a page boy.

Then they had the Coronation. Xentos, who was shaping up nicely as a prelate-statesman of the Richelieu type, crowned him and Rylla. Then he crowned Ptosphes as First Prince of the Great Kingdom, and the other Princes in order of their submission. Then the Proclamation of the Great Kingdom was read. Quite a few hands, lifting goblets between phrases, had labored on that. His own contributions had been cribbed from The Declaration of Independence and, touching Styphon's House, from Martin Luther. Everybody cheered it enthusiastically.

Some of the Princes were less enthusiastic about the Great Charter. It wasn't anything like the one that Tammany Hall in chain mail had extorted from King John at Runnymede; Louis XIV would have liked it much better. For one thing, none of them liked having to renounce their right, fully enjoyed under Great King Kaiphranos, of making war on one another, though they did like the tightening of control over their subject lords and barons, most of whom were an unruly and troublesome lot. The latter didn't like the abolition of serfdom and, in Beshta and Kyblos, outright slavery. But it gave everybody security without having to hire expensive mercenaries or call out peasant levies when they were most needed in the fields. The regular army of the Great Kingdom would take care of that.

And everybody could see what was happening in Nostor at the moment. He understood, now, why Xentos had opposed intervention; Nostor was too good a horrible example to sacrifice.

So they all signed and sealed it. *Secret police, to make sure they live up to it; think of somebody for chief.*

Then they feasted for a couple more days, and there were tournaments and hunts. There was also a minor scandal, carefully hushed, about Princess Amnita and one of Tythanes's cavalry officers. Finally they all began taking their leave and drifting back to their own Princedoms, each carrying the flag of the Great Kingdom, dark green with a red keystone on it.

Darken the green a little more and make the scarlet a dull maroon and they'd be good combat uniform colors.

II

THE weather stayed fine until what he estimated to be the first week in November—*calendar reform; get onto this now*—and then turned cold, with squalls of rain which finally turned to snow. Outside, it was blowing against the window panes—*clear glass; why can't we do something about this?*—and candles had been lighted, but he was still at work. Petitions, to be granted or denied. Reports. Verkan's Zygrosi were going faster than anybody had expected with the brass foundry; they'd be pouring the first heat in ten or so days, and he'd have to go and watch that. The rifle shop was up to fifteen finished barrels a day, which was a real miracle. Fireseed production up, too, sufficient for military and civilian hunting demands in all the Princedoms of the Great Kingdom, and soon they would be exporting in quantity. Verkan and his wife were gone, now, returning to Grefftscharr to organize lake trade with Ulthor; he and Rylla both missed them.

And King Kaiphranos was trying to raise an army for the reconquest of his lost Princedoms, and getting a very poor response from the Princes still subject to him. There'd be trouble with him in the spring, but not before. And Sesklos, Styphon's Voice, had summoned all his archpriests to meet in Harphax city. Council of Trent, Kalvan thought, nodding; now the Counter Reformation would be getting into high gear.

And rioting in Kyblos; the emancipated slaves were beginning to see what Samuel Johnson had meant when he defined freedom as the choice of working or starving.

And the Prince of Phaxos wanted to join the Great Kingdom, but he was making a lot of conditions he'd have to be talked out of.

And pardons, and death-warrants. He'd have to be careful not to sign too many of the former and too few of the latter; that was how a lot of kings lost their thrones.

A servant announced a rider from Vryllos Gap, who, ushered in, informed him that a party from Nostor had just crossed the Athan. A priest of Dralm, a priest of Galzar, twenty mercenary cavalry, and Duke Skranga, the First Noble of Nostor.

He received Duke Skranga in his private chambers, and remembered how he had told the Agrysi horse-trader that Dralm, or somebody, would reward him. Dralm, or somebody, with substantial help from Skranga, evidently had. He was richly clad, his robe lined with mink-fur, a gold chain about his neck and a gold-hilted poignard on a gold link belt. His beard was neatly trimmed.

"Well, you've come up in the world," he commented.

"So, if your Majesty will pardon me, has your Majesty." Then he produced a signet-ring—the one given as pledge token by Count Pheblon when captured and released at Tarr-Dombra, and returned to him when his ransom had been delivered. "So has the owner of this. He is now Prince Pheblon of Nostor, and he sends me to declare for him his desire to submit himself and his realm to your Majesty's sovereignty and place himself, and it, under your Majesty's protection."

"Well, your Grace, I'm most delighted. But what, if it's a fair question, has become of Prince Gormoth?"

The ennobled horse-trader's face was touched with a look of deepest sorrow.

"Prince Gormoth, Dralm receive his soul, is no longer with us, your Majesty. He was most foully murdered."

"Ah. And who appears to have murdered him, if that's a fair question too?"

Skranga shrugged. "The then Count Pheblon, and the Nostor priest of Dralm, and the Nostor Uncle Wolf were with me in my private apartments at Tarr-Nostor when suddenly we heard a volley of shots from the direction of Prince Gormoth's apartments. Snatching weapons, we rushed thither, to find the Princely rooms crowded with guardsmen who had entered just ahead of us, and, in his bedchamber, our beloved Prince lay weltering in his gore, bleeding from a dozen wounds. He was quite dead," Skranga said sadly. "Uncle Wolf and the high priest of Dralm, whom your Majesty knows, will both testify that we were all together in my rooms when the shots were fired, and that Prince Gormoth was dead when we entered. Surely your Majesty will not doubt the word of such holy men."

"Surely not. And then?"

"Well, by right of nearest kinship, Count Pheblon at once declared himself Prince of Nostor. We tortured a couple of servants lightly—we don't do so much of that in Nostor, since our beloved and gentle Prince . . . Well, your Majesty, they all agreed that a band of men in black cloaks and masks had suddenly forced their way into Prince Gormoth's chambers, shot him dead, and then fled. In spite of the most diligent search, no trace of them could be found."

"Most mysterious. Fanatical worshipers of false Styphon, without doubt. Now, you say that Prince Pheblon, whom we recognize as the rightful Prince of Nostor, will do homage to us?"

"On certain conditions, of course, the most important of which your Majesty has already met. Then, he wishes to be confirmed in his possession of the temple of Styphon in Nostor Town, and the fireseed mills, nitriaries and sulfur springs which his predecessor confiscated from Styphon's House."

"Well, that's granted. And also the act of his late Highness, Prince Gormoth, in elevating you to the title of Duke and First Noble of Nostor."

"Your Majesty is most gracious!"

"Your Grace has earned it. Now, about these mercenary companies in Nostor?"

"Pure brigands, your Majesty! His highness begs your Majesty to send troops to deal with them."

"That'll be done; I'll send Duke Chartiphon, our Grand Constable, to attend to that. What's happened to Krastokles, by the way?"

"Oh, we have him, and Netzigon too, in the dungeons at Tarr-Nostor. They were both captured a moon-quarter ago. If your Majesty wishes, we'll bring both of them to Tarr-Hostigos."

"Well, don't bother about Netzigon; take his head off yourselves, if you think he needs it. But we want that archpriest. I hope that our faithful Baron Zothnes can spare us the mess of blowing him off a cannon by talking some sense into him."

"I'm sure he can, your Majesty."

He wondered just who had arranged the killing of Gormoth, Skranga or Pheblon, or both together. He didn't care; Nostor hadn't been his jurisdiction then. It was now, though, and if either of that pair had ideas about having the other killed, he'd do something about it in a hurry. Court intrigues, he supposed, were something he'd have with him always, but no murders, not inside the Great Kingdom.

After he showed Skranga out, he returned to his desk, opened a box, and got out a cigar—a stogie, rather, and a very crudely made stogie at that. It was a beginning, however. He bit the end and lit it at one of the candles, and picked up another report, a wax-covered wooden tablet. He still hadn't gotten anything done on paper-making. Maybe he'd better not invent paper; if he did, some Dralm-damned bureaucrat would invent paper-work, and then he'd have to spend all his time endlessly reading and annotating reports.

He was happy about Nostor, of course; that meant they wouldn't have a little war to fight next door in the spring, when King Kaiphranos would begin being a problem. And it was nice Pheblon had Krastokles and would turn him over. Two archpriests, about equivalent to cardinals, defecting from Styphon's

House was a serious blow. It weakened their religious hold on the Great Kings and their Princes, which was the only hold they had left now that they had lost the fireseed monopoly. Priests, and especially the top level of the hierarchy, were supposed to believe in their gods.

Xentos believed in Dralm, for instance. Maybe he'd have trouble with the old man, some day, if Xentos found his duty to Dralm conflicting with his duty to the Great Kingdom. But he hoped that would never happen.

He'd have to find out more about what was going on in the other Great Kingdoms. Spies—there was a job for Duke Skranga, one that would keep him out of mischief in Nostori local politics. Chief of Secret Service. Skranga was crooked enough to be good at that. And somebody to watch Skranga, of course. That could be one of Klestreus's jobs.

And find out just what the situation was in Nostor. Go there himself; Machiavelli always recommended that for securing a new domain. Make the Nostori his friends—that wouldn't be hard, after they'd lived under the tyranny of Gormoth. And . . .

General Order, to all Troops: Effective immediately, it shall be a court-martial offense for any member of the Armed Forces of the Great Kingdom of Hos-Hostigos publicly to sing, recite, play, whistle, hum, or otherwise utter the words and/or music of the song known as Marching through Nostor.

20

VERKAN Vall looked at his watch and wished Dalla would hurry, but Dalla was making herself beautiful for the party. A waste of time, he thought; Dalla had been born beautiful. But try and tell any woman that. Across the low table, Tortha Karf also looked at his watch, and smiled happily. He'd been doing that all through dinner and ever since, and each time had been broader and happier as more minutes till midnight leaked away.

He hoped Dalla's preparations would still permit them to reach Paratime Police Headquarters with an hour to spare before midnight. There'd be a big crowd in the assembly room—everybody who was anybody on the Paracops and the Paratime Commission, politicians, society people, and, by special invitation, the Kalvan Project crowd from the University. He'd have to shake hands with most of them, and have drinks with as many as possible, and then, just before midnight, they'd all crowd into the Chief's office, and Tortha Karf would sit down at his desk, and, precisely at 2400, rise, and they'd shake hands, and Tortha Karf would step aside and he'd sit down, and everybody would start that Fourth Level barbarian chant they used on such occasions.

And from then on, he'd be stuck there—Dralm-dammit!

He must have said that aloud. The soon-to-retire Chief grinned unsympathetically.

"Still swearing in Aryan-Transpacific Zarthani. When do you expect to get back there?"

"Dralm knows, and he doesn't operate on Home Time Line. I'm going to have a lot to do here. One, I'm going to start a flap, and keep it flapping, about this pickup business. Ten new cases in the last eight days. And don't tell me what you told Zarvan Tharg when he was retiring, or what Zarvan Tharg told Hishan Galth when *he* was retiring. I'm going to do something about this, by Dralm I am!"

"Well, fortunately for the working cops, we're a longevous race. It's a long time between new Chiefs."

"Well, we know what causes it. We'll have to work on eliminating the cause. I'm a hundred and four; I can look forward to another two centuries in that chair of yours. If we don't have enough men, and enough robots, and enough computers to eliminate some of these interpenetrations, we might as well throw it in and quit."

"It'll cost like crazy."

"Look, I don't make a practice of preaching moral ethics, you know that. I just want you to think, for a moment, of the morality of snatching people out of the only world they know and dumping them into an entirely different world, just enough like their own . . ."

"I've thought about it, now and then," Tortha Karf said, in mild understatement. "This fellow Morrison, Lord Kalvan, Great King Kalvan, is one in a million. That was the best thing that could possibly have happened to him, and he'd be the first to say so, if he dared talk about it. But for the rest, the ones the conveyer operators ray down with their needlers are the lucky ones.

"But what are we going to do, Vall? We have a population of ten billion, on a planet that was completely exhausted twelve thousand years ago. I don't think more than a billion and a half are on Home Time Line at any one time; the rest are scattered all over Fifth Level, and out at conveyer-heads all over Fourth, Third and Second. We can't cut them loose; there's a slight moral issue involved there, too. And we can't haul them all in to starve after we stop paratiming. That little Aryan-Transpacific expression you picked up fits. We have a panther by the tail."

"Well, we can do all we can. I saw to it that they did it on the University Kalvan Operation. We checked all the conveyer-heads equivalent with Hostigos Town on every Paratime penetrated time-line, and ours doesn't coincide with any of them."

"I'll bet you had a time." Tortha Karf sipped some more of the after-dinner coffee they were dragging out, and lit another cigarette. "I'll bet they love you in Conveyer Registration Office, too. How many were there?"

"A shade over three thousand, inside four square miles. I don't know what they'll do about the conveyer-head for Agrys City when they go to put one in there. There's a city on that river-mouth island on every time-line that builds cities, and tribal villages on most of the rest."

"Then they aren't just establishing a conveyer-head at Hostigos Town?"

"Oh, no; they're making a real operation out of it. We have five police posts, here and there, including one at Greffa, the capital of Grefftscharr, where Dalla and I are supposed to come from. The University will have study teams, or at least observers, in the capital cities of all the Five Great Kingdoms. Six Kingdoms, now, with Hos-Hostigos. They'll have to be careful; by spring, there'll be a war that'll make the Conquest of Sask look like a schoolyard brawl."

They were both silent for awhile. Tortha Karf, smiling contentedly, was thinking of his farm on Fifth Level Sicily; he'd be there this time tomorrow, with nothing to worry about but what the rabbits were doing to his truck-gardens. Verkan Vall was thinking about his friend, the Great King Kalvan, and everything Kalvan had to worry about. Now *there* was a man who had a panther by the tail.

Then something else occurred to him; a disquieting thought that had nagged him ever since a remark Dalla had made, the morning before they'd made the drop as Verkan and his party.

"Chief," he said, and remembered that in a couple of hours people would be calling him that. "This pickup problem is only one facet, and a small one, of something big and serious, and fundamental. We're supposed to protect the Paratime Secret. Just how good a secret is it?"

Tortha Karf looked up sharply, his cup halfway to his lips.

"What's wrong with the Paratime Secret, Vall?"

"How did we come to discover Paratime transposition?"

Tortha Karf had to pause briefly. He had learned that long ago, and there was considerable mental overlay.

"Why, Ghaldron was working to develop a spacewarp drive, to get us out to the stars, and Hesthor was working on the possibility of linear time-travel, to get back to the past, before his ancestors had worn the planet out. Things were pretty grim, on this time-line, twelve thousand years ago. And a couple of centuries before, Rhogom had worked up a theory of multidimensional time, to explain the phenomenon of precognition. Dalla could tell you all about that; that's her subject.

"Well, science was pretty tightly compartmented, then, but somehow Hesthor read some of Rhogom's old papers, and he'd heard about what Ghaldron was working on and got in touch with him. Between them, they discovered paratemporal transposition. Why?"

"As far as I know, nobody off Home Time Line has ever developed any sort of time-machine, linear or lateral. There are Second Level civilizations, and one on Third, that have over-light-speed drives for interstellar ships. But the idea of multidimensional time and worlds of alternate probability is all over Second and Third Levels, and you even find it on Fourth—a mystical concept on Sino-Hindic, and a science-fiction idea on Europo-American."

"And you're thinking, suppose some Sino-Hindic mystic, or some Europo-American science-fiction writer, gets picked up and dumped onto, say, Second Level Interworld Empire?"

"That could do it. It mightn't even be needed. You know, there is no such thing as a single-shot discovery; anything that's been discovered once can be discovered again. That's why it always amuses me to see some technological warfare office classifying a law of nature as top-secret. Gunpowder was the secret of Styphon's House, and look what's happening to Styphon's House now. Of course, gunpowder is a simple little discovery; it's been made tens of thousands of times, all over paratime. Paratemporal transposition is a big, complicated, discovery; it was made just once, twelve thousand years ago, on one time-line. But no secret can be kept forever. One of the University crowd said that, speaking of Styphon's House. He became quite indignant when Dalla mentioned the Paratime Secret in that connection."

"I'll bet you didn't. That's a nice thought to give a retiring Chief of Paratime Police. Now I'll be having nightmares about—"

He broke off, rising to his feet with a smile. A paratimer could always produce a smile when one was needed.

"Well, now, Dalla! That gown! And how did you achieve that hairdo?"

He rose and turned. Dalla had come out onto the terrace and was pirouetting slowly in the light from the room behind her. It hadn't been a waste of time, after all.

"But I kept you waiting ages! You're both dears, to be so patient. Do we go now?"

"Yes, the party will have started; we'll get there just at the right time. Not too early, and not too late."

And in two hours, Verkan Vall, Chief of Paratime Police, would begin to assume responsibility for guarding the Paratime Secret.

A panther by the tail. And he was holding it.